THAT VAST HUNGER

BREE WILDE

THAT VAST HUNGER

Copyright © 2026 by Bree Wilde

All Rights Reserved.

This is a work of fiction. Any resemblance to actual persons, living or dead, or actual events, businesses, and locations is coincidental.

No part of this book may be reproduced in any form or by any electronic or mechanical means, including information storage and retrieval systems, without written permission from the author, except for the use of brief quotations in a book review.

No AI was used in the making of this book.

ISBN: 978-1945860089

Cover Design by Asterielly Designs.

Map by Ink and Lore Maps.

ALSO BY BREE WILDE

STANDALONE

Between Smoke and Shadow

THE ECHO REALM

This Violent Light

That Vast Hunger

These books are for 18+ readers.

Your mental health matters! Visit breewilde.com for mature themes in each book.

*To the girls
who save everyone
but themselves:*

*I hope you
find your Elliot.*

CONTENTS

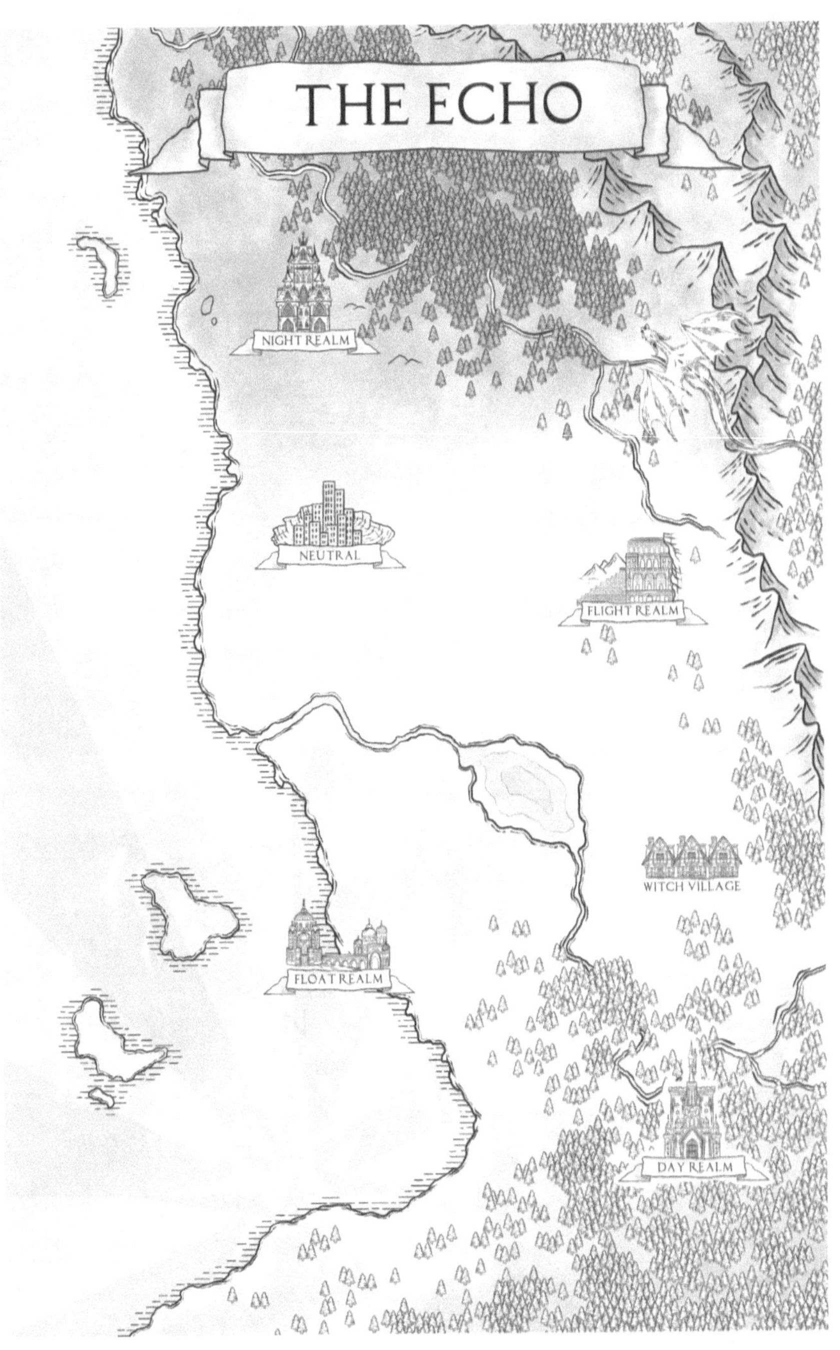

THE ECHO
NIGHT REALM
NEUTRAL
FLIGHT REALM
WITCH VILLAGE
FLOAT REALM
DAY REALM

1

———

NOT EVEN ME

CORA

I keep my memories in jars. Not all of them, of course. Just the bad ones, the unhelpful ones, the ones that take up space and time and energy. Those, I store in jars on the walls of my bedroom, organized by year and neatly labeled with black ink. At night, they glow with desperation. Blues and oranges, yellows and pinks. Vibrant colors, all fighting to escape their glass prisons.

I rarely release them.

Today, the suffering is necessary. I trail my finger across a row of silver-lidded jars, lips moving silently as I read the labels. I'm looking for any mention of Ochre Village, one of the largest witch communities in the Day Realm. I skip any that mention Hayver, the small and dismal place I was born. Where I was first labeled a *Dark One*, where they kept me isolated in a dreary orphanage and told the other children to stay away.

For tonight, I need to see Ochre Village specifically. The buildings, the people, and most importantly, the roadways. I swear I've got a jar here somewhere that mentions a festival. I move to the next row, then the next, until finally...

"Yes," I whisper.

I pluck the jar from its place on my wall, scanning the label as I move to my four-poster bed. I collapse into the black comforter, slouching against the wooden headboard and crossing my legs. The label reads:

Cora Reed
age 12
*Autumnal Festival - Harrison**

I wish it said more, like whether I'll actually see the festival or the village, or whether I'll be stuck looking at Harrison the whole time. I absently touch the star on the second line. It won't *just* be Harrison. That star is my shorthand warning for Elliot. As in, *proceed with caution, Cora! This memory contains an Elliot sighting and will likely send you into a depressive episode.*

If I weren't dragging three others into this mission, I'd probably put the jar right back on its shelf. Memories with both Harrison and Elliot are of the worst variety, and I'd prefer to go in blind than see them together. Amelia, Beatrice, and Milas deserve better though. I owe it to them to check.

With a huffed sigh, I grab the memory stone off my nightstand. It looks like an ordinary rock from the Flight Realm, but it's not. It's a brick-sized cut of Initia Stone. Black and glossy, yet far lighter than one would guess. The edges are smoothed and the top is coated with a thin white film. It's worn from years of use, but it will work for many years to come—likely long after I'm dead.

Once the stone is balanced on my lap, I take the remaining ingredients from a tiny velvet pouch. A vial of freshwater from Lake Astoria. Three dried mermaid scales. One infant dragon claw. A strand of auburn hair, stolen directly from the head of the fae king.

I line the items over the stone. Residual magic hums against my skin, and I close my eyes, savoring the feel. The memory stone, by itself, is cool to the touch. With each added ingredient, it grows warmer. Though the bottom of the stone remains cool on my thighs, the top is starting to smoke. And when I remove the memory from its jar, the smoke builds and stretches, yearning to claim the frantic magic.

I pinch the memory between my fingers. This one is green, vibrant as a spring leaf but far more restless. It thrashes like a wild animal and sends nasty shocks through my fingers. I can feel the sting all the way to my shoulders.

Memories don't like being kept in jars. They crave the soft, malleable give of brain matter, and they despise me for stealing them away.

"If you didn't want to be kept in a jar, you should have chosen a better memory," I tell it, tossing the glass to the side.

The memory shocks me again. I grit my teeth and hold the memory to the Initia Stone, careful to watch my fingers. The memory and the stone call to each other. Within seconds, the memory lays parallel to the stone and magic surrounds me in an explosion of shocking green smoke.

It's all I can see. The stone walls of my bedroom are gone, replaced by thick green smoke and the stark smell of burning flesh.

"Give me something good," I whisper into the mist.

Make the suffering worth it, I add silently.

The smoke grows impossibly thicker until I'm breathing it deep into my lungs with each inhalation. My head swims, my vision blurs, and the steady beat of my heart becomes frantic.

Gone is my bed and the shelves of memories and the weight of stale, trapped air.

The next time I blink, I am outside in an open market. The me of today doesn't recognize it. There are booths with yellow awnings and witches clothed in every shade of orange and white. A few wear blue. Fewer still wear green or violet. They all move in masses, breaking apart to stop at one stall or another. Some booths sell seasonal berries. Others dried meat. Others still, silken scarves and handmade trinkets and woven baskets.

I might not recognize this place, this market, but the me of the past does. She is timid and scrawny and clumsy, moving with hesitant thrill. Her eyes are on a small booth, tucked between a bookseller and a palm reader.

"Look," I whisper. It's not my voice, not really. It's twelve-year-old me. Her voice is higher, squeakier. Her attention is locked on a collection of lizards and snakes, of turtles with painted shells and colorful fish, separated into bowls.

Twenty-seven-year-old me wants to move away, to shrink from the buggy-eyed creatures and find the safety of shadows.

Twelve-year-old me smiles. I feel it, the way my mouth grins without permission.

As much as I want to resist, I've watched enough memories to know better. I force myself to relax, to let the memory take control. With every breath, I melt deeper into the past, shedding my current self like a second skin. Finally, there is only this one, singular moment.

"Are you looking?" I demand. I'm still grinning as I move forward, tugging my sister Margot by the hand.

She keeps close, her blonde braids swinging between us. My brown hair is tied in a neat bun, fastened with the yellow hair tie she gifted me just this morning. Margot loops her elbow through mine, giggling as we shove through the crowd.

"Oh, not this again," she groans. "Mama is not going to approve a single one of these and you know it."

"But look how cute they are," I say. I squeeze her forearm, pulling her closer to my side. "This green one? Are you kidding? It's the most beautiful thing you've ever seen."

"*Snakes are not beautiful,*" Margot says. "*And before you say anything else, fish and turtles and lizards are not beautiful either.*"

I gasp and swat her shoulder.

"*You shush,*" I say. *I touch the fishbowl nearest me.* "*This is Graves, and he's stunning. He wants to come home with us.*"

"*Graves?*" *Margot repeats. She leans forward, pressing into my line of vision.* "*I feel like that's your subconscious, warning you exactly where we'll end up if you buy this fish and bring it home.*"

"*He's only seven hewns,*" I say. "*That's practically free.*"

"*Secora,*" Margot says, snorting. "*That is far from free. We only have ten hewn, and if you think I'm donating two from my half to buy you this hideous creature—*"

Another gasp. Another swat to her shoulder.

"*He's beautiful,*" I insist. "*If I don't get him, I fear I might perish.*"

"*I fear I might perish,*" comes a male voice. It's pitched and condescending, and I recognize the sneer without looking.

Instantly, my timid excitement, my treacherous comfort, dissolves.

"*No one asked you, Harrison,*" Margot says. Her posture stiffens as she tightens her hold on me. Then she rotates, as if to block me from view.

I've only lived with Margot for a few months. I've been her sister —spare sister, that is—for less than a year, but she's undoubtedly the kindest person I've ever known. She's allowed me to feel like I belong, like the things I say are worth hearing. I'm allowed to joke and tease, to whine and complain. To be normal.

I don't want her to have to protect me. I don't want to be her pathetic, orphaned sister. I want to be brave and bold and normal.

Still, I don't step out from behind her. I can't even bring myself to speak.

"*I'm not taunting you, Margot,*" Harrison says. He's the same height as she is, but he's far broader. Wide shoulders, thick arms, a *strangely flat face. He's hideous, though most girls wouldn't agree. Still, I'm positive it's true.*

He looks like an inbred dog, and his eyes hold an indescribable lack of light, as if his soul faded to darkness years ago.

"You're too pretty to tease," Harrison goes on. "Your ugly little stray, on the other hand—"

"I'm not kidding, Harrison," Margot says quietly. When I finally get the nerve to step forward, she places an arm in front of me, keeping me in her shadow. It's where I've lived for the past several months, and as much as I'm ashamed to admit it, I like the darkness. The shelter. The protection. Even if I don't deserve it.

"I'm worried about you," Harrison says. His voice goes soft, and I think he means it. They dated, after all. He was suffocating and cruel, according to the limited information Margot offered, but it's clear he cares. It's hard to hate him for that, even if I'm the thing he sees as a threat.

"You don't need—"

"She killed her parents," Harrison interrupts. "Killed them, Margot. Killed the next family she was with, too. Your parents are—"

"Stop," Margot snaps.

Harrison doesn't. He steps closer, forcing Margot, and therefore me, to shrink backward.

"Your parents are fools for bringing that thing into your home," he continues. "She'll kill you all, and you'll have no one to blame but yourselves."

"I've never hurt anyone," I say. My voice is small. Pathetic. Meek. I'm in Margot's class, but I'm a year younger. Right now, I feel years beneath them, too stupid to handle people like Harrison. "And I'm wearing the bands, Harrison."

I'm shaking as I pull up my sleeves, revealing the golden bands clasped on either wrist. Harrison already knows I'm wearing them. Everyone knows. They're only reason I was allowed to live, to have a semi-normal life. With these bands, I can't cast a simple spell, let alone hurt someone.

"Don't talk to me, freak," he snarls. "And don't ever say my name again."

He presses forward, yanking my arm, right above the golden band. With a movement too fast to track, he rotates, placing himself between me and my protector. I bump against the reptile booth, nearly knocking over the haphazard stack of fish bowls.

I suck in a tight breath, shrinking as small as I can, hating myself for it. Margot attempts to move around Harrison, but he shrugs her off. With a quick glance over his shoulder, as if remembering where we are, Harrison pulls me away from the table. He surges between the reptile booth and the palm reader's, taking off down the narrow alleyway behind them.

I have to stumble to keep up, my short legs requiring twice as many steps. He keeps me in front of him, and Margot remains a breath behind, her fists pounding his shoulder blades. He ignores the strikes as if he doesn't feel them.

"I haven't hurt anyone," I repeat. I'm crying and I hate it but I don't know how to stop. "I didn't—"

He shoves me against the brick wall. The Ochre Autumnal Festival continues in the street, and though I catch more than one person's eye, no one interferes. Even the reptile shop owner, who watched it all unravel, doesn't say a word. He keeps his attention on the flourishing market, and he doesn't look back once.

"Fucking vile," Harrison tells me.

I'm not sure if he means the way I look or dress or simply the way I am. Like Margot, I'm wearing a long-sleeve dress and a pair of tights, but we are not the same. Where everyone else here wears the color of their family season, I wear black. The color of mourning. The color of death.

I stand out in any crowd, surrounded by yellows and oranges and *violets and greens. A black spot of death in an otherwise vibrant field of flowers.*

"I never hurt anyone," I repeat. I'm not even sure if that's true. Mama Perskey promised I didn't. Margot's mama says the same thing. Most people though...they think I did. They think I killed my parents. That I killed Mama Perskey too, even though that's impossible.

"Take this off," Harrison snarls.

I don't know what he's talking about until his hand fists my hair. With a vicious tug, he rips the elastic tie from my bun. It's the loveliest shade of yellow, the same color as the tree leaves all through town.

"Stop!" Margot shrieks, but she suddenly seems so small. Thirty pounds below Harrison, if not more. She grabs his wrist, nearly falling when he easily releases the tie to her.

"It's yours, Margot," he says, that same gentle voice from before. "I wouldn't keep it from you."

"It's Secora's," she argues. She presses the hair tie against my open palm, but I don't dare grab it. It falls to the gravel between us. Now, she stares at me, the first time since Harrison attacked. "Secora, it's yours. You can wear it."

"No, she can't," Harrison says, glaring at me. He presses closer, until I can taste his rancid breath on my lips. "Right, stray? You can't wear it, and you know it."

I swallow. My throat feels tight, like I've taken poison and my entire body is swelling.

"Say it," he barks. "Say it, freak."

"I'll never talk to you again," Margot says. She's crying now, but where my tears are silent, slow streaks down my face, hers are loud. Gasping. Panicked.

That's how Margot is. Alive and bold and striking. Where I barely exist, barely matter.

"I can't wear it," I whisper.

"That's right," Harrison says. He's so close our lips are almost

touching, and I turn my head, pressing it against the cold brick. I'd rather freeze my skin than feel his cruel touch.

"I hate you," Margot cries. She punches Harrison's arm again, then again. "I hate you, and I'm telling Mrs. Raekes."

"Tell her," Harrison says lazily. "See what she does."

He grabs my throat then, hard and fast, like a viper striking. Margot is still crying, still trying uselessly to pull him away. Harrison ignores her, squeezing until I can't breathe. My mouth bobs, searching desperately for air that won't come.

He smirks.

Do something, *I beg myself.* Please, Secora. Do something. Do anything.

I don't do anything but cry.

Harrison squeezes harder until I start to thrash. Until I am nothing but a wild animal, fueled by instinct. Magic surges through me, trapped by the golden bands, but not gone. It swells until it feels too big to contain, as if it might explode and kill us all. Just when I'm sure it will, Harrison loosens his grip.

I suck in desperate breaths. It takes everything to stay upright, to not fall at his feet.

"Vile," he repeats. His hand remains at the base of my neck, mockingly gentle. He's looking at me—I can feel it—but I don't dare raise my eyes from the ground.

Margot is gone and tears are leaking down my cheeks and a pathetic sob rips from my throat.

"Stay away from her," Harrison says. His low voice is an infection, spreading through my body like an incurable disease.

His fingers twitch, as if to tighten again, only to suddenly disappear. Harrison steps away. At first, I think he's grown bored of me. That, without Margot for an audience, he doesn't care to torture me. But then, I hear what he clearly already has.

Footsteps. Not Margot's. Not Mrs. Raekes'.

"What's going on?"

It's him.

My entire body tenses.

"Harrison."

His voice is hard. Loud. Close.

"What are you doing?" Elliot asks.

I don't want to look.

No, I don't want him to look. To see me, standing here, humiliated and pathetic.

Head still lowered, I peek through the tangled mess of my hair.

Elliot Lyrie stands before us. He is the most beautiful thing I've seen in my entire life, and as an orphan, I've met a lot of people. I've lived in orphanages and strange homes, switched schools more than once. I've seen too many people to harbor a guess. And without a doubt, Elliot is the most stunning of them all.

He has dark hair, thick and wavy, with a single strand that curls over his forehead. His eyes are mostly brown with hints of gold and green and even a bit of blue in the right lighting. He's taller than Harrison, but leaner. His muscles come from running and playing groundball, not from terrorizing orphans.

Where Margot is wearing yellow today, Elliot and Harrison both wear shades of burnt orange. It looks stupid on Harrison. Too muddled, too dark, with his pale hair and blue eyes. On Elliot, it looks like art, like the colors were created purely for his use.

"Are you okay?" Elliot asks.

Harrison makes a show of rolling his eyes. He shoves his hands in his pockets, scoffing as Elliot comes between us.

"Really, Elliot?" he asks. It's a condescending yet good-natured response. "We were just talking. Right, Secora?"

My mouth is too dry to answer, not that I would anyway. No one, aside from Margot, will believe that Harrison is a cruel villain. Because while he obviously hates me, he seems to love everyone else. He's created a picture-perfect golden boy persona, and if I weren't so intimately familiar with his cruelty, even I would believe it.

"Oh thank the Mother!" Margot calls.

We all startle to look at her. She sprints down the alleyway, halting at Elliot's side. She's panting hard, face red from exertion.

"I got Mrs. Raekes," she says between heavy breaths. She glances over me before glaring at Harrison. "I told her what you did."

"We were just talking," Harrison says again. He shifts slightly, the first show of nerves, but then looks at me with an expectant expression. "Right, Secora?"

For reasons I can't explain, even to myself, I find myself replying, "right."

Maybe because I want this to be over. Maybe because I can't stand the way Elliot is looking at me. Like I'm a sad, neglected dog.

"You're such an asshole," Margot says. Turning to Elliot, she adds, "He's tormenting her."

I've rarely heard my sister curse, and I don't like it. I hate that it's because of me that she's doing it. That loving me requires this hardened version of her.

"For Mother's sake!" Harrison snarls. "I'm trying to protect you, Margot."

"The only person I need protection from is you," she says. She's crying again, and it's hard not to feel like I'm at fault.

"Are you okay?" Elliot asks.

He's standing right in front of me. Beautiful and calm and far kinder than he has any reason being.

His best friend is a monster. His mother isn't much better.

But Elliot...

"Secora," he says. His voice is as soft as a new blanket, as melodic as a songbird. "Are you okay?"

I can't look at him. I can't speak a single word.

It takes everything I have to force a nod.

Please don't look at me, *I want to say.* Don't see what he sees. What everyone does.

"Time to leave, children!" a woman calls.

It isn't Mrs. Raekes but Virginia. She's an augur, one of the most powerful types of witches in the Echo. There aren't many of them, and they all share an eerie home on the main square. They travel around the Day Realm, identifying different types of magic and scouting witches with promising potential.

And sometimes, like twelve years ago, augurs deem particularly dangerous witches as Dark Ones. It's a label I'll never escape and one I'll detest until the day I die. Still, I can't help but like Virginia. She's one of the few adults who shows me kindness. Just yesterday, she chased off a boy who was making fun of my black clothes.

Now, Virginia stands at the opening of the alleyway, hands planted on her hips. She's frowning, eyes flicking between all of us. Though a part of me hopes she'll punish Harrison, that's foolish thinking. His mama is an augur, like her, which makes him untouchable.

"The trolley is here," Virginia says. "Best not to keep it waiting."

I should be hurt that she doesn't ask what's going on, that she clearly doesn't care. Right now, I'm too distracted by the gentle press of Elliot's hand on my wrist. The way he's staring at me with soft, unreadable emotion. It's too lovely an expression to be wasted on me.

Remembering myself, I pull my hand away and lower my eyes.

"C'mon," Harrison says. He playfully slaps Elliot's shoulder as he heads for Virginia. Torment, temporarily forgotten.

Margot tugs me along moments later, rushing through a surplus of apologies, promising Harrison's cruelty won't go unpunished. I'm barely listening. It's taking every ounce of self-control not to look back at Elliot.

THE MEMORY ENDS, and I come back to my bedroom. The Initia Stone is still on my lap, the ingredients in their careful line, but the smoke has receded. Now, the green memory thrashes over the stone, threatening to fall onto my blankets. I pinch it between my fingers, glaring as I return it to its jar.

Once I've put the Initia Stone and the collection of ingredients back on my nightstand, I grab the waiting vial of Dismemrate. It's dull red and gelatinous, a powerful elixir made of human blood, ghoul's teeth, and raw magic. Enough for only a swallow, Dismemrate is an expensive, difficult spell.

It's also the fastest way to wipe my memory. It'll take the last thirty minutes, give or take. Soon enough, I won't remember the Autumnal Festival or the feeling of Harrison's hand on my throat.

I take the Dismemrate in one swallow. It's foul and bitter, and the only thing that will clear my palate is green tea. Before I make my way to the kitchen though, I scrawl notes on a scrap of parchment. I include anything and everything I knew about Ochre Village and the augur in that memory.

By the time I finish, abandoning the parchment on my nightstand and moving into the kitchen, the memory is all but gone. Ochre Village and Virginia, Harrison and Margot, Elliot and his gentle touch...they all disappear. I chug giant gulps of green tea, letting the dull flavor burn any taste of Dismemrate from my tongue.

Once I'm done, I lean against the kitchen and breathe deep.

Finally, there is nothing but the present, where no one knows the truth of my past.

Not even me.

2

───────

THE LIKES OF YOU

CORA

In the Echo, every realm has a unique landscape. The Flight Realm has jagged mountains and pale sand dunes. The Float Realm has peaceful shores and treacherous waters. My original home, the Day Realm, is lush with thick forests, winding rivers, and a bottomless lake. Even the neutral territory, overpopulated and poverty-stricken, can be categorized as lively. It's filled with colorful markets and schools for all ages, loud restaurants and businesses of every kind, winding neighborhoods and even community greenhouses.

The Night Realm is different. It reeks of death, particularly within the vampiric sector. The land here is unkempt and rocky, spanning aimlessly in either direction. There are no trees or plants for miles. Occasional clusters of buildings, oddly spaced and in different states of disrepair, are the only break in an otherwise grey expanse. Nothing here is measured or strategic. For a species that once terrorized the Echo, the vampires lack practicality and organization.

Perhaps this is why they fell so easily.

They were untouchable for so long, they didn't realize how fragile their power was. They only needed cruelty and bloodlust to rule—until the witches, until *Madam Lyrie,* destroyed them with a single, violent spell.

Cursed to burn in the sun, vampires lost their hold over the Echo in a matter of days. I'd only been a child at the time, but I remember how our entire world shifted. How we suddenly switched from being prey to ordinary people. The vampires could rampage during nightfall, but by daylight, they either cowered indoors or burned until only their bones remained

Sitting here now, sharing a table with three vampires, should feel traitorous. It doesn't. It feels like relief and redemption, all at once.

"We'll meet here," I say. "Midnight."

Amelia and Beatrice nod, but Milas shifts in his seat. They've already agreed to venture into the Day Realm with me tonight. The only reason we're meeting now—in the minutes before Sebastian's clan meeting—is so I could update them on my plan. But of course, Milas *has* to be difficult.

"We could at least—"

I lift my hand, silencing him. I already know what he wants to say. He sits across from me in his usual place at the stone table. We're positioned in the manor's outside courtyard, surrounded by crawling ivy and a dying patch of grass. Overhead, the afternoon sun blazes, mocking those trapped within the manor walls.

Forget the betrayal of sitting with vampires. These particular three—and the two coming—can only be out in daylight *because* of me.

"I'm just saying—"

"Look up there," I say, cutting Milas off again. Without looking myself, I gesture to the overhead windows, where undoubtedly, vampires lurk behind the protective glass. "Do you know how many of them would *kill* to sit where you are now? To feel this sunlight on their skin?"

"Trust me, I know better than you," Milas says. His face tightens, even as his gaze betrays him. He looks up, eyes slowly shifting from window to window.

"You've already agreed," Amelia points out.

At almost the same time, Beatrice releases an exasperated sigh.

"Cora needs witch allies," she says. She taps her sharpened black nails against the table, leaning forward to steal Milas's attention. "Sebastian will throw a fit if he knows her plan for getting them. He won't stop it—he *can't*—but this will at least avoid the theatrics."

Beatrice is right. Ever since Sebastian stepped down as king, making the four members of his inner circle his equals, he can't squash all my good ideas. He *can*, however, be needlessly arrogant and vicious.

"All right, Milas?" Beatrice demands.

He huffs out a sigh. The nod he finally gives looks painful, and it takes all my effort not to smirk. Beatrice is unpleasant and obnoxiously brash. It's why I appreciate her more than the others.

"We'll tell him after," I point out. "Once we've secured some allies, he'll be too relieved to be angry."

I hope, I add mentally. As much as I'd like to pretend I make sunwalker spells for the pure satisfaction of pissing off Madam Lyrie, that would be a lie. At this point, I'd be happier to pretend the Day Realm, the witches, and that horrid woman don't exist at all.

But Sebastian saved my life twelve years ago, and I've been determined to repay the favor ever since.

I open my mouth to say more, but the tiniest shake of Amelia's head stops me. Where Beatrice is blunt and cruel, Amelia is softer, more difficult to read. I pride myself at understanding people. Beatrice, for example, wants love so desperately she makes it her life's mission to convince everyone she doesn't. Milas pretends to scout the Echo for the adventure—and for the vampires' needs, of course—but I know it's deeper. He can't handle being stagnant for long. His soul is restless, as if desperate to find the place it belongs.

Amelia is different. Blurry. Whatever she wants in this life... it's not clear to me. I've never cared to pry. I may be the vampires' resident witch, but I am not one of them. They've all lived much, much longer than I have, and they'll continue to do so, long after I'm dead.

Still, I've known Amelia long enough to read her body movements. That small head shake is a clear warning. *They're coming.*

I don't nod to confirm I've heard her. I don't need to. It's yet another skill I've learned while surviving in a house of the undead. Vampires notice *everything*. If I so much as nod when Sebastian enters the courtyard, he'll sense the unspoken conversation. He'll pry and demand, until Milas inevitably cracks.

I don't say a word. We've already discussed everything we needed in the minutes before our scheduled meeting. They know where we'll go, what they need to wear, and who I plan to recruit.

I only hope I don't let them down.

"THIS FEELS LIKE A TERRIBLE IDEA," Milas says. He stands to my left, clothed in the customary orange of the autumnal witches. To my right, Beatrice and Amelia wear dresses and tights, their hair twisted into matching double braids.

We all look ridiculous. Black is by far the most popular color worn in the Night Realm, and even when I lived amongst my kind, I *still* didn't wear orange or yellow or any other color. Since before my sixth birthday, I've never worn anything but black. The color of death, of mourning, of my long-rotted heart.

With a yellow long-sleeved dress and white leggings, I look like an imposter. I *am* an imposter.

"It is a terrible idea," Beatrice agrees. She plucks at the loose fabric of her dress, lips twitching with distaste. "If the witches don't kill us, Sebastian will."

"He's not going to find out," I say. Harder than I should, maybe. "We'll tell him if we succeed. If we don't, he doesn't need to know."

"Relax," Beatrice says on a lengthy sigh. "Unless it's directly related to Grace's vagina, Sebastian is clueless."

"Gross," Amelia says.

I agree, with both of them.

Rather than continuing *that* conversation, I take stock of our surroundings. We're on the edge of Ochre Village, facing a long-rusted metal archway. It spells out Ochre in black letters, and around the text, a series of bloodied thumbprints stain the pale yellow background.

It's tradition amongst the witches. Every coven leader in history has their fingerprint on their village's sign. My mother's thumbprint is somewhere on the Hayver sign outside my birthplace. Distantly, I wonder if Margot ever became a coven leader like she planned, if her thumbprint is amongst the bloodied marks overhead.

I clear my throat, swallowing an unexpected lump.

I blame this morning's memory. Even though I've since forgotten it, the memory has undoubtedly stirred my emotions. It's made me feel reckless, anxious, uncertain. The Cora of today is *not* afraid, and I remind myself of that as I address the inner circle.

"I'll go alone," I say. "Stay close. Listen for my signal, and don't approach unless you hear it. Remember, you won't be able to come inside, so if she pulls me in, don't try to save me."

"And what, leave you here?" Beatrice asks with a snort. She ducks to my height, eyes narrowing into slits. "Let's be clear, Cora. We're not leaving you with these freaks."

I run my tongue over the back of my teeth. I've got three of five vampiric clan members here, and Sebastian will kill me if I come back without a single one of them. We're here to, *hopefully*, negotiate a deal with Virginia to make more sunwalker spells. It's a long shot, but it's the best option we've got.

"It will be fine," Beatrice continues. She pulls back, glancing between Milas and Amelia. They nod in agreement. "Either make the deal or retreat. Do *not* go inside."

"I'm going to make the deal," is my immediate response.

That earns me an eye roll.

I lead the way beneath Ochre Village's metal archway, a few paces in front of the others. The settlement isn't warded that I can feel, and I'm not surprised. Of all the witch villages, Ochre is farthest from neutral territory. It's a trek to get here from the Night Realm, making the risk too great for vampires to take.

Well, *most* vampires.

Without a sunwalker spell, most vampires would catch fire if we didn't make it home before sunrise. These three will just bitch about having to walk as mortals, rather than running with their typical speed.

I clench my jaw as we walk, scanning our surroundings. The streets are empty. The sun is down, and the moon barely provides enough light to show the cobblestone. The village, it seems, has not been updated in the years I've been gone.

I'm not surprised. Witches prefer history over maintenance.

"What's her name again?" Beatrice asks. She's a step behind me. The other two flank either side, spread out like body guards. It's a comfort I'm not sure I deserve but appreciate all the same.

Most witches don't stand a chance against vampires. Not when the sun is down like this. Not when vampires are powerful and hungry, fast and deadly.

"Virginia," Amelia answers for me.

I'm not surprised she remembers. Where Beatrice and Milas are loud and brash, Amelia has always been one to listen, to observe. When Sebastian brought me into his inner circle twelve years ago, she was the first to welcome me. To trust that I wouldn't betray them like Beatrice feared.

"Is that right, Cora?" Amelia asks.

I blink twice before looking at her. My brain feels hazy, and it takes me a moment to process what she's asking.

"Correct," I say finally. "Virginia is an augur. She has access to a lot of powerful people. She was always kind to me."

I've already told them this. I'm not sure why I'm repeating it now, except that I'm nauseatingly anxious. It's been twelve years. I'm not sure Virginia will recognize me, and if she does, it likely won't be a good thing. At the very least, I know Virginia is still a practicing Augur. Milas found her with little effort, and if there's a chance she can provide what I need...

"Go east here," Milas says.

I follow the direction, tensing as my insides flutter with unease. I may have removed most of my Ochre memories, but I still recognize certain parts of this village. We've reached a strip of half-timbered buildings, framed with dried wood and filled with pale, cracking clay. Before Milas gives further direction, I stop in front of a three-story structure. Now that I'm here, I recognize it as the augur house.

Most of my memories of this place are undoubtedly in my bedroom, labeled and gathering dust. And still, my body knows it. It remembers this augur building and the terrible things that once happened here.

I shift on my feet.

I am *not* afraid.

I study the building as the inner circle presses closer around me. There's a thatched roof that's likely been magicked to withstand the weather. A series of windows with thin orange drapes. A candle flickering in the upper-left room, casting shadows against the curtains. The front door is simple and unassuming, painted yellow, surrounded by an unnatural halo of light.

I pick at the hem of my dress. It might be my imagination, but I swear this thing is starting to itch. It's as if a thousand bugs have hatched in the fabric and are now rapidly dispersing across my skin.

We should go, I think. *Far from here, back to the Night Realm and Sebastian's manor and the safety of our own shadows.*

"Cora?" Beatrice asks. Her voice is hard, irritable in the way it too often is. "What's the deal? Do you think she's in there or—"

Rather than respond, I lift my hand in a silencing gesture. For once, Beatrice quiets. I stride forward, center myself in front of the door, and knock before I lose my nerve.

There's a rustle of movement behind me. The sound of quick, near-silent footsteps that I only recognize from years of exposure.

In the darkness, vampires are lethally fast and quiet. Their bodies are barely human. They don't need to breathe, to blink, to move. They can sit perfectly still for hours and then surge across the room before you realize they've moved.

Without looking over my shoulder, I know Beatrice and the others are gone.

I knock again, a bit firmer.

Overhead, the candle flickers, then extinguishes. Straining my ears, I can just make out the sound of creaking footsteps on an ancient staircase.

Goosebumps trail over my skin. The augurs can likely see

me through their threadbare curtains. The magicked light surrounds me, highlights my stupid braids and ill-fitting dress.

"I know it's late," I say, leaning against the door. "I need to speak with Virginia. Immediately. I need *help*, and it's your Motherly duty to—"

"Quiet," a woman says. Her voice is rough, deep for a woman. I don't remember what Virginia's voice sounds like. This morning's memory has long faded.

I fidget on the stoop before forcing my hands to still. I look guilty. Agitated. If I have any chance of her helping me, I have to play the part.

"What business have you?" she asks.

"I told you," I say, lifting my chin. I speak to the door knocker, imagining a face in its place. "I need to speak with Virginia. *Right. Now.*"

"It is after nightfall," she says. "This must wait until morning."

"No," I say. My voice shakes, and I clench my fists to hide their trembling. "It is not safe for me to wait. Get Virginia. It is imperative—"

"I thought it was you," she interrupts. My skin goes cold, and without conscious decision, I take a step back. "You're as homely as you were in childhood."

I swallow. Her insult doesn't offend me. Of all terrible things about me, my appearance is the least of my concern.

My eleven-year-old self thought Virginia was kind. That she was merciful on the downtrodden, unwanted types.

Clearly, she was wrong.

"Virginia—"

"Do not use my name again," she says, cutting me off. For the first time, *she* sounds as nervous as I do. "You have no business here, Secora Reed. Now get off this stoop before someone sees you and gets the wrong impression."

"Let me inside," I try desperately. "Let me at least explain what I need. You are indebted to the Mother. It is your *duty* to provide aid to witches in need."

The door opens with a violent thrust. I stumble backward again, narrowly avoiding a collision.

"My faith does not apply to the likes of you," Virginia says. She's taller than I expect, and I have to crane my neck to look up at her. She holds a palm toward me, and I can sense the magic, the invisible tension zapping between us. "You are no child of the Mother, Secora Reed. You lost that right the day they clothed you in black. Now, get out of my sight before I do to you what you did to—"

I'm too distracted to hear them coming.

One moment, I'm cowering before Virginia, feeling pathetically small and foolish. The next, I'm gasping for breath, the world spinning out of focus. I squeeze my eyes shut and flail for stability. My hands find the stiff fabric of Beatrice's dress.

"You were supposed to alert us," she snarls. "Not beg to go inside."

She doesn't slow her pace, even when I notice we've left the Day Realm. The neutral territory is covered in street lights and festive music and drunken chatter. I dig my fingers against her dress and will myself not to puke.

We're moving faster than usual.

I should tell her Virginia won't follow us, but it'd be a guess at best. My memories, it seems, can be deceiving.

3

NASTY LITTLE THING

ELLIOT

"Here to see Madam Lyrie?" Vera asks.

The council's attendant is the dreariest person I've ever met. She's the same age as I am, but she acts older than my mama. Her hair splays over her shoulders in perfect blonde ringlets, and she peers up at me through large, round glasses. Why she wouldn't fix her eyesight with magic is beyond me. She certainly has the skill to do so.

Perhaps the glasses are another way to age herself. To pretend she's mature and worldly, rather than a stale over-achiever.

Most people in the council building call Mama by her given name, especially when talking to me. Not Vera though. It's *always* Madam Lyrie to her. And similarly...

"Mister Elliot?" she presses. "Are you here to see Madam Lyrie or—"

"Yes," I say. I can't keep the exasperation out of my voice. "As has been the case *every* time I come, I am here to see my mama."

If my sarcasm hurts Vera's feelings, she doesn't show it. She only offers a prim nod before rising from her desk.

"Let me see if she's available," she says before disappearing around the corner.

I don't point out that I could see if Mama's available myself. Over the past few years, I've learned it's easier to appease Vera's quirks than to argue.

Minutes later, I am led to Mama's office. Upon entering, I'm hit with the overwhelming scent of black tea and an undertone of lemon. It's rare for Mama to be *without* her black tea, and though I don't like the taste, the smell eases something in my chest. This place smells like comfort, like *home*, and for most of my life, Mama has spent more time here than anywhere else.

"Elliot," she says warmly. She places a well-read copy of our family's grimoire on her desk. The spine is so worn the cover splays over her pale wood desk like melting ice.

Mama's office is both overstuffed and organized. It's exactly how I imagine the inside of her head to be. Bookshelves line the walls, overflowing with ancient texts and an assortment of herbs and ingredients. Beneath each item, a dot of paint categorizes its purpose. Mama explained the system to me once—in agonizing detail—but I've long forgotten how it works.

Some things, like Mama's brain, are easier to admire than to understand.

"Hi, Mama," I say. I cross the room, dodging the small ritual set up on her rug. It's a location spell, and from the charred edges of the three herbs, it's already been completed. "Looking for someone?"

"Yes," she says. Her expression plummets as she glares at the location spell. She pushes from her desk and squeezes between two lopsided stacks of books, pulling me into a tight hug. "How was the surgery?"

"Fine," I say. It's the truth, but it'd still be my answer, even if it wasn't. The last thing I want is Mama worrying over it—over *me.* Despite being twenty-eight and a reputable healer, she still looks at me like I'm a gangly teenager.

Mama pulls back, hands on my shoulders. Her eyes narrow as she looks over me. She won't find anything. These are fresh clothes, free of wayward blood or potion spills.

"I changed," I assure her, rolling my eyes. "You really think I'd risk bringing a deadly infection to the council building?"

"Of course not," Mama says. She pats at my clothes, as if brushing them off. I think she's still unconvinced, but then she says, "You're too thin, Elliot. You work too much."

"And you worry too much," I say. I pull back, sliding past her to sit in the chair opposite her high-backed one. Despite being the most prestigious member of the autumnal coven, Mama always makes time for her people. She allows them to enter her office every Monday morning and complain over whatever menial thing is bothering them.

That said, she chose the world's most uncomfortable chair for them to sit.

To move them along, she'd once told me with a wink.

"So, who are you looking for?" I ask, jerking my chin toward the ritual. "Sebastian again? Or the Pruce woman?"

"No." Mama shakes her head. She purses her lips, as if debating whether to tell me.

"Is something going on?" I ask, straightening.

Sebastian Vulce and his clan of vampires attacked us not long ago. They'd stolen one of our prisoners and left over a dozen witches dead. Mama and the council have been uneasy ever since. Though they haven't announced anything, I suspect they have retaliation in the works.

"Sebastian's little witch visited last night," she says finally.

"Ah," is my only response. It doesn't surprise me that the vampires are scheming too. That's how everyone is in this gods-forsaken world. They all dream of power, of wealth, and the destruction of those who stand in their way.

In Mama's defense, the vampires have ruined her life every chance they get. They killed her husband—my father—while she was pregnant, leaving her to raise me alone. And years later, when she agreed to a peace treaty with them, Mama was publicly attacked by Sebastian. They deserved her wrath, her curse. And still, I wish more than anything this would all end. As it is, we're in a constant state of alert, just waiting for the next rebellion.

Mama's expression grows tighter. Her hair is almost entirely grey now, and her wrinkles look heavier than usual. She had me late in life, when most her age had teenagers. She's always been older than my friends' parents, and yet...She looks so much older than she did even last year.

"Secora Reed?" I ask. Mentioning the Day Realm's most notorious criminal—and our greatest traitor—does something strange to my stomach. Like Mama hates the vampires, I have more than enough reasons to hate Secora.

She's a violent criminal. An escaped murderer. A woman who once killed the closest friend I've ever had—and avoided persecution.

I have every reason to hate Secora Reed, but for some reason, I don't. I can't explain why. Maybe it's because, before she was a monster, she was just the lonely girl in my class. Forced to wear black, ostracized by everyone around her. She was the adopted sister of a close friend. Of *Harrison's* close friend.

Simply thinking of him sours my stomach. I clear my throat, forcing the feeling away.

"Yes, *Secora Reed*," Mama says with a sneer. "Nasty little thing can't seem to stop meddling. She was here last night."

My pulse spikes, but I don't let myself react.

"In Ochre?"

Mama nods as she returns to her chair. She takes a long drink of tea, eyes watching mine carefully.

"The augur house," she says. "She approached Virginia and demanded her cooperation."

I blow out a breath and lean back in my chair. The wooden rungs dig against my spine.

"Cooperation for *what*?"

"Unclear," Mama says. Deep wrinkles bracket her frown. "Virginia was too rattled to ask. Anyway, Secora is back in the Night Realm now, but she's clearly after something. I just don't know what..."

Mama trails off on another sigh. Takes a drink of tea.

"She's going to be a problem," she says. "I imagine she'll appear here at some point. We need to have a plan. A way to uncover her motives without her realizing."

"I'll keep an eye out for her," I say. "Maybe ask if any of the other healers—"

"Don't," Mama cuts me off sharply. "She's dangerous, Elliot. Stay away from her, you understand?"

"Well I wasn't planning to get drinks with her," I say, teasing. Mama's posture doesn't ease in the least, and I can't resist rolling my eyes. "She's an escaped murderer. Obviously, I'm going to be careful—"

"You're going to stay away," she repeats. "Say you understand."

This time, I do resist rolling my eyes, but only barely.

"All right, Mama," I say. "If I happen to see her, I'll stay away."

"And you'll tell me immediately."

I arch an eyebrow, as if to say, *obviously*.

"Good. Enough about that horrid woman." Mama swishes her wrist, as if flicking Secora Reed away. "Tell me about the surgery."

It's over an hour before I stand to leave Mama's office. I'd only planned to stop for a short chat, but time got away from us. It's rare we go this long without being disrupted by Vera for one reason or another.

"You'll be at the council meeting?" Mama asks as I pull on my coat. She rises too, crossing to stand before me. "I think it'd be nice for you to—"

"It's not a good fit," I interrupt.

Mama flinches, just like she does every time I tell her. I wish I had an ounce of her passion for politics, but I don't. Ever since I was a kid, my mind has been fascinated by the biological. I can't fathom sitting in an office like this. I don't belong in meeting halls or on stages. I belong at the healing center, undoing nasty curses and healing wounds.

Not *causing* them.

"I'll see you tomorrow?" I ask. I pull her into a hug, if only so I don't have to see that stricken, disappointed look on her face. I keep telling myself she'll get over my refusal to join the council, but it's been years now. Maybe this will always be an awkward divide between us.

"Of course," she says. "You can come over for dinner. I'll make your favorite. You really are getting too thin."

"I promise I'm eating, Mama," I say, chuckling.

She laughs too, pulling back to look at me. She says something, but I don't process it. I'm too busy staring at her wrist. The yellow fabric of her long-sleeved shirt has fallen toward her elbow, exposing dull grey skin.

I've been a healer my entire adult life, and I'm a damned

good one. I specialize in the rare, in the difficult, in the deadly. And still, I've never seen anything quite like this.

Mama tracks my stare and attempts to step away, but I don't let her.

"What in the Mother is that?" I demand.

I grab Mama's arm, shoving the fabric fully past her elbow. Pale grey skin stretches from just above her wrist, all the way up her arm, disappearing beneath her shirt. Despite knowing better, despite the possibility this could be infectious, I touch her forearm. Her skin is brittle and rough, like ancient parchment. No, rougher, like crushed eggshells.

I expect Mama to deflect. To get angry. To tell me it's none of my concern and to leave her be.

Instead, her shoulders deflate. When I look up from her arm, there are tears in her eyes.

"I was going to tell you," she says, voice cracking.

"Tell me *what*, exactly?" I can't keep the horror from my voice.

It looks like my mother is dying, like this part of her might already *be* dead.

"It started with the girl's death," she whispers. She pulls her hand away, tugging the sleeve back into place. "Ever since the Pruce descendant died and became a vampire, it started happening."

"Where?" I ask. I'm mentally tracking the days. Sebastian turned Grace Pruce into a vampire a month ago. An entire *month* ago. Part of me wants to berate her for neglecting to tell me. I will, someday, but not right now. Not when I'm already a month behind whatever the hells is happening to her.

"My chest," Mama says. She rests her hand over her heart, closing her eyes. "Right here. Then down. Then my arms. My legs are the newest—"

"The woman's cell was warded," I interrupt. My thoughts are

whirring too quickly, and my mind isn't processing this as fast as I need it to. There has to be an explanation. Once we have it, I'll figure out the solution. "Maybe when she died, some part of the ward latched onto you. Or maybe—"

"No," Mama says. The word is final, and I realize she already knows. She knows what's wrong and she *still* didn't tell me.

"Tell me," I say. I'm close to falling on my knees in front of her, terrified she'll deny me. "I can fix it, Mama. I'll fix it."

"You can't," she says. A lone tear escapes, tracking down her cheek. "It's the sun curse, Elliot. The Mother is punishing me for my part in it."

My entire body feels cold, and a rough shiver courses through me.

Twenty years ago, the vampires had gotten out of control. Mama did what she had to to protect our kind—and all of the Echo. She cursed the vampires to burn in sunlight, and for the first time in centuries, the Echo knew peace. But even the best intentions have a cost.

Mama's predecessor sacrificed his life to seal the curse, and she always feared the Mother would punish us for it. The Mother doesn't want her children to die, especially not by their own hand.

"I'll fix it," I say again. My eyes drop to Mama's sleeve, to the plague hidden beneath it. With a swallow, I force my attention back to her face. "I have questions, Mama. I'll need you to answer all of them. And please, *please* don't fight me on this."

"This cannot be cured," Mama says vehemently. Now she's the one looking at her arm. "It's the Mother's will, and her vision is greater—"

"Fuck her vision," I interrupt. My eyes burn with unshed tears, but I refuse to accept this. Mama isn't going to die. Mama *can't* die. She's all I have in this world.

Her eyes flash. She grabs me by the upper arms, rougher than she's ever been.

"Don't you ever speak ill of the Mother," she says. It comes out between her teeth, more a hiss than a whisper. "You understand me, Elliot?"

For a moment, I am a child again.

"Yes, Mama," I tell her. I swallow the knot in my throat, letting out a breath once her grip loosens. Speaking carefully, I try again. "Let me try to heal it. If it's the Mother's will that you die, then you will die. But maybe it's her will that I save you. Maybe if we find the woman's brother, it can be fixed. Let me try."

Mama doesn't respond right away. She takes a steady breath through her nose, palms coming to cup the sides of my face. I've been taller than her since I was a teenager, and yet, she's never seemed so small. So vulnerable.

"Ask your questions, Elliot," she says softly. "Do what you can. But please, know that I have made peace with the Mother's decision."

4

____

CAREFUL ISN'T MY STYLE
ELLIOT

"It doesn't make sense," I tell Henry. "Mama thinks the Mother is punishing her for the sun curse. If that's true, her sickness should have started with the ritual itself. Twenty years ago! Not now."

Henry Blume—my closest friend and a top-performing healer at the center—sits on one of the brown sofas in my living room. He's wearing a simple pair of slacks, a lavender buttoned shirt, and expensive grey shoes. Legs crossed, Henry rests his feet on my circular tea table.

"The curse only recently sealed though, when the Pruce woman died. They've yet to find another living descendant, right?" he asks. "There probably isn't one. Grace Pruce died, the curse fully sealed, and now that it has...your mama is facing the consequences."

I pace my living room. This house is too big for one person. Back when I first bought it, Mama insisted I needed the space to raise a family. I'd done it, mostly to appease her, but part of me hoped she was right. Mama raised me by herself, and I'd grown up lonely, on a large estate just like this one. I'd always loved the idea of having a big, rambunctious family.

Instead, I'm nearly thirty, and I've yet to find a serious girlfriend.

I pause at the far wall, leaning between two framed pieces of artwork. Mama picked them both, and it doesn't escape me how little my own preferences have gone into this place. If I'd chosen, there'd be colors beyond the typical autumnal hues. Mama balked when I considered purchasing black furniture instead of brown, and as usual, it was easier to indulge her.

Besides, having this home is less about the details and more about my personal success. Despite Mama's insistence that I join her on the council, I'd started my own healing center. Seven years in, and the Lyrie Healing Center is one of the most profitable in the Day Realm. I bought my home with the money *I* earned, and I'm infinitely proud of that, brown couches and all.

"It doesn't make sense," I say again. *Insist* because Mama can't be dying.

Henry doesn't reply right away. He plucks an olive from a ceramic bowl on the table and drops it in his mouth. Behind him, elongated windows span the length of the entryway, showing off the unobstructed view of Lake Astoria.

"So, what's your plan?" he finally asks. He crosses his ankles and settles deeper into the brown cushions.

"I don't know," I say. I pace toward the kitchen, tapping my fist against the stone counter. On it, I have several medical texts. My impromptu evaluation of Mama's symptoms lies in the center of the mess.

I can only hope she was honest. That she didn't leave anything out.

"Her skin is decaying, Henry," I say. I look over my sloppy handwriting, eyes catching on words like *fatigue* and *stiff joints* and *intermittent breathing pain.* "If it continues this speed of progression, she doesn't have much..."

I trail off. As a healer, I'm embarrassed at my inability to speak about this. Luckily, Henry doesn't mock me. For the entirety of our ten-year friendship, he's been brutish, obnoxious, and relentlessly unserious. I expect the same playfulness now, but his face is surprisingly somber.

"You need to buy yourself time," he says. He continues, even as I keep my attention on the counter. "If your mother is dying as quickly as you believe, you can't focus purely on the cure. You have to slow the progression."

"How do you suggest I do that?" I ask. My voice is a snarl, but I can't help it. "It's impossible to treat if I don't know the source."

"Legally, yes," he agrees.

Only now do I look at him.

Henry is no longer slouched on the sofa. His feet are planted firmly on the hardwood floor, an elbow propped on each knee. Though his blond hair is as messy as ever, his face is solemn.

"You can't be serious," I say. My voice is low, almost threatening.

After all, I *am* his boss.

"You're right," Henry says. He raises both hands in a gesture of surrender. "I shouldn't have said anything."

"It's illegal," I say anyway. If he hears the way my voice wavers, the way my words drop to a whisper, he doesn't acknowledge it.

"Yes," he agrees. "It is also dangerous. Potentially fatal, if not administered correctly."

I swallow.

"She would never allow it," I say. My voice is so quiet now, I'm not sure I've spoken aloud. The fact Henry doesn't reply makes me think perhaps I haven't.

Before long, he buttons his coat near the entryway of my house. I stand across from him, leaned against the metal-and-wire railing. The designer insisted it was a wildly popular trend in the human world, *destined to gain popularity here, too.* It's one of the few features Mama didn't pick.

"I truly am sorry about your mama, Elliot," he says. "If you need anything, tell me."

Something unspoken lingers beneath those words, but I can't bring myself to interpret it.

"Thank you," I say. My throat feels thick. Perhaps because Henry is a better friend than I deserve. More likely because I'm debating sacrificing every value I thought I had.

"You'll get through it," he says. Then, with an impish smirk, he adds, "If you need someone to take your mind off the stress, Mary has a couple friends who would *love* to distract you."

"I'm sure she does," I say, rolling my eyes. "You be careful with her."

"Nah," he says, slapping me on the shoulder. "Careful isn't my style."

I know, I almost say. *It's mine.*

Instead, I stay quiet, offering a final wave as he departs my doorstep. I stand there for longer than I should, staring at the gentle waves over Lake Astoria. When I first moved here, I had great expectations of spending weekends on the water, or at least the shore. I've been here for years, and I've only stood on its sand twice.

Long after Henry has left, when evening approaches and most witches are entering their homes until morning, I walk the path alongside the lake in the direction of the Night Realm.

5

A DAMNED LIABILITY

CORA

I've been keeping strange hours. There's no reason for me to be awake at two in the morning. After being out last night and spending all day stressing over the mission's failure, I should be exhausted. Instead, I'm jittery and filled with endless, half-formed ideas. The next clan meeting is in a few days, and I'll have nothing to report on the sunwalker spells. Again.

It's bad enough that Amelia, Beatrice, and Milas know the truth. I'm an utter failure, and there's a high likelihood I *won't* be able to deliver the allies I promised. Disappointing those three feels humiliating. Disappointing *Sebastian* is downright shameful. I can't help but credit him for my survival all these years. Even if I could survive on my own now, I couldn't have at fifteen. Sebastian saved my life, and I *hate* that I haven't been able to repay the favor.

By three in the morning, I'm too restless to remain in bed. I drink a cup of green tea and wander the halls. I'm in the farthest-most quarters in the western wing. Partly for my protection. Partly for the vampires' sanity. Witch blood smells putrid to them—a handy trick my ancestors came up with to dissuade them from eating us.

It also dissuades them from being in our presence at all.

I stride down one hallway, then another, keeping on my side. The eastern wing of the manor is packed with resident vampires. There are hundreds of thousands of vampires in the Echo, and a few hundred of them live within these walls. They bunk in shared bedrooms, glaring out at the daylight through their protective windows. Many of them despise me for being a witch, for being the same species that brought this horrid curse upon them.

Never mind that *I'm* the one who magicked the windows. Never mind that *I'm* the one trying to fix it.

Not fast enough, I think bitterly. Sunwalker spells are the only way vampires can walk in the sun without catching fire. I've only made one since Grace became a vampire, and it was for *her*.

Forget the hundreds of thousands of vampires in the Night Realm. At this rate, I'll die long before the manor's residents can walk in daylight. I need help, and I need a lot of it.

I grind my teeth to the point my jaw aches. I pace the hallways, forcing myself to study the many oil paintings and to imagine what may lie behind each closed wooden door. After a while, I start counting my steps to try to keep the bad thoughts from overtaking me.

It doesn't matter. I can't escape my own mind, and before long, I've reached the end of the western wing. I could go to the next level. That's what I *should* do, honestly, but I'm inexplicably drawn to the central wing. That's where the ballroom is. The courtyard. The bloodletting room and the extravagant entryway. There's no reason I should go there.

There are plenty of reasons I *shouldn't*.

It's nightfall, the vampires are at their rowdiest, and the fact I stink to them won't stop them from attacking. If they're reckless enough, *hungry* enough, they will. Sebastian would kill them for it, sure, but that's not much comfort if I'm already dead.

I rock onto my toes, then shake my head.

What am I thinking?

Why the hells would I leave my sanctuary, just because I *feel* like it? That's a new level of stupidity.

I shift on my heels, back in the direction of my room. I'll pace these halls again, maybe twice more, and then I'll go to bed.

I barely manage a step when I hear it.

A loud, garbled screaming, coming from the entryway.

I don't think, don't register the who or the what or the why. There's no moment of consideration, no thought of potential consequences.

I'm already moving. Heart racing. Eyes searching. Magic pulsing. Because even without allowing myself to think, my body *knows*. It will know him until the day I die. Maybe even after that.

I don't stop running until I reach the front door. There, a handful of goons drag him in by the shoulders.

It's been twelve years since I've seen Elliot Lyrie, but I swear, my breath catches in the exact same way.

Beautiful.

When we were teenagers, I thought he was the most stunning man I'd ever seen. But he wasn't a man then, not really. He is now. Somewhere over six feet tall. Still lean, but far more muscular than he was at sixteen. His hair is darker. Longer. That curl over his forehead is more pronounced than I remember. Perfect lips, the bottom slightly larger than the top.

His mouth twists into another vicious scream, and my momentary daze evaporates.

Elliot. *My* Elliot is here.

The one place I hoped to never see him.

I should tell the goons to unhand him. These four vampires are under Sebastian's protection, which means they're under mine too. They're not breaking any laws by dragging Elliot into the manor. Witches are forbidden in vampire territory, and by Night Realm rules, these goons can do whatever they'd like to him as punishment. Capture, torture, even kill him.

So yeah, I should tell them to unhand Elliot. It would be the fair, honorable thing to do—and I swear I'm trying to be a better person. But when Elliot cries out again, any thought of playing nice disappears.

I extend both palms at once, letting my magic loose. It latches onto each goon, hurling them in different directions.

One crashes against the door to the bloodletting room. Another smashes through the front window, sending shards of stained glass across the floor. The other two fling somewhere behind my head, their bodies crunching horrifically against the stone pillars.

I look over Elliot, cataloguing every single body part. He's not injured. Not that I can tell.

The two vampires in front of me are unconscious. I imagine the two behind me are, as well. I know better than to look away from Elliot to check.

"Tell me if they move," I instruct him. My voice croaks, raspy and strained. I'm breathing so hard I can barely see straight, and my magic is going haywire. It singes beneath my skin, as if branding me from the inside.

Elliot stares at me. He's impossible to read, and I'm hit with a foul sense of nostalgia. Once again, my body is remembering something *I* don't. My heart squeezes, begging me to approach him. I don't.

"You're—" he starts. He blinks at me, hazel eyes wide, mouth parted. "You look just like..."

An indescribable sensation pulses through me. Good and

bad, all at once. I'm tempted to smile, to laugh at the absurdity of his confusion. He doesn't know me. Not like he should. He's staring at me like a complete stranger, and it's almost funny, the look of bewilderment on his face. As if I am no more than a scary story, a classmate he once had but never really knew. A classmate who once tortured his best friend until his heart gave out.

Maybe, if I wasn't completely gutted by his disgust, by the vile horror in his expression, I would smile. Instead, I force myself to swallow. I keep my posture straight, my expression neutral.

"Keep your eyes on the vampires behind me," I remind him. I think I'll hear them move, but it's better to be cautious. More importantly, it'll keep those hazel eyes off me.

Elliot doesn't immediately respond. His palms are open at his sides, but they're not raised defensively. Despite his impressive lineage, he was never much of a fighter. It went against his every instinct, and by the looks of it, it *still* does. He could have fought those goons off himself. He *should* have, but I don't voice that opinion.

After a strained moment, Elliot's eyes flicker away, shifting between the two goons behind me.

"They're unconscious."

His voice is so much deeper now, like warm velvet. It makes me want to close my eyes and drift to sleep.

Safe, I realize. Elliot's voice makes me feel *safe*, even now.

"What are you doing here, Elliot?" I ask. I force the words out, make them as sharp and cruel as they need to be. "You should know better."

"You remember me?" he asks. His dark brows jump toward his hairline, and I internally cringe at my mistake. In his mind, we were barely acquaintances. We went to the same school. We had the same friend in Margot. But for him, that's where it ends.

If I were to pluck out a few more memories, if I were to screw them tight in my collection of jars, that's where it would end for me too.

I couldn't though, and this is *exactly* why. I needed some sense of assurance that, if Elliot and I ever crossed paths, I would know he's *mine* to protect.

"Answer the question," I say, rather than answering his.

"It doesn't matter."

Elliot looks down at his clothing then, and I can't help but do the same. He's wearing a burnt orange buttoned shirt. Dark grey pants. A pair of shoes that must be brown but are dark enough to appear black. I can almost see myself in them. They're so shiny. It's all so...fancy.

I shouldn't be surprised. Elliot's always been wealthy, and at some point, he had to outgrow his rebellious teenage phase. Back then, he wore grass-stained pants and shirts with holes in them, just to irritate his mama. Now that he's running his own healing center, I suppose he has to dress nice.

I scan over him again. No blood that I can see. No bruises, even. Whatever the goons were planning to do with him, they clearly hadn't yet.

"Are you hurt?" I ask. Then, realizing I shouldn't have, I say, "Don't answer that. Just...tell me why you're here, Elliot. Because if your mama sent you—"

"She didn't," he says. The words come out in a rush, so there's a good chance he's lying. "She doesn't know I'm here. Don't go turning this into an act of war when it isn't one."

His brows are furrowed, lips twitching downward. He's trying to look fearsome, I think. It makes me want to smile, but I restrain myself.

"All right," I say. Then, "Whatever the reason, I hope it's settled. You can't come back, Elliot. This will happen every time. You're lucky I was here to stop it."

"Why did you?" he asks. His hazel eyes flicker over the vampires behind me before settling back on my face. "Stop them, I mean."

"It doesn't matter." I arch my eyebrow in a silent challenge.

"Fair enough," he says tightly.

"Well, now that we've got that..." I trail off, stomach sinking with a realization I should have had *way* sooner. "Fuck."

"What?" he asks. His lips are downturned, brow still creased. It's unfair how handsome he is. Pretty people always look good, no matter the face they're making. It's distracting. A damned liability.

"You can't leave," I say. "They'll eat you alive out there, Elliot. And I do mean that literally."

"I'm a witch—"

"Who clearly isn't prepared to defend himself," I snap. I start for my quarters, pausing when I realize I've given him my back. Whirling around, I say. "Come on."

"You're insane if you think I'm stepping another foot into this place." He looks at me with disgust. He's never looked at me like that. And I know it's unfair to be hurt. I know exactly *why* he's looking at me like that, and still...it does something to my insides. It feels like my organs are melting, like my body is dying piece by piece.

"Fine," I grit out. My voice chokes, and I realize with a wave of horror that I'm going to cry. I clear my throat roughly. "Make a run for it. See how far you get."

I stumble out of the room, stopping in the nearest hallway. Only once I'm out of sight do I allow a few tears to fall. It's pathetic—I know that. I just can't seem to stop it.

Life has always been unfair to me, but this is unjustly cruel. Having Elliot this close, seeing his blatant hatred of me...It's a punishment fit for a villain, not for me.

I lean against the wall, breathing slowly. Silently.

I can't see into the entryway from my position, but there's a window that reflects most of the room. I can see the goons, still unmoving on the floor, and I can see Elliot, shifting on his feet. He keeps looking my way, as if expecting me to reappear.

He takes two steps toward me.

Roughly shakes his head.

Turns and marches through the front door.

"Fuck," I mutter.

Mine to protect.

I run after him, hands already trembling. Even if he doesn't want me to follow, he'll have to let me. He'll be too busy fighting off vampires to worry about fighting me. If I can convince him to work together, we should be able to make it.

Except we reek.

They'll smell us immediately.

We'll be lucky *if they bring us to Sebastian.*

I throw open the front door. I've barely stepped through it when Elliot crashes back inside—and into me. I stumble backwards, and it's only his hands on my elbows that keep me from falling.

He's touching me.

No. He's *holding* me.

"Let go," I say. My voice is breathy, unfamiliar, even to my own ears.

"Sorry," he says.

He releases me. Steps back. Allows a gasp of breath between us. All the while, I stare at him, breathing hard, palms tightened into fists.

"You were coming after me," he says, and it comes out like an accusation.

"Well, yeah," I snap. "You were going to get yourself killed."

"And?" he asks. There's no anger from his word, only naked

curiosity. "Wouldn't your folk celebrate the murder of Madam Lyrie's son?"

My folk? Maybe.

Me?

"It would start a war," I say. It's not a lie. "So come inside. I'll give you a place to sleep. Once the sun is up, you'll be safe to leave."

"Fine," he says. The word is muddled by his clenched jaw. "I'll stay. But if you lock me up—"

"Trust me," I interrupt. "I'm more eager for you to leave than you are."

6

SECORA REED CLEARLY DESERVES IT
ELLIOT

There is something wrong with Secora Reed, and it's not *just* that she's an escaped murderer. It's a feeling I get when I look at her. Like she's a lie. Like there's something twisted in her soul, meant to be unraveled, but too vague to name. I look at Secora Reed, and I see a complete stranger.

Not a former classmate.

Not a friend's spare sister.

Not Harrison's killer.

She is a stranger I've never met, and I can't make sense of that. She is pretty and sharp and *alive*. I should have memories of her. I would have spoken to her in school. At the very least, I would have noticed her from afar. And yet, no matter how hard I try, I can't come up with a single, solid memory of this woman.

"I don't have a guest bedroom," she says. She glances back at me, and if she sees the panic on my face, it doesn't phase her. She stops at an unmarked door, the last in a ridiculously long hallway of them.

"Are those rooms all full?" I ask, tilting my chin in the direction we came.

"They're empty," she says. She pauses, hand on the door-knob, to look up at me. Her large eyes are a deep shade of brown. Her mouth is wide. Only her nose is small, and it makes her look a bit like a porcelain doll. Beautiful. Too delicate for a murderer.

With that, my mind snaps back to the situation at hand. Now is *not* the time and she is *not* the person.

"I'll stay in one of them then," I say. "No offense. I'm sure you're great company—"

"They're not warded," she says, shoving open her door. "So unless you want vampires attacking you in your sleep, I'd recommend staying in mine."

She strides through her doorway and doesn't look back to see if I follow. I'm not sure if this is another bluff. Maybe, if I start for a different room, she'll chase me down like before.

Or maybe she'll let me go, I'll get eaten, and I'll never make it back to the Day Realm.

With a stiff sigh, I force myself into the woman's quarters. They're as dreary and unpleasant as you'd expect for a murderer. The furniture is black. The kitchen is littered with incomplete potions and a sink full of dishes. Stepping farther into the room, I can see an array of rotted plants across from the kitchen. They're alive though. Magicked to look dead while thriving.

Yes, I think. *There is something very wrong with Secora Reed.*

She stands in the kitchen, her back to me. It's a stupid move for a wanted criminal. I could disarm her before she turned around, have her tied up and thrown over my shoulder before she could retaliate. But then, I'd be faced with getting us back to the Day Realm, a feat I've accepted is impossible. Clearly she knows that too.

"I'm not used to company," she says. Then, "I only have green tea."

"Honey?" I ask.

Secora stills, her entire body clenching at once. As if honey is somehow an offensive request.

"No," she says finally. "No, I don't. Sorry."

"It's fine," I say. I watch the tension ease out of her shoulders. Slowly, she starts making a single cup of tea.

"I'll take one," I say. She never offered, but it felt implied.

"You drink green tea?" she asks. Only now does she turn around, one of her dark brows stretching for her hairline.

"Yes?" I say. It comes out more like a question. I'm not sure why she looks shocked. Maybe she forgot tea is a universally loved beverage in the Day Realm. I don't think I've met a witch who *doesn't* drink it. We all have our preferences, sure. Green tea isn't my favorite, but I'll drink any kind other than black.

"Oh," she says. She looks frazzled now, dropping her eyes as she turns back to the counter. "Sure. Of course."

Then she's rattling through cupboards for another mug. They're all mismatched. Many are black, but there are colorful ones too. Red and orange and green. She returns her focus to the tea, and I stand awkwardly near the doorway, just watching her.

"Shut the door," she says without turning.

"I thought it was warded." I don't know why I don't simply close the door. Or maybe I do. Maybe it's the same reason I've yet to take my eyes off Secora as she makes my tea.

"I'd rather no one know you're here," she says.

"You're a murderer," I say. Blurt is a more accurate word. But somewhere between *shut the door* and her not wanting anyone to know I'm here...I can't bear the tension surrounding us. Surrounding me, at least.

I expect Secora to tense again, but for all the grief I got asking for honey, she doesn't so much as flinch now.

"Yes," she says. She swirls both teas, but releases them to face me. Behind her, the spoons continue stirring. Without even looking, she's controlling them by magic.

Powerful, my brain warns me. *More powerful than she looks.*

It's her height, I decide, that makes her look unassuming. That, paired with her large, doll-like features, makes her look innocent. Like something in need of protection.

"The guy you killed," I say. My voice chokes as I speak, until my words are almost too garbled to understand. "He was my best friend."

Harrison Iyle had been my best friend from the time I could walk until the day he died. We'd grown up together. Been more like brothers than friends. He spent most weekends at my house. Taught me how to play groundball. Made me laugh so hard my stomach hurt for days. He could be an asshole, sure, but he didn't deserve to die.

He didn't deserve to be murdered by this five-foot-nothing woman. She'd only been fifteen at the time. What kind of fifteen-year-old murders her classmate?

"Yes," Secora says again. She leans back, crossing her arms over her chest. The movement shifts her black sleeves, revealing her wrists. Her very bare wrists, where golden bands used to trap her magic.

She should be balking at the realization I was Harrison's friend. At the very least, she should look apologetic. She doesn't, and that lack of remorse makes her hideous. She is a monster without chains, and even those weren't enough to protect Harrison.

"I'm not going to hurt you, Elliot," she says, following my gaze on her wrists. Her voice is unsettlingly gentle as she looks over me. "If it's any consolation, I haven't really killed since I was fifteen."

"It's not," I snap. "I don't believe you, for one thing. But for another, even if I did, it wouldn't make me feel better. You *killed* my best friend. Plus three other innocents."

Her eyes narrow, and I wait for her to say something against me. That they weren't innocent. That they deserved it.

If she does...I'm not sure what I'll do. I clench my fists, feeling an unexpected flare of magic in my palms.

She's powerful, but *how* powerful? Enough to take me down? Enough to kill me?

I run my tongue over my teeth, debating. This could be the win the witches need, a way to step back into power after the vampires' recent victory over us. Secora's death would certainly hurt the vampires. She's the only reason they've *won* anything in the past twenty years.

"I could kill you," I say. The words don't come out half as threatening as I intend. I don't believe them, and by the way her face softens, she doesn't either.

"You're not a killer, Elliot."

"You don't know anything about me," I say. I *hope*, because maybe she did. Maybe she stalked Harrison for months before killing him. Maybe she stalked me too, and the only reason I'm still alive is because she had to flee the Day Realm.

"I know enough," she says simply.

My lip curls without permission, desperate to argue with her. She's right though. I'm a healer by nature, and the simple thought of hurting someone makes my stomach turn. I've never been one to get in fights, not even when people deserve it.

But Secora Reed *clearly* deserves it.

She surprises me by turning once again, facing our teas. I've lost count of how many times she's given me her back. This time is objectively worse. She knows I'm debating killing her, and she's still acting like I'm not a threat.

If she remembers me from school—and she's certainly pretending to—she would know I was top of our class. I could have her unconscious already. Could have her lifeless body at my feet in seconds. Just because I'm not quick to violence doesn't mean I wouldn't be good at it.

"Even if you were a killer," she says lazily. She turns back to me, and I feel a flare of shame that I wasted my opportunity. She holds our teas in either hand. "If you killed me or kidnapped me or whatever you're thinking...you'd die for it. Trust me. Sebastian doesn't take kindly to people hurting his own, in case you've forgotten what happened with Grace."

Now I do snarl. That night left far too many dead. It's what initiated the sickness in my mother. Secora may not have been the one to seal the curse, but she undoubtedly played a role in it.

"Here," she says. Remaining at the kitchen counter, she floats my drink across the room. The pale blue teacup hovers in front of me, but I don't touch it.

I shouldn't have asked for it. I don't know why I did. I'm obviously not going to drink tea from a known murderer. Doesn't matter if I watched her make it. She could have all too easily poisoned it—

"And here I thought *I* was the stubborn one," she says on a sigh. Her lips tick into a barely-there smile. When I blink, the expression is gone, and I decide I imagined it.

～

Elliot Lyrie

age 12

Ochre Primary School

"Do you see her?" Harrison asks. He crashes against my side, hard enough I stumble into the tree I'd been using for cover.

Because, yes, I do see her.

When we heard the Blake family was taking on an orphan from the hibernal coven, we couldn't believe it. Harrison was convinced Margot was lying. I didn't doubt her at first. Her family are the nicest people I've ever met. Mama Blake organizes most of the school's fundraisers. Papa Blake runs a free groundball club for families with no money. And Margot makes it her personal responsibility that everyone in our class feels included.

To me, it made sense the Blake family was helping out an orphan. I had assumed it was a baby. At the very least, a normal kid whose parents died in an accident or something.

Not...her.

Harrison crowds against me, until I'm squished between him and the tree. I have to shove him away to lean around it, to catch sight of the new girl again. She's standing all by herself near the swing set, the hem of her dress clenched in both fists.

I've never seen a Dark One before. They usually aren't integrated into society after they're discovered. They're usually imprisoned or killed. But they're not usually little girls with wide, innocent eyes either.

"I asked my mama," Harrison whispers, glancing over at me. His white-blond hair is a wild mess, as if he forgot to brush it this morning. "It's true, Elliot. She killed her parents."

"No way," I say. I peer farther around the tree. The girl seems way too little to be dangerous. She's only a year younger, but she looks so much smaller. She's short and skinny. But she's wearing all black, and when she rocks back on her heels, I catch a glimpse of gold bands beneath her sleeves.

"I wouldn't lie," he says. He turns toward me, nose scrunching. "You don't believe me?"

"She's just..." I trail off, unsure what I planned to say.

"She killed them both," he says. "Only a few months old. Exploded their brains."

"She did not."

"She did!" Harrison punches my shoulder. "Serious, Elliot. The first family that tried adopting her brought her right back. The second, some nice old hag? She killed her too. She's been at the orphanage for years, and for some crazy reason, Mama Blake picked her."

I don't respond this time. I'm too scared my voice will break, and I don't want him to know I'm afraid. It takes all my effort to keep my knees from shaking.

She's killed three people? She's younger than we are. Only eleven. Why would she...

"There's Margot," Harrison says.

Harrison has been dating Margot for all of two weeks, but he's already annoyingly obsessed. He ditched me twice during lunch this week to hang out with her. Like I said though, she's nice. Harrison could certainly pick worse company, even if I don't know why he wants a girlfriend at all.

Seems more fun to play groundball or practice spells or do literally anything else.

Margot glides across the playground, waving ecstatically to the little girl in black. She told us her name—I'm sure of it—but I can't remember it now. They look as polar opposite as physically possible.

Margot wears a pale yellow jumpsuit, her blonde hair twisted into matching braids. A sparkly orange bow fastens the end of each, glinting with the sun's sharp reflection. The new girl wears baggy black clothes, and her long brown hair is loose. Unkempt. She looks...sad.

I wonder if she feels bad for killing all those people.

Slapping my shoulder for the millionth time—I'm sure I'll have a permanent bruise, even when I'm a grown up—Harrison takes off in the girls' direction. I follow after him. I don't bother asking if he'd rather play with the other boys. I already know the answer.

By the time I reach them, Harrison is standing in front of Margot, like he's her personal shield. The girl in black has stumbled several steps away, arms now hugging her middle.

"Stop, Harrison," Margot hisses. "You're scaring her."

"Good," he says. He bares his teeth at the girl, and she again stumbles back. "Don't even think about hurting Margot, you freak."

I suck in a breath. Harrison's always been a little bossy, a little "aggressive", according to Mama. But he's never been mean. I've never heard him call someone a name before.

I grab his shoulder rather than saying anything. When he looks back to me, his expression instantly shifts from one of hatred to determination.

"She needs to understand," he tells me.

I stare at him, widening my eyes, silently willing him to read my mind. He should know better than to pick on a literal murderer. She killed grown ups when she was a baby...who knows what she could do to us now. Golden bands or not.

"You don't touch Margot, you understand?" he asks, shifting back to the girl. "If you do, I'll know, and I'll kill you."

"Harrison!" Margot shrieks. She's crying, which isn't unusual for Margot. Just about everything makes her cry. But for the first time, I feel like crying with her. A nasty knot ties in my stomach.

"This is for your own good," he spits back at her. He steps for the girl, whose brown eyes widen. She mimics his movement, only adding distance when he's taking it away.

"C'mon, Harrison," I say.

"Say it, freak," he says to the girl, ignoring my hand on his shoulder. Ignoring Margot tugging on his opposite arm. "Say it!"

"I won't touch her," she says. She's not crying, but her lower lip trembles, like it's taking everything not to.

"Good," he snaps. Then, turning back to Margot, he says, "We need to talk."

"Yes, we do," she agrees. Her face is red, but her tears have stopped. Now, her terror has transformed into fury. "Not here. Follow me."

Without waiting for him, Margot storms off in the opposite direction, back toward the school. I glance past her, scanning the playground for our teacher. Mrs. Raekes isn't anywhere to be seen. There are other kids though, all watching this interaction unfold.

"I mean it," Harrison says.

I've barely turned back to them when he pushes her. She stumbles backward, not even attempting to catch herself as she falls into the dirt.

"Harrison!" I yell.

But he's already moving. He's taken off after Margot, leaving the girl sprawled out on her back.

I stare at her longer than I probably should. She's blinking up at the sky, hands fidgeting, but otherwise unmoving. I keep waiting for her to get up, but she doesn't.

I shift on my feet. This girl is dangerous. So dangerous Harrison is terrified of her. I could see it in his eyes. Between the fury and the determination, beneath all the hatred. He is scared of this girl and what she's capable of.

I should run like he did.

Instead, I step forward. One. Two. Three. Until I'm standing beside her. My body casts a shadow over her, but she doesn't look at me. She just keeps blinking up at the sky.

"Here," I say. I shove my hand toward her, and the girl flinches. Those wide eyes find mine, looking far more terrified than any natural-born killer's should.

I stare at her.

She stares at my hand.

The seconds tick by, until I'm shifting on my feet again.

"Look," I say. "Just take it. I'm not going to push you or anything." She still stares.

With my arm extended toward her, I glance around again.

Everyone is watching. The eleven and twelve years are all out here. It isn't only Mrs. Raekes' class. There are dozens of kids, all watching me get rejected by our newest, unwelcome addition. The only people I don't see—thank the Mother—are Harrison and Margot. The last thing I need is Harrison pestering me about this for the rest of my life.

"Come on," I say. I lean closer, feeling the edges of my ears heat with embarrassment. "Just take it. Don't be stubborn. I'm trying to help you."

"I'm not stubborn. I'm smart," she says. She pushes onto her elbows, then climbs to her feet. She brushes off her dress, sending bouts of dust into the air. "Get shoved into the dirt enough times, and you will be too."

"I already said I wasn't—"

"People lie, Elliot," she says. I raise my eyebrows, surprised she already knows my name. As if she's caught her mistake at the same time, a faint blush crawls over her cheeks.

Murderers shouldn't blush.

"People lie all the time," she repeats. "Getting shoved into the dirt teaches you all sorts of lessons."

My mouth feels dry. I want to ask why she's always getting shoved in the dirt. I want to know if she meant to kill all those people. I want to tell her I really wasn't going to shove her into the dirt. I wasn't lying.

The girl turns. The back of her black dress is still covered in dust. She storms off, not toward the other kids, but toward the tree I'd just used as a hiding place. It's a solitary willow, rumored to be haunted. Harrison and I never believed it.

"Haunted," I say. When the girl turns back, a scowl on her face, I struggle to elaborate. "The tree. Some people think it's haunted. So, uh, be careful."

"Don't you know?" she asks. "I'm haunted too."

With that, she storms across the field, arms stiff at her sides. It isn't until she's reached the tree, until she's curled up beneath it, that I realize I still don't know her name. And now, inexplicably, I want to.

7

———

WHAT'S THE CATCH

CORA

I spread a blanket on the couch, spending more time smoothing it than I need to. Once Elliot's bed is ready, I'll have to try for more information. If he still refuses, I'll have nothing else to do but go to bed. There are extra wards over my bedroom, so at least I won't have to worry about him killing me in my sleep.

You wouldn't be worried anyway, my brain taunts me.

I ignore it. Tuck the blanket into the couch's crease.

"You realize I'm just going to undo all that," Elliot says from behind me.

He finally closed the door, but he still hasn't moved from the entryway. I'm sure he's expecting me to kill him, but there's no point in trying to change his mind. This will—hopefully—be the last time we ever see each other.

I swallow over the knot in my throat.

"Did you get what you needed?" I ask.

"I don't need anything," is his immediate, sharp response. "I'm not drinking your tea. I don't want food—"

"In the Night Realm, Elliot," I say, cutting him off. I resist the urge to roll my eyes at him and instead focus on his couch bed. I position a pillow at one end. His feet are going to dangle off the opposite side, but there's nothing to do about that.

"It's none of your concern," he says. "What I do here—"

"I need to ensure you don't come back, so tell me what you need," I say, looking at him. I work to keep my voice level, but it wavers. I only hope he doesn't notice. "Assuming it's not an act of war, I should be able to get it for you."

He arches an eyebrow, watching me silently. He doesn't believe me, and for good reason.

"Listen," I say. "If the vampires know Madam Lyrie's son is sniffing around our territory, they're going to get freaked out. And once they get freaked out, they destroy anything that's a threat."

"You're telling me you *don't* want my people destroyed?" he asks. Then pauses, considering. "Our people?"

"Your people. You had it right the first time," I say. "Honestly, I don't care about your people. I care about *my* people. And the more time wasted on you, the less time spent on things that actually matter."

Elliot doesn't immediately respond. He continues staring at me, and I can tell from his posture that he's actively working not to fidget. His fingers give him away, just barely twitching at his thighs. All these years later, and I can still read him so easily. This would be easier if I couldn't.

As he looks at me, regarding me as a stranger, an *enemy* stranger, I wish I could see him the same way.

Instead, I am hit with a wild and dangerous nostalgia. The way he smells and talks. The way his mouth moves, slanting slightly to the right when he speaks. The way he sighs and shifts and...all of it.

I know him, far more than I'd like.

But that is my own punishment to bear.

"I need blood," he says, pulling me from my thoughts. A crease forms between his brows, the one he gets when he's worried. He used to look at me that way all the time, as if I was someone he desperately needed to save.

"Blood?" I echo dumbly.

"Vampire blood," he says. He shifts again, fingers stretching and curling at his sides. He keeps his eyes on me, but I can tell it's taking effort. He's nervous, telling me this.

"You're the best healer in the Day Realm," I say before I can stop myself. "What do you need with vampire blood?"

"I'm not going to tell you that."

"Then no," I say. I finally rise from the floor, patting his black pillow. It's one from my bed, but I don't tell him that. It's not like I had any spares lying around. I've never had a guest before, and after tonight, I doubt I will again.

"Secora—"

"Cora," I correct him. "No one calls me that here."

His jaw ticks.

"I need the blood," he tells me. "I can't tell you what it's for, but I assure you, it's nothing nefarious. Someone is sick. Our typical healing methods aren't working. I need to buy time."

I study him, trying to sense a lie. There's nothing there, not even an inkling of deception. This man may be older—broader —than the boy from my memories, but he's still Elliot Lyrie. The same pure soul I've always known, and he's telling the truth.

He *would* risk his life to save someone else.

"You're in the Night Realm for a patient?"

"I need blood," he repeats. His voice is soft, and my eyes flutter shut without permission. "Please, Cora."

I've never been able to deny this boy anything.

"How much?"

"At least two vials," he says, shoulders loosening. "More would be better, but I can get by with two."

"I'll give you six," I say.

I brush past him and cross to the far side of the kitchen. From his place by the doorway, he watches me with narrowed eyes. I ignore him and maneuver my way onto the counter. I wouldn't normally do this with an audience, but at my height, counter-climbing is an essential life skill. My kitchen cabinets go all the way to the ceiling, and I keep the good stuff—like vampire blood, poison, and rare herbs—up at the top.

"Do you need help?" he asks, voice strained.

Ever the gentleman. My lips twitch into a smile, and because I'm facing away, I let it stay. I've barely smiled tonight, and still, I'm sure it's more than the past weeks combined.

I stretch onto my toes, sift through the various ingredients, and collect six vials of dark vampire blood. All belonging to a deceased vampire, just to be safe. On the off chance Elliot is lying, the witches won't be able to hex this blood for any of their vile hobbies.

I carefully lower from the counter, and Elliot watches me with an unreadable expression. His brows crinkle as I cross the room, stopping in front of him.

"What's the catch?" he demands. His attention drifts to the vials in my hands, and I study the desperation in his eyes. The barely-contained relief.

This blood isn't just for a patient. Vampire blood is illegal in the Day Realm. The Mother despises dark magic, and almost everything in the Night Realm was born of it. For Elliot to be here, he's trying to save someone he knows. Someone he *loves*. The idea guts me.

"Six vials," I say, pushing them into his hands. His skin is warm, soft, lightly calloused. I force myself to pull away. "You take them, and you never come back."

I WAKE to the sound of my name. I bolt upright, heart thundering. I'm moving before I'm fully awake, because it's not Elliot calling for me. It's Sebastian. If Elliot answers the door, there's no telling what will happen.

I fling open my bedroom door, only to falter. My quarters are empty. The blankets are folded on the end of the couch. Our mismatched tea mugs are laid on the drying rack.

He's gone.

"Cora!" Sebastian calls again. His fist pounds on my door in a sharp, rhythmic pattern that's unique to him. I typically find it comforting. Right now, it's grating my last nerve.

"Patience, Master!" I call back.

I shove the mostly-dry tea mugs into the cupboard. I toss the folded blanket on the other side of the couch, out of sight. It won't make a difference, but it at least buys me a few seconds before I have to face Sebastian.

"You don't have to call me master any—"

I throw open the door, letting the knob bump against the wall. I stand before him, arms loose at my sides. After years of practice, I know how to control my own body. How to breathe steady. How to maintain an even heartbeat. How to hold eye contact, even when I'm desperate to look away.

Sebastian glowers down at me. Short blond hair. Haunted green eyes. A slight twist to his mouth that makes him look displeased, even when he's not. He's taller than I am by several inches, but shorter than Elliot.

Stop, I mentally chastise myself. *Do not compare him to Elliot.*

"He's already gone," I say. I lift my chin, swallowing past the knot in my throat.

"I assumed you would deny it," Sebastian says carefully. His voice is level, but I can sense the fury boiling beneath every word.

"Then you assumed I was a fool," I say. I brush past him, into the hallway. "Go ahead and look. I can lift the ward, if you wish. You can investigate every nook and cranny. I assure you, he's gone."

"He left at first light," Sebastian says. Despite his words, his eyes drift away from me, scanning my quarters instead.

I met Sebastian Vulce twelve years ago, when he was the sole king of the vampires. He was rumored to be terrible, monstrous, and unjustly cruel. To an extent, the rumors were true.

By the time his eyes return to me, Sebastian's downturned mouth has twisted into a full grimace. He looks at me in disgust. In disappointment.

I don't take it personally.

"Why?" he asks. His hands tighten into fists, then loosen. Tighten again.

I sidestep back into my quarters.

"An old friend needed vampire blood for healing. He'd gotten himself into trouble," I say. It's not a lie, but it's certainly not the full truth. "I provided some—it was a dead vampire's, don't worry. I instructed him to wait until daylight before leaving."

"You gave him free reign of your quarters?" Sebastian asks. His voice lowers. Grows rougher, and his fingers clench into tighter fists.

"He didn't touch anything. I have this whole place warded, so I would know," I say. "I gave him several doses of Dismemrate. He'll have forgotten everything by the time he returns to the Day Realm."

This is a lie. Warding every item in my quarters would take more magic than I care to waste. And while I could have given Elliot Dismemrate for memory loss...

Why *didn't* I?

I swallow the question down, banishing it from my consciousness altogether.

"Who was it, Cora?"

I don't let myself react, even as my soul hums with gratitude. No one who saw Elliot recognized him. They saw a witch—not a council leader's son. Not the person Madam Lyrie loves more than anyone else.

I run my tongue over the back of my teeth, considering my words carefully.

"It was a boy from school," I say finally. "He was kind to me. When all the others were horrible, he was kind. I felt I owed him."

Sebastian studies me silently. I regulate my breathing, my heartbeat, my eye contact.

"Never again," he says, though I don't miss the way his face softens. "If he—or any like him—returns, you will notify me *immediately*."

"Yes, Master."

"You don't..." Sebastian breaks off on a sigh, as if he knows it's a losing battle. Then, he steps back into the hallway, sweeping his hand for me to follow. "Come. We have a meeting. Grace wanted me to inform you she's made breakfast."

It takes all my effort not to crinkle my nose. I imagine Grace Pruce was a terrible cook when she was a witch, and now that she's a vampire, she's simply terrible. That said, she's also the love of Sebastian's life. We don't have much—or anything, really—in common, but I do my best to support their relationship. She's good for him. She cracked through him in a way no one else could. So if that means eating foul food for the rest of my life, I'll do it.

"Is it...?"

"Tomato soup? Afraid so," he says. He smiles, and it's more

disorienting than the fact he'll never age. "Pretend you like it. I'll have a servant fetch you something better after the meeting."

Together, we walk through the quiet halls of the western wing, and I silently pray to every god we have that Elliot found his way home.

8

KING OF THE VAMPIRES
CORA

I don't retain many memories from my final days in Ochre. There are only a handful I hold inside my head, and they are the most painful of all. By themselves, they are enough to eat a person alive, to devour them whole until death feels like the gentlest option.

Maintaining these memories is an art. I keep them far enough they won't destroy me, but close enough I never forget.

As I lie in bed that night, I feel the scratch of old memories at the edge of my mind. I don't ignore them like I normally would. I sift through them, rejecting any that include Elliot, until I find the one I inexplicably crave.

Cora Reed

age 15
Neutral territory

DON'T STOP, *I beg myself. My legs are numb. Maybe from the stark cold. Maybe from the countless miles they've carried me. I don't know how long I've been running. I don't let myself slow enough to take a guess.*

I keep moving, knees buckling as I cross the neutral territory. The ground here is scarred and black, still reeling from the witches' curse years ago. My people see themselves as the Echo's saviors, and yet, they destroy far more than they protect. The neutral territory is meant as a safe haven, but their magic is a disease here, contained only by the thick black ledge surrounding these cities.

I run for so long, it's too difficult to think. I rely on instinct alone, eyes blurring against the brutal wind.

It is only once I reach an outer ledge that I pause. My legs tremble until I finally allow them to collapse. I fall to the burnt dirt in a heap, digging my bloodied fingers into the soil. I am soaked in blood. It's splattered across my clothes, my face, my hair. It's beneath my fingernails, dark and dried.

I don't know where I am. I'm hoping this is the Flight Realm. In all the times I dreamed of running away from Ochre, I imagined going to the mountains. I can see them from here, but I can't tell if this ledge borders the Flight Realm...or enemy lands.

I have heard terrible things about the Night Realm. Heartless vampires. Volatile werewolves. Monstrous fiends, neither human nor other.

I glance over my shoulder. There's a neutral town less than a mile from where I sit now. Every town I've crossed thus far has been sleeping, and I've been grateful. Sleeping people don't ask questions.

But in the Night Realm, the safest hours come with daylight. Most werewolf packs are deeper north. Vampires are my greatest threat, and until sunrise, I won't risk crossing into their lands.

I may be without golden bands for the first time in years, but that doesn't mean I know how to use magic. The power pulsing through my body feels more like a liability than a strength. It was enough to get me out of the prison, and I'd like to believe I could take any number of vampire attackers. I'm just not sure I'm ready to bet my life on it.

I let out a shaky breath. My vision is going hazy. I don't know if it's fatigue or if it's an effect of using magic for the first time. All I know is I want to throw up and cry and maybe sleep for the next fifty years.

Does Elliot know? I wonder. Has he heard?

I dig my fingers tighter into the dirt and glare at the skyline. There's at least an hour left of nightfall. I could wait here until daybreak, but that's an hour for one of Lyrie's soldiers to find me. To capture me before I even see them. To drag me back to the Day Realm.

I won't escape a second time.

"Go," I hiss under my breath. "Don't think. Just. Go."

I'm back on my feet. Legs pumping, eyes locked on the distant mountains. It's easy to distinguish the neutral territory, but the realms fade into each other. In the darkness, it's impossible to tell where one ends and the other begins.

"Focus on the mountains," I say. And I run and run and run, far longer than my body should allow.

My breath is harsh and ragged. My heart feels ready to burst out of my chest. My vision dances with spots, and maybe that's why I don't see him coming until it's too late.

He crashes against me, and I pummel into the dirt like a wounded bird. I roll twice before coming to an abrupt stop on my stomach. Letting out a rough groan, I rotate onto my back.

Everything hurts. I'm positive I've broken a few ribs. Possibly my ankle too.

"Hello, little one," the man says. He's standing several feet away, watching me with his head tilted.

He wears all black. A buttoned shirt. Straight-leg pants. Shoes that reflect the moon. It's all simple, but undoubtedly expensive.

I've never seen this man in person, and still, I know him with unwavering certainty.

"Sebastian Vulce," I whisper.

I have been taught to fear this man. King of the vampires. The ruler who fed from Madam Lyrie's throat in a show of resistance. The man who brought the sun curse over his people. Madam Lyrie did it to punish Sebastian, but she'd punished them all. And now, I'm at his mercy.

"You're a far way from home, little witch," he says. He doesn't have fangs that I can see, but I don't doubt their existence. He could have my blood drained in seconds, and I'm assuming that's on his agenda.

"I hate her," I blurt. "Madam Lyrie. I hate her as much as you do. Maybe more."

"Is that so?" Sebastian muses. He steps closer, his shoes kicking up dust. The Flight Realm, I realize. We're definitely in the Flight Realm, but I'm not sure why I thought that would protect me.

This is the king of the vampires. He won't fear the Flight Realm's laws. By the time they find my drained body, they'll have no idea who killed me anyway.

"Yes," I say. My mouth is dry.

"What are you doing out here?" he asks. His attention flickers from me, almost bored, as he surveys the space around us. "Dangerous place for a young witch. Though by the blood on your clothes, you may be the danger."

"I'm due for execution," I tell him. There's no point in lying. "Madam Lyrie wants my head, and I wasn't interested in giving it."

Sebastian's expression doesn't change, but his eyes return to me.

"Your crime?" he asks. His voice is chillingly soft, and I get the eerie sense he's playing with his food. Luring me into a sense of calm before going for my throat.

"Murder," I say.

Sebastian's eyebrow ticks. I wait for him to ask whether my victim deserved it. Whether I feel guilty. Whether I'm ashamed.

Instead, he holds his hand toward me. I stare at it, seeing it for the viper it is.

"We cannot delay," he says. He steps closer, roughly grabbing my elbow and pulling me to my feet. I'm shaking before him, trembling so hard my knees knock together. "Sunlight is coming."

"Do it quickly," I say. It comes out as a command, and for whatever reason, I hope I sound brave.

"I will not be killing you," he tells me.

Without asking, he scoops me into his arms, holding me like a child. I shriek, hands instinctively grabbing his collar. My entire body hurts, but I can do one more spell. Just one more, and then I can keep running for the mountains.

"Close your eyes," he says.

There's no time to close my eyes, and there's definitely no time to cast. We're already moving, the world zipping around us faster than I can comprehend. My vision blurs and my stomach tightens. Before I realize it, I lose consciousness.

Some time later, I wake in an unfamiliar place. The walls are grey stone. The air is bitterly cold and unpleasantly stagnant. Dust covers every surface around me, including this bed.

I gasp, surging onto my elbows.

I expect to be alone, but the vampire king stands before me. He leans against the wall, surveying me with a displeased expression. I pat over my body, surprised to find my bloodied clothes still on but my wounds gone.

"You healed me," I say. It's more accusation than gratitude, but I can see the dried blood on his wrist. He's healed me—and a vampire favor never comes without a cost.

"Yes," he says.

"Why?"

"You claim to hate Madam Lyrie," he says. "I'm giving you the chance to prove it."

9

STAY FAR AWAY

ELLIOT

I don't tell Mama about the vampire blood. I know it's wrong, but so was hiding her illness. This is my way of buying time, and as soon as I figure out the cure, I won't ever do it again. For now, I've mixed the blood with enough herbs and Lake Astoria water to dilute the taste. Mama drinks it with a crinkled nose, but she doesn't put it down until the vial is clear.

"You're good at this," she says, wiping delicately at her mouth. She pulls her sleeve up, displaying her grey, diseased flesh. It hasn't spread, but it's certainly not disappearing.

"I wish I were better," I admit. Still, her praise warms something in my chest. Mama has always been stern and demanding of the people around her. Council members, friends, the townspeople she's sworn to protect. Never me though. She has only ever been warm and welcoming.

"This is the first thing to slow the progression," she says.

"You should have come to me," I say. I can't help myself, but as soon as the words are out, I feel a pang of guilt. I glance sheepishly at her. "Sorry."

"No, you're right," she says. She gives me a thin smile, eyes watering. "I didn't...I didn't want to worry you."

She blinks the tears away before straightening. She doesn't look at me, even as I stare at her, searching uselessly for words. Mama tugs her sleeve back into place, hiding the grey skin. She focuses on the grimoire before her, fingers shaking as they trail over her scrawled writing. She's added annotations in every blank space on the page.

I can only see the headings, but it's clearly information on dark magic and its consequences.

"We'll figure it out," I say. "I'll look into some options at work, and if you can come in—"

"No," she says. She closes her book with a sharp snap. "No one can know."

"We wouldn't announce it," I say gently. "We could come up with an excuse so no one knows. It will—"

"I said no, Elliot." Her eyes, a lighter version of my own, flash with all too familiar determination. Once Mama's made up her mind, there's little point in trying to change it.

"Fine," I say. I lift my hands in surrender. "I'll find another option."

"I have a meeting soon," she says. Her eyes are back on her grimoire, hands tapping the well-worn cover. It's been passed down for generations, and it's strange to imagine that someday it will be mine.

I'd like to put that day off for as long as possible.

"I'll see you later," I say. I collect my jacket and messenger bag from the chair. Though I don't tell Mama, it contains my last batch of medicine. After the next treatment, I'll be out of vampire blood—and out of ways to keep her disease from spreading.

"Goodbye, Elliot," she says. She smiles at me, lips pressed together. "I love you."

"I love you too," I say. I start for the door, only to pause.

I've considered asking Mama about Secora Reed since I made it back to the Day Realm. I don't know what stops me. There's an uneasy clench in my gut though, an undeniable urge to keep that interaction to myself. Mama warned me to stay away from Secora, and even though I didn't seek her out on purpose, it feels wrong to hide the interaction.

Telling her feels even worse.

"Say it," Mama commands, startling me.

"How do you do that?" I ask as I turn from the door. I can't keep the guilty smile from my face. "There's no way—"

"I'm your mother, Elliot," she says. She returns the smile, and her previously cold eyes spark with mischief. "Just ask. If it's about my disease or its curability, I can tell you I don't know. But if it's about—"

"Secora Reed," I blurt.

Mama's smile evaporates, and her lips twist into something unrecognizable. I've rarely seen Mama angry. She's always been too controlled, too calculating to lose her temper. Even when Sebastian Vulce attacked her onstage, she didn't let her fear or fury show. She kept it all close to her chest.

I wait for Mama to speak, but she doesn't. She only stares at me, and any plan to tell her the truth withers on my tongue.

"I don't remember her," I say. "You mentioned her the other day, and I realized...I feel like I should remember—"

"She murdered your best friend," Mama interrupts. Though her voice softens, her posture doesn't. "It's normal to want to forget."

I fix my teeth together, resisting the urge to say more. I can tell by her expression this was a mistake. Mama wouldn't understand anyway. I'm not sure I would, had my path not collided with Secora's. The moment I saw her face, I knew something was wrong.

Something is missing, and there's nothing normal about it.

This woman had been my classmate for years. She'd been a spare child of my friend's family. I should have memories of her. I should remember seeing her on the playground. I should remember her voice. I should know what magic she practiced. I should *remember* her.

She certainly seems to remember me.

"Don't bring up that horrid girl's name again," Mama says. She rubs her sternum, as if I've caused her physical pain.

And maybe I have. Secora Reed is one of two people to ever escape her council's punishment.

"Mama—"

"I have a meeting," she interrupts. This time, there's no warmth in her tone. She looks pointedly at the door.

"'Bye, Mama," I say. This time, I actually go.

"I don't know, man," Henry says.

He sits across from me in the employee lounge of Lyrie Healing Center. Like all employees here—myself included—he wears a simple white shirt, grey pants, and black shoes. Only his pale violet blazer sets him apart. Most healers here are autumnal; some are vernal. Of our two hundred employees, only a handful are estival or hibernal.

Henry is one of them.

We met as new students at the Neutral Territory University and shared a fascination with rare and biologically complex ailments. When I'd pitched the idea of opening a new medical center, Henry was eager to join.

Now, he's one of our top surgeons. He's as obsessed with decoding mysteries as I am, which is why we're here late into the evening. His shift ended in the early afternoon. Mine ended over an hour ago.

We're only here because I can't drag him away from his tomes. He's surrounded by ancient books and newer research alike, the parchments cluttering the elongated grey couch. Its decorative orange and yellow pillows are on the floor to make room.

"It doesn't make sense," I continue. Henry is looking far more absorbed in his work than my personal crises. As his boss, I'm thrilled. As his friend, I'm irritated. I thrum my fingers across the oversized round table.

"Trauma does peculiar things to the mind," he says distract- edly. He spins his pen between his fingers, splattering his skin with black ink. As it dries, the color reminds me of Mama's arms.

A sharp chill licks up my spine. Much as I try to ignore it, I can't get the thought of Mama dying out of my head. There's only one thing capable of distracting me, and it's as much of a mystery as her illness.

"I know it does," I say. And it's true. I've seen a number of cases where the patient's traumatic background infested their body, creating their own personal disease. Difficult to treat, strong enough to kill. "It's just..."

Henry pauses his writing to look at me. Without lowering his pen, he runs his hand through his hair. A droplet of ink stains his hair. Normally, I'd laugh. Now, I just stare at the black drop, wondering how long it will be before Mama's overtaken by disease entirely. Will it radiate over everything? Her face, her hair, her nails?

"She killed my best friend," I say, my voice cracking pathetically.

Henry already knows this. Everyone in the Day Realm and beyond knows about the murder of Harrison Iyle. A prominent augur's son, slaughtered in cold blood by a fellow student. Motive, unknown.

"She killed my best friend," I repeat, strengthening my voice. "She was our friend's spare sister. She was *around*. I should...I should remember things about her."

Henry studies me with a watchful expression. Finally, he sets down his pen.

"Why are you worrying over this now?" he asks. His face blanches the longer he looks at me. "Are you...are you thinking of seeking vengeance?"

I stop tapping the table, looking at Henry with both brows raised. We hold eye contact for a long moment before dissolving into laughter. I laugh so hard I start to cough, folding over against the table.

"For the Mother, Henry." I choke down a breath, trying but struggling to get a hold of myself. "*No, I'm not thinking of seeking vengeance.*"

I try to imagine it, me storming into Sebastian's manor and killing this woman I barely remember.

She's evil. She'd deserve it. But I'm no killer, and though I hate to admit it, I wouldn't stand a chance. I'd be dead before I chose a spell.

"So," Henry says once we've gotten a hold of ourselves. "What is it then?"

"I saw her," I admit. I look away from Henry, if only to avoid the expression on his face. Past him, through the wide set of windows, the sky is starting to darken. If we delay much longer, we'll have to take the tunnel back to town. "When I went to the Night Realm for the blood, I ran into trouble. She, uh, helped get me out of it."

"Why would she do that?" Henry asks. He finally closes the grimoire, settling it on top of the scattered parchments.

"Exactly," I say. I run a hand through my hair, fingers tense.

"I can't figure it out. All I know is that she helped me, and that when I looked at her, I felt..."

My words trail, and Henry waits patiently while I search for the right ones. The problem is, I don't know how to explain. My mouth grows dry as I stare out the windows, heart thrumming in rhythm with my racing thoughts.

"I felt like something was missing," I say finally. My voice grows quiet as I talk, almost without permission. We're alone in this room, but speaking of Secora Reed in the Day Realm is close to treason. "Up until I saw her, I assumed I'd blocked her from my mind. She killed my best friend. I didn't *want* to remember her, you know? But the other day, seeing her...I realized I *couldn't*."

"What are you saying, Elliot?" he asks. He leans forward, propping an elbow on either knee. "You don't think—"

"I do," I interrupt. "I'm missing memories, Henry, and I'm inexplicably certain *she* stole them."

"Elliot..." Henry starts, but his voice trails off until we're subdued in strained silence.

Outside this room, the center bustles with healers and aides, with the occasional flashing codes and voices too distant to make out. But here, everything is quiet and still. There is only my unsteady breath and the steady tap of Henry's shoe on the tiled floor.

"What makes you think *she* stole them?"

"I don't know," I say. Then, "She acted like she knew me, like she trusted me, but she wasn't phased that I didn't know her."

Henry lets out a quiet hum.

"I used to be morbidly fascinated by her," he says after a long gap of silence. I look up in surprise, and the next words come out in a rush. "I have a ton of articles on her. Did a few papers. Once I learned of your connection, I stopped researching, of course. But...I have them, if you want to look."

"Yes," I say. If I weren't so desperate, I might feel embarrassed. Instead, I'm shuffling Henry's parchments into a stack. "Show me everything you have."

SEVERAL HOURS LATER, I sit at the kitchen table in Henry's home. His place is similar to mine. Too large for his needs and a bit messy. Where my house is covered in shades of orange, yellow, and brown, Henry's is purple and silver. The color scheme gives me a headache, so I'm faced away from the living room, focusing only on Henry's macabre collection of notes.

I imagine a number of people have a secret obsession with Secora Reed and her infamous murder. As one of the few witches to escape persecution, she's something of a celebrity.

Not that I'd admit that to Mama.

As Henry works on his research, I comb through information, taking notes as I go. I'd come in with high expectations, and I already know I'm going to leave disappointed.

He's hoarded dozens of articles, but there's nothing to tie me to Secora Reed. Nothing besides the Blake family, of course, and I'd already known that one. I sigh as I read through my notes for a third time.

Secora Reed was born a hibernal witch. Both parents died of mysterious brain bleeds when she was eight months old. From eight months until age seven, Secora lived in various orphanages. Complaints were often made of her dark and unpredictable magic. An estival witch, Mrs. Perskey, took mercy on Secora and housed her from age four to five. Mrs. Perskey then died under the same mysterious conditions as Secora's parents. Following this, Secora was fitted with golden bands to make casting impossible. She received specialized therapy while in an orphanage and continued it while under the care of the Blake family. She remained there until the time of her imprisonment.

I tap my pen on the corner of the parchment. Henry's notes paint a picture of a troubled child with a vast hunger for chaos. Multiple occasions of magic gone awry in her presence. People hurt. Questions unanswered. Toward the end, even the bands could not control her power. She set a boy on fire, mere weeks before killing Harrison.

Through it all, multiple teachers and caretakers reported the same warning: *Secora Reed is dangerous.*

They were right, and yet, they failed to stop her.

"Find anything useful?" Henry asks, startling me from my thoughts.

When I look up at him, he's as bleary-eyed as I feel. We've been at this for too long, and I'm only now realizing it's too late to venture home. I'll be stuck crashing on his couch, which means my back will hurt like the Mother tomorrow.

"Not really," I admit.

"Oh come on," Henry groans. "You can't tell me that. I spent over a year obsessing over that case. Did you see she set a kid on fire?

"Yeah, I saw it," I say. I shove the parchments away, letting my head fall against the back of the chair. "It's just...none of this explains *why* she killed Harrison."

"Of course it does," he says, clearly offended. "Harrison was the ex-boyfriend of the Blake girl. I'm sure Margot was heartbroken about something your friend did, and Secora melted his brain for it."

I swallow, closing my eyes.

"Sorry," he says instantly. "Didn't mean to bring up Harrison or the fact..."

He trails off.

"What if I was there?" My voice cracks, and I take a shaky breath before trying again. "What if she came to kill Harrison, and I was there, and I didn't save him? What if I stood there like a coward, and she stole my memories to make sure I couldn't expose her?"

"Then be grateful," Henry says. I don't know when he moved but he's suddenly at my side, rattling my shoulder until I look at him. His expression is somber. "Be grateful she didn't kill you too. Thank the Mother she spared you, and leave well enough alone."

"It's not that simple—"

"It is," Henry interrupts. "It *is* that simple. Leave it alone, Elliot, and stay far away from that woman."

My only response is a forced nod, my jaw clenched tight.

He's right. I *should* leave it alone.

But he's wrong too. It's not that simple. Even if I wanted to stay away from Secora Reed, I can't. I need vampire blood to keep Mama alive until I find a cure—and Secora is the only one who will give it to me.

10

———

THE ENEMY'S SON

CORA

My palms itch with sweat. After more than a decade living with vampires, I'm not quick to anxiety. I've grown harder over the years, more calculating, less reactive. Only Elliot can rattle me like this, and he's not even here. All I have of him is this wrinkled parchment, delivered two mornings ago by an overcaffeinated werewolf teenager.

I thumb the letter in my pocket, smoothing over words I've long memorized.

> *To Secora: I promised not to return. I will respect that agreement. However, my patient needs more blood than I hoped, and we are no closer to a cure. I would like to propose a new agreement. Tell me your desires, and I will make them yours.*
>
> *Respectfully,*
> *Elliot B. Lyrie*

His words stir deep in my stomach, igniting a sensation I thought I'd left in the Day Realm. He doesn't know what he's doing to me, of course. He doesn't know I've been imagining him saying those words against my ear. *Tell me your desires, and I will make them yours.* I want to write him back, assure him there is nothing "respectful" about *my* desires.

"You're late," Beatrice says as I enter the courtyard.

It's enough to pull me back to reality. I remove my hand from my dress pocket, but I swear the letter's ink is stained on my thumb. Dropping my hands at my sides, I stride across the lopsided cobblestone. This courtyard once held a massive statue of Sebastian at the center. After he stepped down as king, they had it removed. Now, the space is filled with overgrown grass and an ever-expanding infestation of weeds.

"I am not a member of your little club," I say. I stop at the edge of the large table in the corner, resting my hands on its stone surface.

The entire inner circle stares at me, but my attention settles on Sebastian. Even after stepping down as king, he maintains an air of importance. He and Grace sit at the head of the table, her with an electronic device unfolded in front of her. Before coming here, she'd lived in the human world, and apparently, some habits die hard. Moving pictures flash across her device, but when Grace inevitably loses interest in me, it's not her entertainment she looks to. It's Sebastian.

She watches him with adoring fascination, and within seconds, he breaks eye contact with me. He can't help but look at her, and it sends a physical ache through my core. The pain settles in the bottom of my heart, a relentless, steady torture.

I shift my attention to Milas and Amelia, who each claim a side of the table, then Beatrice who sits opposite Sebastian. The three of them look ready for a night out, and they're undoubtedly biding their time until they can leave. Though none of them have said it, I suspect sharing Sebastian's rule isn't as glamorous as they imagined.

Between all of them, endless parchments and artifacts cover the table's surface. They're the same artifacts as always, the ones needed for the sun curse ritual. Despite everything, they're still seeking a cure. A fix to the ailment my kind brought over theirs.

They know as well as I do that they're wasting time. There's nothing in those texts that will help them, and those artifacts haven't been useful since the curse sealed.

There's only one thing that can help them at this point, but they're not going to like it.

"Not part of our club, and yet, you've never missed a meeting," Beatrice says sweetly. She rests one hand on top of the other as she grins at me. Her sharp black nails are long enough to brush the tabletop.

She reminds me of the mean girls I knew at school. Bratty. Entitled. Self-absorbed. And yet, she's proven loyal time and time again. It's unsettling how often people prove me wrong these days.

"I have a proposition," I say. I realize I've got my hand in my pocket again, brushing over Elliot's words. I snap out of it, removing my hand and balling it into a tight fist. "An idea."

"An idea?" Grace asks, finally looking away from Sebastian. His gaze lingers on her as she looks at me. "An idea about what?"

Her voice pitches with hope, which is nothing abnormal for her. Where the rest of us are bleak and generally pessimistic, Grace is an unending force of light. Even now, months after she first arrived in our manor, her presence feels unnatural.

I wouldn't admit that though, especially not when Sebastian is sitting between us.

"I've found a potential witch ally," I say. I level my tone, working hard to control my heart.

Beatrice, Amelia, and Milas are all staring at me now. I don't have to return their gazes to imagine their incredulous expressions. My last potential witch ally wanted to kill me—and only their intervention kept me safe.

"You're wasting time trying to break the curse," I say. I glance at Grace as I add, "That door has closed."

"In case we need reminded, I was the one who turned Grace. *I* closed that door," Sebastian says, stiffening. Gone is the fool in love, here is the terrifying king we all once knew. "Not Grace."

"Believe me, we haven't forgotten," Beatrice says. She jabs her index finger toward the middle of the courtyard, to the empty space where Sebastian's statue once stood. "No one here is complaining about how that worked out."

"You have an idea," Grace repeats. She places her hand on Sebastian's shoulder, and whether he realizes it or not, he instantly relaxes against her. He is a cold-hearted monster, and she brings out the best in him. I can't help looking at them, wishing...

"Cora?" This time, it's Sebastian.

"An old acquaintance recently found his way to the Night Realm," I say. "He's a healer in the Day Realm, and he needs vampire blood for a patient. I believe I can work out an agreement with him. Vampire blood for sunwalker spells."

"Fuck that," Beatrice snarls. "That's obviously a trap. Lyrie's up to something. She probably sent him to fuck with us."

It takes all my effort not to flinch.

"I would ward the blood," I say. "It's simple. Quick. He'd be able to use the blood for healing purposes only, not potion-making."

The table falls quiet as the inner circle looks amongst themselves. This is far from the first time I've pitched the idea of a witch ally, but it's the first time I've had an actual lead. Even Virginia had been a shot in the dark—one that *clearly* didn't land.

"It takes months for me to make a sunwalker spell," I say. "I've been creating them for years, and I only have twenty-seven. It's not nearly enough, and it won't be enough, even if I make them until the day I die. With an ally, I can double production. Maybe more. It's still not enough, but it's an improvement."

"I want information on this supposed ally," Sebastian says. "We don't move forward until we're sure we can trust him. Until we know this isn't one of Madam Lyrie's plots."

"It's Elliot Lyrie," I say. I don't let my nerves waver now—I knew coming into this that his name would be a problem. The least of mine, but that's beside the point.

"As in..." Beatrice starts.

"Madam Lyrie, yes," I say. I ignore her shrieked outburst, focusing instead on Sebastian. His expression has darkened, and even Grace's hand on his shoulder does nothing to ease his tense shoulders.

"You didn't mention our visitor's name," Sebastian says, clearly having pieced together the full story.

"I know what I'm doing, Master," I say.

He doesn't correct me on the formal title. He's too busy staring at me, eyes narrowed, as if trying to decipher a hidden message in my expression. He won't find anything.

"Very well," Sebastian says after a lengthy pause.

"This needs to be a vote," Beatrice snaps. When I turn to her, she's openly glaring at Sebastian. "You aren't a dictator anymore."

"You want power," I snap at Beatrice. "You're *desperate* for it, Beatrice. Well, you're not going to get it without an army. And your army dies in the sun. This is a solution, one you clearly need. Don't be—"

"She's right," Sebastian interrupts. He holds a hand toward me, silencing me. "We'll take a vote. Does anyone have comments before we do?"

"I do," Beatrice snarls. "Giving our blood to witches is the most foolish thing we could do. Giving it to Lyrie's spawn? That's past stupidity. That's betrayal!"

"When have I *ever* risked this place?" I ask. I lean forward, palms flattened against the table. My magic hums against my skin, and the stone vibrates beneath my touch. "When have I *ever* risked you? Or anyone else here?"

"I trust you," Grace says. She stares at me, her blue eyes as bright as ever. "If you think it's a good idea, I think we should do it."

"Amelia?" Sebastian prompts. "Milas?"

"I vote we find a different witch ally. Surely—" Milas starts.

"Surely, you remember our last attempt to find an ally," I interrupt. Sebastian raises an eyebrow, mouth opening as if to speak. When Grace quietly shakes her head, he stays silent instead.

"I am for it. I trust Cora, and so do all of you," Amelia says. She starts stacking the loose parchments on the table, wordlessly calling an end to the meeting. "Three against two. That means Cora has the clan's blessing."

I nod again. My hand is back in my pocket, fingers smoothing out Elliot's letter. I should have mentioned that he hasn't agreed yet. That he very well may not, especially if his mama finds out.

"You have more dead blood?" Sebastian asks. When I nod, he rises from the table, holding a hand to Grace. She hands him her human electronic, and he tucks it beneath his opposite arm. "Start with that. Double check the wards."

"I will," I say. Then, because I can feel Beatrice's open glare, I add, "It won't be usable in spells. I promise."

Beatrice doesn't respond. She flounces out of the courtyard, chin tilted high as she brushes past me. I don't take it personally. I also don't expect her fury to last. Beatrice may be volatile and quick to anger, but she's also incapable of holding grudges for long.

"We didn't discuss anything on our agenda," Milas protests

as Grace and Sebastian exit the courtyard. He holds up one of his collected artifacts, a severed werewolf ear from a previous ritual. "We were supposed to figure out—"

"Next time, Milas," Amelia says. She winks at me as she scoops up the rest of the parchments. She's almost past me when she pauses, leaning in close enough I doubt Milas can hear. With vampires, you never truly know. "How long have you been sleeping with the enemy's son?"

"I'm not," I say immediately. My words sound frazzled, defensive, even though it's the truth. My entire face feels like it's on fire. "I've never—"

"Good for you, girl," she says, cutting me off. She pats my shoulder and shoots me a wide grin. "I've seen Elliot at realm meetings...he's stunning."

"I'm not," I repeat, harder this time. My cheeks are bright red, burning hot enough it feels like *I* might be flammable in sunlight.

Amelia only laughs before striding out of the courtyard. Milas is a few steps behind her, juggling the werewolf ear and remaining artifacts. Then, I'm alone, wondering if I've made a terrible mistake.

11

———

LIFE HASN'T BEEN KIND

CORA

Three days later, I'm in the neutral territory, not far from the place Sebastian and I first collided. I'd invited Elliot to meet me here, at this quaint cafe, rather than the manor. Everything—from the walls to the tables to the benches—is made of rough wood and black metal. Whoever runs this place didn't put much into its interior. There aren't paintings on the wall, nor are there curtains over the windows or even coverings on the tables.

It's hard to care when I'm surrounded by warmth and the smell of freshly baked bread. I sit in one of the back booths of the cafe, selected both for its privacy *and* its proximity to the wood burning stove. The few other customers here are near the kitchen, their chatter barely audible through the crackling flames beside me.

I roll my sleeves to my elbows and settle my messenger bag onto the table. In it, there are a few vials of dead vampire blood and the supplies for today's spell. I sort through it all, if only to keep myself busy.

He's late.

By two minutes, but still. He's late, and I'm stuck sitting here, alone and exposed. This is the first time I've traveled to the neutral territory by myself, and it feels wrong. Reckless, without a vampire guard to protect me. Magical violence may be impossible here—it backfires, harming the attacker, rather than their intended victim —so it's supposed to be safe. It doesn't matter. I know better than anyone that you don't need magic to hurt someone.

I shouldn't have come, but I did. Because of *him*.

Luckily, only Amelia knows where I am. When I told her, she'd grinned at me like we shared a juicy secret. It's why I told her and not the others. Sebastian and Milas would've insisted on an entourage. Beatrice would've spied on us. She might've even taken a shot at Elliot.

Better Amelia assumes I'm having sex for the first time in my life than being surrounded by vampires. Nothing would scare Elliot off faster. Though, at this rate, that was an unnecessary worry.

He's three minutes late now.

A human server delivers a steaming mug of green tea. It's a different variety than I use, and it smells disappointingly weak. Still, I cup it toward my chest, breathing the scent deep into my lungs.

I'll take one.

I frown at the dull brown mug, ignoring the server as she stands at the end of my table. She's asking if I want to order food, but I'm too busy thinking about Elliot. He asked for green tea the last time we were together. He hates green tea. He thinks it tastes like rotten grass. At least, he did when he was fifteen. Maybe he grew out of his distaste for it.

My stomach twists as I wonder, not for the first time, just how much I've lost about Elliot. Maybe, somewhere in my bedroom, there's a jar containing a memory of Elliot trying green tea and realizing he liked it after all. Or maybe, he realized it in the years since we've been apart.

I pinch my eyes. Force myself to decide it doesn't matter.

By the time I open my eyes, the human server is gone. She must have returned to the kitchen.

The front door opens. Elliot hurries inside, bringing with him a rush of wind and the bright shades of autumn. His hair is carefully styled, and his cheeks are tinged pink from the cold. His shirt is orange today, buttoned except for the two nearest his neck. He stands with hands loose at his sides, looking over the cafe. Maybe he's checking for potential witnesses. Someone who could see him here, with *me*, and report back to his mama.

It's risky, him coming here. And yet...

I look back to my tea, feigning disinterest. In all reality, I could stare at Elliot for hours on end. I used to, when we were kids. I'd study the way his mouth moves and the sound of his breathing. Now, it feels wrong to look at him, as if I'm stealing something that isn't mine.

"I apologize," he says as he reaches the table. The bench creaks as he pulls it out to sit. Even as he stares with blatant distrust, he nods his head in greeting. "This place is farther than I realized."

"I assumed you'd prefer distance," I say, arching an eyebrow. "We're as far from Ochre as we can be within neutral territory."

"As far from Ochre...and as close to the Night Realm as possible," he says. I don't miss the accusation in his tone.

"I'm not the one lying to my leader," I say. Rather than waiting for his response, I take a long drink of tea. As I suspected, it's weaker than I like. At least it's warm. The heat spreads through my chest, settling pleasantly beneath my ribs. It steadies me somehow. Makes it easier to breathe.

There's no reason to bicker with Elliot. Though he doesn't realize it, we're not enemies.

"Let's focus," I say. I clear my throat and dig into my dress pocket. I place a single vial of blood onto the table between us. "As promised, one vial of blood in exchange for one session."

Elliot visibly swallows, staring at the vial, rather than me. I've realized there's a lot I don't know about this man. So much has happened in the years we've been apart, and so much more exists in my bedroom, locked away for my own sanity.

It was easy to ignore the memory jars when I didn't have to look at Elliot. But now, I'm desperate to *remember*. I want to know why Elliot drinks green tea now, and it's killing me that I may already have the answer.

"How does it work?" he asks, drawing me from my thoughts. "The sunwalker spell, I mean. There's obviously no literature on it, so I presume..."

He trails off. For reasons I won't explore, I *want* him to acknowledge the simple truth. I want him to be impressed that I created the spell on my own, without a team of brilliant healers or endless resources. It was just me, a scrawny and traumatized fifteen-year-old, against his mama's curse.

When Elliot doesn't continue, I pull a well-worn piece of parchment from my pocket. It's my original theory. A few ingredients have changed, and the final ritual is vastly different. It would be easier if he knew *exactly* how the spell works, but I couldn't bring myself to do it.

While Elliot may be mine to protect, he's not mine to trust. Not anymore. I'd be a fool to give him the true formula. For all I know, this is an intricate plan with his mama to undo years of my work.

"It's not overly complicated," I say. I smooth out the paper, twisting it to face him, rather than me. "I have all the ingredients, and I should be able to perform the ritual without you. *This* is where I need your help the most."

Elliot looks over the parchment, then back at me. His eyebrow arches in an almost bemused expression.

"A protection spell?" he asks. "You need help casting a protection spell? On what? Surely you can—"

He breaks off as I rummage through my messenger bag. From it, I remove a small white stone, a splintered piece of metal, and a twig blackened with smoke. They're the simple ingredients for a protection spell, and Elliot doesn't look impressed. It's only when I remove the final item that his brows furrow.

I hold the tiny vial toward him, and he takes it, removing the cork. He peers inside before hesitantly sniffing the opening.

"It's...empty," he says.

"Yes," I say. "It's the only way this works. If I attach it to anything, it dissolves during the ritual. The spell doesn't work, and the person I think I've saved bursts into flame. It's rather disappointing."

Elliot looks at me like he's trying to decide whether I'm kidding.

I'm not. Three of my first attempts ended this way, all because I couldn't figure out where the spell was failing. Three people, dead at my hand. My only consolation was that they had *agreed* to be test subjects. Not exactly murder.

"I don't understand," he says. He sets the vial on the table, and I organize the remaining items into a triangle around it. "How do we protect *nothing*?"

"It takes a lot of magic," I admit. "It can be painful. I'm hoping between the two of us, it won't be as intense."

Elliot nods, silently looking over the items.

"And you plan to make how many?" he asks. He lays his hands on the edge of the table, fingers tapping restlessly against the cheap wood. "These sunwalker spells of yours. When will you have enough?"

"When every vampire has one," I say. Elliot gapes at me, and I sigh. "These spells don't undo your mama's curse, you know. They allow the vampires to be in the sun, but not as true vampires. They're weaker. Slower. Softer. They're mortal, basically harmless."

Elliot doesn't look convinced. He's scrutinizing my face, searching for something he won't find. But his stare is too intense. Before long, I'm not worrying whether he believes me. I'm only wondering *who* he sees, and whether he likes her. When we were teenagers, he thought I was pretty. This stunning, perfect man used to think *I* was pretty.

I doubt he does anymore. Life hasn't been kind to me, and these past years have been filled with stress and more work than any one person should have. I've spent so long in survival mode, I'm not sure I'll ever escape it.

He must think I'm hideous. That's what everyone else thinks, what they've *always* thought. It shouldn't bother me that he thinks it now. It's better actually. Yes, it's a good thing—

"Show me what to do," he says.

So I do, relieved to think of something other than our lost past.

Two hours later, we've made less progress than I hoped. Elliot is bent over the table, breathing hard. Exhaustion flushes his cheeks, and his eyelids droop with fatigue. We've been at this too long. I'd suggested calling it twenty minutes ago, but he insisted he could do another round.

"One more," he says now. Even gasping, even struggling, he looks more determined now than he did when we first began.

"No," I say. I open my bag on the chair next to me and collect the items from the table. Elliot, still panting, moves as if to stop me. I level him with a hard look, and his hand pauses in the air. "Don't even think about it."

"One more," he insists, but thankfully, he doesn't reach for the ingredients again.

I stuff them into my bag, carefully capping the magic in its vial. It's the same amount I would have gotten in two hours by myself, but I can't deny it was far easier with Elliot's help. Usually, I'd look a lot more like him right now. My heart would be pounding. My head would be dizzy. My eyes would be blurry from hours of strain.

So yes, while we didn't get as far as I hoped, it was easier. Now, I should be able to go home and work on it for at least another hour before bed.

"Why aren't you dying?" he demands. He chugs the water our server delivered. It's his fourth glass since we got here.

"This comes easier to me than it does to you," I say.

He doesn't immediately reply. He's watching me, an unreadable expression on his face.

"How do you know?" he says. It's both a question and an accusation, and my heart misses a beat. It was a stupid mistake, speaking as if I know him, and it takes all my effort to keep still. Much as I want to, I can't panic.

"Well, not to hurt your feelings," I drawl, "but you weren't exactly pulling your weight back there."

"No," he says. "You know I've always been bad at it. How?"

"We were classmates, Elliot."

"Yeah," he says. "And yet, I remember *nothing* about you. Not your strengths or your weaknesses."

My heart spikes in my chest. Thank the Mother he's not a vampire, or he'd hear the panic in my every breath.

"Is that my fault?" I ask, lifting an eyebrow. I'm doing my best to maintain control, but it's hard when he's looking at me. His hazel eyes are so pure, so desperate for the truth. The weakest parts of me are tempted to give it to him, no matter the consequence. "I was bound as a child. I wasn't exactly practicing magic in front of you."

He grows quiet for a long moment, and my insides relax, one by one. Everything I've said makes sense, and he knows it. Even if he suspects the truth, there's no proof.

"If that's all, let's call it a day. We'll meet back here in a week. Same time."

I push to my feet while Elliot remains in his seat. He's staring up at me with an expression I don't recognize. At least, not directed at me.

Fear, I realize. *Elliot is afraid of me.*

"You stole them, didn't you," he says. It's not a question. His breathing has finally leveled, and the heat has cooled in his face. "You stole my memories."

I don't respond. I stare at him, keeping my voice perfectly still. Though my heart pounds, I don't let myself outwardly react. He has no proof, and as long as I don't give him any, this is where it ends.

"You're a good liar," he says after a moment. "A good liar. A good thief."

"I don't know what you're talking about," I say. The words tumble from my lips, so frantic it's humiliating. Of all the things I worried about with today's meeting, him figuring out the truth was *not* one of them. I've never prepared for a scenario like this.

A cocky liar. A cocky thief. That's what I am. So arrogant with my magic that I assumed I'd never get caught.

"Secora," he says.

"Cora," I snap back. I'm flustered now, so unsteady there's no hope of regaining control. All I can do is get the hells out of here. I throw my bag over my shoulder and speed for the door. "My name is Cora."

"Say it," he says. He rises from his seat, crossing to stand beside me.

I freeze, hand on the doorknob. The entire cafe blurs around me, until there is only me, this door, and Elliot's heavy presence next to me. He places a hand near the top of the door, sealing it.

"Say it," he repeats. "Admit you stole my memories."

Say it, freak.

How many times did Harrison say those same words to me? How many more times did he say it that I can't even remember?

A single expression, and I am a child again. The truth is sour in my mouth, desperate to be spoken.

I stole your memories, I want to say. *I'm sorry.*

But weak as I may feel, I am *not* a child anymore.

"Move," I say instead.

To my surprise, he does. His hands fall slack at his sides as he steps to the side.

I open the door, only to pause with one foot outside the cafe. My heart pounds, but I can't bring myself to leave. Elliot and I need each other.

"Look," I say, letting the door fall shut again. I turn back to face Elliot, unsurprised he's still watching me. "I don't know what you think, but—"

"I have a friend," he interrupts. I'm too caught off guard to be offended. "His name is Henry. He's brilliant with magic, with spellcasting. We might've filled that entire vial if he'd been here."

I don't say anything, unsure where he's going with this.

"He might even have ideas on how to increase production," Elliot continues. "I can ask him to help. He's trustworthy. Won't cause problems."

"Why would you do that?" I ask, terrified I already know.

"Memories," he says. "I'll bring my friend. You give me a memory. One for every vial we complete."

"Absolutely not," I say. I'm back to the door, twisting the handle.

"Please, Cora," he says. His voice is somehow both familiar and entirely new. It fills me with a warmth I forgot existed.

I wish I could say it's logic that makes my decision. A third person could make a huge difference, especially if he's as good as Elliot claims. It's a completely rational argument, but that's not why I agree. For the first time in longer than I can remember, this decision comes straight from my heart. An organ I thought died twelve years ago, but apparently still clings to life.

"Fine," I whisper. "One memory for one vial. But *I* get to pick the memory."

Before Elliot responds, I shove out the door and into the blistering wind.

12

WE ARE NOT FRIENDS

ELLIOT

"You don't have to do this," I tell Henry.

"Yeah, you've mentioned." He walks beside me, hands stuffed in his pockets. While I opted to wear darker colors, near-black shades of burnt orange, Henry is wearing his usual estival attire. A lavender suit jacket. Light beige slacks. A golden watch, gifted to him by an old friend.

Even beyond his bright clothing, Henry doesn't belong here. He's smiling, for one. I'm certain people in the Night Realm don't smile. His chin is tipped toward the sky, breathing in the air like it's the freshest he's ever smelt.

It's not. This place smells like werewolf fur and spilled blood and filth...or at least it *should*. I'm certain there are undertones of it, lingering between gusts of fresh wind from the neutral territory.

"I'm serious, Henry," I say. I stop walking, catching him by the shoulder. We're only a few miles into the Night Realm. That leaves us plenty of time and space to get the hells out of here before reaching Secora Reed's lair.

"You?" Henry asks, a grin splitting his face. "The Elliot I know would *never* be serious."

"We can go back," I say, ignoring his mocking. "I'll never mention it again—"

"Look, I know this woman ruined your life, so I'm trying to be courteous," Henry interrupts. "But I've been fascinated with Secora Reed for years. I'm intrigued by her. I've dreamt of meeting her someday to figure out what goes on in that twisted little head of hers. I'm *excited* to meet her. If anything goes awry, we're skilled enough to get back to the Day Realm. All right?"

I swallow. My throat is suddenly too dry to speak. *Excited?*

"I told you I was trying to be courteous," Henry says. He sighs as he starts walking again, and my hand falls from his shoulder. I force myself to keep pace, even as my mind races and my entire body begs me to turn around.

It was stupid to bring Henry into this.

And why? To get memories I didn't realize I was missing until a couple weeks ago? To potentially discover I was a useless bystander at my best friend's murder? To learn some other, horrible truths? I should have accepted Cora's obvious lie and pretended she *didn't* steal a damned thing from me.

"Is that where you tried to buy vampire blood?" Henry asks.

Much as I wish he'd picked a different subject, I'm thankful for the distraction. We've reached the first cluster of buildings in the Night Realm. They're not well-maintained, and they clearly don't have building codes here. The structures are close enough together, if one falls, they all will. From the looks of it, it's only a matter of time.

"Yes," I say, glancing at the dreary stone building. It doesn't have a proper name that I can tell, but there's a sign in its front window that reads: *High Quality, Quick Blood!* I hadn't even made it through the door before Sebastian's men grabbed me.

"We could probably just steal blood now," Henry muses, dropping his voice. The entire strip of businesses is dark and quiet. It'll remain this way until nightfall, at which point vampires will fill the street like it's a holiday festival.

"Yeah?" I ask. I look over the shadowed building once more before giving Henry an unimpressed look. "And what will we do if there are vampires *in* there?"

By his slackened expression, Henry hadn't considered that. Of course, I have. I've considered every option other than the one we're pursuing now. If there was some other way to save Mama's life, I'd do that instead. As it is, Cora's her best chance—and therefore, mine.

"To the vampire manor, then," Henry says. By the way his lips tilt, he's not particularly disappointed.

I don't respond, focusing instead on the walk ahead of us. Overhead, the sun hangs high in the sky, warming the cool fall air. We have several hours before nightfall, and Cora's only criteria for us meeting at the manor—rather than in public— was that we be gone by dark. She didn't want to be responsible for getting us to the neutral territory once the vampires were out.

As if we'd be begging her, a literal murderer, to protect us.

The strip of businesses abruptly comes to a stop. The Night Realm is so poorly designed it's actually funny. A random cluster of buildings here, a few miles of unused rocky landscape there. To the west, another section of buildings rests against the skyline, but it's too far to tell what they are. More businesses, maybe, or a subdivision of vampiric fortresses.

To the east, Sebastian's manor sits isolated amongst jagged rocks. It looks like a miniature castle, all rough stones and over-grown vines. There's no proper lawn. No trees or bushes, vegetation or flowers. A short set of stairs leads to a neglected porch, and I'm so busy studying it, I don't realize Henry has stopped.

As soon as I pause to look back at him, he lurches forward to grab my arm. His grip is painfully tight, but his eyes aren't on me. They're on a small, darkened figure as she approaches from the far side of the manor.

Cora cuts across the plane of dark stone. She's not using the main trail, as we are, yet she glides effortlessly all the same. Her hair is pulled tight, accentuating her large features. Her clothes are baggy. Her body scrawny.

And yet, there's something about the way she moves that captures attention. That makes your spine straighten. Secora Reed may be small, but she is undoubtedly fearsome.

"She looks pissed," Henry says from beside me. He's still gripping my arm too hard, and now, his magic is pulsing into his palms. I can feel the heat through my jacket, threatening to sting me.

"She's a murderer," I remind him. "Of course she's pissed."

Henry doesn't have a response to that, but his posture has changed. Gone is the boyish charm and nonchalance. Now, he looks as nervous as I've felt this entire journey.

"You look like Harrison," I blurt. I'm not sure why. It's not a good time to say such a thing. I know that. I *know* that. And yet, I can't stop the word vomit from spilling out of me. "You might remind her of him."

"You're telling me this *now*?" he asks.

"It's fine," I say. I don't know who I'm trying to convince.

Now that I've spoken the words aloud, I can't stop seeing the similarities. Harrison and Henry. Even their names are similar. Both with blond hair and boyish smiles and outgoing charm. What if I've just hand-delivered Cora's next victim?

To my surprise, she barely looks at Henry as she approaches. She's glaring at me, those wide dark eyes narrowed. She stops directly before us, tilting her chin in a way that makes *me* feel like the small one, even as I tower over her.

"You were supposed to wait," she says. She has the same bag

from our first session strapped over her shoulder. It's bulkier this time, stuffed with Mother knows what.

"It's daylight," I say.

"Some vampires can walk in the sun," she says. She may not be a vampire herself, but she certainly has the countenance of one. Ungodly pale. Eerily still. Impossible to read. "In case you've forgotten why you're here."

"I haven't," I say. Then, nodding toward Henry, I add, "I brought my companion. As promised. And the memory?"

"I have it," she says. She glances at Henry, face revealing nothing. She doesn't ask his name. She doesn't introduce herself, even as he gawks at her. "Sunwalker spell first. Memory second. Understood?"

"Yes ma'am," Henry blurts. His voice is sharp, like he's addressing a war general. "Honor to meet you, ma'am. Woman. Lady."

Cora raises a single black eyebrow. She watches him as blush turns his entire face red, then looks back to me.

"He's the competent one?"

I can't tell if she's mocking or genuinely asking.

"With spellcasting," I clarify with a forced smile. "In other areas, not so much."

She doesn't smile in return.

"Let's go," she says. She turns on her heel and starts back for the manor, once again avoiding the flattened pathway. Instead, she leads us over the steep, rocky terrain. She's sure-footed. Confident. So graceful I can't help but think of vampires again. Perhaps she's lived here long enough she's becoming one.

"Elliot," Henry hisses from beside me. Despite his fumbling introduction, he's back to his typical, goofy self. I suppose a bit of distance from Cora helps with that.

"What?" I ask. I'm studying her back, admiring the gentle slope of her neck.

"I'm in love," he says. "You should've warned me she's pretty. You know I'm a fool for mean, pretty women."

I grind my teeth. I know Henry's teasing, but it pisses me off all the same. Because this woman killed my best friend. Because her cruelty goes far beyond *mean*.

Because despite all of that, I've noticed she's pretty too.

THE LAST TIME I was in this manor, I was running for my life. I'd slipped down the twist of hallways in the early hours of morning, and I'd vowed to never return. I hadn't paid attention to the primitive architecture or the dark furnishings. Now, with Cora as some sort of miniature body guard, I allow myself to study Sebastian Vulce's infamous home.

The wood floors are scratched and in need of proper cleaning. The walls are dark and the decor is minimal. There isn't any furniture in the main entryway, but I spot a few velvet couches as we maneuver the halls. Oil paintings surround us, depicting various scenes of vampiric gore.

Vampires are far too proud of their own cruelty.

When we take an unexpected turn, away from Cora's quarters, rather than toward them, I halt. I press a hand to Henry's chest, stopping him too.

"Where are we going?" I ask.

"The courtyard," she says. She pauses. Turns to look at us. Regards me with an unimpressed, raised eyebrow.

"Not your quarters?" I ask. Then, though she obviously knows, I add, "They're warded."

"The courtyard is open to the sun," she says. "We'll be safe there."

Before I can ask a follow-up, she takes off again. Her steps are quicker now, more determined, as if she's expecting me to back out of our deal. It wouldn't be the worst idea. Finding vampire blood is not an easy feat, but there has to be another way. Ways that don't include betraying Mama and aiding Vulce's army.

Then again—and I wouldn't admit this to *anyone*, not even Henry—I think sunwalker spells are far more humane than my mama's curse. The vampires clearly spiraled out of control twenty years ago, but forcing them to burn in the sun *forever*? It feels unjustly violent. Sunwalker spells are a happy medium: the vampires can't easily kill, but they also won't instantly die.

Henry lurches to a stop. This time, he doesn't let me pass. He throws his arm in front of my chest, and I crash against it.

"Is that..." he trails off, frozen beside me.

It isn't until he's spoken that I notice the figure at the end of the corridor. I'd been lost in my thoughts, carelessly so, and I'd missed the obvious predator watching us from the shadows.

"I don't need a babysitter," Cora informs the man.

It's enough to draw a surprised breath from my lungs. I may not have seen Sebastian Vulce since I was a child, but I've heard stories of him in the years since Mama cursed him and his kind.

He is a monster. A villain. A cruel and vicious leader.

My pulse spikes. This man publicly hurt my mama. Made an example of her, of us. And yes, she'd put him in his place...but not without enraging him. Not without giving him a good reason to kill us without a spare thought.

Cora assured me we'd be safe here. She promised no harm would come to Henry or me, so long as we helped with the sunwalker spells.

Now, that feels like a foolish hope.

"I am not here to watch you," he tells her. There's something strange about the way he looks at her. His expression is one of concern and thinly veiled adoration. He looks at her as if she were a child. *His* child.

I shake my head, forcing the thought away. Vampires are many things—evil, violent, dangerous. They are not paternal or protective or gentle.

"No?" Cora asks. She crosses her arms over her chest, glancing back at me and Henry as we cower like children. "Well, then if you don't mind, we'd appreciate privacy. You're terrifying my guests."

I grind my teeth and force myself to stand at full height. Mama would be repulsed at how I'm acting. I straighten my shoulders, step forward in a brief surge of confidence, and close the distance between us.

Sebastian is a frightening man, but he's shorter than I am. I'm nearly a head taller, and I focus on that tiny, inconsequential detail to ground me.

"Elliot Lyrie," I say, extending a hand.

Sebastian stares at my hand, face blank. His green eyes shift to mine, then to Cora's. A flicker of *something* crosses his face, but it's too quick for me to decipher.

"Sebastian Vulce," he finally returns. Rather than shaking my hand, he tilts his head, regarding me for a long, uncomfortable moment. "How's your mother?"

Magic pulses through me, shooting from my chest and through my limbs. It coils in the base of my fingertips, desperate to slice through Vulce's throat. I clamp my teeth and tighten both hands into fists. It's taking everything—slow breaths, clenched muscles, steady eye contact—to keep from reacting. From launching every ounce of magic straight through Vulce's chest until his heart lays at my feet.

"We have a lot of work to do," Cora says. She steps between me and Sebastian, capturing my wrist in her hand. Her skin is soft and delicate, but her grip is strong. She pulls hard enough I have no choice but to follow after her.

Henry is only a step behind, giving Sebastian a wide berth as we step into an open-air courtyard. I slip out of Cora's hold, feeling a rush of relief as I step into the cool air. Sebastian remains in the doorway, half his face cast with sunlight.

We don't know how many vampires have sunwalker spells. Mama's been trying to figure out a number for years, but her spies have reported anything from five to a hundred. I mentally add this to my to-do list. Maybe Mama will be less infuriated if she knows I found useful information while risking my life.

Not if she knows I helped increase their numbers.

I take a deep breath and try to shake the anxiety from my lungs. It's bad enough being here. But being around *him* feels like an unnecessary torture.

Cora leads us to a large stone table in the corner, positioned next to a vine-infested stone wall and a strip of elongated windows. Without taking my eyes off Sebastian, I sit beside Henry nearest the stone wall. Cora remains standing, turning away from us to nod at the vampire king.

"Master," she says. Despite her nauseating nickname for the vile man, her voice is hard. Almost as if in warning.

"Signal if you need anything," he says. His green eyes flicker over Henry, then me. His lip snarls before he forces his attention back to Cora. "Don't give them your back again."

If Cora responds, it's not out loud. She sharply faces me and Henry, cheeks stained pink with blush. I'm so busy watching her, it takes me several seconds to realize Sebastian is gone.

"I told him not to come," she says, glancing between us. Her blush grows darker, and it's inexplicably charming. She's apologizing for this terrible man like she's a teenager being embarrassed by her father.

Murderer, I remind myself. *Both of them. Murderers.*

"You call him master?" I ask. I'm not sure why. The question slips out, and my judgment is so loud even I flinch.

Surprisingly, Cora doesn't.

Her face hardens though, lips folding into a flat line.

"We're doing the sunwalker spell first," she repeats. Any lingering embarrassment washes from her features as she removes her bag. She takes a collection of items from its main pocket. "Once we're done..."

She trails off, eyes darting toward Henry.

"He knows," I say, answering her unasked question. "I told him what you did."

The disgust is heavy in my voice, and that same pink blush from before lights her face again. Cora clears her throat, and too soon, the color disappears.

"We'll do your memory second," she says. With her attention on her bag, she adds, "I even brought two, if you're feeling up to it."

"How generous," I deadpan.

Cora glares at me, nose wrinkling.

"This is the deal," she says. "If you don't want—"

"I do," I interrupt her. "Let's just get it over with."

So we do. We work the next several minutes in tense silence, only speaking for instructions or questions. As time passes, the atmosphere changes. Softens. Henry is undoubtedly better at spellcasting than I am, and it's clear Cora is pleased. She doesn't smile, exactly, but her lips tilt at the edges, as if she's tempted.

Even with me dragging us down, we make impressive progress. In a matter of two hours, we've done it. An entire vial is filled with a loose, furious protection spell. The stringy orange magic thrashes in its glass container.

"Wow. We're done," Cora says. Like last time, she seems utterly untouched by all the magic we just produced. Henry is struggling, but not nearly as terribly as I am. I'm sweating, gasping, unable to catch my breath.

"I'm much better with potions," I say. I'm not sure why, other than to prove I'm not a complete loser. "And biological magic, obviously. I've done...I'm good with surgeries. But this is not my..."

I trail off. Henry claps a hand over my shoulder, laughing gently.

"No one is questioning your witchcraft," Henry says.

"I am," Cora says. Another unimpressed lift of her eyebrow. She does that too much. Looks at *me* like that too much. With the way her lips twitch, it almost looks like she's teasing me. But no. This woman is a monster, and she's obviously judging me.

"Who knows," I snap, "Maybe I was once good at spellcasting. Maybe you stole that from me too."

Cora drops her eyes and swallows. I see it, the way her throat tightens. I wait for her to defend herself, but when she doesn't, I feel like *I'm* the asshole.

"So," Henry drawls. He pats the edge of the table, looking almost as uncomfortable as I feel. "Speaking of memories...do we want to look?"

Without responding, Cora digs through her bulky bag again. She keeps her gaze down as she removes a shiny black stone and a drawstring velvet bag. She places the stone at the center of the table and removes a strange collection of objects from the little bag. As she lines the items—I spot a mermaid scale and an animal claw—I frown.

"What is this?"

Cora looks up from what she's doing. Her eyes are wide, and in the sunlight, I can see all the different shades of brown. Soft and hard, light and dark, all surrounded by long, thick eyelashes.

"A memory stone?" she says. It comes out more like a question, and her gaze darts between me and Henry. "Mrs. Raekes showed us. Second year—"

"I want my memories back," I interrupt. "I don't want to watch them, and I certainly don't want to watch them with *you*."

She flinches, eyes locking on the stone instead of me. This woman is a literal murderer, and still, my stomach sours at the way she's curling in on herself. As if expecting *me* to hurt *her*.

"Just give it to me," I demand. I hold my palm out, keeping my eyes on her, even as she refuses to look at me. "Secora."

"Don't call me that," she says, eyes snapping to mine. "I told you I don't like it. So *don't*. Be pissed all you want, but don't disrespect—"

"Really?" I ask. "You're going to talk about disrespect? You *stole* my memories. They're *mine*. You have no right to them, and you're acting like you're the good guy for doling them back, one by one."

"Let's take a breath," Henry says. I don't know when he moved, but he's closer now, hand heavy on my shoulder. "We're all friends here."

"No. We are *not* friends," I growl. I shove his hand off me, twisting to face him. "She *murdered* my friend. She stole my memories. I've agreed to her fucking requirements to get them back. I'm not leaving them with her, so she can keep my thoughts in her twisted little collection, watching them whenever she's bored. They're—"

"I haven't watched them since the night I took them," she says. Her voice is level, devoid of emotion. It is only the slight curl of her upper lip that gives her away, that indicates there's *something* more behind her icy mask. "I'm not some obsessive stalker, all right? I was going to give it to you. But I figured you wouldn't have a memory stone. You can't just go sticking random things in your head, Elliot. I could've fucked with it. You have to watch it like this first. Which you *know*."

I grind my teeth. I hate this woman. I hate more that she's *right*. I do know better than to stick a random strand of magic in my head. It could be laced with poison. It could be manipulated.

It could be *a lot* of things, and if I didn't check with a memory stone first, I could have killed myself.

I just assumed Cora wouldn't care if I did.

I assumed she'd leave it to me to find a memory stone, not that she'd offer up her own.

"But you don't have to use it," she says. She grabs the ingredients from the memory stone, shoving them back into their velvet bag. I don't remember much about memory stones from school, but I know these ingredients are hard to come by. If I ask Mama for them, she'll know I'm up to something.

"Wait," I say.

I can feel Henry watching me, but I don't take my eyes off Cora. She's paused her movements, and her stormy eyes stare up into mine. If they weren't so angry, they'd be pretty.

Fuck. Even angry...

"I'm sorry," I say. It feels like I'm choking on the words as I speak them, as if I'm personally stabbing my mama with this tiny betrayal. Apologizing to the henchman of my mother's greatest enemy. "I'm sorry. I wasn't thinking. I...can we still? Please?"

She doesn't respond. I can see her jaw working. She's grinding her teeth so hard I'm surprised I can't hear it. She doesn't move to put the ingredients back, but at least she's stopped taking them away.

"I'm sorry," I repeat, harder.

Cora lets out a shaky breath. She's going to agree—I can see it in her softened expression. I've already won, and yet, I find myself continuing anyway.

"You can watch it too, if you want."

Without looking, I can see Henry's shock from my peripheral vision. Both blond eyebrows are raised as he stares at me.

"She's probably memorized them anyway," I say. More as a way to convince myself than him.

"I haven't," she says. Her words are level, steady.

I don't respond, and she somehow knows I'm not going to. She lines the ingredients once again onto the black stone and removes two jars from her bag. Both are labeled with silky ink and the same description: *Elliot Lyrie, age 12, Ochre Primary School.* Within each jar, a vibrant memory thrashes against the glass. One is blue. The other is somewhere between orange and red.

"How many?" I ask. My voice is hoarse, almost unfamiliar. "How many jars do you have?"

"A hundred, maybe more," she says. "Only some are yours."

"Only," I repeat. Nausea pinches my gut, threatening to eject this morning's breakfast. Part of me wants to lash out, to tell Cora exactly what I think of her and her cruel, twisted games.

Maybe it's the exhaustion from spellcasting. Maybe it's the surreal realization I'm about to learn something new about my own life. Either way, I'm too tired to fight.

"All right," I say. "I'm ready."

Cora carefully places the memory onto the stone, and an instantaneous burst of blue smoke surrounds us. I can't see Cora or Henry. There is only a thick wall of blue around me, slowly dissolving into a past world. By the time the smoke has cleared completely, I am no longer in the present. Sebastian Vulce's courtyard is gone, replaced by the outer fields of my primary school.

13

————————

STAY FAR AWAY

ELLIOT

*H*arrison isn't in school today, and neither is Margot. Mrs. Raekes said he's sick, but I doubt it. He was just fine last night when we were playing groundball at Rowan's. Then Margot called, he took off early, and now he's sick.

Well, guess who's also sick?

Margot.

I glare at their empty desks from where I sit. I've been glaring for most of the day, and I don't have any plans to stop. Last I heard, Margot didn't want to be Harrison's girlfriend anymore. Now, they're skipping school together and not even telling me. I'm stuck sitting here like a complete loser, and it's almost time for lunch.

Lunch always sucks when Harrison is gone. I have to eat lunch with Stephan and Gregg, and they only want to talk about their latest experiment. They're probably still trying to reanimate the hog from Gregg's family farm. It died last week, and supposedly, they're "this" close to bringing it back to life.

Stephan and Gregg are liars. Harrison and I would've started a game of groundball with the older boys. I could probably go out there by myself, but I'm not half as good at it as Harrison. What if they won't let me play? What if they laugh right in my face?

No, I'll be stuck sitting with Stephan and Gregg and hearing about their half-reanimated hog.

Mrs. Raekes dismisses the class for break. I take my time collecting my lunch from the shelf, only to pause when a glimpse of black catches my attention.

Secora Reed.

I don't know much about her. After her eventful first day, I've mostly steered clear of her. Secora typically clings to Margot like a fifth limb, and I've done everything in my power to keep Harrison from terrorizing her. It's not that I'm not afraid of the Dark Ones. I am.

It's just...I've yet to see her do anything mean or violent. She certainly hasn't pushed anyone into the dirt.

With my lunch bag draped over my arm, I follow Secora through the crowded halls. Everyone is headed for the auditorium, the over-sized room where we eat when it's too cold to go outside.

Secora, of course, doesn't follow everyone else.

I hardly blame her. No one aside from Margot wants anything to do with her, and since she's not here...

Secora disappears out a side door, leading to the playground. I'm not sure if we're allowed to go outside. I should at least ask someone if it's okay. I can see one of the younger class's teachers near the auditorium entrance. I could ask her. I could...

I'm already moving for the door. I shove through it, and I'm instantly struck with a harsh gust of wind. I shrink against the side of the brick building, wrapping my arms around myself.

The playground is empty. The swings jostle in rhythm with the wind, but otherwise, the world is quiet and still. Secora was only a minute ahead of me. She should be here, on one of the slides, or even sitting in the dirt. Instead, it's like she vanished.

"Secora?" I call.

I don't know what I'm going to say once I find her. I don't have a reason for following her out here. I haven't spoken to her since her first day, and I only know her name because Mrs. Raekes calls it every day when taking attendance. It's probably weird I'm out here.

I should go back inside and accept my boring fate of lunch with Stephan and Gregg.

Instead, I venture farther onto the playground. The wind whips around me, rustling my clothes and burning cold against my cheeks.

I'm on the verge of giving up—or maybe getting help from a teacher—when I spot her. A quick flash of black clothing, stirred by the wind.

She's back at the haunted tree, leaned against its trunk, head tilted to the sky.

I move across the playground and the grassy field separating us. Now that I can see her, I feel an unexpected sense of determination. This girl is going to like me. She's going to like me, and if she ever decides to kill her classmates like she did her own parents, she'll spare me.

That's what I tell myself anyway. It feels like a good enough reason.

When I arrive at Secora's side, I realize her eyes are closed. She might be sleeping. She's definitely not eating lunch. From the looks of it, she doesn't even have one. Maybe she forgot. Maybe she's not hungry.

I stare at her for too long. Her eyes open before I have the chance to announce myself, and she yelps in surprise. She slams back against the tree, tucking her knees to her chest. Her fists come up toward her face, braced for impact. Her sleeves fall at the movement, revealing those shiny gold cuffs.

"I wasn't trying to scare you," I say. I take a small step backward and raise my palms. "I was just...what are you doing out here?"

Secora blinks at me, eyes wide, mouth unmoving.

"We're supposed to eat in the auditorium," I say stupidly. As if she doesn't know. As if she cares.

"I know," she says. Her voice is raspy.

I wait for her to continue, but she doesn't. I shift on my feet, consider going back inside, decide I most definitely should. Then stand stock still.

"Is Margot sick?" I ask. "Because Harrison is supposedly sick, but I don't believe him."

One shoulder lifts in a half-hearted shrug.

"Come on, Secora," I say. "You can tell me. I promise I won't tell anyone."

Now she wraps her arms around her knees, pulling them tight. Her eyes are still on me, but they're different now. Calculating.

"Are you hungry?" I ask. I hold my lunch bag toward her. "It's mostly vegetables, but they're not bad. Mama buys the good stuff."

A slight shake of her head.

"It's not poisoned, I swear. Here," I say. I sit at her side, trying not to be offended when she shifts away. I remove a handful of eggroot and drop it on the skirt of her dress before she can say no. Then, I pluck one off and toss it into my mouth. "See? Not poisoned."

That earns me the world's tiniest smile.

"Mama Blake feeds me," she says. "I forgot my lunch on the table this morning."

"I do that all the time," I say. "I bet she would've brought it if you sent a message."

"She would," Secora agrees. She takes an eggroot off her lap and scrunches her nose. I almost expect her to throw it back in my lunch bag. Instead, she takes a tentative bite.

We eat in silence for the rest of lunch. It's only when Mrs. Raekes sticks her head out the door and yells at us for being outside that I realize how much time has passed.

"Whoops," I say, grinning at Secora. I shove to my feet. "We should go."

Secora drops her eyes, and for some reason, she looks ready to cry.

"We won't get in trouble," I say. I extend my hand to her, and only once I have, do I remember she wouldn't take it last time. "I'll tell her it was my fault."

"No, don't," she says. She jolts to her feet, ignoring my outstretched hand. She's already jogging for Mrs. Raekes, and I have to hurry to catch up with her. "Trust me, Elliot. It's better if you stay far away from me."

WE'RE BARELY OUT of the memory before I'm reaching for the second one. Cora says something, but I'm dizzy with desperation, with an unfamiliar need. *More.* I want to know more. I don't want time to process what I've just seen. I want answers, and the only way to get them is with another memory.

"Is this in order?" I ask as I uncap the second jar.

"No," Cora says. She looks as disoriented as I feel. She's busy returning the blue memory back to its jar. "I mean, roughly. That one is age twelve too, but it won't necessarily be consecutive."

From beside us, Henry watches with silent fascination. I'm too greedy to acknowledge him, to ask if he saw the first memory, or whether he'd like to see the next one.

"Do you want to take a minute?" Cora asks. "We can—"

"No," I say. "I'm ready. You can watch or not."

I drop the red-orange memory onto the black stone, sucking in a deep breath as smoke flares up around me. The world immediately blurs, and I lean into the sensation, desperate to see it all.

Elliot Lyrie

age 12
Ochre Primary School

I*T's winter in the Day Realm, but it's uncharacteristically warm. The sun shines brightly overhead and reflects off piles of snow. About half of the school is outside for lunch. We're all bundled in thick coats and pants, boots and wool caps. I'm late getting outside because Mama didn't have time to pack me a lunch and I had to buy it from the school's store.*

Harrison and Margot are inside today, and I've never felt more relieved. Now that they're dating again, Harrison wants her all to himself. That means he'd rather I not come around, and more importantly, that he doesn't notice where I eat lunch instead.

I think Margot knows I've struck a tentative friendship with her spare sister, but I'm certain Harrison doesn't. He'd throw a fit if he found out and undo whatever progress I've made. It's taken me months to gain Secora's trust, and I don't doubt Harrison's ability to ruin it.

I cross the playground and trudge through the snowy field. Of the kids outside, they're mostly contained in the playground. With all the snow, it's too slippery to play groundball or any other game.

I follow a solitary line of footprints through the deep snow until I arrive at Secora's tree. She's sitting on her coat, curled up and chin tilted to the sky. Her lunch bag sits open at her side, filled with a couple of empty pouches. She's already eaten, and now, she's leaned back with her eyes closed. She's not sleeping though.

I just like to daydream, *she told me once.* Think about the way things could be, you know what I mean?

I didn't know what she meant, but I said that I did. I want her to think I'm smart, that I understand things. No, that I understand her.

I'm still several feet away when Secora's eyes open. She studies me as I approach, offering a hesitant wave as I reach her side. I grin down at her, pathetically pleased with the way she's relaxed around me.

Months and months of torture, but finally, she looks at ease when I sit next to her.

"Sorry I'm late," I say. "I tried to convince Mrs. Raekes to let me go early, but she wasn't having it."

"You don't have to be sorry," she says, giving me a tiny smile. "You didn't have to come over here at all."

My grin fades. Months and months of effort, and Secora still seems to think this is some form of charity.

I lean back against the tree, close enough our arms touch. She moves, just enough to keep a gap between us.

"Why do you do that?" I ask. I lay my head against the tree and close my eyes, if only so I don't have to look at her expression. "Why do you move away? I'm not going to hurt you."

"I know," she says.

"Then why?" I ask. "Do you not want me to touch you?"

"People don't want to touch me, Elliot," she says. Her voice doesn't crack. She doesn't sound bothered at all. "It's okay. I know, and I understand. You don't have to—"

"I want you to," I say, cutting her off. I can feel myself blushing. Even my ears are hot, and I'm begging the universe that Secora isn't looking at me. "I don't mind if you touch me, Secora. You can touch me whenever you want."

She's silent for long enough I know she isn't going to reply. She's not going to say she wants me to touch her too. Maybe she doesn't. Maybe she wishes I'd leave her alone.

It'd be smarter for me to keep my mouth shut. Easier too. But I've been planning to ask this all week, and today is my last chance. If I don't ask now, I'll be mad at myself later and I'll have no one to blame but myself.

"We're going to the Hibernal Festival tomorrow," I say. My voice cracks and I clear it, hoping she doesn't notice. "In Hayver."

"I know," she says.

"There's a dance there," I say. My heart is beating so loud, there's

no way she can't hear it. Harrison can probably hear it from inside the school. "We could go together. Margot and Harrison are going together anyway. We might as well—"

"Elliot," Secora says. Her voice is utterly horrified, and I feel my face light up with embarrassment.

"Forget I said anything," I say. I force my eyes to open, and I'm mortified to find her already staring at me. She's shifted onto her knees, hands floating in the air, as if debating whether to reach for me. Of course, she doesn't.

"I get you want to help me," she says. "But that's just going to make things worse."

I don't know what she's talking about. I'm not sure how me taking her to the dance would be helping her, but I decide it doesn't matter. She obviously doesn't want to go. Not with me.

"Forget it," I say again. I shove to my feet, and without looking back at Secora, I make the long walk back to the playground.

I come out of the memory gasping. Henry is saying something to me, but I don't register it. I don't register anything but Secora —no, *Cora*—looking at me. Large brown eyes, slightly parted lips.

Fuck. I had a crush on her. I liked her. My best friend's killer, and I...liked her.

"Keep that one," I say. I stumble off the bench, grabbing the blue memory from the table as I go. Looking over at Henry, I add, "Let's go."

"What in the Mother did you see?" he asks.

Relief surges through me. He wasn't watching. He doesn't know—and he won't need to. I can keep this to myself, buried so deep, maybe I'll forget it too.

I storm out of the manor, ignoring Sebastian Vulce's

watchful gaze. He was no more than twenty feet from the court-yard, fully prepared to come rescue Cora from me.

I liked her.

"Elliot—"

"Drop it," I snap. Then, weakly, "Please."

Henry doesn't push me. He keeps my frantic pace out of the manor and across the Night Realm. We don't speak a word, and I do everything I can to erase that memory from my brain.

14

IF THIS IS AN EGO THING

CORA

I sit at the stone table long after Elliot and Henry leave. I planned to walk them back to neutral territory, or at least through the manor. Instead, I watched them leave. Watched Elliot leave with that horrible look on his face.

Shame.

He was mortified that he could like someone like me, and I don't blame him. Even as a kid, I was used to people reacting that way to me. Disgust. Horror. Hatred. The thing is, Elliot never reacted that way. He'd only ever been kind and gentle with me. Witnessing the opposite felt like years of trauma, all packed into one anguished look.

"Are you planning to sit out here all day?"

I startle at the voice. Vampires are notorious for their stealth, but after living with them for so long, I'm typically good at detecting them. I'm too distracted sitting out here, and that, more than anything, means it's time to return to my quarters.

"I was just leaving," I say. I loop my bag over my shoulder and stand, finally looking at Amelia.

She's wearing skin-tight black pants and a sheer black top. As usual, she has bold red lipstick and her thick curls are loose around her face. She's one of the youngest vampires in physical appearance. Maybe twenty. Twenty-two at most. It's only her eyes that make her seem older, wiser.

When she looks at me, I get the unsettling feeling she sees *everything.*

"You've been out here for hours," she says. She strides into the courtyard, the soft afternoon sun gleaming off her dark skin.

There's only one way she'd know that.

"Master should mind his own business," I grumble.

"In his mind, you *are* his business, Cora," she says. Her voice is gentle, but there's an edge of concern in her words. "Perhaps you should tell him of your...relations with the Lyrie boy."

"I'm not sleeping with him," I say. I brush past Amelia, striding into the manor with the confidence of a king. This time, I'm paying enough attention to hear Amelia follow. "We were friends in school. That's all."

"Do friends steal each other's memories?" she asks. Her voice is low, mockingly sweet.

I stop so abruptly she has to step backward to avoid hitting me. She's not much taller than I am, but I still have to tilt my chin to look at her. My chest heaves as I glare at her, as I try to keep my magic from spiraling out of control.

"Sebastian had no right to eavesdrop," I snap. My voice shakes, trembles so hard it beats in rhythm with my racing heart. "Elliot has nothing to do with the sunwalker spells. And what...what happened in the past is none of his—or *your* —concern."

Amelia doesn't immediately respond. She stares at me for an uncomfortably long pause, dark eyes wide and full of knowing.

"I've never heard you call Sebastian by his name," she says.

It's not the comment I expect. I reel backward, only now realizing she's right. I never call Sebastian by his name. He's always been Master. He's always been some high, untouchable figure in my life. My savior in more ways than one. I've never doubted, never challenged him, not really.

"It slipped," I say. Then, with a shake of my head, I add, "It doesn't matter, Amelia. Just...let it go. All of this. Please."

"I'm worried about you," she says. Her voice is still low, but the curiosity has mostly evaporated. Now, there's just pure, raw worry. And I hate that even more. "Elliot was clearly more than a friend—"

"Amelia," I snap. "Let it go. I've got it under control."

With that, I spin on my heel and march the rest of the way to my quarters. I keep my ears on high alert, but thankfully, Amelia doesn't follow.

I AM HORRIDLY DRUNK. I have no idea what inspired me to be such a disastrous moron, but for the first time in my twenty-seven years, I am hopelessly intoxicated. I have slipped far past the point of numbing my mind, and that had been the reason for the first drink. Even the second.

Now, I've had five drinks and everything is spinning. I'm stumbling around my room like a toddler learning to walk, tears streaming down my face and an unpleasant nausea settling in my gut. I am, inevitably, going to puke.

"Fuck you, Amelia," I say.

She's not here. I'm not drunk to the point of delusion—yet—but the words feel satisfying all the same. Maybe even *more* satisfying, seeing as she can't defend herself.

"You're stupid," I declare to my empty quarters. "You don't know anything."

I stumble over to my wall of dead but thriving plants. Stick my finger deep into the soil. Dry. I forgot to water them.

"Stupid plants," I say. I stagger to the kitchen, fill a pitcher of water, then stagger back. By the time I reach the wall, I realize I've lost a good amount of water on the floor. That's a problem for tomorrow. "Here, drink your stupid water."

I hiccup.

"Elliot was a friend," I say. I don't know if I'm telling imaginary Amelia or the plants. "Elliot was a stupid friend. And...and just because...If you saw the way he reacted now...Stupid."

I hiccup. My stomach twists, and I briefly consider running for the toilet.

"No vomiting," I instruct myself. Then, because I'm sloppy drunk, I start to laugh. My words are slurring. I hardly sound like myself, and though it's probably not, it *feels* hilarious.

I laugh as I return to the kitchen, leaving the empty pitcher on the counter. Then, I go to my bedroom and glare at the jars and jars of memories.

"Stupid," I tell them. "All of you."

I sit on the end of my bed and wrestle my tights off until they're in a tangled heap on the floor. My entire body feels like it's on fire, like I'm roasting from the inside out. I have no idea if this is supposed to happen when you drink alcohol. For all I know, I'm having a horrific allergic reaction and I'll die before morning comes.

Here's to hoping.

I peel my dress over my head. I'm in nothing but my underclothes, and I'm still hot.

I shove from the bed, run my fingers delicately over Elliot's memories. I should watch each and every one of them. That way, I'd know which to show Elliot. If he even wants to see more. Maybe, hopefully, he'll be scarred enough from today's session that he'll never want to see another memory. He'll help me with sunwalker spells, and we can pretend our past never happened.

I assumed if I stuck to his twelve-year-old memories, we'd be safe. I didn't know he liked me back then.

I wasn't lying when I told Elliot I hadn't watched his memories since the day I stole them. I haven't watched my *own* memories in nearly as long.

"Fuck." I stumble past the jars around the doorway and move to the final wall of memories. These are mine. Dozens of them, silver-lidded. Detailed with ink. "I'm going to have to watch you, aren't I? I'm going to have to take you back."

Memories of every color thrash in their jars. Purples. Reds. Oranges. Blues. Greens.

They're all desperate for escape, and right now, in this drunken stupor, I see them for what they are. Protection. The only way to protect me *and* Elliot, is for me to remember what I've forgotten.

"Fine," I tell the jars. I stumble along them, reading the labels until I find the one I want.

In the morning, I'll be ashamed of what I pick. Maybe I feel the shame even now, but alcohol is nothing if not stubborn. It demands I pick this one, the same one I eye all too often.

～

Cora Reed
age 14
*Astoria Lake**

THIS WAS A TERRIBLE IDEA. I knew it when Margot invited me. I knew it when I attempted to say no, and I knew it even more when I reluctantly agreed. There was never a point I thought this was a good idea. As I put on this stupid dress. As I let Margot apply goopy makeup on my eyelashes and sparkles on my cheeks. As I followed her and her friend group down to the shores of Astoria Lake.

Still, it's never felt like a worse idea than it does right now.

Margot Blake is an absolute angel. She's only ever been kind to me, only ever done her best to include me, to chase away those who are mean to me. She broke up with Harrison because of me, even though she won't admit it.

I wonder if he'll be here tonight.

I don't see him. I'm sitting back at the trees, leaned against the wide base of one. It's only a matter of time before Margot notices I'm back here and begs me to join the party. I hope she doesn't. I hope she has the best birthday of her life and is too busy with her friends to realize her spare sister is in the shadows, lurking like an uninvited guest.

Margot's friends tolerate me. I'm not delusional enough to believe they like me, though they pretend. There's only one person in our school who seems to enjoy my presence, and I've spent too much of tonight hoping he'll appear.

He probably won't come. I know Harrison wasn't invited, so maybe they're off doing something together. It's strange knowing they're friends. Best friends. Close enough that it's been years since Harrison openly tormented me. At first, I assumed it was to win back Margot, but even once that door fully closed, Harrison kept his distance.

Because of Elliot, I've realized, not Margot.

I settle deeper against the tree. I'm comfortable enough I could fall asleep—not that I'm stupid enough to do that. Just because Harrison isn't here, doesn't mean none of my tormentors are. If they think they can get away with kicking dirt in my mouth while I sleep, they will.

I scan the shoreline, looking. There are nearly fifty people here, most people from our class, but some are older. They showed up with large jugs of dark liquid. It took me an embarrassing amount of time to realize they'd brought alcohol. And now, the majority of guests are drunk.

If they're worried an adult might stumble upon this party, they sure don't show it.

Margot may have had more to drink than anyone. She's currently sitting on Preston Wright's shoulders, pumping her arms to the booming music. She's smiling. Laughing. And that alone makes me feel better about coming.

I'm still watching her when a group of guys show up. They're singing a birthday song to her, voices loud and undoubtedly drunk.

I find Elliot immediately. He's always been tall for his age, and he's almost a head taller than the other boys. I scan through the faces of his friends, shoulders relaxing when I confirm Harrison isn't with them.

Margot claps and hollers as they approach, shimmying off Preston's shoulders to meet the group of boys. They hug and chat, and I feel pathetic watching from the shadows.

It's my own fault. If I forced myself over there, Margot would be nothing but kind. And maybe, if I played it just right, this party could mark the night other people accepted me too. Maybe I could finally fit in. Make friends. Be happy.

I tuck my knees to my chest.

"Pathetic," I whisper. Because even now, I know I'm not going over there. I can too easily imagine everyone's faces if I did. Some would be annoyed, some angry, but the most hurtful would be the ones who were scared. The nice kids, who stay away not because they hate me, but because they're terrified I'll kill them.

The group of guys disperses through the party, until it's only Elliot and Margot together. They'd make a lovely couple. She's tall enough he'd barely have to lean to kiss her. And they're both unjustly beautiful and kind and—

Oh no.

Margot points over at me, and Elliot's head snaps my way. He lifts a hand, and it takes all my nerve just to wave back. A beautiful grin stretches over his features. Waving was a mistake. Now he's coming over here.

Out of pity. Out of mercy. I don't know.

My stomach twists into a hideous knot. Because, yes, I'm an unde-niable outcast, sitting alone at a party. That's fine. Doable. Normal.

Elliot witnessing this and pitying it is so, so much worse.

"Hey Secora," he says. He's smiling as he reaches me, words slur-ring softly. There's a slight haze over his eyes, like he's perfectly intoxi-cated. "I didn't think you'd be here."

"Margot invited me," I say. My voice is rushed, defensive. I can't help it, just like I can't help the flare of blush that scours my cheeks.

"I know," he says. He laughs, and it soothes something in my chest. "I figured you wouldn't want to come. If I'd known you were coming, I would've been here sooner."

My face burns hotter.

"You don't have to look out for me," I say. I untangle my knees from my chest, hoping it makes me look less pathetic. "No one has bothered me. I promise."

"I like looking out for you," he says. He sits in the dirt beside me with far less grace than he normally would. He bumps against my side, and his face is too close to mine. It's impossible to think straight.

"I know," I say. I gently ease back, creating much-needed distance. "But you don't have to. You should be having fun with everyone else. I'm okay. I promise."

"Maybe I'd rather have fun with you," he says. His lips tilt lazily, and his eyes roam over my face.

My heart stops. Full on stops in my chest, until I'm convinced I might have just died. Elliot's words may be slurring, but he's looking at me with complete steadiness. His attention keeps snagging on my lips, and for one glorious, horrifying second, I think he's going to kiss me.

But then, he pulls back.

"You don't even know, do you?" he asks. He twists until his back is against the tree too. Our shoulders are touching, but at least his face isn't so close to mine. I breathe unsteadily and he lets out a quiet laugh. "You're impossible, Secora."

"I don't understand—"

He shifts again, kneeling in front of me. Bracing one hand on the trunk behind me, he uses the other to cup my face. His hazel eyes study mine, flicking occasionally to my mouth.

I suck in a breath, holding it there until it's painful.

"Elliot—"

He runs his thumb across my lower lip, and I gasp.

Everything stops. My heart. My lungs. My thoughts.

"I'm drunk," he says. He stares at my mouth, at his thumb still tracing my lower lip. "It's hard to keep my thoughts in my head, so I might just let them out."

I'm too stunned to speak. Luckily, Elliot doesn't seem to notice.

"You've got the prettiest mouth," he says. "Prettiest eyes. Prettiest everything. It's very unfair. I don't know how I'm supposed to concentrate when you're this pretty. How I'm supposed to not kiss you all the time."

His eyes drift back to mine. The warm alcohol haze is still there.

"I keep trying to ask you out," he says quietly. His thumb swipes my lip again, moving to trace the upper one too. "You always say no. I tell myself it's because I'm not making it clear. That you don't realize I'm interested, and I'm too much of a coward to make sure you know."

Elliot moves his hand from my mouth, and I almost cry out at the loss. He cups my chin, tilting me until I'm looking up at him.

"But I'm drunk now," he says. "So if you reject me, I can hide behind my intoxication the next time I see you. We can pretend it was only a joke."

"Is it?" I ask. My voice is shaking, and I'm dizzy from the fact he's still touching me. That Elliot Lyrie is touching me and saying these impossible things. "Is it a joke?"

"No," he says. His thumb is back on my lip, and his throat bobs as he swallows.

"Because if it's a joke, it's not funny," I whisper. "You obviously know I wouldn't reject you, so if this is an ego thing—"

He kisses me. So suddenly I'm not prepared for it. One moment,

I'm rambling, and the next, his lips are on mine. Soft and warm and sure. He's kissing with the confidence of someone who has kissed a lot of people, and I'm scrambling to keep up.

Our teeth clank. Our noses bump. I'm trembling so hard I can't concentrate on what I'm doing.

"You're shaking," he says, pulling back abruptly. The alcohol haze is still in his eyes, but there's intensity there too. "Do you want me to stop?"

"No," I say, and tomorrow, I'll be mortified at how needy I sound. "I just—I don't know how."

"You're doing good," he says. He brushes his thumb across my jawline. "I can slow down if you want."

I shake my head.

"Just...I've never done it," I say. As if he hasn't figured that out, as if he doesn't already know. "Tell me if it's not good."

"It's good," he says. Then he kisses me again, slower, firmer. His lips taste sharp, like the alcohol he's been drinking. I wouldn't know how to name it, but I decide it's my favorite flavor in the world. Between soft presses of his lips, he whispers. "It's so good, Secora. So fucking good. I knew it would be."

With shaking hands, I grab the shoulders of his shirt, pulling him closer. I don't let myself think beyond this moment, not about whether he meant what he said. Not about whether he'll regret it once he's sober.

I lose track of the minutes, of the hours. I have no idea how much time has passed, only that my lips are numb by the time he pulls away. He places a hand over my head, against the tree, briefly scanning my face before looking over his shoulder.

It's only then I realize why he stopped.

"Sorry, Secora and I have to go," Margot says. Her voice slurs and she breaks into a fit of giggles. She stumbles to the side into my line of sight. She's grinning at me, and when she gives me a cheesy thumbs up, I'm certain I'll implode from humiliation.

"All right, give us a second," Elliot says. "I'll walk her over."

Margot giggles again and stumbles across the rocky shore. I realize most of the party has taken off, leaving only a handful of stragglers. I wonder how many people saw Elliot kissing me.

A lot, probably.

"Is it a joke?" I ask again. My voice cracks, and I'm horrified at the tear that slips down my cheek. Now that I've already made the leap, I'm terrified it was the wrong decision. I acted out of desperation, out of neediness, rather than logic. If this was a ruse, some elaborate plan by the popular kids, I'm not sure I'll survive it.

"No, it's not a joke," he says. He kisses me again, and this time, his tongue swipes out, darting across my bottom lip. When I gasp against his mouth, he smiles. "I'll take you on a proper date, all right? We'll go on a date, and then I'll teach you how to kiss with tongue."

15

THAT WASN'T REAL

ELLIOT

"Well, now I know why you didn't tell me she was hot," Henry says. He lays on the lounge's couch, pillows once again spilled across the tile floors. We're alone, but Henry is still on shift.

Luckily, I'm not. I'm too fucking stressed, too scattered to have people's lives in my hands.

Henry is the opposite. He's relaxed and stretched out, enjoying the last of his lunch break before he goes into another surgery. He takes a bite of apple before tossing it up in the air like a ball and catching it.

"She's not—" I break off. I can't finish the sentence, and Henry smirks knowingly at me.

Cora Reed *is* hot, and until today, that was fine. It was easy to ignore her attractiveness when she was nothing more than my best friend's killer. Who cares if she's hot if she's psychotic?

"She was my friend," I say finally, gritting the words through clamped teeth. "She was my friend. She was probably Harrison's friend eventually. And she killed him. That's completely fucked, Henry. It makes it worse, if anything."

"To be fair, you were twelve," he says. He takes another bite of apple before sitting up, resting his elbows on his knees. He studies me, blue eyes quietly assessing until I'm squirming. "I think you're overreacting."

"I think you're under-reacting," I argue. I run a hand through my hair and slouch back in my chair. "I *liked* her, Henry. What if we ended up dating or something? Maybe she killed Harrison because he tried to get between us. Or maybe she killed him because I broke up with her, and she wanted to get back at me."

"You were twelve," Henry repeats, slowly, as if I'm stupid. "You having a crush on the hot, spooky girl isn't nearly as monumental as you're making it. I'm sure half the guys in your school wanted to get it on with the freaky outcast."

"There's a reason she took those memories," I say. I'm starting to spiral, but I can't help it. This woman stole my memories, and I'm terrified of what I've forgotten. Of what I'll learn if I keep digging.

"I feel like I should tell you to leave this alone," Henry says, grinning. "But clearly you don't like that advice."

"Would you?" I challenge. "Would you leave it alone? Knowing that you might know something about your friend's death? That maybe—"

"It won't bring Harrison back," Henry says. His smile falls, voice softening. "I know you feel like you owe him, but...you don't. Nothing you figure out now will change what happened. It's only going to bring more hurt."

"Maybe," I agree.

Henry chucks his apple at me, and it smacks against my shoulder.

"Shit!" I grab my shoulder, glaring at him. "What the Mother was that for?"

"I can already tell you're going to ignore my advice. *Again*," he says. He rises from the couch, carelessly stepping over the apple as he heads for the door. "We both know you're going to dig until you've shattered your own heart, so be strategic. Get closer to the date he died. She's giving you memories from when you were twelve. That's not going to tell you shit, and you know it."

"Yeah, but—"

"Tell her you want the good stuff," he interrupts. "You were, what, sixteen when Harrison died? Tell her you want those memories."

"I doubt she'll—"

"There are other ways to get vampire blood," Henry says, cutting me off again. "I'm pretty sure she doesn't have other options for witch allies."

"We are *not* her allies," I say quickly.

"Yeah, yeah." Henry flaps his wrist at me as he tugs open the door. Beyond this room, healers bustle up and down the hall, and somewhere in the distance a baby is crying. "Now, if you're done complaining about your childhood crush, I've got a life to save."

He's out the door before I have time to respond.

THE FOLLOWING WEEK, Henry and I are back at the stone table in Sebastian Vulce's open-air courtyard. We're nearest the ivy-covered wall, facing Cora, and beyond her, the doorway into the manor. Though I can't see him, I assume Sebastian is lurking somewhere within the shadowed halls.

"I only brought one this time," Cora says, drawing my attention.

We've just finished our work on the protection spell, and as usual, I'm feeling it more than anyone else. As I heave to catch my breath, Henry taps his fingers rhythmically against the table and Cora readies today's memory. I haven't let myself look at her for longer than a few seconds since we arrived today, but with both of them distracted, I allow myself the indulgence.

She's wearing her typical baggy black dress and heavy tights. Her hair is in its tight ponytail, and she's not wearing any makeup. She's pretty in a startling way. Her large, yet delicate features demand attention, and I can hardly blame my younger self for being smitten.

There's something different about her today. I can't quite place it, but she looks sadder. Less put together, like she's a stitch away from falling apart.

I hate that I notice.

Still breathing hard, I force myself to look away. I swipe the jar she's placed in front of her, twisting to read the label.

Elliot Lyrie

age 12

Ochre Primary School

"No," I say. I push it back toward her, barely restraining a smile when her brows furrow. She glares at me, mouth puckering.

"No, what?"

"No, I don't want that one," I say. "I want an older memory. From when I'm sixteen."

"That's not how this works," she says. She grips the edge of the table, and her attention flickers to Henry, as if expecting him to back her up.

I almost expect him to. After all, he *does* like mean, pretty women.

"Sorry, sweetheart," he says. "I'm on his side, remember?"

"Never call me sweetheart again," she says. She's speaking through her teeth, almost growling.

Once again, I'm holding back my amusement.

"Yes, ma'am," Henry says. He offers a small salute, earning him a sharp scowl in response.

"Either you want this memory, or you don't," she says. She starts unpacking her bag, placing the stone and its ingredients on the table. "You don't want it? Fine. You can go."

My heart punches against my ribs. I knew she wouldn't back down easily. This was one of her rules, after all. *She* gets to pick the memories.

"If you haven't watched them anyway, what do you care when they're from?" I ask.

Cora doesn't reply. She lines the ingredients over the top, finishing with a few drops of liquid. I risk a glance at Henry, and his stare says everything he can't out loud: *don't look at me, dummy!*

"I could find blood elsewhere," I say. I focus on Cora and do my best not to fidget when she holds my gaze. She's unflinching, untouched by the threat.

"That's a grand idea," she says lazily. The stone starts to smoke beneath her, filtering up to her barely-restrained smile. "Remind me, how did that go for you last time?"

"Yes, well, now I've got Henry for back-up," I say. It's a stupid argument. Makes me look weak, pathetic. Still, it's the best I've got.

"And now I know you're looking for vampire blood," she says sweetly. She finally pulls back from the stone, but only to uncap the memory. "I'm close with the vampire king, in case you've forgotten."

She subtly tilts her chin, nodding at the manor's doorway.

"I haven't forgotten," I say. "He's got quite the hold over you."

I expect her to flinch. To frown. To get defensive in one way or another.

Instead, she offers a one-shoulder shrug.

"Yes," she says. "I suppose he does. He also has quite the hold over our blood vendors."

"We'll come twice," I blurt. "Twice a week, if you'll give me older memories."

Beside me, Henry stiffens. We both know we don't have time to make bi-weekly trips to the Night Realm. Especially not him. I may not have a life outside of the healing center and this psychological warfare, but Henry does. He'll have to cut back on time with friends, on time with Mary and other women.

I glance at him again, trying to convey I'll make it up to him.

"Fine," Cora says. By the time I look back to her, she's already rising from her bench. Unsurprisingly, she's taking the memory stone with her. "I'll be right back."

"No way," I say. I'm out of my seat and standing in front of her before she's fully on her feet. She blinks at me in surprise when I grab her wrist. "You're not taking this. For all I know, you'll go watch the memory in advance."

"For all you know, I've already done that," she snaps. Her attention drifts to her wrist, to my hand around it. I expect her to demand I release her. Instead, a heavy blush scours her cheeks.

"Unhand my witch, Lyrie," comes a voice from the doorway.

Out here in the daylight, I shouldn't be terrified of Sebastian Vulce. He might not burn in the sun, but he's weak like this. And yet, he walks across the courtyard with slow, predatory steps.

"I have this handled," Cora says. She glares at the vampire king before roughly stepping out of my hold. One of the mermaid scales falls, hitting the cobblestone. Cora curses as she crouches to pick it up. She glances at me and Henry, but her attention settles on Sebastian as she speaks. "I'll be right back. Don't kill anyone while I'm gone."

Breath held, I wait for Sebastian Vulce to put Cora in her place. Instead, his lips twitch, as if fighting a smile.

"Very well," he says. The look is there again, the one that suggests she is far more than mere weapon to him.

Once Cora disappears into the manor, I return to my seat. Sebastian Vulce remains standing, and he stares down his nose at me as if I'm a repellent insect. I force myself to hold his gaze, even when I'm sure I can't bear another second of his scrutiny.

After nearly ten minutes, Cora finally reappears. I watch her through the stretch of windows as she approaches the courtyard. Her dark ponytail swishes behind her, chin tilted high. She's still carrying the memory stone and another jar. I can only hope it's a memory from age sixteen. Even if it's from age ten, I'm going to watch it, just to escape this ungodly place.

As she reaches the doorway, Sebastian leans in front of me, blocking her from view.

"Touch her again, Lyrie, and I'll remove your hands," he says. He straightens without giving me time to respond. "Yell if you—"

"Yes, Master," she says, heaving a sigh. "Now, please. I've got it handled."

He regards her for a long moment before finally nodding. With a final glare in my direction, the vampire king crosses the courtyard and returns to the manor's darkened interior.

"He cares for you," I say.

I'm not sure what compelled me to say it, and it clearly catches Cora off guard too. She raises both eyebrows, attention shifting from me to Henry. Her mouth opens, but nothing comes out. Finally, she clears her throat and sets her items in front of me.

"A new jar," she says. "Age fifteen."

"We agreed sixteen."

"Age fifteen," she repeats. She uncaps the jar, piercing me with a stubborn glare. "Do you want it or not?"

I don't let myself glance at Henry, even though I'm annoyed. Even though we absolutely agreed on age sixteen.

"Fine," I say. "Whatever."

She places the green memory onto the stone, and together, we watch the color burst into smoke.

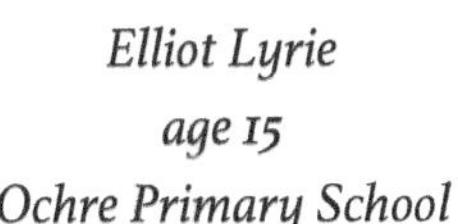

Elliot Lyrie
age 15
Ochre Primary School

"Come on," *she whispers. She's giggling and running so fast I can barely keep up. I don't mind. I'd cross treacherous landscapes, mostly blind, any day of the week if it meant I was getting time alone with Secora Reed.*

Time alone, because Mama thinks she's a bad influence.

Time alone, because Harrison thinks she wants to kill me.

Time alone, because Secora thinks people would hate her if they knew.

Time alone, because I'm terrified she's right.

"You're so slow," she complains, but I can hear the smile on her face. "Our tree misses us!"

"You think?" I ask. I'm grinning too. I feel drunk, even though I haven't had a drop of alcohol. It's simply Secora. Intoxicating. Beautiful. Wild. "Because I think our tree might be glad for the break—"

I don't get the chance to finish my sentence. We've reached our tree, the same one I once warned her was haunted. The same one we sat beneath for countless lunch breaks and more than one afternoon date. Even after moving to our next school, we still come back. There's something special about this place, something distinctly ours.

Secora grabs my shoulders, tugging me down to her height. Every year, we grow farther apart in height, and closer together in every other way. I bend to meet her, capturing her mouth with my own. She tastes like the dessert we just shared and fresh air and crisp winter mornings.

I break away from her mouth to kiss her neck. I've got her dress bunched in my fists, tugging her skirt higher and higher, until she's nearly exposed to me. We haven't crossed that line, not yet, but the moment she gives any indication...

"We should do this more often," she says. She's gasping, head tilted against the tree. "Like, maybe all the time."

I hum in agreement, too focused to pull myself away. I'm still kissing her neck, still gripping her waist and teasing her skirt, when I realize she's gone still. She shudders before making a terrible choking noise.

When I pull back, she's crying.

"What's wrong?" I ask. I drop her skirt, cupping her face with both hands. "Fuck, Secora. I'm sorry. Was I—"

"No, sorry, it's nothing," she says. Tears streak down her cheeks, and she hiccups, scrunching her eyes shut. "Keep going."

"Tell me what's wrong," I beg. I wipe her tears, but they're falling too fast for me to keep up. "Hey, look at me. What's—"

"You're going to do this with someone else someday," she says. She's crying so hard she can barely breathe. "And that's good. It's fine. It just—it breaks...it breaks my..."

"Secora, look at me," I say. I wipe her tears again, tightening my hold over her face. I tilt her chin, forcing her to do as I say. "I'm not doing this with anyone else. Okay? Just you."

"I'm a Dark One," she says. She's still crying, and my heart is breaking, and I don't know how to fix any of it. "Dark Ones don't... they can't—"

"Shhh," I say. Because I know as well as she does the laws for Dark Ones.

They can't marry.

They can't reproduce.

They can't do so many things.

"We're going to get your ruling reversed," I say. It's something we've talked about dozens of times. She was a kid when those people died, and there's no proof it was actually her fault. "We'll get it reversed. And once we do—"

"Your mama would never allow it," she says. She's still crying, but she swallows the sobs. Soon, there are only silent tears. "You know that, Elliot. She'd never—"

"I pick you," I say. My stomach clenches as I speak the words. Not because I'm lying, but because I'm telling the truth. "She'll either learn to accept it or she'll lose me. Because I am not losing you, Secora. Understand? I love you—"

I'M YANKED out of the memory so abruptly my vision spins. Or maybe that's a side effect of what I just saw. Of the horrible, terrible memory I'm certain can't be real. I would have kept watching. It wasn't me who pulled us out, but Cora.

"Was that real?" I demand. Cora doesn't reply. She's shaking as she takes the memory off the stone, shoving it roughly into its jar. I lean forward, trying to force myself into her eyeline. "How did you do that?"

That memory looked like mine. It felt like mine. But it clearly wasn't. Clearly this woman manufactured it, twisted reality to convince me she's not the enemy at all. It's some sort of ploy. A tactic to get me to make more sunwalker spells. To betray my people.

"I'm sorry," she blurts. She's on her feet, bent over the table, scrambling to put everything in her bag. Her hands shake as she plucks the ingredients off the stone. "I thought...It was a school memory. I didn't think..."

She's crying, I realize. Tears stream down her face, an eerie reflection of the Secora in my memory.

"That wasn't real," I spit. "I didn't...I didn't *love* you."

"Oh shit," Henry mutters.

Cora chokes out a sob as she fastens her bag.

"You're saying that was real?" I demand when she doesn't speak. "That we were in love? Forgive me if I don't fucking believe you."

"Leave, Elliot," she says. Voice shaking. Tears falling. If this is an act, it's a damn good one. "*Please.*"

She runs—actually runs—from the courtyard. I collapse back onto the bench, dropping my head into my hands. Though I consider chasing after her, Sebastian Vulce's lingering shadow convinces me otherwise.

16

______

SHE IS NO MONSTER

ELLIOT

I've never been in love. At least, that's what I thought until Cora showed me that damned memory. Looking through my eyes at fifteen, I absolutely *have* been in love. I have been in the soul-consuming, beautiful, reckless love I recently believed didn't exist. Even though I left the physical memory with Cora, I remember watching it all too well. I can still feel that wild love in my chest, lodged somewhere deep between my ribs.

Two days later, and I'm sick with it, this realization I once loved Harrison's murderer. It doesn't feel possible, and I cling to the hope it's not. Cora and her vampire clan might have manufactured the memory, and there's one person who should be able to confirm it.

At least, I hope.

I step off the tram, my body vibrating with coiled tension. People jostle around me, all clad in soft yellows and browns. A man mutters about the dismal weather, and a cluster of children start a game of groundball long before they've cleared the crowd. I stand in place, hands tucked into my pockets, and watch the children take off into Ochre.

I know this place better than anywhere else. The weathered sign with its bloodied thumbprints. The cobblestone streets. The clay and timber houses, all similar yet slightly different. Empty booths line the walkways, still standing from the recent autumnal festival, but clearly vacated.

With a quick glance at the address in my pocket, I follow the crowd to the east. It's early enough in the afternoon that shop doors are propped open and the occasional vendor calls out to passerby. I've done this, walked the streets of Ochre, too many times to count. And yet, for the first time, I'm forced to acknowledge the strange sensations coursing through my body.

I've felt them for over a decade. Inexplicable flutters in my stomach when I pass the primary school. A sharp pinch in my chest when I walk main street. The feelings blossom into something darker, something heavier, whenever I pass the augur house. I stare at the unremarkable building now, at the threadbare curtains covering each of its square windows. Though I'm tempted to slow, I don't.

I never understood what those feelings were. I assumed they were my imagination. There was never rhyme or reason to tie the sensations to anything meaningful.

Now, I think I get it.

My body is reacting to memories I no longer have. I might not consciously be able to name everything that's happened here, but my body remembers. I'm reacting to a history I've forgotten, and if this last memory is true, no one else remembers it either. At fifteen, I was dating Secora in secret. I hadn't told Mama or Harrison. We hadn't told *anyone*.

Still, I'm hopeful there's one person who would have known —and she wasn't just Secora's friend. She was mine too.

I turn to the east and walk a series of near-identical subdivisions. It's late afternoon, and despite the cool air, the direct sunlight makes it feel warmer. I've got the sleeves of my white buttoned shirt rolled to my elbows, but it's not enough to keep the sweat from collecting on my palms. I wipe my hands against my pants as I reach the house at the end of the street.

It's an ordinary timber and clay house. Only the overflowing flower boxes beneath the windows and the array of kids' toys on the lawn set it apart. I smile at the sight, at the rush of nostalgia that warms my chest.

Margot Blake's home today looks much like the one she had when we were children. Simple, but beautiful. Messy, but charming. Imperfect, but in a lovely way.

She doesn't know I'm coming. There's a chance she won't be home at all. Maybe that's why I didn't tell her, why I chose to come in the early afternoon, when she might still be at work. There isn't much information on her in the autumnal directory, but she's currently employed at a nearby children's center.

The last time I spoke to her—nearly ten years ago now—she still talked about pursuing a position in the council.

I follow a colorful brick pathway across her yard and to the front stoop. An empty bin labeled "frogs" sits to the left of the door, and several pairs of shoes line the right side. From the shoes alone, I can tell Margot has as many children as her parents.

Taking a sharp breath, I go to knock on the blue door, only for it to swing open before I touch it. A young boy, maybe five, with white hair and blue eyes stares up at me, a spitting image of Margot.

"Sorry, there's no time!" he shrieks. He dodges around me, shortly followed by an identical set of girls, not much older than he is. All three of them carry a toad. The boy has one in each hand, and one of the girls snags the empty bin as they pass.

"Mama's inside!" the other girl calls.

Their shrieked giggles fill the neighborhood, even once they've disappeared into one of the adjacent yards. Moments later, the laughter doubles, triples. Somewhere, just out of sight, there's a whole cluster of kids screeching and cackling.

Despite where I am—and *why*—a smile tugs at my lips. Harrison and I used to get into all sorts of trouble when we were their age. We'd play pranks on the neighbors. Catch and capture every type of bug, only for one of our mothers to release them when we inevitably forgot about them. We'd play groundball past our bedtime and make stink potions to release during mathematics. We'd been terrible and wonderful, and Secora Reed *ruined* it.

I swallow and force my attention back to Margot's home. Her door is still open, revealing a short landing that splits to upper and lower floors. Aside from the tiled entryway and the wooden steps, I can't see anything. I can only hear the tone-deaf singing of a young girl, followed quickly by her frustrated screech.

"Mama!" she screams. She's got bright red hair and she leans over the upstairs balcony. Her face is stained with tears and heavy blush. "I can't do this. I'm going to be the worst one—"

She cuts off abruptly when she sees me. Her face, which was already bright red, explodes with heat. Her pale hands cover her cheeks and eyes, and she collapses to the ground, out of sight. She must be fifteen, far too old to biologically belong to Margot.

I open my mouth to explain. I can't imagine what she's thinking...some strange man standing in her doorway, eavesdropping on her family. The problem is, I don't know *how* to explain.

Your siblings left the door open? They were on a frog quest, and I got caught in the middle?

"Nadia isn't accustomed to handsome men on our stoop. You'll have to forgive her."

I startle and turn in the direction of the basement. Margot Blake climbs up the final stairs, arms crossed over her chest, smile broad and blindingly beautiful. She's always been stunning and charming and kind, and Mama used to constantly encourage me to ask her on a date.

I told Mama it would be weird. She was Harrison's first girlfriend. She shared a home with his killer. Those excuses felt easier than the truth: Margot Blake was beautiful, but for some reason, I wasn't interested.

"Mama!" the redhead—Nadia, apparently—screeches. "Why would you say that?"

She's crying now, and Margot glances toward the upper balcony, an affectionate smile on her face.

I still haven't said a word, but now, I'm not even trying. Instead, I have a palm to my chest, feeling the steady beat of my heart. Everything within me moves exactly as it should, and yet, I am hit with that eerie sensation again. That same one I notice more and more now that I know what Cora did.

My body remembers things about Margot Blake that I don't. It's a terrifying, world-tilting sensation. Were the memories about her good or bad? Safe or dangerous?

"Let's step outside," Margot says. Then, to the girl upstairs, she adds, "Keep practicing, love. You're getting better all the time."

I don't dare ask what she used to sound like.

I step back onto the porch, leaning against one of its wooden pillars. Margot closes the door behind her, moving carefully around her family's haphazard collection of shoes, and mirrors my stance against the opposite pillar. That blinding smile is back as she scans over me.

There's nothing sexual in the way we regard each other, only a nostalgic fondness that warms my chest. Margot Blake is as beautiful as ever, but she's undeniably different. Older. There's a soft crease between her eyebrows now, and her blonde hair is darker than it was in my memories.

"Did you come to inform me you've lost your voice?" she teases. "Or to stare at me like I'm an endangered creature?"

"Secora Reed," I say. They're the first words I speak to her, and my voice is so raspy, it doesn't sound like mine. Cora's name is a terrible combination of curse and anguish coming from my lips. "I'm here because of Secora Reed."

Margot's expression falls. Goes blank. Even her eyes, forever gentle and kind, go distant.

"Not here," she says quietly. The words tremble from her mouth, and her gaze darts down the street, as if expecting someone to be lurking nearby. "We can't do this here, Elliot."

"Can't do *what*?" I ask. I lower my voice to a whisper, stepping to bridge the distance between us. Down the street, the children have started shouting again. Margot looks toward the sound, but I keep my eyes locked on her. "Margot. You have to tell me."

"This place doesn't know her like we do," Margot says. She steps closer, angling her body so that she's facing the house, rather than the street. "Anything you say will get you in trouble, Elliot. You never know who's listening."

Another flicker of her attention.

My stomach twists, sinks, distorts into something unrecognizable.

I came to get confirmation on what I wanted to be true: Secora Reed and I are strangers. We were acquaintances, at most. We weren't friends, and we definitely weren't lovers.

But the way Margot speaks...as if she and I knew Cora better than anyone else. As if I—Madam Lyrie's son—wouldn't be a threat to whatever twisted secret she has.

We have.

"You shouldn't be here," she says. There's an urgency in her voice I've never heard before. I think back to our last conversations, but they were always quick. Easy. I never mentioned Cora, and neither did she. "Whatever you and Secora are doing now, I can't be part of it."

"What makes you think I would be doing anything with *her*?" I ask. It's meant to be a snarl, but it's a whispered, pathetic question. A burning desperation that claws up my throat, laced with self-loathing.

Tell me, Margot. Confirm what I now know is true. Tell me I once loved a monster, and she loved me back.

Margot flinches, putting space between us once more. She stares at me, brows furrowed, eyes darting between my features. And then, all at once, her face softens. In a single moment, she looks years younger.

"Oh, Secora," she says. She's not looking at me as she speaks, but off in the distance, as if speaking though the realms, all the way to that horrible, vampiric manor. When she looks back to me, her eyes are watering. "I suspected it. That she may have taken them. I guess I just hoped..."

"Margot, if you're fucking with me, if this is some ploy that you and Cora conjured—"

She huffs out a silent laugh, the tears remaining unshed in her eyes, making them impossibly blue.

"I haven't spoken to Secora since the night they took her," she says. "Clearly, you have. I can tell from the look on your face, I'm right. Did she take them all?"

"How would I know?" I snap. "She stole my memories, Margot. I barely remember her. And now, she's giving them back, piece by piece, making it look like we were *dating*—"

A surprised laugh sputters from her lips.

"She's evil," I snarl. "She *killed* Harrison. My best friend. And I'm supposed to believe—"

"She loved you more than anyone, Elliot. Even herself," Margot interrupts. She wipes at her eyes before finally looking back at me. Something like anger ripples beneath her expression, and her words echo through my mind like a pulsing drum. "If she took your memories, it was for *you*. Not her. You may not remember Secora, but I do, and you will not speak ill of her."

"That doesn't make any sense," I say. It's an accusation. A demand. A plea. "Why the hells—"

"It's almost impossible to steal memories," she says, once again cutting me off. "Did you know?"

"She's powerful," I spit. "Her magic...it's not like ours. Normal witches can't steal memories, but she's not normal. She's a monster. She—"

"Secora is no monster," Margot says softly. She steps away, touching the door but not opening it. "The fact you're here, confused on my doorstep, is proof enough of that."

"You should hate her," I say. Demand. "She *killed* Harrison."

"Yes, she did," Margot says. "She killed him, and they imprisoned her for it. Beat her. Starved her. Planned her execution as the event of the century."

She's shaking as she speaks, fists so tight her hands lose color.

"If *his* death is what makes you angry, perhaps you gave her too much," she says.

"She stole them," I say. "I didn't give her a fucking thing."

"Are you sure?" she asks. She finally opens the door, stepping inside, where sounds of her spare daughter's off-key singing persists. "Because I promise you, Elliot, you loved her more than anyone, too. Even yourself."

17

A MIDNIGHT SNACK

ELLIOT

Mama watches me with detached curiosity as I treat her the following morning. We stand in her office, surrounded by ancient texts and various documents for the upcoming, annual witch council meeting. Heads from all different covens will attend, and Mama will be at the forefront of it all.

Fielding questions.

Planning budgets.

Assigning roles.

And, most notably, pretending she isn't dying.

"Well?" she asks.

I have her hand clasped between mine as I rotate her arm between us. Dull grey flesh stretches from her wrist to deep beneath her long sleeves. The darkened skin is dry and flaking, and something tells me the decay goes far beneath the surface.

She's already had three vials of blood this week.

"It's not enough," I say. My voice cracks, but I'm quick to clear it, to steady my next words. My emotions won't get me anywhere, earnest as they may be. "You're dying, Mama."

"Slower than I was," she says. She stares at her arm, attention only briefly flicking to my face before returning. "You've done well, Elliot. Better than I dared to hope."

"You're dying," I repeat. I release her hand, chest clenching as she tugs her sleeve back into place. Like this, she doesn't look sick. She looks normal. Powerful.

How much longer until it's everywhere? How much longer until it kills her?

"You need to come to the clinic," I say. I step back, putting distance between us, doing my best to look at her, not as my mama, but as an extremely sick patient. "This isn't enough. Once we get a better idea—"

"The annual meeting is in two weeks," Mama says. She lets out a breathy laugh and brushes a strand of graying hair over her shoulder. Even in the face of death, she's fearless, and I hate it. "There's too much to do, Elliot. Besides, I already told you I won't go to the clinic. As soon as people know, I'll lose any semblance of control."

Don't you want to stay? I want to scream. *Why am I fighting when you're not?*

"You're going to lose your control or your life, Mama," I say through a tight jaw. "I think it's clear which you should prioritize."

"My life belongs to the Mother," she says. She offers a soft smile now, but it's far from comforting. It's a punch in the stomach, a slap to the face. It's every form of physical pain, wrapped into the minimal tilt of her lips.

"I'll put together a team," I say. When she opens her mouth to interrupt, I only speak faster. Louder. "They'll come to my house. They won't know the reason. I'll have them diagnose you. I'll get enough Dismemrate for the lot of them, and they'll forget it ever happened. No one will know, Mama. All right? So let's—"

"Since when do you condone Dismemrate?" she asks.

It's an illegal drug, so normally I wouldn't. Maybe it's my tentative alliance with Cora Reed that's messed with my head. Or maybe it's my aggravating, stubborn mother who won't accept help, even when I'm desperate to give it.

"Mama," I say. "You can't put me through this. All right? You're all I have here, and—"

A sharp knock on the door cuts through my pathetic rant.

"Come in," Mama calls. She doesn't breathe out in relief, and that, more than anything, makes me realize just how hopeless my arguing is. For Mama, it doesn't matter what I do or say. There's nothing to sway her stubborn mind—she's merely letting me vent like she would when I was a child.

I grit my teeth as the council's attendant steps through the office door. Her ringlets are tighter than I remember. Her glasses bigger. Her curled lip more pronounced.

"Madam Lyrie," Vera says. Then, nodding to me, "Mister Elliot."

"Yes?" Mama asks. In a quick movement that Vera likely doesn't notice, but I sure as hells do, she checks her sleeves. She only looks up once she's confirmed her decaying skin is hidden.

"Mister Rierson is here for you," Vera says. She glances at me with a fake, apologetic grimace, before looking back. "For your ten o'clock."

"I'll come to him," Mama says. She rises from her chair, crossing the room in a few strides. I tell myself I'm imagining it, but I'm certain she's walking differently. Staggered, almost, as though in pain.

"Mama—"

"We'll continue this next week," she says. She places her hands on my face, soft fingers splaying either side of my jaw. "You have to trust me, Elliot."

I glance over her shoulder, confirming Vera is gone.

"We might not have that long," I say. "It's spreading. With the medicine I'm giving, it shouldn't possibly be spreading. But it is. We don't have time."

Mama doesn't immediately reply. She keeps her hands on the edges of my face, her eyes carefully looking over my features. She's looking at me like it might be the last time. There's no fear in her expression, only nauseating acceptance.

It makes my eyes burn, and before I can stop it, tears leak down my cheeks.

"I'll meet Mister Rierson in the lobby. It'll take at least thirty minutes," she says quietly. "Collect yourself, Elliot. Don't make a scene here. Understand?"

Then, she's gone, and I'm alone in her office, surrounded by the smell of her perfume and black tea and brutal complacency.

"Coward," I whisper. Not sure if I mean it, not sure if it's fair.

I glance up at the clock on the wall, then at my bag on the floor. Thirty minutes is a long time. I look at the clock again. The bag. The rows of books and documents. The locked desk drawers and filing cabinets.

This place has always been a treasure trove, but for the first time in my life, I see the potential. There isn't just history in these books; there are clues. Keys to old curses...and perhaps a cure for the woman who made them.

I arrive to the Lyrie Healing Center just after eleven. There are stacks upon stacks of paperwork waiting on my desk, but I ignore them. Prior to my visit with Mama, I'd intended to catch up on all the work I've put off. Now, I take the stairs two at a time, not so much as glancing at my office door. Instead, I run all the way to the seventh floor, crashing into the break room with the grace of a freshly winged harpy.

It's empty.

"Dammit," I mutter.

Henry was scheduled for a nine o'clock surgery, and I hoped he'd be done by now.

I pace the room while I wait, then find a stack of blank parchment and sit at the rough table. I scrawl one idea after another, tossing each rejected scrap to the tiled floor. By the time I have a fully-formed plan, I've used up all of the parchment.

"Oh for Mother's sake..."

I jolt, looking up from the table to find Henry standing in the doorway. He's wearing a bloodied surgeon's coat, his transparent face mask hanging around his neck. His eyes are half-open, dark bags beneath them.

"Rough surgery?" I ask. I glance at his vibrating hands, at the magic that's undoubtedly been stripped from his skin.

"What are you doing, Elliot?" he asks, rather than answering. He disposes of his surgical attire as he looks over my discarded mess of parchment.

"I figured it out," I say. My hands are stained with blank ink, and I'm sure I look about as disturbed as he does. I hold the final piece of parchment on the table, pinching it between my thumb and index finger. "The sunwalker spell. I know how to mass produce it."

Henry grimaces and looks over his shoulder, as if expecting someone to be behind him. He's right to be cautious, and yet, I can't bring myself to care. My entire world has imploded in the past few weeks, and not even imprisonment would make it worse.

"Since when was that part of your plan?" he asks. He takes a careful step toward me, and his expression is so timid it's almost comical. The brave and reckless Henry looks mortified by me, and if it weren't such a shit situation, maybe I'd laugh. "Mass sunwalker spells, Elliot? That's past the point of a fair trade."

"Mama thinks the Mother is punishing her for the sun curse, right?" I say, ignoring him. "We can't undo it, obviously, but we can stop the harm. Maybe, if we make the vampires mortal in sunlight—rather than dead—the Mother will forgive her."

"Elliot—"

"I know it sounds crazy," I interrupt. "But she won't be seen in the clinic. She won't be seen at my house. She's determined to let the Mother decide, so fine. We'll let the Mother decide. I'm just going to make that decision a little easier. Once the curse isn't actively killing people, the Mother will have mercy. She will."

I sound like an absolute deranged lunatic, but I don't care. I look away from Henry to go over my notes again.

"This will undermine your mama's life work," Henry says slowly. He's reached the side of the table now, bumping it gently as he looks over my work.

Good, I want to say. *Maybe it will give her a reason to stay.*

I swallow, pressing my tongue against the back of my teeth, trying to keep in the words I've wanted to say for too long. Yes, I want Mama to live. And yes, I'd love to be the one to keep her here. More than that though...

"They're people, Henry," I say. I stare at the parchment, rather than him, as I speak. "Maybe they're terrible. Maybe they deserved it. But it's been twenty years. They've paid long enough."

"Your mama would disagree."

"I know," I say.

There's a heavy silence between us. I'm not sure why I'm telling Henry all of this. When I first came here, I'd wanted his help in forming a solution. Now that I've figured it out on my own, there's no reason to stay. I don't need him for any of this, but I continue speaking all the same.

"I'm going to work out a trade with Cora," I say. "All of my memories for a widespread sunwalker spell. She won't be able to say no."

Another heavy silence. I don't allow myself to look up from the parchment. I've got a list of ingredients we'll need for the sunwalker ritual. Seeing as Cora's already made several spells, she'll have most of them. It's only one specific one, found deep in the archives of Mama's office, that she won't.

And it will change everything.

"I hope you know what you're doing," Henry says. He steps away from the table, staring at me as if I might be a stranger.

"Yeah," I say through a heavy breath. "Me too."

THE FOLLOWING EVENING, I find myself at the border of the Night Realm. I left later than I should have, but I couldn't bear the thought of waiting another day. Now, with the sun falling dangerously low behind me, I trek through the shadowed streets of vampire territory. I'm weighed down by my overstuffed pack. It contains more items than I could possibly need for my planned journey, but I didn't want to risk missing something important.

If Cora agrees to go, that is.

By the time I arrive at Sebastian Vulce's doorstep, I've convinced myself this was a monumental mistake. Cora isn't going to agree. Or, if she does, she'll insist on a vampire entourage. She'll deny the memories I want most. She'll refuse to let me into the manor at all, and I'll become one of her clan's victims.

I pound on the door, stepping back to survey the endless

stretch of windows overhead. Pale vampires leer down at me from between dark curtains. A glance at the skyline confirms what I already know: mere minutes separate us. As soon as the sun drops, I'll be as good as a plate of food on their master's porch.

The front door swings open, and I audibly gasp. I haven't decided whether it's in fear or relief until my eyes settle on Amelia Cyrtev. She's one of the few vampires I've actually met, and I'm *hoping* she knows better than to eat me.

Her brows lift as she glances at the sky behind me.

"Cutting it close, Lyrie," she says.

The hazy interior lights cast a red glow over her, making her look far more terrifying than she ever has at Echo meetings. She's the representative of the vampires, the only bloodsucker the Day Realm willingly allows through their gates.

"Cyrtev," I reply.

I belatedly realize there's blood on her face. It drips from the corner of her mouth and disappears beneath her chin.

"Is our resident witch expecting you?" she asks. Her bright lips curl into a smile, and for the first time, I question whether her characteristic red lipstick is lipstick at all.

I should have a lie ready. For all the traveling I did, I had plenty of time.

"No," I admit. "But I need to see her. Please. At least ask her."

"And if she says no?" she drawls. "Shall I feed you to our hungry men? The bloodletters have retired for the evening. I'm sure—"

"Elliot."

It's unsettling, how instantly I recognize her voice. How, rather than causing my muscles to tense, her voice loosens my shoulders. I look away from Amelia Cyrtev to find Cora staring at me from the back of the room.

Only now do I realize how crowded the entire entryway is.

Just beyond Amelia's shoulder, opposite Cora, a mass of vampires linger in an adjoining room. More are visible at the mouth of the eastern corridor. They're all staring at me, eyes bloodshot. Starving.

"Your timing is uncanny," Amelia says. She's still looking at me, but it's clear her words are for Cora. "I was ready to offer him as a midnight snack."

I think she's joking. I can't tell.

"Come inside," Cora says. She strides across the room, faster than I'd expect for someone her height. She brushes past Amelia and the watching vampires. Grabbing my arm, she yanks me into the entryway. She scowls all the while. "What are you doing here?"

It's a question, spoken like an insult.

"The memory you gave me," I say. I shoot a sideways glance at Amelia. I have no idea how much the clan knows about our arrangement. As much as I need answers, I need to be careful too. "I have questions."

"Sounds hot," Amelia muses.

Again, she must be kidding. It doesn't stop the blush from rising in my face, all the way to my ears.

"This way," Cora snaps. She turns on her heel and takes off in the direction of her quarters. Without looking back, she calls over her shoulder. "You can tell him, Amelia. But let him know I won't answer the door. I have it under control."

I hurry after Cora, doing my best to watch for the bloodthirsty vampires Cyrtev mentioned.

"Do you though, Cora?" Amelia teases, still standing in the open doorway. I realize she's likely about to leave. To *hunt*.

Cora doesn't reply. I tear my eyes from Amelia and the sprawling hallways beyond her. There must be hundreds of vampires in this manor. Maybe a thousand. Every time I enter this place, it could very well be my last.

Despite the overwhelming number of predators living here, Cora walks with confidence and ease. As if this home is hers as much as it is theirs.

I quicken my steps to reach her and match her pace. She doesn't look at me, but her face is pale. She stretches her fingers. Scrunches her nose. Purses her lips. Does *everything* but look at me, even as I stare at her.

"I went to—"

"Not yet," she interrupts.

And so, we walk. Past dreary paintings and ugly sculptures and endless unmarked doors. Until, finally, we reach the door to her quarters and slip inside. The moment the door closes, she turns on me, stepping close. I imagine it's meant to be intimidating, but she's too short to make the look effective.

Cute. She looks cute and vicious and precious, and I *hate* the wild range of emotions coursing through me. They don't make sense. I can't piece them together, and it's *her* fault.

Why do I want to kiss you?

What does Margot know that I don't?

Did I help you escape? Am I a monster and I don't even know it?

"You are more foolish than I ever imagined possible," Cora says. She's pale and shaking—and holy Mother, I think she's going to cry.

"What are you doing?" I demand. My hands itch to touch her. I have to clench the sides of my pants to keep myself from reaching. It's taking all my self-control not to console my best friend's killer.

What have you done to me, Secora Reed, and how do I make it stop?

"You can't be here," she says without answering me. She presses her fists to her eyes, but it only makes them redder when she pulls away. The tears are still there, and unlike with Margot, they actually start to fall. "You can't just show up whenever you feel like it. Master doesn't like unexpected guests, and he *certainly* doesn't like guests with your name."

I grind my teeth. Much as I'd like to point out that her *master* is the bad guy here, not me, I don't have the energy. After the past two days, I don't have it in me to argue with Cora over whether I should have written before visiting.

"I found something," I say, rather than arguing. "In my mama's office. If it's what I think, we should be able to create enough for all of them."

"Enough of what? All of who?" Cora asks. The tears stain her face like translucent tattoos. I could wipe them away so easily.

"Sunwalker spells. The vampires," I say. I swallow past the lump in my throat, the one that fears I'm doing the *wrong* thing.

Cora tilts her head, surveying me in silence. It's hard to read her expression, but I think that's *hope* I see in her eyes. Hesitant, disbelieving hope.

"Why." A command, not a question.

"In exchange for the final memories," I say. When her entire body clenches, I finish in a torrent of words. "The final memories, and I'll get you what you need. I deserve to know, Cora. It's...it's killing me."

"You want them that desperately?" she asks, cheeks flushed. "You're ready to betray your entire species?"

"Our species," I say. Then, "Yes."

"I don't believe you," she says. She wipes at her eyes, frowning at the wetness she finds there. "If this is some sort of trap, Sebastian will—"

"I'm not going to hurt you, Cora," I say. "All I want are answers."

Answers, and a chance to save Mama. The latter, I decide, is better kept to myself.

"I figured out an ingredient, important to the original curse,"

I say. "I can't guarantee it, but if I'm right, this will make all the difference in your sunwalker spell."

She doesn't reply right away, large eyes studying me. Pretty. Why is she so fucking pretty? Why does it physically hurt to look at her, as if she's stolen far more than just memories?

"Where," she says finally. It's another non-question.

"Flight Realm," I say. "A two day trek, I think."

"Fine," she says. She swallows, lifting her chin. "Give me the directions. If I'm able to collect it, you'll get your memories when I return."

"Absolutely not," I say. Despite the seriousness of the moment, I find myself grinning. "We'll go together, Reed. Just the two of us. You'll bring the memories. Once we've got the ingredient, you'll show me the memories."

I brace myself for her inevitable no. It'd be too easy, too simple for her to agree, not to mention foolish. We may have fooled around as teenagers, but there's no way she can trust this isn't a trap. Too much time has passed for that level of trust.

I prepare myself for the debate. She'll inevitably demand at least one chaperone. I'll advocate for Amelia. At least she'll be—

"When do we leave?" Cora asks.

I'm too caught off guard to speak. Instead, my mouth hangs open as I gape at her.

"The sooner, the better," she adds. If she notices my shock, she doesn't acknowledge it. "If we leave at first light, we'll have the best chance of evading Master."

"I could kill you," I say. I can't explain the pinch of anger in my chest, the annoyance at her lack of self-regard. "This could be a trap, Cora. You said it yourself."

"Yes," she agrees. This time, it's her lips ticking into a smile. "It could be a trap, but I don't think it is. And you certainly won't kill me. I might kill *you*, however, if this is all a ruse."

"No," I say, unsettled by the certainty of my own voice. "You won't."

"Tomorrow then?" she asks. She steps back, and it's the breath of oxygen we both clearly need.

I blink, slowly, using all my concentrated effort not to stare at her mouth, at that subtle half-smile she's doing her best to hide.

"Tomorrow at first light," I say with a nod. Then, dropping my pack unceremoniously to the floor, I add, "I've brought everything we'll need. Tonight, I just need a place to sleep."

18

THERE'S NO REASON
CORA

I haven't done many dangerous things, a fact that would probably surprise people. Being an escaped murderer and a traitorous witch, many would assume I like to live recklessly. The truth is, I rarely make impulsive decisions. I am typically cautious, detached, and above all, strategic. If I do something, it's for the big picture, for the greater good, or at least the lesser evil. I don't do things for myself, for selfish want or greed...but today, I'm not sure that's true.

This morning, I'm fussing over my reflection in the ornate bathroom mirror. I'm tucking my hair behind my ears, then undoing it. Then throwing my hair in its tight ponytail after I'm positive I look ridiculous with it down.

As much as I'm tempted to lie to myself, I know I'm not going on this quest for Sebastian and the vampires. I'm not following Elliot into the unknown with the selfless determination to make sunwalker spells.

Truthfully, I'm not convinced Elliot's ingredient will change much at all. I've done more than a decade of research on the sun curse, on its different properties and rituals, and I highly doubt there's some unknown ingredient I missed.

No, the secret ingredient is nothing more than a convenient excuse. It is a way to ease my guilt, to clear my conscience if I'm discovered.

If.

I sound like a fool. I *am* a fool.

Whether Amelia tells him or not, Sebastian will come looking for me at some point today. He'll be expecting to reprimand me and my overnight visitor. Instead, he'll only find this scrawled note, posted haphazardly on the door to my quarters.

Master,

Following a lead. I shall return in four days, five at the most. I have everything under control.

Respectfully,

Cora Reed

Resident Witch

Elliot stands at my side as I fasten it to the door with a slightly bent tack. He raises both eyebrows when I glance back at him.

"Don't say a word," I command. "I've always called him *Master*, all right? I always will. So—"

"I'm *actually* judging your signature. 'Resident witch'? Is that your official position title?" he asks. "I assumed it was more of a pet name."

"Do I look like a pet?" I ask. Then, before he can respond, I turn on my heel and storm down the elongated hallway.

Elliot keeps close behind me, his hand slightly lifted, floating near my waist, as though prepared to grab me. To protect me? Doubtful. To use me as a meat shield? Probably.

"Once we—"

I quiet him with a wave of my hand. Then, pressing my index finger to my lips, I look pointedly around us. Elliot nods. It isn't until we're out of the manor, walking in the chilly air of early morning, that he speaks again.

"Do you want to put that in my pack?" he asks.

I follow his gaze to my messenger bag. It's the same one I always use: a canvas bag with a long shoulder strap. Within it, I've packed the memory stone, two jars, and all the needed ingredients.

Nothing to clean my teeth or brush my hair. No food or drinking water. Not so much as a blanket for nightfall.

I'm an absolute fool, and there's genuinely no excuse. I accepted this adventure on pure, selfish impulse. I saw an opportunity to see Elliot beyond the walls of Sebastian's manor, and I took it.

Not for his mama's ingredient.

Not for Sebastian and the vampires.

Not for the satisfaction of foiling the witches' curse.

But for this. To walk beside someone who once knew me better than anyone, and *loved* me as I was. To feel his presence without worrying something will happen to him for being beside me.

Out here, there are no threats, not like the ones within the manor. I'm strong enough to fend off an attack in daylight, and Elliot has a plan for nightfall.

"Cora?" he asks. He shifts, his tall frame slipping into view. Something about that heavy pack makes him seem even larger than he typically does. He could probably carry my bag *and* me. I wonder whether he would, if I asked.

"I'll carry it," I say. Despite my chaotic thoughts, my voice is calm. Steady. There's even the typical undertone of annoyance clipping through the words.

"Afraid I'll steal the memories?" he asks. His legs are long, and I have to walk twice as many steps to keep pace with him. I wonder if now is a good time to inform him how out of shape I am.

Yet another thing I should have considered before agreeing.

"Of course," I say. "Just because you won't kill me, doesn't mean you won't fuck me over."

He lets out a breathy scoff, something between a laugh and a groan. We walk in silence after that, surrounded only by the sound of our boots on rough stone. The crisp morning air warms slowly, but soon enough, the sun stretches high into the sky, and we pause to remove our jackets.

This time, when Elliot offers to carry my jacket, I don't protest. I hand it over, feeling a strange twist in my stomach when he carefully folds it into his bag, right over his own.

"You don't have to carry it," I say, even as he's tying the pack closed. "I can carry my own—"

"Can I ask you something?" he interrupts. He straightens and adjusts the pack between his shoulders. "And try to be honest, all right? I know that's against your nature, but at least try."

"What's your question?" I ask pointedly. I straighten my shoulders as we start walking again, letting my mask fall back into place. To him, I likely look untouchable.

I pretend it's true.

"Did you steal them?" he asks.

I lift a brow, turning to him in surprise. Of all the things I thought he might ask, that wasn't one. I figured he'd ask about Harrison or my imprisonment or even our sordid love affair as teenagers.

"Your memories?" I ask. Then, following his nod, "I think we've already established that, haven't we?"

We stare at each other as we walk. His jaw ticks as he looks over me.

"I swear, I haven't taken anything more," I say. My eyebrow is still lifted, but a sickening twist clenches my gut. "You should know I took them, Elliot. We already—"

"I didn't ask if you took them," he says, cutting me off. "I asked if you *stole* them. Did you take them without permission? Or did...did I..."

He trails off, and despite my best efforts, I can't keep my gaze on him. I look ahead, at the mountains towering above us. The Flight Realm belongs to the dragons, to the harpies, to the frightening winged ghouls. Where the Night Realm is dark rock and beautiful decay, the Flight Realm is soft sand and rigid mountains and the ever-present scent of dust and land scorched by dragon fire.

Sometimes, I imagine what my life would be like, had I been born not to the witches, but to the dragon riders. Even if I weren't fit to fly, I like to imagine my life would have been better there. I wouldn't be dangerous, not like I am here.

"Cora," he says. He slows his steps, but I shake my head, pressing forward with longer strides.

My heart beats too fast, until I'm almost sickened by my own pulse.

"Is that what this is?" I ask without looking at him. "Is this a fake quest, Elliot? Are you actually just planning to interrogate me while we walk?"

"Fuck," is his muttered response. From my peripheral, I watch as he runs a strong hand through his hair. It tousles, only momentarily, before falling back into place. That damned curl hanging near his furrowed brow.

"Let's just focus on where we're going," I say. My voice is sharp but weak, as brittle as a thin stone. "I'm not answering anything."

"I gave them to you," he says. He laughs, but it's clear he's not amused. He's horrified. Haunted. "Fuck."

"Elliot," I say, but I realize I have nothing to follow up with. There's a lie at the edge of my lips, but something stops me from speaking it. I fidget with the realization that I'm exhausted. Tired of lying. Tired of twisting reality to protect us.

"Fuck," he says again. This time, when I try to talk, he waves me off. "I think you're right. Let's just focus on where we're going."

WE TREK FOR HOURS. We don't speak unless Elliot has a comment on our direction. *A little more to the east,* he'll say. *That's where we're headed. Toward that peak.*

I spend most of the walk wondering where the hells we could be going. It's clear we're going somewhere in the Flight Realm, but it doesn't appear to be toward any sort of town. We bypass the settlement where Sebastian's closest Flight Realm ally lives, and for that, I'm grateful. If Nicassi saw me parading around with some unknown witch, he'd run straight to Sebastian, likely dragging me with him.

I scowl. Would Nicassi do that? Would he throw me over his shoulder like I'm one of Sebastian's lost possessions? Or would he look the other way, take our own friendship into consideration?

"What's wrong?" Elliot asks from beside me.

The sun is high in the sky now, and despite the late autumn season, it's warm. Too warm. I'm sweating through my long sleeves, and my tights feel like heavy wool blankets. We haven't stopped to take a rest or to drink water since we've started, but obviously I'm not going to be the one to ask for a break.

I'm not sure we even have water.

"Cora?" he says. His steps slow, then stagger to a stop.

I have no choice but to do the same. Or, maybe I do. Maybe I'm just that desperate for an excuse to stop walking.

My legs ache, calves cramping with each step. It's shameful to admit how little I exercise my muscles. Right now, they're operating purely on adrenaline and pride.

"Nothing," I say. I prop my hands on my hips, then touch one to my face. Sure enough. "I'm sweating."

"Yeah," Elliot says. He shrugs his pack off his shoulders and unbuttons the top. He rummages through the bag before finally pulling out a rectangular canister. He untwists the top and offers it to me.

It's nice that he's giving me the first drink. It makes me scowl harder.

"It's not poisoned," he says with a hefty sigh. "Here, look—"

I swipe the canister from his hand before he can take a sip. No part of me thought he'd try to poison me, and for reasons I don't want to evaluate, I need him to know that.

I take a long drink, tipping my head back. My eyes flutter shut at the cool water. He must have magicked it to stay cold. It's pure bliss. I didn't realize how dry my mouth had gotten, but a few swallows, and I feel like I've been revived, pulled from the desert and given a second chance at life.

"Thank you," I rasp when I finally stop drinking. I shouldn't be surprised to find the canister still full as I hand it back to Elliot. He's thought of everything.

"You're welcome," he says. He's staring at my mouth as he speaks, and I'm not sure he even realizes it. His pupils are wide, nearly swallowing the irises. I don't know if it's the show of trust or the actual act of chugging water.

He blinks, mutters something under his breath that sounds like *fuck*. I'm tempted to ask when that became his favorite word. I'm tempted to ask him a lot of things.

While Elliot drinks, I adjust my bag over my shoulder. A tight knot is forming beneath my neck, and I imagine a night sleeping in the forest won't help. I peek sideways at Elliot, just as he's capping the canister. There's a lot I don't know about this adventure of ours, a lot I most definitely should have asked before agreeing.

Especially since I told no one where I was going.

I don't even know where I'm going.

Elliot is still placing his canister back into his pack when I start walking again. There's nothing I hate quite like introspection, not even exercise. I glance at the contents of my bag as I walk, more to keep myself busy than to check I have everything.

Two jars. The glossy black Initia Stone. A miniature container, filled with Astoria Lake water. A separate pouch with the fae king's hair and the mermaid scales and the dragon claw. It's all still in place, but the memories look more anxious than they did before we left. It's like they know something is changing.

Do they think I'm going to release them? Allow them to return to their owner?

I'd sooner absorb them myself.

"More to the south now," Elliot says. I'm not sure when he caught up to me, but he's steadily keeping pace. His pack is back in place over his shoulders, and he looks all too comfortable for someone who has been walking all day.

I puff out a breath, staring straight ahead, rather than at him. In front of us, massive craggy mountains sprout from the desert and stretch for the gray sky. Overhead, a slender green dragon whips between the mountain turrets. Not far behind him, a harpy follows suit. A male, whooping at the top of his lungs.

A teenager, I'd guess.

"Have you ever thought about it?" Elliot asks from beside me. Both of his hands are on the straps of his pack, the only possible sign he's more fatigued than he looks.

"About what?"

"Flying," he says. He nods to the harpy, then the dragon. I realize the latter has a rider, clinging haphazardly to its back.

"I have no interest in that," I say. I tilt my head slightly, following their trajectory until they disappear between mountain peaks to the north. "I've found the ground to be challenging enough."

"Have you?" Elliot asks. His lips tilt into a subtle smirk, but within seconds, it blossoms into a full smile. "I suppose you *are* sweating."

"I've noticed you aren't," I say. Blush scours my cheeks as soon as the words are out. I rush forward, hoping he won't read into my words. "Are you one of those people who *enjoy* this? Walking. Trekking. Exercising."

He barks out a laugh, and it shoots dopamine through my entire system. The blush on my cheeks grows hotter, and pride swells deep beneath my ribcage.

Make him laugh again, my body begs. *Let us hear it again.*

"I do enjoy this," Elliot says. He's looking at me, but I do not allow myself to look back. "Even with you, Cora."

"I'm honored," I say. My words drip with sarcasm, and I can only hope it's enough he thinks I don't mean it. When, truly, my body is humming.

We walk in quiet for several minutes. We are officially in Flight Realm territory. The ground has fully transitioned from grey rock to pale sand. Mounds and mounds of it, the color of powdered clay and as fine as dust particles. Every step sends a puff of it into the air, and before long, I can feel the scrape of it on my throat.

"You see that?" Elliot asks. He points at the same peak he has multiple times now. "That's where we're going."

"You've mentioned," I deadpan.

"No, look closer," he says. His hand remains lifted, finger directed at that same, lopsided pinnacle. It's one of the shorter mountains, maybe technically a hill, tucked between two enormous peaks.

I ignore my instinct to argue with Elliot that I *do*, in fact, see the peak. I lean forward, eyes squinted at the peak. There's nothing remarkable about it. The mountains of the Flight Realm are broad and jagged, a collection of freestanding crests and interconnect stretches. They're all sandy and grey, dotted with dark trees and scattered boulders.

I'm still blinking dumbly at the small peak when Elliot steps closer, crowding into my space. I can feel his body heat. It should be miserable in this desert and with my skin already sticky with sweat. Instead, I welcome the gentle brush of his arm against mine. I let his heat consume me like the loveliest of fires.

"Don't look at the top," he says. He takes my hand, and my breath catches without permission. He doesn't comment, and for whatever reason, I don't pull away. I let him hold my hand in his, let him point my index finger as if it's an extension of his own body.

"There's the peak, right?" he asks. His voice is a rough mumble as he leans closer, his chest pressing against my shoulder.

"Right," I say. Barely a whisper.

"Good," he says. He lowers my hand, guiding my pointed finger down the mountain.

There's no reason he needs to be using my hand. There's no reason he should be touching me at all.

I haven't taken a breath since the moment he did.

"Right there," he says, stopping abruptly. "Look."

I follow my own finger, still wrapped in his hand. My thoughts are mush, completely incapable of thinking beyond Elliot and his voice. It takes all my concentration to do as he commands.

I don't see anything, not until he whispers an unfamiliar spell against my ear.

I blink, and then, it's there. A blurred rectangular rock, about one quarter from the bottom of the mountain. Amidst the light soil and the sparse trees, the black rock is like a blot of spilled ink.

"What is that?" I ask. My question lingers in the air, as unsteady as I feel.

Because though I've asked, I don't need Elliot to tell me. I know *exactly* what I'm looking at. I just didn't believe it existed. The realization twines between my ribs, a pulsing beat that warns me of dangerous, incomprehensible magic.

"Do you know?" he asks.

He still hasn't released my hand.

"It can't..." I trail off. I'm foolish to even think the words *the Cursed Grounds*, and I can't bring myself to say it out loud. As much as I want to make Elliot laugh again, I certainly don't want him to laugh *at* me.

"It can," he says. He drops my hand, fingers trailing reluctantly over my wrist, as if he's debating holding on.

I let my hand drop at my side. I'm still staring at the mountain as Elliot surges forward again, back onto our mission. I keep my attention locked on the black rock and press a hand to my chest, counting my heartbeats as they spin out of control.

Everyone in the Day Realm—and likely beyond—has heard of the Cursed Grounds. It's named in our history books and whispered in scary stories, but I've doubted its existence for years. I'd once gone looking for these grounds with Milas, and after weeks of searching, I decided it was nothing more than another clever myth, thought up by the witches to seem more powerful than they are.

"Are you coming?" Elliot calls, looking back at me. He's not smiling, but there's an unexpected tone of amusement in his voice.

"I didn't think it was real," I say finally. I walk quickly to catch up to him, my hand still pressed to my sternum. "I—I've looked for it before."

"It's veiled," he says. "Mama showed me a few years back. You can't see it unless you're shown."

"And you showed me?" I ask. I don't bother trying to mask my shock. "Why would you do that?"

Elliot slows, and I do too. I stare at him, fighting the strange flutter in my stomach. I hate the way he seems to see me. It's like he's tracking every detail, noticing things no one else ever has or will.

I hate it almost as much as I love it.

"I met with Margot," he says. He's watching me, face carefully blank, and I have to work hard to do the same. "She spoke highly of you."

I swallow. My tongue suddenly feels two sizes too big.

I haven't seen Margot since the night I was imprisoned. Even now, I can picture her tear-streaked face. Black lines of makeup on her cheeks. Her hair messy from having woken in the middle of the night. Mama Blake holding her against her chest, telling both of us that it would be all right.

She was wrong, of course, and I think she knew it.

"That's it?" I ask. My voice is brittle, sharp. "She spoke highly of me? And that was enough for you to change your mind?"

I don't know why I sound angry—or even surprised. I knew Margot would speak highly of me, even after everything. She probably assumed I was innocent all along. Perhaps she assumed Elliot knew the truth. Perhaps she knew he and I were more than the acquaintances we pretended to be. She knew we kissed at her birthday party...but maybe she knew about other times, too.

Maybe she simply knew I was in love with this man, and that once upon a time, he was in love with me too.

"She didn't change my mind," he says. He steps closer, tilting his head as he looks at me. His lips part, but for a long moment, he says nothing at all. He just studies me like there *must* be something he's missing. "She simply reminded me I don't know the whole story. She made me realize how much I need it."

I don't know how to respond, so I don't. Eventually, Elliot turns to face the mountain. We're hours from the base still, a thought that makes my stomach tighten. Soon enough, we'll have to stop for the night. There are too many dangers to be unprotected, even in the Flight Realm. We're not nearly far enough from the vampires to feel safe, and since we'll be out in the open...

"I hope there's a secret cave you know about," I say, rather than commenting on his little epiphany. *Thanks a lot, Margot.* I shift my bag higher on my shoulder, just to give my hands something to do. "We're going to get slaughtered if we're sleeping in the open. You know that, right?"

"Fine, we don't have to talk about it now," Elliot says evenly. He sighs, sounding far more content than he should. "As for caves, I unfortunately *don't* keep a record of them. That said, I'm honored you trusted me to take care of you. The Cora from a few weeks ago would've wanted a printed itinerary and had it cleared by her precious *master*."

I roll my eyes and opt not to comment.

"I'm not going to let you get eaten, don't worry."

"Big words for someone incapable of taking on a couple drunken, vampiric goons."

"There were four," Elliot says. He laughs though, and the sound is too delicious not to smile. "But anyway, I could have taken on the goons. I would have, eventually. And I promise, if any find us tonight, I won't let them hurt *you*."

I swallow, stomach twisting. *That* is exactly what I'm afraid of.

19

—————

I WANT TO SKIN MYSELF

ELLIOT

I feel like a kid again. Despite the fact Cora has most of our shared teenage moments trapped in jars and hidden somewhere in her bedroom, I am certain this is how I felt back then. I am a tangle of pride and giddiness, determined to make this dark cloud of a woman smile. She's done it precisely twice on our hours-long trek.

Once, when I reminded her there were four vampire attackers, not two. That smile only lasted a few seconds, but it was enough to energize me for the rest of the day.

The second was more unexpected. I'd been in the process of showing off my warded tent—to keep us from being eaten or attacked in our sleep—when it came out of nowhere. I was tying one of the tent poles to a nearby tree, explaining how Henry had helped check the wards right after his shift at the healing center, and she just...smiled.

A full, broad-mouthed grin that caught me so off guard I stumbled. Literally tripped over flat ground and nearly took out our tent in the process.

"What was that smile for?" I asked.

"Nothing," she'd been quick to say. "You just reminded me of you, that's all."

I wasn't entirely sure I understood, but I didn't care. Even now, three hours later, I still don't. I'm just trying to do it again, one more time before we go to sleep.

Cora isn't smiling. She's busy setting up a haphazard wall between our sleeping mats. They're thin but relatively comfortable. If I'd had more time, I would have magicked them to be luxurious and soft.

"I'm not going to cuddle you in your sleep. I promise," I say. I'm propped on my elbow, snacking on a collection of vegetables. I didn't have time to go shopping before our trip, so everything I have was pulled from my own kitchen. Miscellaneous vegetables, half of a watermelon, some bread that's likely stale.

Cora still hasn't eaten. The bread is sitting next to her on her sleeping mat, but she's focused on her fortress. Everything between us, I notice, comes from my own pack. Her bag, on the other hand, is tucked safely behind her.

"I'm not worried about cuddling," she says. Though she doesn't look up, a pale blush softens her features. She takes her lower lip between her teeth, eyebrows scrunching as she moves a bundle of my clothes to make her wall symmetrical. The watermelon is mixed in with the spare blanket and the pack itself.

"No?" I ask. I trail my finger over the top of her fortress, tapping on a pair of bundled socks. The pillow I brought for her is also in the lineup. Apparently, she's planning to go without.

"No, I kick in my sleep," she says. She's still blushing, still gnawing on her lower lip.

While she straightens her wall, I let myself admire her. Big brown eyes, straight nose, pouty lips and a wide smile she so rarely shows. I wonder if she knows how pretty she is.

"Well, I'm not worried about that," I say. A grin stretches over my features as I stare up at the pale yellow tent. Outside, the final rays of sunlight are disappearing behind the mountains. Mountains we've just barely reached the base of. We have a lot more to go tomorrow, but I'm not sure I mind.

"Why are you smiling?" she asks, accusation thick in her voice.

I can see her from my peripheral, and her lower lip is puffy from where she was biting it. I force my eyes closed.

"It's nothing. Just...you're a violent criminal, fussing over kicking me in my sleep. It's ironic, that's all."

Cora doesn't respond.

When I crack an eye open, she's disappeared from my line of sight. I instantly surge upright, looking around the darkened space.

"Relax, I'm not going to hurt you," she says. She's turned away, rummaging through her own bag. "Just because I *could*, doesn't mean I will. But if you don't feel—"

"I know you're not," I say quickly. My stomach drops as I watch her, shoulders hunched. That bag doesn't have much in it. She can't be looking for anything. She just doesn't want to look at me.

The realization I've hurt her feelings flares through me. It's stupid to care. Almost as stupid as sharing a tent with my best friend's killer. I don't dwell on the logic. I move by pure instinct, crawling over Cora's fortress with little grace.

She only turns once I'm at her side, those wide eyes flashing up to mine. Defiant, hurt, angry.

"I'm sorry," I say. "I shouldn't have brought it up."

"It's fine, Elliot," she says. Her eyes go back to her bag, but she doesn't make a show of searching it.

"Look at me," I say. Beg.

When she doesn't, I curl my hand around the back of her neck. Not firmly, not even enough to make her turn.

Still, she does. Eyes wide, mouth parted.

She's not afraid. No, she's fucking leaning into my touch, looking up at me like she wants me to—

I don't think. I just move, crashing my lips against hers and biting the same lip she's been teasing all night. Our movements are thoughtless. Easy.

Without so much as breaking the kiss, she's in my lap. I pull her even closer, until our chests press together. I slow the kiss, exploring, claiming, devouring her mouth. There's nothing but the sound of wind against our tent and her gasping breaths. When I groan against her lips, her hips snap against mine.

Instinctual.

Familiar.

Perfect.

"Fuck," I say against her mouth, the word a garbled mess.

Cora whimpers, and I'm absolutely done for. I pull her harder to me, until her hips align with mine, and her warm cunt grinds over my cock. I can't remember the last time I felt this hard, this desperate for sex. Have I ever?

The want ricochets through my entire body. Any blood reserved for my brain has moved south, until I am nothing more than *hers*.

Hers to use, to enjoy, to devour.

And she, she is mine.

"Fuck, Cora," I say. It's a prayer, a plea, a promise.

I don't recognize the sound I make next. It's somewhere between a growl and a hum, and it's filled with a vast hunger I didn't realize existed until she fell back into my life. Until I felt the warmth of her skin and saw the things I once did to her... things she *made* me forget.

With my hand still on her neck, my thumb settled in the

hollow of her throat, I kiss her deeper. She tastes like green tea and winter wind and something so viscerally *Cora* that I'm sure there's no proper name for it. All I know is she's the most exquisite thing I've ever tasted, even better than my memories promised.

I am ruined. Gone is any concern of right and wrong, of guilt or uncertainty. I don't care who she is or what she's done. In this moment, I only care to get closer. To taste this perfect woman, new and familiar, all at once.

Cora's hands slide up my shoulders, cool fingers locking behind my neck, keeping me close. She's trembling against me, honest-to-Mother shivering, nails digging into the back of my nape.

"Gods, Cora," I say. The words are muffled against her lips, but I don't move away as I continue. "How do you taste this good? You're fucking unreal."

I'm dizzy with lust. Arousal. Endless and overpowering need.

Cora doesn't respond. She's too busy kissing me, soft lips trailing from the corner of my mouth to my jawline, down the length of my throat. When she reaches my shoulder, she bites softly. Sucks the tender spot, just above my collarbone.

"Fuck," I groan. My head swims, and the control I thought I'd already lost, disappears completely. "Hold on, I need...I have to..."

My cock strains against my pants. I could come from this alone, but I'm not ready for it to end. I want to feel her come on my hand. My tongue. My cock.

I slide a hand up her skirt, trailing up the thick tights until I reach her damp center. She's fucking soaked for me. Ready. As desperate to be fucked as I am to fuck her.

"Can I—"

"Stop."

Cold dread washes over me, and several things happen at

once. I pull my hand from the warmth between her legs. I slide her off my lap, keeping a hand on her shoulder when she wavers. Her eyes are still dark with desire, her lips swollen and red. She's breathing almost as hard as I am.

"We can," she says. "I just need to tell—"

I shove backward, knocking over her carefully built wall. Reality crashes over me, over what I've just done.

Whether I kissed this woman when we were kids or not... that was before. Before she killed Harrison. Before she aided the vampires. Before she became a monster.

And I was moments away from fucking her in this tent.

I collapse on my side, and this time, it's Cora who moves toward me.

"Stay there," I say, and she freezes. I hold a hand up, as if she's a threat.

Dammit. She is *a threat.*

"Elliot–"

"No," I say. I'm horrified. Nauseated. Wishing I could undo every second that led to this moment. I knew better than this. Not just kissing her, but putting myself in this position. Having her close to me and smelling perfect and giving me those rare smiles...

Cora's face falls. The same lip I just had between my teeth juts out, trembling, like she's about to cry. And I can't take it. The warring emotions inside me. The way I hate her for what she did. The way I hate myself for bringing that look to her face. I want to skin myself for making her sad. I want to skin myself for being anywhere near her.

"Please," I say. I collapse forward, head against my knees. My breath is ragged as I look up at her. "Please, Cora. I can't take it. I need them back. I need to understand. You...you're destroying me."

Tears stream down her cheeks, but I know what she's going

to say. She'll give vague answers. Barter another deal. Tell me she will once she's gotten Mama's ingredient for the curse.

I'm expecting anything but the stiff nod she gives me.

"Okay, Elliot," she whispers. Her entire body is shaking as she repeats, "Okay."

20

JUST THIS ONCE
CORA

Elliot sits on one side of my pathetic—and clearly ineffective—wall, and I sit on the other. The memory stone rests between us, and I force myself to solely focus on it. Elliot hasn't spoken a word since I started readying it, lining the ingredients one by one. The first of the two jars lies in my lap, still capped.

The memory lashes against the glass, and it's how I imagine my pulse must look right now. My stomach is in my throat. My hands shake like they never have.

"I have a condition," I say. I keep my attention steady on the memory stone, but I don't miss the way Elliot stiffens.

In the back of my mind, I can't help wondering if I knew this would happen. If I knew from the moment I made that deal with Elliot, I'd give him everything back. Maybe part of me has always felt rotten for what I did, and this was the inevitable end. I would show Elliot everything I stole, and he would...what, exactly?

I close my eyes and force a deep breath.

"What's the condition, Cora?" he asks. His voice sounds as stiff as his posture looks.

I keep my eyes closed.

"I'll show you everything. Give you everything, even the memories back at my quarters," I say. My voice wavers, growing shakier with each word. "Then, you decide. You can keep it, or give it back. If you give it back, we'll never do this again. Okay?"

Elliot is quiet for so long, I have no choice but to open my eyes. I stare down at the stone, at the carefully straight line of mermaid scales. Beyond it, I can see the edge of Elliot's knees. Dirt stains his pants from when he was knelt on the ground, putting up our tent. He props forward, tilting, as if to force himself into my line of vision.

I swallow and make myself look at him.

He's still the single most beautiful thing I've ever seen. The thought that even with distorted memories *and* the knowledge of my past, he still kissed me...it's too much. Too much to believe.

He kissed me.

Despite everything, he still wants me. Maybe only physically, but maybe...

"Agree?" I ask, cutting off my wandering thoughts.

"That's it?" he asks. "That's your condition?"

"Yes," I say. My voice cracks, so I steel my spine. I will not cower, not now. "You decide whether you want them, once and for all. It will be your choice. I'll understand, whatever you decide."

"All right," he says, brows furrowed. "I agree."

I nod in response. My throat is too tight to speak.

"Which one are we doing first?" he asks. His voice is raspy as he peers at the jar in my lap. The label is turned away, facing me.

I stare at the jar too. I'd planned to show him his final memory with me, the one that led to everything else, that led to the *now*, with him looking at me like I'm a stranger.

"Actually, neither of them," I say. I twist slightly, shoving the jar into my bag. Elliot immediately starts to protest, but I cut him off. "I'll show you them, I promise. But first...I need to show you one of mine."

I look down at my palm and rub my fingers together. My magic pulses beneath my skin, zapping just beneath my fingernails.

"One of yours?" he repeats.

"Yes," I say. Another nod. Another stubborn refusal to cower. I stare at Elliot. "It's important. I promise."

"All right," he says finally, reluctantly.

With magic stinging my skin, I press my hand to my forehead, pulling the memory from my head. The pain is similar to extracting a tooth. The memory strains to hold its place in my brain, but I am nothing if not gifted at forgetting.

"What can I do?" Margot asks.

She sits beside me on the hard wooden bench outside of the headmaster's office. Her hands rest on my knee. She just painted her nails yesterday, and I study the pale yellow polish, rather than meet her eyes.

"I didn't do it," I say. My voice wobbles, and before I can stop it, tears leak from my eyes. "I swear, Margot. I couldn't have. I didn't—"

"I know," she says. She squeezes my knee, so hard it's painful. "Look at me, Secora."

I swallow the lump in my throat and do my best to blink away the lingering tears. When I finally meet her gaze, she leans closer.

"I know you didn't," she repeats. "I'm going to talk to Mama, and they're going to figure this out, okay? We'll get it taken care of."

She means every word, but it's a hollow promise. Mama Blake won't be able to save me, not from this one.

"They're going to send me back," I choke out. "They'll make me go back, and they'll n-never reverse my sentence. They might even k-k-"

I break off. I can't make myself say it out loud.

The tears fall again, and this time, there's nothing I can do to stop them. I sit here and cry, while Margot helplessly rubs my back. She promises again and again that Mama Blake will help, until my sobs are too loud to talk over.

"Oh, Secora—" she starts.

"Elliot," I interrupt. I'm mostly-incoherent now, but I know she's heard me. "Get Elliot. Please."

I know better than to ask for him. We're not supposed to be friends, let alone close enough for me to beg for him. Margot knows we've kissed, that we're kind to one another. She doesn't know how many stolen moments we've shared. She doesn't know he's told me his dreams or that he talks about having a family with me someday.

She doesn't know how devastated he'll be when they drag me away.

He'll forget me. I know that. But right now, he'll be devastated.

"Okay," Margot says. She doesn't sound confused like I expect. She only squeezes my knee again before standing. "I'll find him."

"Secora."

I look up. I'm still on the bench outside of the headmaster's office. I should have left with Margot to find Elliot, but I feel so tired. I'm not sure I'll be able to walk home with either one of them. Mama Blake might need to come get me.

Ignoring the voice at the end of the hallway, I peer down at my wrists, checking they're covered. I've worn golden cuffs for most of my life. They've kept me from producing magic, from being the killer the augurs swear I am. One on each wrist, pronouncing me as unworthy of the Mother's gifts. I'd gotten used to the shame of wearing them.

But now, I have two additional pairs. Both silver. They're made to weaken witches, to deplete their energy.

Not even the worst criminals wear golden and silver cuffs. But when Gregg Larson caught fire during study session, Stephan insisted he heard me casting a Burnish Spell. Within minutes, I was out of the classroom and in the headmasters' office. There, they'd fastened the two new pairs around my wrists.

"It's just a precaution," the headmaster said as I sobbed. She'd added, "It's temporary, just until the council decides on next steps."

But I know it's the start of a death sentence.

The first set of bands make it impossible to cast magic. The second two are making it difficult to breathe. To blink. To keep myself upright. Whatever hesitation they'd had in killing me before, it's clear they've lost it.

If I wear these long enough, they'll kill me, and no one even cares. They've left me alone in this hallway, and I can't help but wonder if they're hoping I will die. If they'll claim it was an accident to avoid the Mother's wrath.

I look away from my wrists and finally acknowledge the boy standing beside me.

The Mother has a sense of humor, sending Harrison my way today. Both he and Elliot missed school today, but of course he's here to witness this.

"Secora," he says again.

I tuck my hands under my thighs, trying to hide the number of cuffs I now wear. Harrison's attention flickers toward them anyway, and I stiffen. He already knows. Of course he knows. He's probably the reason I'm here to begin with.

"I didn't set Gregg on fire," I tell him. I steel my voice and straighten my shoulders. I try to make myself look as big as possible, even as I sit cowering before him. My confidence is as thin as orphanage blankets, and I have no doubt he sees through it.

"I know you didn't," he says.

He isn't smug. He doesn't sound pleased or amused. Instead, he looks unexpectedly compassionate. It's an expression I've seen on him plenty of times—just never directed at me.

"You know?" I repeat. My voice wavers, gives me away. I do my best to sharpen it again, but it's useless. I sound exactly as desperate as I feel. "Then you need to tell the headmaster. If you know—"

"That's why I'm here," he interrupts. He shoves his hands into his pockets, eyes flicking away from me.

Right now, the school is dark and quiet. Classes ended hours ago, and once the headmaster dismissed me, she left too. It's only me here, until Margot returns. I shift on the bench, unpleasantly aware of my own helplessness. I have rarely spent time alone with Harrison, and not one of those times has ended well for me.

I force myself to stand, stumbling from the effects of the cuffs. My stomach clenches with unfamiliar nausea.

Harrison doesn't step forward like I expect. On any other day, he'd use his height to tower over me, to make me feel small and weak. Today, when I'm more powerless than ever, he keeps his distance.

"Why are you here?" I demand. I take an unsteady step backward, expecting him to mirror the movement. Instead, he doesn't so much as flinch. His hands are still in his pockets. His face still looks soft and kind.

"Elliot sent me," he says.

I don't let myself react. Even as my heart pounds and my body stirs with unease, I don't move. I don't so much as blink out of rhythm, terrified I'll give something away.

Elliot and I haven't told anyone we're together. I'm a Dark One. It's forbidden. And even if Elliot doesn't know his best friend torments me, he must realize Harrison wouldn't take it well. He didn't like Margot being around me. Elliot loving me would be an unacceptable level of betrayal.

"Look," Harrison says. He finally removes a hand from his pocket, and I flinch, bracing myself. His lips twitch into a frown at the movement. "I know you and Elliot are hooking up, all right? He told me a couple days ago. When he heard what happened with Gregg, he sent me to get you. He's stuck with Madam Lyrie."

I study his face.

Look for any sign of deception. Of lies. Of hatred.

"He told me to come get you," he repeats. His expression is earnest in a way it's never seemed before.

"And go where?" I ask finally.

"Well first, we'll get the extra cuffs removed," he says. "My mama is at the Augur House. She can remove them. I'll take you there myself."

I follow his gaze to my wrists, and despite the stirring in my gut, I decide to trust him, just this once.

I CAREFULLY EXTRACT myself from the memory, letting Elliot watch the ending by himself. I forced myself to retain this horrible moment, to harbor the anger and the hurt, to remind myself why I can never return to the Day Realm. Why I would never want to.

I ease out of the smoke, but I still know what Elliot sees:

Harrison leading me to the Augur House.

Me realizing the augurs aren't there.

Harrison punishing me for corrupting his friend.

Me trying and failing to fight back.

Harrison trapping me against the desk in his mama's office.

Harrison yanking off my leggings.

Me watching the office fish tank, praying someone would find me.

Harrison threatening to kill me if I ever talked to Elliot again.

Me crying, still face down on the desk.

Harrison leaving me with my underwear around my ankles.

Me walking home with a foreign pain between my legs and a hideous ache in my heart.

21

MY SECORA

ELLIOT

The memory ends. I stumble backward, scrambling to the tent's exit. I don't care that it's dark or that dangerous predators are out for the night. I can't think straight and the only way to fix it...

I stagger to the bushes and everything comes out. My meager breakfast, lunch, dinner. My scoured heart, lungs, soul. I'm suffocating, surrounded by oxygen. Dying without a single injury or illness.

Magic sparks through me. Courses through my arms and pulses at my fingertips. I've never been quick to anger, never felt this disastrous recklessness before. It's all-consuming, wracking through my body until there's nothing else left. There is only red-tinted vision and bone-rattling fury.

I clench my knees, staring as my vomit drips between the bush leaves. I'm prepared to stand here all night and wait for some ungodly creature to kill me. It is only Cora's small hand on my back that snaps me back to reality.

Cora is consoling *me* after watching what happened to *her*.

It's enough to regain control, to snap me out of the trance threatening to consume me whole. I blink and grind my teeth together, taking several deep breaths before I stand to my full height. My magic doesn't calm, even as I force my mind to focus.

I look at Cora.

She's a foot shorter than I am. Short. Thin.

Without meaning to, I look at her wrists. They're free now—have been for years—but they weren't in that memory. She was defenseless. Half his size. Without magic.

My stomach tightens again. *Harrison.* Everything I thought I knew of him is suddenly false. Every aspect of his personality I've spent years mourning is nothing but an illusion.

He *raped* her.

He raped a defenseless girl, half his size. He held her down, uttered horrible things in her ear, then left her, bloodied and alone.

Magic sparks from my fingertips before I can stop it. It's directionless and shapeless, shooting between the trees before dissolving into air. And still, my hands burn.

I want to kill him. I want to destroy him for what he did to her. And I barely remember her.

I look over her again. Her wide brown eyes are on me, her full lips parted as she stares. She looks nervous, frightened. Ready to bolt, yet still standing here with her hand on my back.

"Cora," I say. My voice is ragged, tortured, full of blistering hatred and pathetic helplessness.

"You should sit down," she says. Her lips keep twitching, like there's more she wants to say. "I'll make some tea if you've brought some and—"

"Cora," I say again. Her name cracks in my mouth.

"It's over," she says. She lifts her chin, clenching her teeth so hard her jaw sharpens. "He's dead."

She looks proud of that fact, and for the first time since I learned what happened to my best friend, I don't pity him at all.

Please. Please. Please. Please.

That's what she'd been thinking while he raped her. She was begging for someone to find them, to stop him. And I could feel it: she wasn't hoping for just anyone. She was hoping *I* would find them, stop him. Save her.

But I didn't.

"I'm sorry," I say. My eyes burn, and my mouth feels like it's been stuffed full of cotton. "I don't—I should have—"

"It's over," she repeats. She grabs my hand, only to immediately pull away. Though her fingers are cold, I feel a loss of heat when she moves. "We need to go inside. It's not safe out here."

She returns to the tent, leaving me no choice but to follow behind her. She rummages through my pack, finding two bags of green tea. I stare at her, frozen, as she focuses on making our drinks. She blinks hard, but it's not enough to keep tears from welling in her eyes.

"Cora, come here," I say. Beg might be the better word.

She turns, that chin still fiercely lifted. Despite her watering eyes, she almost glares at me as she speaks.

"I didn't show you that to make you pity me," she says. "You wanted to know the truth, so there it is."

"Cora—"

"You don't have to feel sorry for me, and you don't need to change your mind about me," she says. She opens the canister of water, lip trembling. "It's not your job to look out for me anymore."

"Yeah, and whose decision was that?" I snap. My skin itches with magic, pent up and desperate for release. "That wasn't my choice, Cora. Don't punish me for it."

"I know," she says. Her voice cracks, and she angrily wipes at her eyes. "I know, I'm sorry, okay? I was trying to—"

"Come here," I interrupt. I haven't moved from the tent's entrance, too afraid I'll fuck things up if I move.

"Elliot—"

"Let me hold you," I say. A request that would have seemed ridiculous an hour ago feels essential now. "Please. I'm begging you."

A faint blush rushes across her cheeks. She is beautiful and soft and vicious and perfect and...*how dare he touch her?*

She nods, the movement choppy and stiff. She moves toward me, arms tucked in front of her, and buries her head against my chest. It is the purest sensation in the world, unfazed by guilt or worry or confusion.

This is how life was meant to be. I can feel it now. She was always supposed to be here, wrapped between my arms.

Did she let me hold her? I'm desperate to know. After that horrid walk from the augur house, did she find me? Did she tell me what happened? Did she let me hold her like she is now?

Cora sobs against my chest, her hands loosening just enough to grab my shirt. I lift her, cupping beneath her thighs until she wraps her legs around my waist. Unlike before, there's nothing sexual in my touch. I just hold her as close as physically possible, letting her cry against my shoulder.

"I'm sorry," I whisper against her hair. Again and again, until I'm crying too.

I WAKE with sunlight on my face. It's early morning, but it's light enough that the vampires will be trapped inside. The other predators—the werewolves and Nectoa—should be home, asleep. We should be up by now. We've got hours between us and the Cursed Grounds, and I only packed for two more nights of sleep.

I make no move to leave. I only shift Cora farther onto my chest, letting her breath tickle my neck. When she shifts, burrowing closer, her lips brush my collarbone.

I don't remember falling asleep last night. I only remember holding her and letting her cry.

Now, I'm dizzy with the sensation of her skin pressed against mine. It's beyond my control, the flashes of last night that flicker through my mind. Images of Cora straddling my lap, moaning and gasping against my kisses. I'd been ready to fuck her. I would have. I would have fucked her until she only knew my name and the feel of my cock stretching her cunt.

"You're hard," she whispers against my neck.

I startle, twisting my head to look down at her. I have no idea when she woke up, only that her brown eyes are now open and wholly focused on my pants. The outline of my erection is fully visible. When her hand brushes against it, a shock of pleasure rocks through my entire body. I jolt like I've been burned, and Cora immediately pulls back.

She lifts her chin to look at me.

Her lips are so close, it would take minimal movement for me to taste them. To suck her pouty lower lip between mine until she begged for more. I'm just not sure if that's appropriate, if she'd even want me to.

"Sorry," I say.

"For what?" she asks. Her gaze flickers to my pants, then back to me. "I don't mind."

"I'm not..." I trail off, unsure what to say. My throat feels thick and dry, but I'm having a hard time explaining the thoughts in my head. "I don't want you to think...after last night...I'm not trying..."

"I was raped, Elliot." Her voice is quiet, but her tone is more resigned than anything else. "It was terrible, and everything that followed was terrible too. What Harrison did changed the trajectory of my life, but it's still *my* life. I am not ruined. I am not broken. I am okay."

"I know," I say. "I know, Cora. It's just—it's hard for me to think straight. I want to *kill* him. He's dead, and I still want to kill him."

Cora looks away, eyes drifting to the top of the tent. Her breath is steady, eyes clear.

"A couple nights ago, I started watching some of my old memories," she says. "I didn't *just* take yours, Elliot. I took mine too, because after I left...it was hard. It was awful being without you."

Then why did you? I want to ask. *Why would you do that to yourself, to us?*

I don't let myself speak. I force myself to slow, to feel the warmth of her body pressed against mine. My erection has died, but I still feel the high of her closeness. This moment is as close to perfection as I've ever felt, and I'm terrified of saying the wrong thing. I don't want her to leave. I don't want her to ask *me* to leave.

"I've watched several in the past few days," she goes on. "I kept them. Can I show you some of my favorites?"

And so, we do.

One by one, Cora pulls a memory strand from her temple and drops it onto the memory stone. We sit with our shoulders pressed together, fading in and out of her teenage memories. These ones all feature me, and unlike the one from last night, they are *good*.

From her perspective, I watch the first time we kiss. The first time I sneak into her bedroom with a piece of cake to share. The first time I try to hold her hand in public, and she quietly shakes her head. The many times we meet at the haunted tree at Ochre Primary School. Sometimes to kiss. Sometimes to talk about the future or our hobbies or whatever gossip exists in that moment.

Every time, I watch my face heat with embarrassment. Objectively, fifteen-year-old me is terrible at pursuing the girl he likes. He blushes every time he talks to her, all the way up to his ears. He trips over his words. He's awkward and dorky and so transparently smitten. Yet somehow, young Cora doesn't see it.

Can't you tell? I wish I could ask her. *He's enamored with you. He's desperate for you.*

Even when sixteen-year-old Elliot tells her he's in love with her, that she's everything he's ever wanted, she doesn't believe him. She assumes his affection is fleeting. I haven't seen the memory from my perspective. There's so many things I still don't know, and yet, I know.

We come out of the memory, and Cora busies herself with the stone. She carefully returns this memory—a sharp pink shade—to her mind. Then, she straightens the stone's ingredients and readies for another. Instead, I gently grab her wrist, stopping her. She looks at me, mouth parted in surprise.

"He meant it," I tell her.

"What?"

"He was going to love you until the end of time," I say.

"Maybe," she says. She lowers her gaze to my hand, still clasped loosely around her wrist.

I rub my thumb over her soft skin, and she shivers, letting out a breathy gasp.

"You know, I never dated anyone for long," I say. I continue making small circles over her skin. And though her eyes are down, I keep my focus on her face. "Mama always wanted me to find a nice woman, settle down, give her a dozen grand babies. I couldn't though. I never found anyone who held my attention. At least, that's what I assumed."

Cora swallows. Her eyes dart to mine, only to lower again.

"I forgot we existed," I say. "I forgot *you*, Cora, but I don't think my body did. I think it remembered. I think it knew what made me whole, and it wasn't interested in settling for less."

"Elliot," she says. She sighs, soft and resigned. "I've just thrown so much at you. You shouldn't—"

"For Mother's sake, Cora," I say. I cup her face between my hands again, resting my thumbs on her cheekbones. "Stop deciding what I should do. My choices are not yours to make. If you don't want to kiss me or care about me or be near me, then say it. Don't tell me *I* don't want it."

Her brown eyes meet mine, and I hate how scared she looks. Terrified, as if this is a trick. Worried, as if I would ever hurt her.

"I want it, Cora," I tell her. When her gaze flickers to my mouth, I lean closer, daring her. "I want *you*."

We remain still for a long moment. I move my hands from her face to her shoulders, light enough she could easily pull away. She stares and stares and stares, until finally, her cool fingers trace up my arms and settle around the back of my neck.

She's breathing hard, unevenly.

I am tuned into her every movement, no matter how small.

She's waiting for me to kiss her, I think. But this time, I need *her* to take control. To admit she wants it too, much as she pretends otherwise.

She grips the back of my shirt, and with an adorably determined scowl, she leans into me. Her lips brush mine, soft at first, then firmer. I drop my hands to her waist, settling them over her hips. I don't let myself do anything more. I force myself to wait, to let her set the pace.

It's fucking excruciating in the best way imaginable. She kisses slow, leisurely, as if exploring my mouth for the first time. Her teeth nip at my lower lip, then my jawline. She kisses down my throat, once again finding that spot just above my collarbone.

It switches something animalistic inside me. I clench her hips and tug her onto my lap before I think about what I'm doing. Grinding her over my rapidly hardening cock is *not* letting her set the pace.

But she's moaning into my neck, letting out pleased whimpers as she rubs against me, and I can't bring myself to care.

"Fuck," I hiss. "Fuck, you're the best thing I've ever felt."

She doesn't respond. She's too busy kissing my neck again, humming softly against my skin.

"Where's the line?" I ask. I play with the hem of her skirt, then inch my fingers beneath it. I keep my hands on her thighs, not daring to drift higher. "I need to know, Cora. I can't remember what we've done. I don't know what you like—"

"You," she breathes out. "I like *you*."

She kisses her way up the column of my throat, and it's like a fucking rush of magic through my veins. It's almost impossible to think straight, but I *have* to. I'm ready to fuck her just about any way imaginable, but only if she's ready for that too.

"Tell me what you like," I insist. "And what you don't."

"Okay," she says between kisses.

She's trembling as she touches me, but I know from her memories that it's not from fear. She's aroused. So turned on she can't find an outlet. And I've never been more eager to please, to be everything she needs and more.

In a swift movement, I rotate us until she's on her back and I'm propped over her. I keep my weight on my elbows, lowering myself just enough that our hips and chests brush every time we breathe.

Cora stares up at me, but if she's startled from the sudden position change, she doesn't show it. A hazy glaze settles over her eyes, her pupils dilated and intensely focused on me.

"You're so pretty," I say. I capture her lips with my own, gently sucking her tongue in my mouth. Now it's my turn to explore *her*. "And you taste so fucking sweet."

I shift onto one elbow, letting my opposite hand trail up her thigh. She's trembling still, arching against me, until her pelvis rubs against my cock. I bite back a groan, forcing enough space to get my hand between us.

Like last night, she's already wet. I brush my thumb over her leggings, pressing against her heat. She thrusts her hips in rhythm with my touch, letting her head fall back and her eyes drift shut.

"Is this okay?" I ask roughly.

"Mmhm," she murmurs. When she briefly opens her eyes, she appears half in another world. She grabs the collar of my shirt, tugging my mouth down to hers. Just before our lips touch, she whispers, "More. I need more. Please."

"Tell me if you want me to stop," I say.

Her only response is to thrust her hips harder against me. The frigid and distant Cora I've seen over the past few weeks has evaporated, replaced with someone whose vast hunger nearly matches my own. She claws at my neck, and I slip my hand into her leggings.

She's wet. Warm. Perfect.

"Gods, Cora," I whisper, letting her name drag from deep within my lungs. I drop my head against her shoulder as I press into her tight heat. She writhes against me as I press deeper. Just one finger, then two.

The room is filled with our heavy breaths and the obscene sound of my finger fucking her cunt.

"Okay?" I ask again. I start to pull back to look at her, but she wraps her arms around my neck, pulling me closer.

"Don't stop," she begs. "Please, Elliot. I'm going to—I think I'm going to—"

She breaks off, but there's no question what she was going to say. I massage her clit with my thumb and kiss her neck, rubbing my cock against her leg. It's ungodly euphoric, so blissful the world around us stops existing.

My thoughts blur. My movements jerk. There is nothing

except me and this impossibly perfect woman coming beneath me.

She cries out a garbled version of my name, and I come hearing it. I fuck her through the end of her orgasm, leaving my hand in the beautiful mess between her thighs. I've never been particularly interested in eating a woman out, but right now, it's all I can do to resist.

I want to claim every inch of this woman, and I vow to myself, I will. Someday, there will be no part of her I haven't kissed, licked, devoured.

For now, I settle my hand between her thighs and kiss her mouth until I'm sure she must be tired of it. When I pull back though, her puffy lips curl into a smile. It's soft, hesitant. The smile of someone accustomed to being knocked in the dirt.

"I don't think I've ever sucked your cock," she says. "If I have, it's in one of my jars. You might have to talk me through it."

"There is nothing I'd like more than your mouth on my cock," I tell her. I brush my lips down her throat as I speak, relishing the trail of gooseflesh that follows. "But it'll have to wait until next time."

"Oh," she says. Faint red decorates her cheeks. "Do we need to leave?"

"Not just yet," I say, even though we probably should. I rotate onto my side, tugging her against me, until her ass is tucked against my already hardening cock. "I just need a minute before I can go again."

"Did you actually?" she asks. She pushes onto her elbows, blush growing deeper as she notices my pants. The cum stain shows through the grey pants, but so does the outline of my cock. She looks long enough I laugh.

"Yes, I did," I say. "You keep looking at me though, and I'll be ready in no time."

"Good," she says. She quirks her lips into a quick smile

before laying down again, her back pressed to my chest. I tug her hips, until I'm fully pressed against her firm ass.

Cora's breathing slows and steadies until I'm sure she's fallen asleep. I kiss the back of her head and wrap my arm across her middle, anchoring her to me.

"I missed you," I say. "I'm not sure I know just how much, but I know I really fucking missed you, Cora."

"Secora," she says after a long pause. She takes my hand and cradles it against her chest. "You can call me Secora again."

"Secora," I whisper against her hair. "My Secora."

22

———

EVERY WAY IMAGINABLE

CORA

I know better than to feel hope. I've spent the past twelve years warding away positivity like it's a bad smell. I didn't dare believe I would ever find myself here. Not here, staggering up the steep slope of a mountain, but *here*, with Elliot keeping pace at my side.

I sneak a glance at him, relieved that he's too busy looking ahead to notice. I'm able to study his sharp jawline and the sharp line of his nose. His hazel eyes are bright in the sunlight. I can pick out a dozen colors, different shades of brown and green and yellow.

"Do you want to make out?" he asks without looking at me. His voice is perfectly level, but his lips twitch, betraying him. "We'll *really* be risking our timeline, but I'm willing to chance it."

I roll my eyes, unable to keep from smiling.

This is the life I once imagined as a teenager. Before Harrison raped me, before I had to leave the only person who made me feel whole, I dreamt of a future like this.

"Or I could talk you through that blow job," he says. His voice is as calm as ever, but blush has made its way up his neck and across his cheeks. I watch the color spread, only responding once it's touched the tips of his ears.

"Out here, in the open?"

"Afraid a squirrel might see us?" he counters. Finally, *finally*, he looks at me. His eyes spark with mischief, and despite our current mission, I feel at peace for the first time in as long as I can remember.

"There are plenty of harpies around. Dragon riders."

Elliot glares up at the sky. Today is cooler than yesterday, but between the fronds of trees, the sky is blue. Not a cloud in sight.

"In the tent then," he says with a solemn nod. He looks at me, brows furrowing. "Or perhaps I'll taste you. Do you know if we've done that?"

Now it's my turn to blush.

"Hells, Elliot," I say, blowing a breath between my lips. "You can't say things like that. Since when are you so horny?"

"I imagine it started about the time you climbed into my lap last night," he says. He shrugs, grins. "Or maybe when I saw you in the foyer of the vampire king's manor. Throwing grown men around like it was your favorite hobby."

"Perhaps it is," I say. I look back to the rough terrain in front of us.

"You've yet to throw me," he says.

"Maybe *that's* what we'll try in the tent," I say. A small laugh escapes my lips, surprising me as much as it does Elliot.

"Whatever you want," is his immediate response. Then, "I have every intention of making you do that more."

"What, laugh?"

"Yes. When we get done with this, once we've made enough spells for your whole extended vampire family to live happily ever after, I'm going to find a thousand ways to make you laugh."

"A thousand ways," I repeat, humming. "That's going to take a while."

"I'm a patient man," he says.

He nods toward a nearby rock, large enough to use as a bench, and I almost sob in relief. My boots are rubbing my heels, and I'm certain my left foot has started to bleed. While I massage my ankles, Elliot removes the canister from his pack and offers me the first drink.

I could get used to this, I think. And what a dangerous knowledge that is, dreaming for something that can never be.

But why not?

Perhaps, if Elliot never sees the two final memories, those two jars tucked at my side, perhaps we could make this work. He understands now that Harrison was no horrific loss to the world. He was vile. Evil. We are better without his energy demanding space.

He could get used to this too, I whisper to myself. *He could be happy with me, and he would never need to know.*

"Ready?" he asks, standing entirely too soon.

"I think so," I say. Not to walk, because truly, I think my skin is torn to shreds beneath my socks.

I'm ready to give this an honest try, and if he's willing to part with just two pieces of the past, maybe we can.

WE HAVEN'T SPOKEN in over an hour, and my once sore feet now feel like they've been shred to pieces. I'm limping more than I'm walking, and I've been waiting for Elliot to demand I hurry. Sebastian certainly would. Or rather, he'd make us wait until night so he could throw me over his shoulder and zip the rest of the way to our destination.

Elliot does neither. Instead, he keeps a slow and steady pace with me, one hand tucked in his coat pocket and the other hanging free at his side. It's the one closer to me, and though I've felt oddly tempted to grab his hand, I haven't. My willpower is apparently stronger than I knew.

"Did you tell me?" he asks, abruptly pulling me from my thoughts.

"Tell you...?" I trail off, eyebrows raised as I look over him. He looks as relaxed as he did yesterday morning, save for the slight crease between his brows. He's still thinking about what I showed him. All the while, I'm doing my best to forget he knows.

I was so sure he would *never* know that I don't know how to feel.

"Before you stole my memories," he says. Then, softly, "before I *gave* them to you."

"You didn't give them to me," I say. Mostly, because it's true. Partly, because I can tell he needs to hear it.

"Did you tell me what happened?" he presses.

I breathe a puff of air between my lips and tilt my head toward the sky. It's cold today. Not to the point breath turns to fog, but enough that I'm barely sweating.

According to Elliot's estimate, we'll reach the Cursed Grounds shortly before nightfall. It's less than ideal. I can think of *many* better sleeping places that don't include the term 'cursed'.

"Secora," he says. His hand catches my elbow, lightly enough I could pull away if I wanted.

I don't.

"Yes, Elliot," I say, forcing myself to face him. My hands are shaking, so I clench them into fists at my sides. Take a few steadying breaths. "I told you."

"And?"

I stare at him, trying and failing to come up with an adequate response. With another heavy breath, I start walking again. Elliot's touch on my arm drops, and he falls into step beside me.

He's more patient than I deserve. Even as I can sense him twitching with discomfort, as though it's taking every drop of self-control not to press, he doesn't say a word.

"You believed me," I say after nearly a minute of pained silence. There is only the sound of our boots crunching over fallen leaves and dried sticks. I have to swallow to keep my voice from cracking. "You believed me, of course. Never questioned whether I was lying. You were angry and wanted to help however you could...but it didn't matter, Elliot."

I sigh, pausing again. I can tell Elliot wants to ask more, so I put it off as long as I can. I gesture to a nearby fallen tree and sit.

"I need a second," I say. Without looking at him, I untie my shoes. My feet will only hurt more when I put them back on, but right now, I need the relief. A break, no matter how brief.

"Hells, your feet, Secora."

"I know," I say. Blush rises through my cheeks as I pull off the second boot. My socks are black, but somehow, the blood is still visible on the fabric. I hiss as I unroll the socks, revealing my blistered skin. "I should have mentioned how rarely I hike."

He blows out a breath, scowling as he takes off his pack. Sitting beside me, he gently takes my left foot and props it on his lap.

"You don't have to—"

"What happened?" he asks, cutting me off.

I watch as he plucks a deep maroon bag from his pack. It's small, but it's stuffed with different ointments and herbs. Elliot tsks under his breath as he applies something—maybe clay root —to my bleeding and cracked ankle.

I don't immediately reply. I weigh my words carefully before finally responding.

"Harrison's mama found out," I say finally. I lift my chin to the sky, staring at the grey-blue as I speak. Elliot continues working on my foot, his touch impossibly soft and gentle. "She took over everything. Made sure it was all kept quiet. Kept it out of the public."

"Secora," Elliot says. It's a hiss. No, a snarl. One of his hands shifts higher up my calf, squeezing, as if he can't help but tense —but that he doesn't dare stop touching me. "Did my mama—"

"No," I say. I make it sound as believable as I can. Elliot's hands are both still on my foot, but his eyes have fluttered shut. "But it wouldn't have mattered. I was a Dark One, Elliot. It was the safer option—"

"Safer option for who?"

Despite the violence in his tone, his touch remains perfectly gentle. He switches from my left foot to my right, and it isn't until he returns my first foot to the ground that I realize how much better it feels. The wounds still look as red, as angry, as they had, but now, they're numb to the touch.

"The council believed Harrison had great potential," I say. This time, I don't bother to conceal my own anger. My blood-soaked wrath. "And me? I was an inconvenience all along. They weren't going to let someone like me ruin his future."

"You didn't," Elliot says. With my foot still in his lap, he leans closer, until our noses almost touch. "*He* was the ruiner. Not you."

"Yeah," I say with a stiff laugh. "I know."

I try to lower my foot off Elliot, but his hold tightens.

"Hold on," he murmurs. "I'm not done yet."

"We're running out of daylight," I say. Even though I know this will only take a few minutes longer. Even though I want to *cry* at how much better my left foot feels now.

"Hush," he says.

I don't have any memories of him saying this to me, and yet, my body recognizes his tone. I've heard it before, I think, likely many times. That single word makes every muscle in my body relax, until I'm halfway melted, leaned against his shoulder.

"Thank you," he says, as if I'm the one helping him.

He finishes tending to my foot, and I almost whine when he places it back on the forest floor. He crouches in front of me, gently guiding one foot into my boot, then the other.

"Feel okay?" he asks. He looks up at me from beneath dark lashes, and my mind is flooded with filthy thoughts that have nothing to do with hiking and everything to do with the heat between my legs. I'm dizzy with arousal, and it isn't until Elliot clears his throat that I remember myself.

"Um, yes. Sorry. Yes."

"You sure?" he asks. He has a lace in either hand but waits before tightening them. "I have plenty of tricks in my bag."

"I'm sure," I say, smiling despite myself. "You're good at this."

"I *am* a healer, you know," he says. He rolls his eyes, but he's smiling too. "I happen to do this for a living. You didn't think I'd go on a quest without medicine, did you?"

"I'm sorry for underestimating you," I say. I try but fail to wipe the smile from my face. Then, after staring at him for entirely too long, I finally sober. Say something I've wanted since the day he was dragged into Sebastian's manor. "I'm glad you went into healing. I always worried..."

I trail off, unsure how to finish. Or rather, unsure what he would think if I was honest.

"Worried what?" he presses. He's still knelt in front of me, and his large hand rests carefully on my knee. I memorize the way it looks, his long fingers stretching up my thigh.

"I don't know," I whisper. "I always worried you'd end up in politics."

He nods. When I glance at him, he's staring at his own hand. He's mesmerized too, I think, by the way his touch looks on me.

"I thought about it," he admits. "Mama always wanted me to follow in her footsteps. I just...I like helping people. Not that the council doesn't..."

It's his turn to leave the sentence hanging, and I get the feeling it's because he doesn't want to lie. All too often, the council *doesn't* help people. They drag them through the mud, only tending to them if it's mutually beneficial.

"I'm glad," I say, filling the silence. "It seems like a good fit."

"I enjoy it," he says. He's still looking at his hand. He stretches his fingers over my knee and thigh, rubbing slow, smooth circles against my leg with his thumb. It's not sexual—or at least, it shouldn't be. His thumb is barely above my knee. And yet, there's something indescribably erotic about it. About the way he's touching me. Reverent. Fascinated. Smitten.

I force myself to breathe, but it comes out as a shaky exhale. Elliot's eyes snap up to mine, and his pupils widen. He swallows, and I watch the way his throat moves, feel the way his hand tightens, just slightly.

"We should keep walking," he says, but he doesn't move.

I do.

Not to continue the hike. I lean forward, grabbing him by the shoulders and pressing my lips against his. He takes a surprised breath, but that's it. Then he's kissing me back with as much— no, more—desperation than I am. He moves with swift, urgent movements, surging to his feet and easily bringing me with him. He stands with me in his arms, hands cupped under my ass.

My back meets the rough edge of bark. A tree. He's pressed us against a tree, our chests so close I can barely breathe. Elliot readjusts his hands, slipping one beneath my skirt. The heat of his palm scorches through my tights, and without permission, my body bucks against his touch.

"Can I—"

"Please," I say, too eager to let him finish the question. "Touch me."

He grunts against my mouth, and were I not so desperate for relief, I might laugh. As it is, I wind my legs around his back and tighten my hold on his shoulders, helping him as he yanks at my tights. When a sudden ripping sounds through the quiet forest, I gasp, and he pulls back.

"I'll buy you new ones," he says. His dark gaze sweeps over me, and his free hand comes up to trace my lower lip. "Fuck, Secora. You're so pretty. Do you even realize it?"

He doesn't give me time to answer. His mouth is back on mine, hungrier than before. He kisses me like he's studying my taste, like he's memorizing my flavor and the feel of my tongue against his.

Maybe I'll bottle this memory one day too, not to hide it from myself, but to memorialize it. To watch it every night and every morning in vivid, undisturbed detail. Without time blurring the reality of this moment, the perfection of it.

And then, Elliot's thumb brushes the wet fabric of my underwear, and I forget everything else. Nothing exists but this moment. I cry out as he shoves my underwear to the side, thumb pressing against my clit. He's rougher than I've ever been with myself. I don't know if he's just so eager he can't help it, or if he somehow knows this is what I need. His unrelenting touch and the scrape of his unshaved face against mine.

"Okay?" he asks. He doesn't pull all the way back as he asks. His lips are still on mine, hand still pressed between my legs.

"Yes," I say. Then, "Please."

He groans against my mouth before trailing kisses across my cheek, down my throat. He's sucking hard enough against my skin that he'll likely leave a mark.

I've never hoped for anything more.

When he sinks his finger into me, the sound I make is so obscene I should be horrified. Maybe I would be, were it not for Elliot's echoing groan, for the filthy praises he whispers in response. He adds a second finger, and it's almost too much. I bow against him, tightening my legs around him.

"You're so fucking sweet," he says against my neck.

I'm too mindless to respond. I'm grinding against his hand, head slanted to the side, nonsensical words falling from my lips. The heat builds and builds inside me, until I'm certain I can't bear another second. Before long, I'm begging, pleading for him to touch me where I need it.

A brush of his thumb against my clit is all it takes. I come and come and come, breaking apart while he holds me against him. I sag against the tree, hands limp on his shoulders. He still has his hand between my thighs, in the mess of my arousal and ripped tights.

His eyes are dark enough to look black, and they're roaming over me, cataloguing every tiny detail.

When he moves to put me down, my legs tighten on instinct.

Not yet, I want to scream. *I'm not ready.*

I expect him to speak, but he doesn't. He only readjusts his hold and presses his free hand to the hollow of my throat. His thumb trails over my skin, settling right above my sternum.

"Our first kiss was under a tree," I tell him. I tilt my head back, looking at the layered branches above us, filtering out the daylight.

"Yeah," he says gruffly.

I'm looking up, and I'm glad I can't see his face. I'm not sure I'd have the nerve to continue if I was.

"I always wanted you to be my first," I say, talking to the clouds. "For a long time, I was sad I'd lost my virginity to a monster. But eventually, I decided I didn't. Rape isn't sex. It's *rape.* Sex...sex is between two people. Two people who want it."

I can feel Elliot's hitched breathing, can tell he's desperate to say something. I'm worried it will be about Harrison, that he'll think I want to talk about our past and what his friend stole. I make myself look down now, let myself study the colors in his eyes.

I don't lose my nerve. I find patience, love, encouragement.

"I want it now, Elliot," I say. My voice is strained. "I want it with you."

His lips part. He moves his hand from between my thighs, balancing one on my hip and the other under my butt. He swallows, and I follow the movement in his throat.

"It's okay if you need to think about it," I say. "I know this is all new, and if you're not interested or ready—"

"In the tent?" he rasps. His fingers dig against my hipbones. "I can have it set up in a few minutes. Or back at the manor? We could do it at my house. I've got a nice bed. I could—"

"Here," I interrupt. "Right here."

Elliot presses closer, forcing my legs wider. I relax against him, letting him spread me with his hips.

"Here," he repeats. His attention lowers to my messed skirt and his straining erection.

"If you want," I say. I'm tempted to offer him other options, to make it clear it doesn't *have* to be against this tree, if he doesn't want it to be. But he already knows.

He lowers my feet to the forest floor, but he's moving fast enough I don't have time to feel disappointment. His hands are already on my tights, ripping them down my legs and pulling my boots off with them. My underwear is next, and I don't miss the way he tucks them into his pants pocket, rather than tossing them to the dirt.

I try to keep his pace, but I'm trembling too hard. I've barely got the button of his pants undone when I'm being lifted again.

"You're so sweet," he groans against my ear. His warm hands cup my ass, one trailing down my thigh, then back up, all the way into the wetness between my legs.

"I'm already wet," I inform him, even though he obviously knows. I'm not sure if it's more or less than I should be, but I can't help the flare of self-consciousness that works through me. "Is it—"

"Perfect," he interrupts. Presses two fingers into my cunt, curling them and groaning against my neck. "You're the most perfect thing in the whole fucking world."

I buck against him, moaning against the side of his neck.

"I need you to tell me," he says. He shifts to hold me with one hand and uses the other to unbutton his pants. "If you want it harder. Softer. Slower. Faster. If you want me to stop. Okay?"

I'm nodding. I'm trembling so hard it should be humiliating. I'm too needy to care. I clench my thighs, dig my heels into his back to try to bring him closer. He pulls his cock out in a smooth motion, and I can't hold back my whimper.

He's long and hard and ready for me. *Me.* After all these years, he's looking at me like he used to. Like there's nowhere he'd rather be. No *one* he'd rather be doing this with.

"Say it, Secora," he says.

"Do it however you like," I say. I arch against him, only to whine when he leans back, denying me.

"Trust me, I'm going to love it," he says. He strokes himself, keeping his eyes locked on mine. "But only if you love it, so tell me."

"I'll tell you," I say. Mostly out of desperation.

"Good," he says. "How do you want it, Secora?"

"I–I don't..." I arch again, feeling a flare of heat rush through my face. "I don't know, Elliot. I've never..."

"We'll start slow," he says. His voice is ragged, the only indication this is torture for him as much as it is for me. "Then, you'll tell me. All right?"

"Yes," I say. It's a plea more than an agreement.

Luckily, it seems to be enough.

He shifts me higher and notches himself at my entrance. I

clench my legs around him, shocked at the immediate sense of pressure. *Too big. Too much.*

"Relax," he whispers. "I've got you."

It's what I need to hear. I relax my legs, allowing them to part farther. Elliot cups one hand behind my neck to keep my head from hitting the bark, and the other beneath my ass. He presses a soft kiss to my temple, then the edge of my mouth. When his lips finally meet mine, and his tongue smooths over mine, he presses forward.

I whimper as he inches into me. I make myself as pliant as I can, letting myself soften. With each shallow thrust, I become fuller and the pressure becomes more overwhelming, until it's all I can feel. Just when I'm sure it's too much, when I'm on the verge of asking him to stop, Elliot grunts against my mouth.

Animalistic and unfiltered. Satisfied in a way I'm sure I've never heard him. Heat scorches through me, and I buck in response, making room where I feared there wasn't any. He slides farther, filling me until he is fully seated. His hips dig against the soft flesh of my thighs.

I open my eyes, only now realizing I'd closed them. Elliot is looking at where we're joined, his mouth parted, chest heaving with barely restrained breaths. He looks up, eyes dark and desperate and alive.

"Okay?" he asks. His grip tightens over my neck, and I arch in response, clenching around him. He grunts. "Fuck. Careful. You'll make me come."

"Sorry," I say. But I'm not, not even a little bit. I'm smiling, glancing between Elliot and the place he's buried inside me. I shift again, and we both groan. "You have to move, I think. It's too...you're too..."

He pulls out, and the pain is more than the pleasure. I suck a breath through my teeth, my features crinkling.

"It will get better," he promises. Another thrust. Another. "I promise. If it doesn't, tell me..."

I dig my fingers into his shoulders and relax into him. The pain...I remember. When Harrison raped me, it's all I felt. Panic and pain, helplessness and shame. For a fleeting moment, I'm terrified that's how sex will feel too. That though I'm not afraid, I won't like it either.

But then...

"Oh," I whisper. The pain subsides, shifting into something softer yet stronger. It coils through my insides, building with heat and pleasure and it's suddenly so good I can't fully process it. I become a mess of discordant mumbling as he fucks me with steady, slow strokes.

"Better?" he asks gruffly. He shifts, moving his hand from my neck to my skirt. He twists it out of the way and presses his thumb to my clit, massaging in tight circles.

It's too much. Only now, it's in the best way imaginable. I don't remember how to work my mouth, so I communicate with my body. I dig my heels harder into his back, urging him closer. I scrape my nails over his shoulders. I shift my hips, meeting his steady thrusts with my own, clumsier movements.

"I should've taken this off," he mutters.

It takes me a moment to realize he's talking about my skirt. He's flipped it out of the way again, exposing my cunt to the cool forest air. His cock pumps in and out, shiny and slick with my arousal.

"Next time," he says. His words are so mumbled, I'm not sure whether they're for me. "We're doing this in my bed. Lights on. I'll memorize every. Fucking. Piece. Of. You."

Between each word, he thrusts, gradually pumping harder and faster. I tighten my hold on his shoulders and accept that I can't keep up. He's fucking me like an animal, too fast and too skilled for me to contribute. I stare at him, at *us*, in fascination.

"I'm going to come," I say. It's breathless, and I'm not sure he's heard me at first. I'm still staring where we're joined, feeling halfway in this world, half in another.

"Look at me, Secora," he says. "Let me watch you come for me."

I do as he says, but only barely. The intensity of his dark gaze pushes me over the edge immediately. My eyes roll to the back of my head as he thrusts, so deep I can feel him everywhere. I cry out in pleasure, so lost in euphoria I don't care how loud I'm being.

Elliot surges forward, capturing my mouth with his. He swallows my sounds, claims them as if they're his, and his alone.

I'm so consumed by my own pleasure I don't realize Elliot has pulled out until his hot cum spurts against my thighs and the edges of my skirt. He keeps me held to him, hand under my ass, mouth tracing leisurely kisses along my jaw.

"I've made a mess of you," he says. He takes a ragged breath, nipping the edge of my ear before pulling back. "I should say I'm sorry."

"Are you?" I ask. I'm dizzy and sated, and I must be a masochist for asking such a terrible question.

"Not even a little," he says. He rests his forehead against mine, his reddened lips curving into a smile. "I'll clean you up. And then we'll do this again. And again. And again."

"Perhaps in your bed next time?" I ask. I'm trying to tease him, but I'm too breathless to pull it off. I sound wistful. Dreamy. "With the lights on?"

"Everywhere," he says. His lips brush mine before he pulls back. "We'll do this everywhere. In every way imaginable."

"Promise?" I ask. I hate the way my voice dips, the way it weakens.

"I swear it," he says. "However you'll have me, Secora, I'm yours."

23

———

THE ONLY PLACE

ELLIOT

Four hours later, we're almost to the Cursed Grounds. We're high enough that the temperature has dropped and the trees are thicker, hiding us from the sun. Secora is wearing my sleep pants, rolled multiple times at the waist and her ankles. Her ruined tights and messed skirt are folded in my pack. Her underwear is still tucked in my pants pocket, and I've decided I'm not giving them back.

I steal a glance at her. She's a half-step in front of me. She's slowed immensely since we first started walking, and despite the chill in the air, she's sweating. She doesn't exercise much now, but I wonder if she did when we were younger. I wonder if she'd be interested in doing hikes in the future or if she'd scowl at the mere suggestion.

I smile and look back to the trees around us. The forest has never seemed quite as sexual as it does now. Every single tree has potential. I bet I could convince Secora to hike if I promised to fuck her on a new tree each time.

She stumbles over a rock and I touch her elbow to steady her. For all the strangeness we've been through these past few weeks, this feels inexplicably natural. The irresistible urge to touch her? Now, I can. I don't have to think about it. I don't have to feel guilty. I don't have to wonder if I'm evil.

Now, I'm thrilled to do it. Pleased to touch her and help her and kick a little more dirt onto Harrison's metaphorical grave.

Secora offers me a small smile. Then she's focused again, brow furrowed as she walks up the steep terrain. If it gets any worse, I'm going to demand her bag. She's going to fall three miles if she trips, and then who am I supposed to christen the forest with?

"Secora?" I ask after a few minutes of walking.

"Yeah?"

"What's after this?"

She stumbles, and again, I steady her elbow. As much as I'd like to grab her hand, for the peace of mind if nothing else, I don't. I need to know what she's thinking, and if I'm touching her, there's a good chance I'll get distracted. I'll end up fucking her again, and besides the fact we need to have this conversation, she also needs time before we have sex again.

My lips tick without permission. I've regressed into a teenage boy, horny and tunnel-visioned, sights set solely on her.

"We'll do some trial and error," she says shakily. "If this new ingredient is what you think, I should be able to incorporate it into the ritual. It'll depend on—"

"That's not what I meant," I say. Then, "You know what I'm asking, Secora."

She drags her boots through the dirt, slowing her steps until she finally stops. We can't see the black stone from where we are on the mountain, but she stares in its direction.

"I'll take you to the ingredient either way," I say quickly. "So you don't have to agree to anything to get your end of the bargain. I'll still show you. I'll still help with the spells."

"But only if I give you the last two memories, right?" she asks. Her cheeks have a pink tinge to them. I can't decide if it's purely from the cold or her exertion, or if there are nerves there too.

"They're my memories, Secora," I say. As fucking gently as I can, because I don't want her to spiral. I don't want her to shut down or turn away or ruin this before it's even started. "They won't change how I feel."

"They will change *everything*," she says. Her voice catches so abruptly even she seems surprised. She wipes at her eyes, attention flicking from me to the hike ahead. "They don't matter, Elliot."

"They matter to me," I whisper.

Secora's hands open and shut, fingers flexing, as if she's fighting off surges of magic. She could hurl me all the way down this mountain. I don't question her strength, but I no longer fear it. I step toward her, taking one of her shaking palms in mine.

"Breathe, Secora," I say. Her brown eyes meet mine, wild with secrets only she knows. "It's going to be okay. I promise. Your old offer can stand. If I want to give them back—"

Secora rips out of my hold. She marches up the mountain, slightly angled to the north. If she keeps that direction, she'll miss the black rock entirely. I should let her go. I should follow after her and let her exert all her energy until she's too tired to fight this losing battle anymore. If she got tired enough to drop her walls, maybe she'd realize I'm nothing to fear, not even once I know every ugly and terrifying truth.

"Secora!" I call. I jog after her, eating the space between us with a matter of three paces.

She stops again, scowl twisting her doll-like features. Her chest heaves as she untangles her bag off her shoulder and throws it haphazardly at my feet.

"You want the memories?" she asks. She's crying and shaking and looking at me like I'm trying to hurt her. "Fine. You can have them. But–but you watch them, and *this* is done. All right? It's over."

She takes off again, this time running. Without her bag, she's faster. She darts between the trees and doesn't so much as look back at me.

I curse. Throw my pack to the ground and replace her bag on my shoulder. I sprint after her, calling her name as she desperately puts more distance between us. When I finally catch her elbow, she spins around so fast she loses her footing. She's still crying as she collapses into the dirt, breathing so hard I'm afraid she's going to pass out.

"Breathe, honey," I say. I tuck her hair behind her ears, and for the briefest of seconds, she lets me. She leans into my touch, allowing me to wipe the tears from her cheeks. Then, her eyes hone in on her bag on my shoulder. She glares at me, mouth twisting into a violent snarl.

"*Don't*," she says. "If you watch that, you'll—"

I lunge forward and cut her off with the press of my lips against hers. It's a messy, clumsy kiss. More teeth than tongue, more frustration than passion. She falls back against the dirt, and I cage her in with my hands on either side of her face. I keep my weight off her and my lips far enough away to make it clear she can say no.

"If I watch that, I will still love you," I say. Her eyes widen with my words, so I lower my head, touching my nose against her. "I will still love you. I will still want you. I will still belong to you."

"Can't you just trust me?" she asks. Her face is wet with tears, and I kiss them away, chasing the ones that have trailed down to her neck. "Please, Elliot. Just love me without them. Be with me without them. Why can't you just let it be?"

I don't answer at first. I lower onto my elbows, carefully

settling my body over hers, until we are touching everywhere through our clothes.

"Because, I have this feeling," I say quietly. "The reason you don't want me to see the memories isn't to protect yourself, Secora. Is it? They're to protect me, and you've done that long enough."

"Elliot—"

"It's my turn," I say. I kiss the hollow of her throat, placing my thumb on the bruise above her collarbone. I didn't mean to leave a mark when I kissed her earlier, but I don't regret it. I'd like to do this every morning for the rest of our lives. Let everyone know she has someone who fucks her exactly the way she needs.

"Elliot." My name is a whisper this time, swallowed up by the immensity of the forest around us.

"Secora," I return. "My Secora. I'm going to watch it, and I am going to love you. Okay?"

She doesn't answer right away. I remain close, planting a few more kisses on her throat before rotating off her. I don't want her to feel pressured to answer. And as much as I hate to admit it, I'm not going to watch them without her permission. I can be patient. I can wait as long as I need to gain her trust, to make her understand I'm not going to leave, no matter what these memories hold.

I lay beside her, both of us looking up at the grey sky, barely visible through the thick trees. Leaves and twigs rustle when she finally turns her head to look at me.

"You love me?" she asks. So vulnerable and soft, so sweet and lovely.

"Yes," I say, dropping my chin to meet her gaze.

"And you'll let me take it away if it's too much?" she whispers.

"I promise," I say. Silently, I add, *it won't be.*

"Okay," she says. She looks back up at the sky, but her hand moves through the tangle of leaves, only stopping once her fingers find mine. "Okay, Elliot. You can watch them."

∾

Elliot Lyrie
age 16
That Night

DARK.

It's dark in the augur house and quiet. The augurs will be gone through the end of the month, so these halls will be abandoned for a few more days. Harrison will be here. I know that now. Even while he should be with his uncle who lives near the river, he'll be here.

Drinking.

Smoking.

Raping.

I stop. Lean against the hallway wall for support. This place has always unsettled me. Mama Iyle has been an augur for as long as I've known her, so this is far from my first time wandering the halls unsupervised. It is, however, the first time I realized how many horrible, terrible things could happen here.

My fingernails draw blood. I force my hands to relax. I didn't realize I'd been clenching my fists, but blood decorates my palms, shaped like tiny crescent moons.

I swallow. I need to stay calm.

The council may be ready to hide Harrison's crimes, but I'm not. I'm ready to drag him into the light, hang him from his wrists in the town square and strip him naked. Let the world see him for the cruel, heartless beast he is. Let them punish him for it. Let them do as they please to the monster I lay before them, only having my turn once his body is bruised and broken.

And if they don't? If they are all cowardly, I will do it for them. I will torture him until he's incapable of hurting anyone ever again. I'll scrape his tongue from the bottom of his mouth. I'll cut his cock clean off his body and feed it to the sirens.

"Elliot?"

I startle, spinning around so fast I almost lose my balance.

I am rage in human flesh, but I am also inexperienced. I've never hunted someone. I've never planned revenge. I've never broken into a house with the intent of harming someone.

Looking at Harrison now, I know the same isn't true for him.

He's a twisted, vicious monster, and I only wonder how I didn't see it before. That unnatural gleam in his eye. Excitement, almost.

Does he know why I'm here?

How could he not?

"Sorry I've been out so long," he says. He leans on the wall opposite me. He's come from the kitchen, knife in hand, spinning it lazily.

I assumed he would be asleep. I assumed he wouldn't know I was here until I was standing over him. Until I was snapping these cuffs over his wrists.

They're the ones Secora has worn her entire life. I used Mama's grimoire and ingredients to remove them, along with the two silver pairs. Secora tried to resist. She warned I could be imprisoned for life. I didn't know how to explain that I didn't care. That her safety meant so much more than mine.

She'd eventually allowed it. She let me remove the cuffs and replace them with a defunct pair from Mama's office. For the first time in her life, she has magic.

In a matter of minutes, Harrison won't.

"I'm making some boar," he says. I look up from his knife, and he grins. "Late night treat. There's plenty, if you want some."

I might believe him, if I didn't have the cuffs hanging at my side.

There's no way he hasn't noticed them. There's no way he thinks this is a friendly visit.

My mouth is dry. It's been nearly a minute since he said my name, and I've yet to speak a word. I can't. I can't think about anything except his hands on her body. His hand on her neck when she tried to run. His cock forced between her legs, tearing her deep enough she needed stitches.

Magic pulses through me. It's sparking from my fingers, through my toes. I've never been more acutely aware of my power than I am right now. I could kill him, I realize. Forget the town square. Forget the world knowing his empty heart. I could end this right now, before he so much as thinks of inflicting more pain.

"Elliot," he says. He speaks slowly, like I am a dangerous animal.

And maybe I am.

Maybe, I just didn't realize it until he stripped away logic. No, until he hurt the one person logic doesn't apply to. Secora Reed has been mine from the moment I saw her all those years ago. She has been mine in every breath, every tortuous, hard-earned smile.

"Why?" the words tear from me. "How could you... She..."

I can't make the words string together, can't make my rage make sense. A flicker of fear and recognition cross his eyes. My rage pulses through my entire body as I realize...he thought he got away with it. The council excused him, and so he thought there would be no consequence.

"I shouldn't have done it," he says. "I know you liked her."

He knew I loved her. I'd told him a day earlier, after he'd made a snide comment. I'd told him I loved her. That I was going to marry her. That if he had a problem with her, he would be the one I cut out, not her.

He hurt her to punish me, and I'll never forgive myself for it.

I clench my fists, loosen, clench. There's more magic pooling beneath my skin than I've ever felt, than I know what to do with. I try to control my breaths, because if I act now, I might just kill us both.

"I'd gone to talk to her, to apologize," he says. "Truly. We got to talking, and I realized you were right. She's really cool. One thing led to another. She came onto me, man. That doesn't make it right, but—"

I throw him before he finishes the sentence. He flies down the hallway and crashes against the far wall. He collapses in a heap on the floor, and a hanging portrait of his mother crashes on top of him. Between us, his knife lays on the floor, reflecting the hall's dim light.

Harrison gapes up at me, staring at me like I'm a stranger. As if I have done something unforgivable. As if I am the one who betrayed him.

The irony of it is too much. I let out something between a laugh and a scream that has Harrison scrambling to his feet.

"Secora wouldn't touch you if you begged!" I scream. My voice echoes around us, filling this small, dusty house of secrets and lies. His mother reads magic as a living.

I wonder if he inherited any of her skills.

I wonder if he realizes just how powerful I am. Just how much darkness I carry, now that he's called for it.

"Elliot—"

"She would have been kind!" I scream. I storm down the hallway, kicking the knife back into the kitchen as I pass. Whatever protection he thought it'd offer, it won't. "If you apologized for the years of torment, she would have been kind. You wouldn't have deserved it, but she would have forgiven you, you fucking miserable asshole!"

He cowers against the wall, hands shaking, lifted at his chest. He's ready to strike, but he doesn't stand a fucking chance. He's already lost.

He just doesn't know it yet.

"She's a Dark One! She's evil!" he screams. "She was never supposed to live! Don't you get that? Everything I've done is to protect the people I care about. Margot. Our classmates. You. If it weren't for those cuffs on her wrists, she would have eviscerated me, Elliot!"

"That's right! If it was a fair fight, she would have killed you. And *gods, do I wish it'd been a fair fight. I wish you weren't such a fucking coward, and I wish she'd killed you! Once people know the truth, they'll wish the same—"*

This time, I'm the one sent backward. I land on the final stairwell, the one leading to his mother's office. Where it happened. Where he held her down and—

I'm back on my feet. There's blood on my chest, and I realize a moment delayed that it's mine. He's cut through my chest with a form of magic I've never even seen.

I'm out of my league, fighting someone better. Someone stronger. Someone far more ruthless.

By every mark of logic, I know I should lose.

And yet, somehow, I know I won't.

I can't.

Because the most precious girl in the world is at home in her bed right now. Her face is stained with tears after hours and hours and hours of sobbing. Because he got away with raping her. With torturing her. With hurting her and shattering her and—

"Let's just talk, Elliot," Harrison calls. He walks toward me, hands still raised, ready to fight. "I don't know what Secora told you, but it's her side of the story. Not mine. Like I told the council, it was consensual. If she regretted it later, that's on her, all right?"

Even if he weren't trying to blame Secora, I'd know he was lying. Because for as much as I thought I knew Harrison, I know Secora. I've listened to her heartbeat while she falls asleep. I've listened to her fears and her hopes and those rare laughs when she forgets to shrink herself.

I know Secora.

I don't need to hear Harrison's side, because I know hers. I sat at her side at the healing center while they gave her stitches. I held her when she was too scared to fall asleep that night. I stroked her hair while she sobbed that no one would ever believe her. I told her I believed her.

I told her I'd fight until everyone else did too.

And I failed.

I failed and Harrison got away with it, and Secora isn't going to get the justice she deserves unless I do something right now.

"Trust me," Harrison says. He's still walking toward me, only a few paces away now. His pale eyes study mine, searching for signs I'm about to lash out. I'm not. I'm frozen still. Reconciling everything I thought I understood about this ugly world. "Secora Reed is dangerous, and this is just further proof. If they don't send her away, which they obviously should, you need to keep your distance. For real this time. It might feel strange at first, but I promise, it's for the best."

He stands before me. Close enough I could grab him. I could wrap both hands around his neck and squeeze until there's no life left. There might be more satisfaction in that, overpowering him the way he did Secora.

"Is that what you think?" I whisper. I don't recognize my own voice, and by the way Harrison flinches, he doesn't either. "You think you're going to rape my girlfriend, have her sent away, and things will go back to the way they were?"

I'm vibrating again. Not just my hands now. My legs. My lips. My body.

"You think because you fucking tortured her, I'm going to love her less?" I ask. I'm screaming. Loud enough someone could hear us. It doesn't matter. Even if they do, they won't get here in time. "You think I'm going to side with you?"

Harrison's eyes don't narrow. He keeps his features cool and collected. He is both puppet and puppet master, carefully controlling his reactions. I can see it. The way he thinks he can twist this situation in his favor, so long as he finds the right words.

"You are a pathetic, entitled, worthless shell," I say, lowering my voice. "The world will be better without you in it."

He scoffs. Makes a show of rolling his eyes. He's too exaggerated in *his movements, too transparent in trying to distract me. He thinks I won't notice the way he shifts. The way his hands lift to strike.*

He doesn't understand that's exactly what I'm hoping for.

Magic flares from his fingertips, but instead of hurling me back to the stairs, it pulls me close. Our noses are almost touching as Harrison's power digs through my flesh. It slices from one shoulder to the next before slicing toward my stomach. I have no idea how deep he cuts, only that the blood is instant. It pools over my pale orange clothing, coating everything crimson red.

I scream, knees buckling. But I do not feel the pain. There's too much adrenaline coursing through me. I'm wholly focused on my movements. Not too fast, but quick enough he doesn't see it coming.

By the time he realizes, it's too late. I've already got one band around his wrist. He tackles me sideways, and we collapse to the wooden floors. My blood pools around us, but I stay focused.

I wrestle him beneath me. He buries his fingers into the open wound in my side, and I choke out a scream. Louder and louder, ignoring the pain. Thinking only of her. He had her beneath him, just like this.

The second band clasps with a tiny, metal clink. It's too quiet for me to hear over my screaming and Harrison's yelling, and yet, I swear I do.

I swear the whole world goes quiet in that moment.

I may be cut open and bleeding, but for the first time in Harrison's miserable life, he doesn't have magic.

"Really?" he rasps. He's working hard to be calm, to act like he's not a breathing dead man. "Is this your grand plan, Elliot? Make me feel weak? Show me how it feels? Do you want me to beg for mercy like she did? Would that make you feel better?"

I stare down at him. I'm straddling his waist, holding him down by the wrists. If he tried, he could probably shove me off him and make a run for it. But we both know he wouldn't make it far.

"Did it make you feel better?" I ask. I study the golden bands on

his wrists. Imagine him doing the same to Secora. My Secora. "Did you feel like a man when you hurt her?"

"What, are you going to rape me?" he screams. "Will that make us even? Are you going to rape me so you can tell your whore that I suffered like she did?"

He's screaming so hard he's spitting, his face a mask of red. My blood, mixed with his fury.

"No," I say quietly. "Only a monster would rape someone."

His face relaxes. He tries to hide his relief, tries to replace it with forced nonchalance, like he's not still chained.

"All right," he says. Scoffs. "Then will you get off me? We can figure this out. Take these stupid things..."

He trails off. He moves slowly, turning his head with almost comical delay. His eyebrows furrow as he studies the skin of his right wrist. There's nothing visible, but he must feel it.

I stare at his arm too, at the space just above where I hold him. Where I send my magic through his skin in droves.

"What are you doing?" he asks. It's a horrified whisper that instantly pitches. "Elliot, what the fuck are you doing?"

His wrist splits open. I'm pulling so violently at the blood in his veins, I've broken through his flesh. Blood sprays from his wrist, and Harrison screams. He thrashes against me, tries to break free, but it's far, far too late. I concentrate only on my magic and the weight of his blood. I pull and pull and pull, coating us so heavily in his blood it's impossible to know what's his and what's mine.

Beneath his shoulder, a pool of blood seeps into the hardwoods. He thrashes until he's lost too much blood, until he's barely conscious. Only as he falls still do his blue eyes return to mine.

"Please," he cries. "Please. I'm sorry. Please, Ell—"

I look away from Harrison as he dies. I stare at his wrist, at the blood running thin, until I am certain his evil has left this world.

"You deserved worse," I whisper.

I don't really register what I've done until I've left the augur *house. Until I've hit the main streets of Ochre, where weeks ago, Harrison and I debated which classes we'd take at university. Then, all at once, reality sets in.*

I just murdered my best friend.

Harrison is dead.

I'm hurt. Badly.

I look down at my chest and my stomach. The cuts are deep. I don't think it's enough to kill me, so long as I get to a healing center. But there's somewhere I need to go first.

Secora deserves to hear this from me. I need to warn her what might happen, but assure her that I'll never regret killing him. I need to tell her how much I love her—how much I will always love her— and that I only want her to be safe and free and happy.

Keeping a hand on my stomach, I limp toward the Blake house.

24

HAVE MERCY ON ME

ELLIOT

Secora comes into focus slowly. I don't know if she left the memory sooner than I did, but she doesn't look half as ruined as I feel. I blink and focus all my energy on her features until they sharpen to their finest details. The tiny freckle next to her ear. The strand of hair that's fallen from her ponytail. The cracks in her lips from this dry weather, or perhaps from being kissed too much in the past twelve hours.

"Secora," I say. My voice sounds too loud and too quiet at the same time.

She doesn't look at me. She's focused on the memory stone, extracting the neon yellow memory with her fingers. It thrashes as it leaves the warm stone.

It should be red, I think.

For blood.

For murder.

For rage and hatred and—

"Did you know?" I ask. "Did you know, all this time, that it was *me*?"

She still doesn't look at me. She drops the yellow memory into its jar, carefully screwing the lid into place. I try to be patient. I wait until she's tucked it back into her bag, but when she grabs the next memory—the last one—I speak again, louder.

"Did you know?"

"I owe you this last memory," she says. Her voice sounds fuzzy, far away, like she's speaking from across a canyon.

We're sitting in the same patch of dirt from before, separated only by this black memory stone. We haven't moved, but we suddenly feel a thousand miles apart.

"Once you watch it, you can decide," she says. Her words tremble, even as her hands don't. "I can take it all back, and I'll never make you see it again."

"I don't want to watch the memory," I say. I try to sound calm, but it's impossible. "I want to know if you *knew*."

"Of course I knew," she says. She sounds miserable and angry and desperate, and still, she won't look at me. She's trying to uncap the jar, but it's stuck, and that only pisses her off more.

"You said I wasn't a killer," I say. "That first time I came to the manor, you said—"

"You're not," she says. "That wasn't a lie. You aren't a killer, Elliot. *I* made you one."

"No, you didn't. I made that decision all by myself. If I couldn't handle it, if that's why I made you take them—"

"Just watch the memory, Elliot," she interrupts. "Take it, and you'll understand. This last one is when you came to see me that night. You'll see how upset you were. You were scared and I promised to make it better. You opened your mind because you *trusted* me, Elliot, and I violated that trust. I stole your memories because I was fifteen and scared and you had just ruined your whole life for me! I didn't know what to do. Okay? I loved you, and I didn't know what to do."

"Secora," I say. She's curled into herself, still clinging to the jar and avoiding my gaze. "Look at me."

"It wasn't your fault, Elliot," she says. She hugs the jar against her stomach. "It was mine. Everything comes back to me and I tried to fix it, and I think I did. It was all fine until you came back, and I don't...I never should have made that deal with you. I was just..."

"Breathe, honey," I say. I extract the jar from her clenched fingers and place it in the dirt. Then, I take her into my lap, pressing her chest against mine, until I swear I can feel her heart beating against mine. "I am so sorry, Secora."

"Don't hug me," she says. But when I loosen my grip, she surges closer, burying her head against my chest. Her hands clench the fabric of my shirt, and a wild sob wracks from deep within her soul. "I don't deserve it."

"You deserve every good thing in the world," I whisper. "That's what I thought at sixteen. That's what I think now."

Tears burn my eyes and I let them fall.

"I'm sorry," I say again. "I am sorry for *everything* bad that happened to you, but especially the parts that were my fault. I'm sorry for making it worse."

"You were the good, Elliot," she says, words muffled against my shirt. "Then. Now."

WE DON'T TALK MUCH for the remainder of the trek, but I keep Secora's hand in mine. Though she hasn't explicitly said, I know she's waiting for the fallout. Maybe she thinks I'll blame her for what I did to Harrison. Or that I'll hate myself so much for it, I'll beg her to take the memories again. Maybe she thinks I'll abandon her once we get back to the Night Realm, that I'll need distance or time or a chance to think things through.

Though I haven't explicitly said, I couldn't feel more at peace than I do now. Ever since I laid eyes on Secora in that vampiric hellhole, my world has felt broken. There were pieces missing from an otherwise perfect puzzle. Now, the puzzle has flipped, but all the pieces are in place.

It makes a better picture than before, since she's part of it.

"The Cursed Grounds were first used for the gargoyles," I say. I'm sure Secora knows the lore already, but I'm desperate to end the quiet. And as much as I'd like to create a to-do list of wrongs to right, I doubt Secora would welcome *that* conversation. "Two hundred years ago, the council made a deal with the Flight Realm. A certain harpy tribe had become a problem, terrorizing their lands. The council offered to resolve it for them, in exchange for this little slot of land—and more importantly, the black sand that's only ever been found here."

Secora nods along. She's staring straight ahead, so I can't tell if she's interested or just humoring me. I continue regardless.

"The council arranged a meeting with this rebellious tribe, under the guise of an alliance. So the harpies show up, only to find no witches. Just this ashy sand and a massive black table. They wait, and wait, and wait, but no witches come. Eventually, the harpies get pissed and decide to leave...only to realize they can't." I pause for dramatic effect, and Secora's lips twitch into the tiniest smile. "Their wings aren't working. Too late, the harpies realize they've been betrayed. The council had laced the table with magic, cursing anyone who touched it to turn to sand and stone. By nightfall, they were all completely calcified, their bodies carved from the same material that cursed them. The harpy tribe had fallen, and the Flight Realm was safe once more."

"Is this your round-about way of warning me not to touch the table?" Secora asks. Now, she's smiling for real.

"They deactivated that magic ages ago."

"That's what they told the harpies," she quips.

"Exactly," I say. I glance down at her, enjoying the tinge of pink on her cheeks.

Up ahead, I can just see the glimpse of black stone through the trees. It feels like we've been walking toward this destination for hours, days, weeks. Yet now that we're here, it feels entirely too soon.

Secora's steps falter. She stops and squeezes my hand hard enough she might break a bone.

"Secora?"

"You don't have to do this," she says. She looks up at me and swallows. "Those memories were yours, Elliot. I'd kept them because I thought it was best for you. I never should have bartered them. It wasn't fair."

"This was never just about the memories," I say.

"We can go back down," she presses. "I'll tell Sebastian it was a dead end. I'll pretend I never heard about the Cursed Grounds or this missing ingredient. You don't owe me anything, Elliot."

"I know," I say. When her eyes widen, I smile. I keep one hand around hers, but I use the other to cup her face, trailing my thumb along her lower lip. "My mama's punishment has gone on long enough. She has her reasons for despising the vampires, but I have mine for admiring them."

"Is it that right?" she asks skeptically. "That's news to me."

"They welcomed you, Secora." I let my words hang in the air for a moment before continuing. "After the witches failed you for too long, it was the vampires who gave you a chance. For that, I will *always* admire them."

"Elliot," she whispers, eyes filling with tears. "If anyone discovers what you've done—and they probably will—your life will be ruined. Do you understand that?"

"Secora," I say. I press firmly against her lip, curling until my thumb meets her teeth. "You've spent enough time worrying about me."

Her eyes flutter shut and her breath falls into a steady rhythm.

"Have mercy on me," I whisper. "Let me take care of you, just this once."

When she opens her eyes, something has shifted. I don't know how to describe it, exactly, but it feels a bit like trust, and a lot like love.

"Okay, Elliot," she says. "Okay."

THE CURSED GROUNDS are as bleak as the one other time I was here. Mama showed it to me shortly after she became *Madam Lyrie*. Looking back, I realize she was trying to sway my future, to pull me into her shadow without forcing me there. She showed me all the exciting and fascinating secrets of the council. The location of the Cursed Grounds. The intricacies of the neutral territory spell. The many, *many* ways in which we held more power than anyone knew to fear.

Back then, I wasn't particularly interested. I suppose I'm still not all that interested, save for the information that's useful to the woman in front of me. Secora wanders the desolate land of the Cursed Grounds, scuffing her boot through the black sand.

Where the past few miles have been packed with lush trees and bushes and flowers and weeds...the Cursing Grounds are stripped. It's a half-mile stretch of land, covered not by dirt but by ashy sand. Trees line the far edges of the circular space, bowed, leaning as from this wretched place as their roots will allow.

In the center, the massive stone table reflects the setting sun. We only have a couple hours of daylight left. We'll get one more night in our shared tent, but then, we'll be forced to return to reality. A reality I'm not sure I understand anymore.

Secora kneels a few feet from the table, using magic to move ashen sand into three containers. It's excessive. We won't need one container for the ritual I'm thinking, let alone three, but it's better to be safe. If we need more—for the sunwalker spells or something else entirely—it might not be simple to get it. Once Mama realizes my loyalties are closer to this woman than to her, she will likely hide this place.

I run my tongue over the back of my teeth as I step forward to collect the first jar from Secora. As she continues filling the next container, I do a quick protection spell over this one before putting it in my pack. Even if I take an epic tumble down this mountain, the glass container won't break. I don't *think* the sand, on its own, is particularly dangerous, but I'm not interested in risking it.

When Secora hands me the next container, she doesn't turn back to the final jar. She watches me, brown eyes trailing from my face to my feet to my hands. Back to my face. I wait for her to say something or ask something, but she doesn't. She only looks and looks and looks.

Even without uttering a word, I somehow know what she's thinking: everything is about to change. I can't have Secora *and* keep my life in the Day Realm. At least, not as it's been. I'll have to confess to Harrison's murder. I'll have to convince Mama to lift Secora's death sentence. Worse, Mama will have to accept I'm a killer. That I'm in love with her enemy's greatest weapon.

I don't want to believe Mama would let the council kill me, but maybe she would. Maybe I'll have to go into hiding, right alongside Secora and her vampire clan.

Secora finally opens her mouth, but whatever she's going to say, I'm not ready to hear it. For once, I'm the one leaning away.

"We have another night," I say. I busy myself with the second jar, readying it for the protection spell. "We don't need to figure everything out right now."

"Elliot..."

"One more night," I say. I clutch the container in my hands. "One more night to be together and not have to think about the rest of the world. I know we'll have to, but just...not yet, all right?"

I feel like a coward. Maybe I am. But when Secora sighs, it's a happy sound, and I can't bring myself to feel sorry at all.

"One more night," she agrees.

She turns back to the final container. The steady sound of sand against glass fills the silence, until finally, we're ready to leave.

25

IS THAT A BAD THING
CORA

When I left the manor with Elliot, I convinced myself I knew what I was getting into, in more ways than one. I believed I could get the ingredient without revealing any memories. Then, I believed I could keep Elliot without revealing his. I was wrong, on both counts, but it's hard to feel bitter about either. I ended up with Elliot, the ingredients, *and* a light conscience. I didn't even know my conscious was capable of feeling light.

My greatest lie upon leaving the manor, however, had nothing at all to do with Elliot, and everything to do with the shadowed man I see now.

"Fuck," Elliot breathes. "Is that..."

"I wonder how long he's been standing there."

I swallow and shake out my hands, determined not to tremble once I reach him. We're far enough away that he won't see me cowering now, but he'll eat me alive if I step onto his stoop with buckling legs.

"Is there a chance he'll try to hurt you?" Elliot asks. He looks sweaty and exhausted, which means I undoubtedly look worse. It was faster walking downhill than up, but not by as much as we hoped. We were racing the sun all day, and we're only now getting back.

The sun is setting.

Another hour, and we would've been caught in darkness.

"I can handle Sebastian," I say.

Elliot stops abruptly, catching my elbow.

"I know," he says. He lowers his voice, pulling me closer. "But if he tries to hurt you, I'm going to lose my mind, and we both know how that ends."

I smile despite myself, despite the seriousness of his expression. It's not that I doubt him. It's that I know he would. Forget the consequences, Elliot would absolutely kill the vampire king to protect me.

"He's not going to hurt me," I say softly. "Sebastian is many things, but he's not stupid. I'm his best defense when it comes to the witches. He needs me."

I start walking again, clasping my hand around Elliot's. It's one of the few times I've so much as touched him in front of someone else, and that fact alone makes my cheeks heat. I don't drop his hand though, even as old insecurities flare to life. I might not deserve Elliot, but he loves me all the same.

"You sure?" he asks.

"He'll know anyway," I say. My cheeks, impossibly, burn hotter.

"I can keep my emotions in check."

"First, I highly doubt that's true, given we *both know how that ends*," I tease. My bravado falters as we cross the final stretch to the manor, crossing its rocky, neglected landscape. The falling sun surrounds the manor with warm oranges and purples, making the stone structure look even bleaker than usual.

Sebastian descends the porch steps. To the ordinary person, his expression looks blank, but I've known Sebastian long enough to read his subtle tells. The flare of his nostrils. The twitch of his left eyebrow. The way his fingers stretch, resisting his urge to clench them into fists.

"And second," I say, my voice dropping. "He can already smell it."

Elliot's pace stutters, and he nearly loses his footing over the rock pathway. I give his hand a final squeeze before we stop, only feet in front of Sebastian.

"Master," I say. I offer him a stiff nod. Polite, acknowledging, but certainly not cowering.

Sebastian's nose crinkles. He looks from me to Elliot, back to me. I'm doing everything in my power to keep my expression controlled, but Sebastian knows me as well as I know him. I'm sure he can hear my heartbeat and the way I can't quite regulate my breathing.

Ever since we started back down the mountain, I've considered what his reaction might be. I left without permission. I went with his enemy's son. I told him nothing of the plan, even in the note I posted. For all he knew, I could have been in the Day Realm, betraying him.

Will he care that we might have a solution to the sunwalker spell? Will it be enough to keep him from exiling me? From killing me?

Sebastian looks at Elliot again. His upper lip snarls, and his hands finally lose their battle. As soon as they clench into fists, I move by instinct, stepping to place myself between the two men. Elliot's reaction is immediate. His hand leaves mine, brushing my hip as he steps forward, back to my side.

The men stare at each other for a long, impossibly silent moment. No one is breathing.

When Sebastian finally speaks, it's not to Elliot. His attention shifts back to me, eyes wild with an unreadable emotion.

"You're sure?" he asks.

My lips part, but I'm too stunned to speak. Of all the reactions I expected, this wasn't one of them. I had already accepted he would be angry and likely violent. I had braced myself for the possibility I might have to hurt him to protect Elliot and myself. I would never injure him, not seriously anyway, but there was a chance he would never forgive me, all the same.

"I'm sure," I say finally.

Maybe I imagine it, but I let myself pretend his expression softens.

"Fine," he says. He looks back to Elliot, and now I'm certain I didn't imagine it. One look at Elliot, and the hardness is back. The slight curl of his lip, the narrowing of his eyes. "I have killed many people, Lyrie."

"I do not doubt that," Elliot says, impossibly calm.

"I would not mind killing you."

"Master—"

"I do not doubt that either," Elliot says. Then, tipping his head slightly, he adds, "I won't give you a reason."

It isn't until now that I realize how much I wanted—maybe even *needed*—this. I'm not fool enough to believe Sebastian sees me as a daughter, but a part of me will always see him as a father. Regardless of titles, he's the only person who has ever seen the darkness in me and smiled. Even as a traumatized fifteen-year-old, I found peace in his house of horrors that I'd never felt elsewhere.

Sebastian looks away from Elliot. His green eyes pierce mine, filled with emotion I don't know how to name.

"I do not forgive you," he says. "Of all the things you've done, this is the worst."

"Understood," I say. "If it helps, the lead was successful. We found something big. It could make the difference—"

"It does not," he interrupts. He looks behind himself, at the falling sun. The sky has darkened into a deep purple. Within a few minutes, we'll be in complete darkness—and the vampires will be out for the night. When he faces me again, the snarl is back on his lip.

I keep my posture straight and do my best not to flinch under his unrelenting gaze. I wait for him to speak again, but he doesn't. He turns on his heel and marches up the stairs, disappearing into the manor without looking back. If I was a fool, I'd assume he stormed all the way back to whatever he'd been doing before this.

No. Sebastian Vulce, feared vampire king, is undoubtedly lingering at the door to make sure we come inside before night officially strikes.

"That went well," I say.

"It did?" Elliot asks, so incredulous that I smile. I realize the expression is starting to feel more comfortable, more natural.

"Yes," I say. I take his hand, squeezing softly as I pull him toward my home. "Very well."

Elliot doesn't respond at first, but he stops me before I enter. His gaze flickers to the closed heavy door, then back at me.

"To be clear," he starts, lowering his voice. I smile, knowing Sebastian can still hear him. If Elliot becomes a regular visitor here, and I hope he does, he'll have a lot to learn. "You're telling me he could *smell* that we're together."

"More specifically, that you fucked me," I say. When Elliot's eyes widen, I grin. "Your scent is on me, *inside* me, and probably—"

The door swings open, and if Elliot's expression was comically horrified before, it's fully terrified now. He grabs my hand again, tugging me slightly behind him, squaring his shoulders. He's taller than Sebastian, but he hardly looks intimidating.

"That is enough," Sebastian growls. "Get inside. Both of you."

I'm still smiling, but it falls the second I realize how empty the entryway is. Usually, at this time of night, the main level of the manor is full of bloodthirsty vampires, rabid for a night of hunting and partying. Instead, there are only five vampires here, and they're the same ones I see at every clan meeting.

"What's going on?" I demand. I release Elliot's hand, brushing past Sebastian to stand in the center of the room. "Where is everyone?"

My eyes shift around the space, moving from one face to another. They're placed strategically, braced for conflict. Beatrice and Grace stand at one hallway opening. Milas and Amelia at another. Then Sebastian, squared near the front door. Otherwise, the house is silent. There's no sound of movement, even when I strain my ears.

I spin, facing Sebastian again.

"What happened?"

To my surprise, he looks irritated. Before he can utter a word, Grace laughs, and her pealing sound breaks through the quiet of the room. The tension ebbs out of Sebastian with that singular sound. Something about Grace has *always* done this to him.

"You think he had vampires running around loose while you were out there, unaccounted for?" Beatrice drawls. "C'mon, Cora."

I whirl around, gauging everyone's expressions. They all look amused, sharing glances like troublesome teenagers, giggling over an inside joke. They're not geared for battle at all, I realize. They're *babysitting*, making sure the exit is guarded against stubborn vampires.

I wasn't stupid! I'm tempted to yell. *I was safe, warded. I took care of myself. You didn't need to look out for me.*

But when I turn back to Sebastian and his scowling expression, I surprise us both by whispering, "thank you."

"Go to your quarters," he replies, voice strained. "Before I lose my fucking mind."

I BARELY SLEEP. I've never shared a bed before, and it's surreal having *Elliot* beneath the covers with me. I lay with my back pressed to his chest, the heat of his bare skin burning against mine. I don't typically sleep naked, but after we had sex last night, I couldn't fathom putting clothes on. It's too lovely, the feeling of his skin against mine.

For as long as we have this, I'm going to enjoy it. Even if that means I can't sleep, too intoxicated by his presence to do anything but count his steady breaths. He doesn't move in his sleep, not like I know I do. By the time morning rolls around, he's in the exact same position as when he fell asleep. His chin is tucked against the top of my head, and his arm is wrapped protectively over my waist, snaking up between my breasts. I keep my hands on his forearm, lightly brushing the skin of his wrist.

We're surrounded by memories. They line the walls of my bedroom, filling the small space with endless colors. The thrashing greens and blues and reds all make up years of hard-earned control. It's difficult to imagine giving it up.

Elliot's breath shifts. It's almost indiscernible. If I hadn't spent all night noticing him, I might have missed it.

"You're awake," I say.

He jolts like I've stabbed him.

"Hells," he gasps. "I thought you were asleep."

I don't respond. I study all the jars on the walls. It will take days to reabsorb them. We probably shouldn't do it all at once either. I'm not sure if memory overload is a thing, but if it is, we definitely have enough to cause it. There are *years* of memories around us, and it will likely be unpleasant, putting them all back.

"Secora?" he asks.

His voice is gravelly with sleep as he untangles himself from me. He props onto his elbow, gently rotating me until I'm flat on my back. His skin is golden and smooth. His hair is an absolute mess. Until we shared a tent, I had no idea how long it took him to make his hair look like it normally does.

"What're you thinking?" he asks. He traces my jawline, stopping to press his thumb against my lower lip.

"Nothing," I say. "Just...enjoying this."

"Yeah?" he asks. Despite everything, he looks unsure.

"Yeah."

"Good," he says. He presses a feather light kiss to my lips, then my temple. When he glances at the wall to my right, his eyes reflect the colorful memories. I expect him to say something, but he only kisses me again, firmer this time.

"We'll probably want to do it slowly," I say. When he smirks, I roll my eyes. "The memories, I mean. At least in the beginning, we should make sure there aren't side effects. It'll be better to do a little bit at a time."

"Whatever you want," he says. Another kiss on the side of my mouth. "Slow. Fast. Rough. Gentle. Against a tree. In the lake..."

I shut him up with a kiss, and I don't let up until we're both breathing hard and he's cleaning remnants of himself from my thighs. I touch myself as he gets dressed, feeling the pleasant soreness, the subtle ache that's already desperate for more.

"You keep touching yourself like that, and we're going to be here all day," Elliot says as he tucks his shirt into his pants. He's already wearing his shoes, and his hair has been styled.

Meanwhile, I'm still naked in bed, fantasizing over what we just finished.

"Is that a bad thing?" I ask innocently.

"Most days no," he says. He holds a hand to me, keeping his

eyes locked on mine, even as I keep my hand between my legs. "But today, we have a lot to do."

"Like?" I ask.

"You need to educate your clan on our plan for the sunwalker spell," he says. His hand doesn't falter, even as I glare at it like it's a serpent. "And *I* need to go back to the Day Realm. Henry's been covering for me, but I need to make an appearance before Mama sends out a search party."

A sour twist punches through my gut.

It's not that I forgot our reality. It's that I hoped it would stay away, if only for a while longer.

"I'll be back," he says. "I won't be long. I'll just need to treat Mama, and I should at least stop by the center to make—"

"Your mama," I interrupt. All at once, pieces fall into place, and I feel like a fool for not realizing it myself. "She's the one who's sick."

It's not a question, but any doubt is washed away when Elliot swallows. For the first time, his attention shifts away from me. His jaw tightens as he looks over the displayed memories.

"I'm sorry, Elliot," I say, surprised at how much I mean it. Maybe I don't care for his mama, but Elliot's affection for her has never been a question. Vampires killed his father before he was born, so that woman is the only family he has. To know he might lose her...

"I'm figuring it out," he says quietly.

"Does she know?" I ask. "About the blood?"

It's hard to imagine the infamous Madam Lyrie approving something as vile as a vampire blood treatment. When Elliot doesn't answer, it's answer enough.

"I'm sorry," I say again. Two words have never felt so useless.

"Yeah, me too," he says on an exhale. With another deep breath, he looks back to me. There's nothing guarded in his expression. I can see it all: the sadness, the disappointment, the rage. And encompassing it all, the determination. "She thinks the Mother is punishing her for the sun curse. I'm hoping the sunwalker spell might change things. If the death stops, then maybe..."

He trails off, glancing away.

"The Mother will show mercy?" I guess.

"Yeah." He nods. Then, looking back to me, he adds, "I know it sounds stupid."

"It doesn't," I say. I don't think it will work, but it doesn't sound stupid. "Do you think she'll agree?"

"No." He shakes his head and sits on the edge of the bed. His hand spans the width of my waist, and his thumb moves in small, rhythmic strokes. "I'm hoping it works anyway. I'm not going to ask for her blessing. This disease, this punishment, is going to kill her unless I do something. Unless I convince the Mother to spare her."

I struggle for something more to say. It's been years since I've honored the Mother. I'm not sure I even believe in Her, but from what I remember, She wasn't the forgiving type. If Madam Lyrie's affliction is truly from the Mother, the sunwalker spells won't change a thing.

When Elliot's head hangs, chin dropping toward his chest, I move to straddle his lap. I may not know what to say or how to help, but I can be here with him. I rest my head against his chest, relieved when his arms wrap around me. A hoarse sob breaks from his throat, and I lean into him, praying I am enough to hold him together.

26

THE SHARPEST OF GLASS

ELLIOT

By the time I step off the tram, it's nearly noon. Mama won't be expecting me, but she'll have to make time. I won't be able to make our planned visit tomorrow. I'll be too busy trying to single-handedly save her life.

"Here to see Madam Lyrie?"

I blink, bringing Vera into focus. As usual, she's sitting at her primly organized desk, staring up at me from behind her large glasses. Her curly hair is shorter than usual. It makes her look older, more proper. I'm sure it's exactly what she was hoping for.

"Yes," I say. My voice cracks, and I try to disguise it with a cough. I'm certain I don't succeed.

"Let me see if she's available," Vera says. She pushes from her seat, swishing past me with a flare of her knee length skirt.

Despite wanting to shove past her and lead myself into Mama's office, I force myself to be patient. The less frantic, the less emotional I seem, the more likely Mama will listen to what I say. She sees emotion as a weakness, and considering what I'm about to ask her, maybe she's right.

"Right this way, Mister Elliot," Vera says, coming back into view. She leads me down the narrow twist of hallways, stopping in front of Mama's closed door. With a sharp nod, she leaves me there, returning to her desk.

When I enter Mama's office, I'm hit with the familiar scent of old books and heavy black tea. It's a darker variety than normal. T'mavy, maybe. A cup of it sits on Mama's desk, surrounded by stacks of loose parchment. A precarious stack of weathered books sits on one corner, and the other is cluttered with candles burnt to the wick.

At the center of the chaos, Mama sits with her typical sharp posture. Despite her body being destroyed from the outside in, much of my mama remains the same. Her astute gaze studies every detail of my appearance. She may not be a vampire, but I wouldn't doubt she can sense a difference in me.

Do I look happier? Fuller? Do I seem more whole than I ever have, despite the fear that wreaks through me? When I passed my reflection in the neutral territory, I thought so. Even facing my greatest fear, I feel stronger than I ever have.

"Henry said you've been ill," Mama says. She stares at me for a beat too long, and I work hard not to fidget.

"I'm better now," I say. My mouth feels dry. I may be nearing thirty, but my body still rebels at lying to her. It's been years since I felt like I needed to. These days, I lie to Mama more often than I tell the truth.

This lie, at least, feels harmless. For now, I can't tell her the truth. I promised Secora three times before leaving the manor I wouldn't say a word about us to her. Not yet, anyway. Whether Secora likes it or not, I do plan on confessing the truth to Mama and all of the Day Realm. It's important to me that they understand who the true villain is in our history. It's not Secora. It might not even be me, though I'm happy to carry that judgment.

More than anything, I need people to know Harrison was a monster, not someone to be mourned.

"I've brought your treatment," I say, finally moving into the room. The floor creaks gently under my feet as I cross to the chair. It's as uncomfortable as ever, the rungs pressing into my back. I balance my bag on my lap, quickly taking out my concoction of blood and pungent herbs. "I won't be able to make tomorrow's session."

"I'm surprised you didn't send Henry yesterday," Mama says. She arches an eyebrow in challenge, but she rolls her sleeves all the same, placing her grey skin on display.

"I promised I wouldn't tell anyone, and I haven't," I say. I bite down on my tongue at the lie, letting the taste of blood fill my mouth.

Just for now, I remind myself. *I'll tell her eventually.*

First, I need to get other things in order. The sunwalker spell, for one. The Mother's forgiveness for another.

The blood concoction is in a black vial, dark enough it's hard to see what's inside. I add a few more herbs, swirling gently before setting it to the side. While the flavor infuses, I take Mama's hand, gently tracing my finger up the inside of her wrist. The skin feels brittle enough to break. I could, I think. I could dig my nail against her arm and cut straight to the bone.

"It's getting worse," I say. I place her arm back on the desk, not bothering to check the other. I don't need to check it to know: "You're dying, Mama."

Mama only sighs. She rolls her sleeves back to her wrist, hesitating briefly before unwrapping the scarf at her neck. She's wearing thick clothing today. A buttoned yellow sweater. A floor-length skirt. A bright orange scarf, made of thick wool. I knew why she was carefully covered.

Seeing it is different.

With her scarf on the desk between us, Mama undoes the top two buttons of her sweater. It's not necessary. Even with her sweater buttoned, I could see the hazy grey of her skin. It disappears beneath her shirt and stretches up toward her neck. It won't be long before the grey touches her face, her hands, her everything.

Even if we increase her treatment to three, four, five times a week. We're playing a losing game.

"Mama—"

"I know, Elliot," she says softly. She fusses with the parchments, and I get the distinct impression it's to avoid looking at me. "I know, sweetheart."

"Mama," I say again, voice cracking. "If the Mother is punishing you, it means she doesn't approve. She doesn't approve of the curse, and so long as it's in place, this is only going to get worse."

Her expression smooths, and she finally looks at me. I have no idea what she's thinking, but when she sighs, I know I won't like it.

"I told you, I have made my peace." She buttons her shirt and replaces her scarf as she speaks, still avoiding my gaze.

"Well, I haven't," I say. "We already know the vampires have started making sunwalker spells. Perhaps, if we ease the curse, the Mother will—"

"She won't," Mama says calmly. "The Mother has decided."

"So what?" I ask, voice harsh. "You're giving up? You think you know, so you won't bother trying?"

"I've made my peace," she says firmly. It's as close as she's come to raising her voice since I walked in here. "You need to do the same."

I swallow. My throat feels thick, scratchy. I'm undoubtedly allergic to the horrid words she's saying.

"No," I say. Command. "We at least need to try. If the sunwalker spell could be the difference, we'll at least try."

"And undo the peace we've claimed?" she asks. "Listen to yourself, Elliot. I stand by everything I did for that curse. It doesn't need to be eased. If anything, it needs to be strengthened."

"What?" My brain lags at her words, unable to make sense of them. "Strengthened? What does that even mean?"

Mama sighs. She plucks a few parchments from her desk, stacking them together before offering them to me.

"I will be informing the council of my illness at tomorrow's meeting," she says as I take them. "I do not have much time left, but take comfort, my son. My death will not be wasted."

I flick through the parchments, and my stomach sinks further with each word I read. Mama has years of information here, documenting finances and budgets, potential threats and species-specific curses. It's her life work, broken into digestible segments.

When I reach the final parchment, I only read a few lines before dropping them all on her desk.

"You're going to kill them all," I whisper. I can't hide the horror in my voice, and I'm not sure I would if I could. "They'll all die."

"Yes," Mama says. She tidies the parchments I've just strewn over her desk, focusing on them rather than me. "I believe my death can expand the curse, as I'm the one who made it. The vampires will burn in the sun, and they will burn in moonlight. They'll burn, Elliot, and they'll never terrorize this world again."

"Mama." I say her name like a curse, like an unforgivable sin. "You can't."

"I have already decided," she says. "If this is the last gift I offer the world, I will rest easy in death."

"Gift?" I repeat. "You're going to kill them. They're people, Mama."

"They are *monsters*," she snarls.

I grab more parchments off the desk, flicking through them as Mama watches me with visceral disappointment.

Tomorrow. She's planning to announce this tomorrow, after which, our realm will inevitably fall into chaos. The council will be frothing at the mouth to sacrifice Mama, the same way they were to sacrifice Grace's father for the original curse.

"You need to push this back," I say, throwing the parchments back to her desk. I lean on both palms, staring hard at Mama. "The annual meeting. Postpone it. At least give me a few weeks. We can figure something out."

Something to stop your death. To make you rational. To stop everything I love from collapsing at once.

"That wouldn't change anything," Mama says sternly. She straightens the mess of papers on her desk, but her attention flickers back to me.

"A week," I beg. "At least give me a week. Let me work through this before everyone else knows."

A week is nothing, and I'm sure she'll agree, if only to placate me. It's not much time, but it's enough. I'll be able to work out a plan with Secora. Mama will agree. She has to.

Instead, she shakes her head. She pauses her organizing to cover my hand with her own. Though it still holds her natural color, I swear her skin feels different. Softer, more fragile than ever.

"I can't."

"Why?" I ask, my voice cracking. "Please, Mama. Just give me a few more days."

"The augurs leave for their retreat the day after tomorrow," she says softly. "They won't be back for a month. We both know I don't have that long."

The world halts. For all the horror I've just absorbed, none of it compares to this. Everything I've known staggers in this moment, erupting in a way I didn't know was possible.

After what happened with Harrison, I should know not to be surprised by the people I thought I knew best.

I reel out of Mama's touch, staring at her as if she's a stranger. Maybe she is. She *must* be, because I've realized something I should have before. Something so obvious I can't help wondering if I knew, subconsciously. If I protected myself, buried the realization, just like Secora did with my memories.

"The augurs' retreat," I say. The words feel numb falling from my lips. I clench the arms of my chair, staring at Mama as she looks back in pure confusion. My mind is reeling, and I don't know how to make it stop.

The augurs go on a retreat every year for an entire month. They travel from village to village, looking for promising witches. Mama Iyle goes every year. She was gone when Harrison raped Secora. And she was gone when I killed her son.

That means she was gone when Harrison evaded punishment. That means it wasn't *her* who got him out of trouble. It was the council. And if it was the council...

"Mama," I say. My heart is shattering, slicing through my internal organs like the sharpest of glass. I am being destroyed from the inside, and it's happening too quickly for me to process, for me to school my expression.

Mama knew.

She knew what happened to Secora. She knew Harrison raped her, and she covered it up. And suddenly, I realize what I would have if I hadn't hidden from the truth.

Mama would have been the first on scene at Harrison's murder. She would have seen the way his blood was drained from his body. She would have known Secora—an infamously dangerous mind witch—wouldn't have killed him like that. She wouldn't have needed to bleed him dry. But I...that's *exactly* how I would have done it.

She knew I killed him. She knew, and she blamed Secora. She let her go to prison. She called for her death, knowing she was innocent. That she was the *only* innocent.

"Mama," I say again.

My body goes slack in the chair.

Did you know I loved her? I want to ask, but I can't.

I promised Secora I wouldn't say a word, and right now, that's the only thing sparing Mama from my wrath.

Did you know she was mine when you destroyed her? When you ruined her life?

It doesn't matter, of course. Whether or not Secora was mine, she was innocent. She was pure. She needed Mama's help, and Mama, the council...they denied her. For me, for Harrison.

Because it was easier.

"I've made peace with it," Mama says.

"I haven't," I say. I swallow thickly as I look in her eyes, silently telling her everything I can't yet say. "But I promise, I will."

"Elliot—"

I'm out the door before I have to hear another word.

27

RETAINED MEMORY
CORA

Elliot looks intoxicated. He stumbles down the final stretch of cobblestone street, relying more on me than himself to stay upright. I've got both arms wrapped around his middle, fingers digging into his blood splattered shirt. If anyone happens upon us right now...

I look to my left, then the right. I don't know what time it is, but the stars are still visible, and the moon is high in the black sky. I'm relying on the natural light to guide us to Elliot's home, a place I've never dared to go. More than once, Elliot has encouraged me to meet his mother, to at least show up as his friend. I always knew it wouldn't end well, so denying him was easy.

Now though, I wonder if this all would have ended differently if I had. Maybe, if Madam Lyrie met me before Elliot brought me to report Harrison's crime. Maybe, if she'd known me as one of Elliot's friends. Maybe, if she knew me at all, she would have believed me. She would have punished Harrison, and Elliot never would have...

I swallow. It doesn't matter.

"Hey, that's my house," Elliot slurs.

My head throbs at the sound of his voice. I've got too many memories stuffed in my head. Every single piece I stole from him is now *trapped in my skull, desperate to escape. I don't have room for both his memories and my own.*

I'll need to empty his at some point. For now, there are bigger problems at hand.

"That's right," I say. My voice is soft and smooth, gentle, as if I'm talking to a child.

I've never wiped someone's memories. I've read about it, but up until a couple weeks ago, I've never had the magic to attempt it. Elliot had replaced my true cuffs with these false ones, but I've hardly had time to master my magic. I've managed a few small spells, but this was far out of my league.

Still, I think I did it right. It's too late to question it now.

I glance up at Elliot. He's looking at his house before us, blinking slowly. I think he'll be okay. His brain should heal around the stolen memories, and he should be exactly as he should have been all along: whole without me there to ruin him.

Without consciously deciding to, I slow my steps, taking in every detail of the way he looks. I'll never see him again after this. I'll never run my hands through his soft hair or feel those hazel eyes on me. I'll never fight to get 'Dark One' removed from my file. I'll never marry him or bear his children.

It was foolish to hope for those things anyway.

We reach the Lyrie house. It's large and white, with black shutters and a well-kept lawn. I've seen it multiple times, but only ever in passing. At night, it feels even more ominous than it does during the day. There are too many trees clustered around the front of the house, their skeletal branches looming above us.

"Step up," I tell Elliot as we reach his porch. There's a porch swing on one side with brightly colored pillows and a thin rug that stretches to the opposite corner. A wreath hangs on the door, heavy with violent orange and red and yellow leaves. Mama Blake has one like it, but the Lyrie one is larger, fuller. More expensive, undoubtedly.

"You smell nice," Elliot murmurs, his breath tickling the crown of my head. "Like honey."

I don't. I smell like sweat and anxiety, a potent combination from hours of nightmares. Visions of Harrison holding me down, of those fish watching from the corner, letting it happen.

A flash of Elliot's memories flares through my own. Harrison's lifeless eyes, staring up at the ceiling.

It's an impossible, unbearable combination of relief and guilt. He's dead and I am relieved, but it was Elliot and it's my fault and if I don't fix it, his entire life will be ruined because of me.

"Have we met before?" Elliot asks.

The question eviscerates my heart, but it's a good thing. The best possibility. He doesn't remember me, and yet, he sounds more lucid than he did a few minutes ago. Now, I can only hope he's disoriented enough to forget everything that's happened in the past twenty minutes.

This long walk from Mama Blake's house to his own, the fact I'm here at all, dragging him to his front door.

"No," I say. The word catches in my throat, garbled enough I'm not sure he's heard it.

"You're pretty," he says. "What's your name?"

He's definitely still disoriented. It took Elliot years to confess he found me pretty, and he'd been drunk then.

I swallow, steadying him roughly against me. We're at his front door, the wreath glaringly bright between us. Elliot stumbles forward, and this time, I let him. He slumps against the white stucco of his house, staring at me with confusion and wonder and...

I close my eyes. That's the last time he'll ever say those words to me, so I let them absorb into my skin. I inhale them with each unsteady breath.

You're pretty.

You smell good.

I killed him, Secora. He'll never touch you again.

I open my eyes. My entire body is trembling as I look back to Elliot. It's a relief, truly, that he's fallen asleep. His chest rises steadily, mouth parting softly. I've never seen him sleep before.

I never will again.

I knock on the door, harder than I should given the circumstances. I should have checked Elliot's pockets first. If I weren't a trembling, emotional mess, I would have. I wouldn't risk someone else in this fancy neighborhood hearing me, peeking through their expensive curtains to see us standing here. Me in my nightclothes. Elliot in a blood-soaked shirt.

The door opens.

I've seen Madam Lyrie many times before, but this is the closest I've ever stood. I'd seen her across the playground, picking Elliot up from school. I'd seen her give speeches on big stages, making grand promises that too often didn't come to fruition. And I'd seen her last week, in that horrible auditorium, surrounded by a select few council members.

Elliot wasn't allowed to come with me. I'd stood there alone while she told me there was no proof of Harrison's wrong-doing. There would be no trial. No viewing of my memories. No justice. And as for me, my trial for Gregg's injury would still be forthcoming. I was dismissed, never being allowed a word.

Up close, Madam Lyrie looks...pleasant. She seems like the type of woman Mama Blake would have as a friend, though I knew they weren't. I'd never questioned that before now. Even with Elliot and Margot's friendship, Mama Blake never spoke of Madam Lyrie at all.

Maybe that should have been a warning in itself.

Madam Lyrie's hair is braided, and she's wearing simple orange pajamas. Her feet are bare, and she looks like she'd been fast asleep. When she blinks, I realize it might not be sleep alone that's given her this hazy expression.

He drugged her, I realize. Gave her something to ensure she wouldn't catch him leaving.

"You've been drugged," I inform her. My words are fuzzy in my ears, sounding foreign, even to me. "You'll need to sort that first."

Madam Lyrie blinks at me. Her eyebrows scrunch, and though it's hard to tell what she's thinking, she manages a nod. Her attention flickers from me to Elliot, who is still asleep against the wall. If she notices the blood on his shirt, she doesn't mention it.

She only nods again and steps back into the house. She leaves the door ajar, and I follow, dragging Elliot behind me. He mutters something incoherent as I guide him to a sofa. Like almost everything in this entry room, it's dark orange and looks both vintage and expensive.

Elliot collapses on the sofa, his feet hanging over the end. He blinks heavily at me, and it's only a few seconds before he's asleep again, a tender smile on his face. I watch him, jaw clenched so tight I might break a tooth.

He'd done this for me.

I wish you hadn't, I want to tell him. I wish you didn't love me at all.

A tear slips down my cheek and I wipe it roughly with the back of my hand. I'm still watching him when Madam Lyrie returns to the living room. She's still dazed, her steps wobbly, but she's gripping an empty vial. Remnants of something purple color her lips.

With every blink, she's more lucid, until she looks less disoriented and more horrified. She looks from me, a Dark One standing in her living room, to Elliot, her only son, covered in blood.

I meet her furious gaze, counting the seconds until she speaks. I've almost passed two hundred when she steps closer. She tosses the vial onto a side table and crouches at Elliot's side. She touches him, hands gingerly moving down his body, tugging at the hem of his shirt. With his stomach and chest exposed, I tell her what she clearly already knows.

"He'll need a healer," I say. "The sooner the better."

"What did you do?" she asks.

I swallow.

Nothing, I could say.

Everything, might be better.

"He came to me like this," I say finally. It's a simple truth, easier than the full story.

Shock flickers over Madam Lyrie's face, but it's gone in an instant, replaced with a carefully blank mask. She already knew Elliot and I were friends. He came with me to make my official report, after all. She knew her son was someone I trusted, but I doubt she expected he trusted me the same.

Rather than responding, she turns back to Elliot. She smooths his shirt into place, careful not to disturb the wound on his stomach. Then she inspects his arms, the sides of his throat, the top of his head. She's so intent on him that I doubt she realizes she's given me her back.

She's too worried over Elliot to protect herself from me, and it gives me all the confirmation I need. For all the cruelty Madam Lyrie has shown me, she undoubtedly loves this boy as much as I do. I didn't know that was possible until this moment.

She loves him, and that means I can trust her.

"He killed Harrison," I say.

Madam Lyrie whirls around. Her hands are still on Elliot, but now, her gaze is wholly focused on me. She scans my body, head to toe, lip curling at what she sees. Even though it doesn't matter, I impulsively add, "I wasn't there."

"And yet, here you are," she says. Her voice is pure venom as she shifts, facing me. She places herself like a shield before Elliot and the absurdity of it—of her protecting him from me—should be ludicrous. It should make me laugh.

Instead, the bitter taste of bile crawls up my throat. He clearly does need protection from me. If only I'd let Elliot introduce me to his mama like he wanted, she likely would have prevented any of this from happening.

"Explain everything. Now." She keeps one hand on Elliot and

raises the other toward me. Though I can't see her magic, I can feel it. It sizzles through the air, stronger than any other I've felt, except perhaps my own.

"I don't know the details," I say. "Only that Elliot killed him. I imagine there's a terrible mess."

Madam Lyrie doesn't immediately respond. Her jaw works as she looks at me, and her upper lip curls into a snarl. I tilt my chin, leveling her with a stare. I hope she can't see the way my knees shake, the way my breath hitches

"What do you want?" she asks finally. Her magic pulses again, but she doesn't strike. She's too smart. There's too much at stake. If she kills me, she won't know how to cover for Elliot. The council might ignore the rape of a Dark One, but they likely won't do the same for the murder of an augur's son.

"You need to clean it up," I say. When Madam Lyrie doesn't react, doesn't even breathe, I continue. "I don't have the right ingredients to conceal his involvement. I'm hoping you do."

She still doesn't move. She only stares and stares at me, one hand locked on Elliot's arm, as if bracing him for impact.

"Why?" she asks.

"Why?" I echo. There are too many questions that could start with that single word. Why did Elliot kill Harrison? Why did he come to me? Why do I want to protect my rapist's best friend?

"Why," she repeats. This time it's not a question.

"You already know," I whisper.

Her eyes flash, and it's the only confirmation I need. Elliot promised me he wouldn't fight with his mama about her ruling, but I feared he would anyway. He's too good. He can't help but defend the defenseless, especially when it's me.

"This is all for your little accusation?" she spits. Her magic pulses again, and this time, I feel it stretch for me. She's ready to hurt me, to kill me, to ruin me. If only she understood, I'm ruined already. Ruined, with no hope of recovering.

"We don't have time," I say, rather than responding to her question. I glance past her, to the brightening sky visible between her orange drapes. "The sun will rise soon, and someone is bound to discover him. You need to go."

Her glare hardens, only to soften when she glances over Elliot on the couch. He's starting to snore, and despite everything else, that makes me want to smile.

Mind magic can be a powerful sedative. Despite his wounds, he's sleeping peacefully. I imagine he will for the rest of his life. He won't remember killing Harrison. He won't remember what his best friend did to me. He won't remember me at all, and as much as that burns my insides, it's for the best.

For him, at least.

"He gave me his memories," I say. Madam Lyrie's attention snaps to me, mouth falling open. "No one will know the truth of what happened. Not even him."

The silence stretches between us, and I watch as a dozen emotions flash over her features.

"Where's the body?" she asks finally.

"I need your word first," I say. Madam Lyrie's face scrunches, a snarl twisting her lips. Before she can protest, I continue. "Promise me you won't give me the death penalty."

"You're trying to barter?" she asks. "My son is bleeding out. His best friend is dead. And you...you're using this to your advantage?"

"Blame Harrison's murder on me. Exile me. Send me to the farthest reaches of the Echo," I say, ignoring the malice in her tone. "Spare my life, and I promise, I'll never come back."

Madam Lyrie's jaw works, but she can't deny me. She knows as well as I do. Elliot's all over that crime scene, and if I don't tell her where that is, he'll spend the rest of his life in prison. I only hope she doesn't know I would never allow that to happen.

"Help me get him upstairs," she says. She rises to her feet before looking expectantly at me. "Once my healer arrives, we'll go."

"*Your word,*" *I demand.*

"*You have my word,*" *she bites out.* "*I'll exile you, and you'll never come back.*"

And that is that.

Two days later, *the council guard arrives at Mama Blake's house. They tear me from Margot's outstretched reach and drag me down their front porch. Neighbors all down the street poke their heads out to watch, and not one of them looks surprised. They don't know what I'm being taken for, but they all assume I deserve it.*

Maybe I do.

I don't fight the guards. I enter the trolley and stare at my cuffed wrists. I'm wearing three pairs again, but no one knows the golden set is false. These silver ones are debilitating. Heavy. Exhausting. But they do nothing to my magic. I'd barely have to move, and I could kill every guard in this trolley.

I won't.

I will give Madam Lyrie the chance to keep her word. And if she breaks it, I will be long gone before she destroys me again.

28

THIS IS AN ACT OF WAR

CORA

"I can't believe it exists," Milas says.

The clan sits around the behemoth stone table in the courtyard, bathed in afternoon sunlight. Two worn pieces of parchment lie between us, along with the three canisters of Cursed Grounds' sand.

Milas lays his severed werewolf ear—which he inexplicably carries everywhere these days—on the table. If I weren't so eager to get started on the sunwalker spells, I'd ask why the hells he always has that thing with him. Milas takes one of the canisters and carefully unscrews the lid.

"It exists," I say. I stand to Sebastian's right, too anxious to remain seated. I look from Milas to the others, scanning each of their expressions.

Beatrice looks skeptical, of course, but the others are intrigued. Excited, even. They should be, though I hold back from saying that. The plan speaks for itself. If Elliot's right—which after reviewing his notes, I think he is—this sand will be strong enough to conjure a widespread ritual. Within a few weeks, we'll have every vampire in the Echo walking in sunlight.

"You're amazing, Cora," Amelia says. She leans back,

slouching against the ivy-covered stone. "I knew you would figure it out."

"I didn't," I say pointedly. I know everyone is suspicious about Elliot, but this should prove exactly who he is. "Elliot did. It will cost him greatly."

"Who knew you were so good in bed," Beatrice scoffs.

I smile. If I didn't know Beatrice as well as I do, I'd feel insulted. Instead, I recognize the envy in her voice, the held-back praise. She's happy for me, whether she's willing to admit it or not.

"Enough," Sebastian barks. "Go over it again."

My smile doesn't waver. Sebastian doesn't need to hear it again. The new ritual isn't all that different from the one I've been using for years. The only difference now is a few minor tweaks and the addition of the black sand. It was an essential ingredient in Madam Lyrie's curse against the vampires, making it the perfect vessel for setting them free.

"Do all the vampires need to be in the circle?" Grace asks. She snatches one of the parchments off the table, squinting to read the smudged ink. She rolls her eyes and glares at Sebastian. "What do you people have against modern conveniences? You could go buy a few reams of paper and some pens, but no, here's some paper a kindergartner made out of pulp and glue."

Sebastian smiles at her, as if she's the most precious thing in the world.

"No, they don't need to be in the circle," I say. "The ash will go around the other ingredients. I'll stand at the center. I might need some vampire blood or maybe a fang—"

"Your lover is here," Milas interrupts. He's holding the werewolf ear again, absentmindedly tracing the outer shell. It's disgusting enough it takes a moment to process his words.

"Elliot?" I say. I look over my shoulder, expecting to see him.

The courtyard is empty though, and the only movement I see through the manor's glass wall is a wandering vampire.

"Yeah," he confirms. "Even with dulled senses, I can fucking smell him. He's almost as potent as you are."

I don't take time to respond or feel offended. I'm already off, running down the corridors until I reach the entryway. The only vampires I'd trust with Elliot are in the courtyard, which means someone else met him at the door. And if they so much as—

I skitter to a stop. Elliot stands at the front door as a pair of vampires leer at him. They're standing too close, pupils blown as he stammers through his reason for being here. One of them grabs his shoulder and presses her nose against the side of his throat.

Within a second, I've got that vampire across the room. She'd been holding Elliot hard enough to pull him down. I throw the second vampire as Elliot gets to his feet. He stares at me with an intensity I feel straight between my legs.

"That one wasn't touching me," he says. He's breathless, chest heaving as he brushes the dust off his pants.

"Yet," I say. Then, "What are you doing here?"

He was supposed to stay in the Day Realm for the next couple of days. If he's here, something happened. Or he changed his mind. He's realized he can't let me use the Cursed Grounds' sand after all. His mama threatened to disown him, and he realized I'm not worth the risk. He'd rather have peace amongst his people than mine.

It'd be more than fair. I won't blame him. I'll—

"I missed you," he says.

I don't respond right away, sure he'll continue, but he doesn't.

"You missed me," I repeat finally. I cross the wooden floor, glancing at the two unconscious vampires. One's neck looks broken. She'll be out for at least the day. The other will be up shortly, but if he's smart, he won't cause problems.

"Yeah," Elliot says. He releases a breath, so tight it seems painful. He closes the distance between us, capturing my mouth in a kiss far too passionate to be in the middle of Sebastian's entryway. Still, I don't deny him. I lean into it, letting his tongue smooth over mine, gasping when he finally pulls away.

"You were supposed to wait a few days," I say, as if perhaps he'd forgotten.

"I missed you," he repeats. He trails his thumb over my jaw and glances over my shoulder. Without looking, I know we're no longer alone.

"Which one?"

"Sebastian," he says, looking back to me. "A couple women. I don't know anyone's names, Secora."

"Secora," a voice echoes. Without looking, I recognize it as Grace's. "Is her name *Secora*? Why am I just learning this?"

I finally look over my shoulder. Sure enough, Sebastian stands at the mouth of the hallway, Grace leaned against him and Beatrice lurking behind his shoulder. She glares at Elliot in a way that warms my chest. She is the terrible big sister I never wanted but begrudgingly appreciate anyway.

"We're going to my quarters," I announce. I grab Elliot's hand, but I only make it a few steps before he stops me.

"Actually, I'd like to speak with them," he says. He meets my confused gaze with a soft smile. "We need to adjust our plans."

"I knew you didn't miss me," I accuse.

"Believe me, I did," he says.

He leans forward to kiss me, but Sebastian steps forward, clearing his throat.

"You want to speak?" he growls. "Then speak."

~

"I can't tell if you're serious," I say.

We're back in the courtyard. Sebastian and Grace sit at the head of one side, and Beatrice sits opposite them. Milas and Amelia take the bench nearest the stone wall, and I sit with Elliot on the other side.

"Unfortunately, I am," he says. He pulls a parchment from his pocket and smooths it over the table. Everyone leans forward, clambering to read it at the same time. "She says she's found a way to strengthen the sun curse. If she's right—and I'd be shocked if she misjudged—you'll burn beneath the sun and moon alike."

The ritual on Elliot's parchment is half-formed and scattered. It's written in his hand, and it's clear this was done from memory.

"This implies she would die," Beatrice says, looking up from the parchment. She arches a thin brow. "We're supposed to believe your mother is *that* determined to kill us?"

"She's already dying," he says. He swallows as he speaks, hands fidgeting, but he holds Beatrice's unrelenting stare. "A consequence of the curse sealing. She's got less than a month. This is her way of making it a meaningful death. She was the one to cast the curse; she's the one who can strengthen it. "

"What does this mean for us?" Grace asks. She twists to Sebastian, grabbing his shoulder. "Are we going to die too?"

"No, love. Nothing is going to happen to you. We have the sunwalker spell," Sebastian says. He kisses the crown of her head, but he pointedly avoids my gaze as he looks back to Elliot.

Truthfully, I don't know if the sunwalker spell will be enough to protect them. I'll have to test it before any of them venture outside.

"How do we stop it?" he asks.

"I have a plan," Elliot says. Beneath the table, he grabs my knee, squeezing firmly. "It will require a lot of trust."

"In you?" Beatrice snarls. She looks between the rest of us. "This is obviously a trap."

"It's not," I say. I ignore her scathing glare and focus only on Elliot. "What's your plan?"

"They're meeting tomorrow afternoon," he says. "We'll need to reach her before then. Once they're in the augur house, it will be far more difficult to interfere."

"And do what?" I ask.

"Change her mind?" Grace suggests.

"Kill her?" Beatrice offers at the same time.

"No," Elliot says. He closes his eyes and moves both hands to the table, tapping erratically. "We'll have to take her somewhere. I'm not sure where, but I'll figure it out. We'll have to hold her until we can mass produce sunwalker spells. We'll make sure they can withstand moonlight too, if it comes to it."

"What you're describing..." Sebastian trails off. He looks between his inner circle, to me, and finally back to Elliot. "This is an act of war. Do you understand? If we hold your mother hostage, people on both sides will inevitably die."

"If we don't, *all* of your people will," Elliot says. Then, "I know it's a lot to process, but time isn't on our side. I don't think they'd attempt the ritual right then and there, but we can't risk them finding out. We need to get to her before she reveals anything."

It's honestly repulsive how much I believe the words. It's been over a decade since Elliot killed Harrison on my behalf. He could be a changed man. He could have spent the past twelve years being manipulated by his mama. Our past several weeks together might be nothing more than careful groundwork, a way to trick me into trusting him.

But I know it's not. I wouldn't only bet my life on it—I would bet everyone's at this table.

As the others whisper amongst themselves, Sebastian turns

to me. His jaw works as he studies me, and even before he speaks, I know what he wants to know.

"He wouldn't betray us," I say. "If he says his mama's planning this, she is. If he has a way to prevent it, we should listen."

Grace presses against Sebastian's side, her blue eyes widening in horror. Sebastian's green ones close, briefly, before opening with renewed determination.

"All in favor?" Sebastian asks. He doesn't look around the table, but he doesn't need to. Within seconds, everyone has agreed.

My brows lift in surprise, but Amelia only scoffs.

"We're trusting you, Cora, not him," she says. Then, sliding her attention toward Elliot, she adds, "Though I do trust you too, Elliot. For the record."

"I don't," Beatrice snarls. "But if your plan includes wreaking havoc over the Day Realm, I obviously want in."

"It's settled then," I say, turning to Elliot. "What exactly is the plan?"

"According to Mama's assistant, she should be at her office until the meeting tomorrow," he says. "I'll stop to see her first thing in the morning. I'll pretend to feel ill. If we're lucky, she'll offer to help me home. If she doesn't take the bait, Secora should be nearby to help transport her by whatever means necessary."

I close my eyes. Elliot speaks as if he's talking about a strange enemy, rather than his own mama. He loves her—I know he loves her—and yet, he's so ready to go against everything she's ever wanted. Is it because he knows better? Or is all of this because he thinks I'll demand it.

And wouldn't you? I can't help thinking. *Wouldn't you beg him to save your family?*

"Where are the rest of us in this little plan of yours?" Beatrice asks.

"Indoors, seeing as it will be mid-afternoon," Elliot says

dryly. "A few of you can stand guard at my house. You can help us once we arrive. We'll need to move locations as soon as it's dark. If you could have backup ready during nightfall, that would be ideal."

"And then?" Sebastian asks. "How long do you imagine this hostage scenario can last? How long before the council arrives on our doorstep?"

"We wouldn't need to keep her *here*," Elliot says, balking.

"Where else are you planning to keep a prisoner?" Sebastian counters. "She'll come here. Just tell me how long she'll be here."

"A few weeks at least," he says. "That should give us enough time to get the sunwalker spell ready. Even if there's no curing Mama, that will ensure the safety of your species."

Sebastian and Elliot regard each other for a long moment, and I hold my breath in the painful silence. I'm desperate for something to say, but I can hardly think straight. Every time I feel the ground solidly beneath my feet, the whole world shifts again.

"Very well," Sebastian says finally. He rises from the table, offering his hand to Grace. "We'll leave tomorrow at first light."

29

MY MIND IS STRONG

CORA

Once the meeting ends, I lead Elliot to my quarters. My heart thrums heavier with each step, propelled by unanswered questions. *Are you sure you want to do this? Why didn't you tell me? How does this all end?*

I can feel Elliot's eyes on me as we walk, but I don't return his gaze until we've reached my door. Only then, once we're closed inside my quarters, do I turn to face him. My mind stalls on the list of questions, but I can't bring myself to ask a single one. Still, Elliot waits patiently for me to speak. He must have things he wants to say too. He must be shocked by his own mama's decisions, afraid of what might happen to her now.

And yet, he's clearly more worried about what's going through *my* mind. It sends an unexpected rush of emotions through me, and before I waste another second, I surge onto my toes, pulling him into a tight hug. I bury my head against his chest, feeling my own stresses fade as he wraps his arms around me.

I pull back, just enough to kiss him, trying desperately to convey everything I'm too afraid to admit out loud.

Thank you.

I missed you, too.

I love you—so much it terrifies me.

I'm the one to finally break the kiss. If we'd gone any longer, I'm confident we wouldn't pull apart until we were naked and sated in my bed. As appealing as that sounds, there are too many things to do.

"You should have talked to me first," I say finally. My voice comes out sharp, reprimanding almost. "This...there will be no coming back from this, Elliot."

"Secora," is all he says. Where my voice is a vicious snap, his is melted butter as he touches my face. His fingers rake through my hair, pausing to release the fastened band. As I gape at him, he works his fingers through my hair, massaging my scalp. "My Secora."

"You're distracting me," I accuse, but I don't try to stop him either. I let my eyes flutter shut as he plays with my hair.

"You shouldn't have lied," he says, ignoring me. "You should have told me what my mama did to you."

I still, but Elliot doesn't. As my pulse quickens, his touch slides from my hair, down the sides of my neck. His hands are gentle and slow, pressing softly against my skin.

"I should have realized it," he adds. "But you shouldn't have lied."

I try to swallow uselessly. My throat is too dry.

"It makes sense," he continues. "I would've gone to Mama for help, and when she failed you...I killed him. I killed him because I couldn't handle that he got away with it. That my *mama* let him get away with it."

The word mama has never sounded more like a four letter curse.

"Did she know *I* killed him?" he asks. His fingers continue playing with my hair, and though I'm desperate to look at his face, I can't bring myself to open my eyes. "Did she know, Secora?"

My chest is hollow. I scramble for something to say, something to excuse what happened. Even after Elliot knew most of the truth, I wasn't sure I'd ever tell him this. He loves his mama, and despite her endless faults, I know she loves him too.

But he also loves *me*, and he deserves to know.

"Yes," I whisper finally. My voice is so quiet, I'm not sure I've spoken aloud. It is only the way Elliot tenses that I know I have.

"Tell me," he says. He's closer to begging than demanding.

"I brought you to her," I say finally. "I *offered* to take the fall, Elliot, for what it's worth."

He doesn't respond. Doesn't move or breathe. His hands rest on my shoulders, no longer playing with my hair.

"I couldn't cover it up by myself," I explain. Now that Elliot's stopped moving, I can't stand still. I wrap my arms around his waist, pressing myself almost desperately against his chest. "I agreed to take the blame. In exchange, your mama promised not to seek the death penalty. She was supposed to exile me."

Still no movement, no reaction. I keep my eyes closed, too afraid of what I'll see if I look up.

"I like to think she meant it. At least in the beginning," I say. I rub my hands across his back, then up and down his spine. "She wanted your memories though. She couldn't stand that I had them, and I understand why. I'm sure she thought I would turn on you at some point, that I'd expose the truth of what you did to Harrison. She refused to exile me until I gave them.

"So I was kept in that prison." My voice cracks, and I pause to take a steadying breath. "They tried everything to get the memories out, but my mind is *strong*. Nothing worked, and I refused to let them in. They beat me. Starved me. Humiliated me. Until finally...your mama realized there was an easier solution to destroy them."

Elliot lets out a strangled sob, and the sound is like frigid water over my head. I snap out of my dazed recount, pulling back to look at him. He'd been perfectly still seconds ago, but now his whole body shakes. Tears streak his face as he takes heaving breaths, failing to regain control.

"Don't, Elliot. You're the reason I escaped," I tell him firmly. I speak the words against his chest, right next to his heart. "After Harrison raped me, you took off those cuffs. You replaced them with a faulty set. They all thought I was powerless, but I wasn't. Whether you knew it or not, you got me out of that prison."

"I was the reason you were in it," he says through a shaky breath. "And my mama..."

"She was *wrong*. She made the wrong choice, but I understand her," I say softly. It's the truth. Much as I despise Madam Lyrie for betraying me, I've always understood her fear beneath it all. "She's still your mama, Elliot. This plan with the vampires won't end well. There will inevitably be bloodshed, and if the vampires feel it's in their best interest—"

"They'll kill her," he finishes for me. Strangely, that comment seems to ground him. "I know."

I swallow, but my throat feels impossibly tight.

"Don't do this because you're angry," I whisper.

Elliot lets out a soft scoff, hugging me tighter against his chest.

"I am angry," he says, voice steadier than it was moments ago. "I am angry at what she did to you, to me. I am angry at what she undoubtedly did to other innocent people. But the sacrifice she's planning...This isn't about anger, Secora. She's planning a genocide. She has her reasons, but I'll never forgive myself if I allow it to happen."

I breathe Elliot in, letting the soft scent of his cologne flood my senses. He's so good, and not for the first time, I wonder how it's possible. With Madam Lyrie as his only parent, with

Harrison Iyle as his childhood friend, Elliot has every reason to be terrible, and yet, he is the purest soul I've ever met.

"I love you," I whisper. Because I still haven't said it. I'm not sure I ever have. I've kept the words tucked to my chest, too scared what will happen if I let them out.

But love doesn't disappear just because you don't acknowledge it. It lingers, multiplies, takes over every breath, whether you accept it or not.

"I love you so much," I say. "And I'm really happy you're here. I hope...I hope you stay."

I don't mean *here*, in my quarters, in this vampiric manor. By the way he kisses my head, still hugging me impossibly close, I think he understands. He pulls back, cupping my jaw between his large hands. He looks at me like I'm precious, like I'm beautiful, like I'm exactly as I should be.

"I love you," he says. He traces my lower lip. "I'm not going anywhere."

THE NEXT MORNING, we travel to the Day Realm in strategic groups. Elliot goes first, alone. He's by far the most likely to be recognized in Ochre, and showing up with an entourage of vampires would foil our plans immediately. The council would realize he's a traitor, and our odds of getting Madam Lyrie alone would diminish to near-zero.

After Elliot, the rest of us travel in pairs. Sebastian and Grace. Me and Amelia. Beatrice and Milas. The first couple was a hard-won battle for Grace. Sebastian wanted her to remain at the manor. She refused because, in her words, *if you all die, there's no way I'm taking over your psycho vampire kingdom.*

With only Beatrice and Milas yet to arrive, the rest of us are spread out within Elliot's home. It's a spacious house, far bigger than the one we once dreamt of sharing. While the others prepare a holding room for Madam Lyrie, I wander the grand space and imagine myself living here.

It's a childish game. I was never going to live here. I don't belong in the Day Realm, and I'm certainly not wanted here. I torture myself all the same. I run my hand over the smooth counter. I imagine sitting on it while Elliot cooks dinner. I've never been much of a cook. I suppose I don't know whether he is either, but I can see it. Me here with my legs crossed, him at the stove, grinning back at me.

Maybe there'd be tiny footsteps upstairs or maybe it'd just be us. It'd be lovely, far more than I deserve.

"They have many homes like this in the Night Realm?" Elliot asks, startling me. He stands just behind me, a soft smile playing on his lips. I turn to face him, feeling blush scour my entire face. Though he can't possibly know what I was thinking, I feel exposed.

"I don't know," I say. I lean back against the counter and tip my chin to look at Elliot. "I doubt it. Maybe some nice, dilapidated stone castles though."

"Dilapidated castles are my favorite."

I roll my eyes and start to turn back to the counter, but Elliot stops me. He steps forward, bracing one hand on either side of my hips. We're close enough I can feel the heat from his body. He's wearing a buttoned shirt, rolled to his elbows, and he smells impossibly divine. I glance toward the living room, relieved the others aren't paying attention. When I look back, Elliot's face is a breath from mine.

"Would you live there with me?" he asks. Rather than pulling back to speak, he moves closer, until his lips ghost my cheek.

"In your dilapidated castle?"

"Anywhere."

I lean back, studying his bright hazel eyes, gauging his seriousness. Before I have the chance to answer, there's a knock at the door. Sebastian answers it, but Beatrice and Milas are stuck waiting on the front porch. Elliot steps away from me, his hand trailing down my arm as he reluctantly turns to the door.

"You can come in," he says.

Beatrice and Milas fight to be first, and though Milas wins, it's Beatrice who lets out a victorious whoop.

"I win," she taunts. Turning to Milas, she adds, "Your knife, please."

Behind her, Milas already has his knife in his palm, the handle turned toward her. He rolls her eyes as she takes it and kicks the door shut with his boot.

"Do I *want* to know?" Sebastian asks.

"I bet Milas that those two would hook up in the few hours since they had breakfast in the courtyard." Beatrice fastens the knife to her hidden thigh sheath. She smirks, looking between me and Elliot. "Couldn't believe he'd bet against them."

"A simple no would have sufficed," Sebastian grumbles.

"As if you didn't already know." Beatrice slaps him on the back as she crosses the room, her smile growing as she looks at me. "Good for you, Cora."

I roll my eyes, but it's the most I allow myself to react. Beatrice feeds on insecurity and embarrassment, and I'm not about to offer her either.

"Enough," Sebastian says. It's the tone that makes spines stiffen, even mine. "We cannot afford distractions today. Understood?"

"Yes, Master," I say. I'm surprised to realize I'm not the only one. Amelia and Milas both echo the title. Sebastian may no longer be king of the vampires, but the respect is there regardless.

"Let's finish with her holding room," Sebastian says. He

crosses to the open doorway near the kitchen. It leads into a small bedroom, containing only a narrow bed. "Milas, you have the supplies?"

Moments later, we're all too busy to pick at each other. Milas and Amelia prepare the ingredients and artifacts. I ward the room to contain Elliot's mama, and he provides a droplet of blood to strengthen its hold. Sebastian, Beatrice, and Grace remain in the living room to discuss the many scenarios that could occur *after*.

A hoard of vampires will arrive as soon as it's safe, and they'll ensure we transport her without getting intercepted. If all goes according to plan, it should be easy. Hopefully, the council won't realize Madam Lyrie has been kidnapped until we're long gone from the Day Realm.

"Get her into the bedroom by her own volition if possible," Sebastian states once we're all back in the living room. He stares at Elliot as he speaks, ankle crossed over his opposite knee.

"She'll sense the wards," I say, shaking my head. "We should take her down as soon as she's inside."

"Can your magic handle her?" Sebastian asks, looking between me and Elliot.

"Mine can't," he says. "Secora's can. If I'm able to get Mama here without Secora's help, she can take her down. But in case this gets messy, you should be prepared to intervene."

"How do you suggest we do that without decapitating her?" Beatrice asks. "Personally, I'd rather not end tonight with my heart ripped outside my body."

"*Carefully*," I say, voice mockingly sweet.

At the same time, Elliot says, "With these."

He pulls his messenger bag onto his lap, and with a quick glance my way, he pulls out a pair of dull golden cuffs.

I can't help the gasp that sucks between my teeth. I haven't seen those cuffs in over a decade, not outside of memories.

Despite everything I've survived and all the ways I've grown, I tense at the sight of them. Without consciously deciding to, I scoot back in my armchair and tuck my hands beneath my thighs.

Elliot passes the cuffs to Sebastian in a monumental display of trust. I'm not sure anyone in this room even realizes it. As the vampires study the bands, Elliot moves from his armchair to mine, maneuvering so I'm on his lap. Normally, I'd be mortified at the public display of affection. But right now, with my childhood trauma being passed around like an interesting artifact, I don't care.

"I love you," he whispers against the side of my head.

"I love you too," I say. My voice is barely audible, but I'm well aware the others can hear me. Despite this, I add, "Are you sure you want to do this?"

At my question, the vampires fall quiet. They make a show of looking at the cuffs, but I know they're listening. I don't care. My question is for Elliot and Elliot alone.

"I'm sure," he says. He kisses my temple before looking to the others in the room. "Those cuffs will rob her of magic. Once they're on, she'll be powerless."

"You wore these," Sebastian says. He doesn't look up, but I know the statement is for me. I'd been wearing the false pair the day we met.

"Yes. They are horrid."

"Excellent," he says, and his mouth twists into a blood-curdling grin.

30

I'VE LEARNED FROM THE BEST
ELLIOT

I was supposed to leave two minutes ago. It's not like me to procrastinate, but I've never faced a moment like this. I'm all too aware of how terrible today will be, and my body doesn't want to carry me a single step from this porch. A porch that, after our mission, will no longer be mine. I imagine the council will sell it or give it to Mama once all is said and done.

If she's still alive to receive it.

I close my eyes and tilt my head back, letting the sun touch my cheeks. It's too cold to feel its warmth, but it's nice all the same. This will be my last time at the home I worked so hard to afford. The home I rarely appreciated, this view most of all.

"Elliot," Secora says, startling me. I turn away from the bannister to look at her.

I'm not sure I've ever seen her in a color other than black. She looks good in yellow, though I imagine she'd look good in any other color too. The autumnal dress hugs her body far better than her typical black ones, showing the soft curves of her chest and hips. She's absolutely stunning, even when she scrunches her nose at me, eyes narrowing.

"I know I look ridiculous," she says. She crosses her arms and juts out a hip. Her hair isn't in its typical ponytail. Instead, it's been carefully divided into two long braids and fastened with bright orange bows.

"You look beautiful," I say. I touch one of the bows, tugging gently on her braid. "I like these."

A faint blush dances over her cheeks, but she doesn't immediately reply. Instead, she looks out at Lake Astoria.

"Our first kiss wasn't far from here." She's looking at the shoreline, and the sun makes her dark eyes brighter.

"Maybe that's why I moved here," I say. I'm still holding the end of her braid, like a stubborn child vying for a girl's attention. "Maybe my body knew this place was important."

When Secora looks back at me, her scowl is back. I don't take it personally. I only smile at her, twisting her braid between my fingers.

"Did you mean it?" she asks. Her voice is sharp, but I can hear every bit of insecurity within it. "About the dilapidated castle?"

She's not talking about the castle, not really.

"Yes, Secora," I say. "I mean it. I imagine I won't be welcome in the Day Realm after this. It might take me some time, but I'll establish myself in the Night Realm. And once I do, once I have a house—whether it's dilapidated or not—I'll ask you to live there with me. Nothing would make me happier."

Her eyes shine with tears, but she blinks rapidly, chasing them away. With a rough clear of her throat, she returns her attention to Astoria Lake's shoreline.

"I kick in my sleep."

"I can take it," I say, rather than pointing out she's yet to kick me in her sleep. "Whatever your quirks, I can take them. I *want* them."

Secora makes a strange, choking sound. Then she's surging into my arms, wrapping all four of her limbs around me. I easily adjust her weight, holding one hand beneath her bottom and the other on the back of her neck. She buries her face against my chest, squeezing me in a tight hug.

When she finally pulls back, she takes a small glass vial from the pocket of her dress. It's smaller than my thumb, filled with an off-white mist, and secured with a wide cork. She presses it into my palm.

"Break this if anything goes wrong," she says, staring at the vial, rather than me. "Anything at all, Elliot, and I'll be there within two minutes."

"Nothing will go wrong," I assure her. "But if it does, I promise, I'll signal."

"Okay," she whispers. She kisses my neck, right above the collar of my shirt. Though I haven't checked, I imagine there's a bruise on my skin beneath it. A wonderful mark in the shape of Secora's mouth, a beautiful, temporary brand.

"Okay," I repeat. "I'll see you back here in one hour."

Secora untangles herself from me, and I gently return her feet to the floor. With a final kiss to the crown of her head, I leave the porch and don't allow myself to look back.

I TAKE the trolley to the main square in a haze of urgency and uncertainty. I know it's my own anxiety clouding reality, but I swear, time is moving differently now. I'm all too aware that Secora is likely already on the trolley behind this one. She'll be across the street from the council building, ready to interfere if Mama doesn't willingly help me home.

She will though, of course. It's Mama's way. All through

secondary school and university, my friends teased me for the way she coddled me. I'd act embarrassed and annoyed, but truthfully, I never minded. I knew that I was loved and that if I ever needed help, Mama would be the one to offer it.

I'm a grown man now, but I know her answer will be the same. She'll fuss over me and insist on walking me all the way to my bedroom. Secora won't need to get involved until we're safely on my property. At that point, the possibility for failure goes way down. Then it's only a matter of subduing her and transporting her to the Night Realm.

Once she's safely in the Night Realm, I'll be able to sort the logistics of everything else. I'll figure out a way to heal her. Secora and I will find a way to strengthen the sunwalker spells. Hopefully, Mama will eventually understand my point of view. She'll realize peace is possible between the witches and the vampires, and someday, she'll forgive me for what I'm about to do.

I'm still trying to convince myself of the last part when I enter the council building. The entryway looks the same as ever. It's a large rectangular room with dreary yellow walls, deep brown hardwood floors, and a few antique paintings on the walls.

However, there is one stark, worrisome change.

I stare at Vera's desk. In all my years visiting Mama, I've never seen her desk empty. I presume she takes breaks to go to the bathroom and eat, but I've never seen it for myself. She's *always* here with her dramatically inflated sense of importance.

I glance up at the wall clock hanging above her wide desk. It's four minutes past ten o'clock. Too early for a lunch break. Too late for her not to be here yet. On the day of the annual meeting, it doesn't make sense for her to be elsewhere. Her desk should be a chaotic mess of last-minute notes and sorted parchments. Instead, there is only a small message in the center of her tidied space.

Vera Pilskey is at the annual council meeting. She will return by four o'clock.

My stomach sours. I look up at the clock again. The meeting isn't due to start for two hours.

Vera is precisely the kind of woman who would arrive hours early to a meeting, but if she's already gone, there's a good chance Mama is too. Luckily, I don't have to worry for long. Within seconds, I hear the sharp tap of Mama's heels coming from the direction of her office.

I force myself to be calm, to act natural. Just because Vera's schedule is unexpected doesn't mean anything is wrong.

"Elliot," Mama says as I turn. She's wearing an orange dress with long sleeves and a neckline that almost reaches her chin. Her fingertips are just visible at the end of her flowing sleeves, but it's enough to see their sickly grey tint. They're decaying, dying along with everywhere she's hidden.

"Mama," I say. Breath rushes from my lungs, and guilt hungrily claims the space it's left. "I thought I missed you."

"Oh, no," she says. "Vera left to help Mister Rierson with prep. Apparently our numbers are larger than ever this year."

I nod, relief surging through me. That makes sense.

"Mama—"

"I wasn't sure when I'd see you again," she interrupts softly. "You were quite upset."

"I'm not here to change your mind," I say. I'm surprised how normal I sound, even as my heart beats erratically against my ribs. *Yes, not here to change your mind. Just here to lure you into a trap that could very well lead to your untimely death.* "I thought you might want a treatment before your meeting."

"I have an hour or so," she says, glancing at the clock above Vera's desk.

"Perfect. I can make that work," I say. "It should at least mute the discoloration for a bit. Get you through your meeting."

Mama doesn't smile now. Her eyes water, and her mouth parts. But rather than say a word, she turns for her office, leading me down the cluttered halls. I study the artifacts as we pass, mentally cataloguing them. Without consciously deciding to, I'm making note of anything that could be useful to Secora and her vampires in the future.

Traitor, my heart taunts.

Justice, my brain returns.

I sit in the chair across from Mama's desk and settle the messenger bag over my lap. I pluck the ingredients from the side pockets and line them on the desk, mentally tallying my time-line. I'll need to start acting sick within the next ten minutes. By thirty, Mama will be encouraging me to—

A sharp click cuts through my thoughts.

I turn toward the sound, shoulders tensing. Mama stands at her office door, faced away from me. Her hand is still on the doorknob, still clutching the lock.

"Mama?"

"You ungrateful, insolent child," she says. The words come out choked, broken by heaving sobs. Mama faces me, her cheeks lined with tears, her lower lip trembling. "After everything...how could you be such a fool?"

I don't respond. I try to regulate my body the way Secora so easily does, but it doesn't work. I can feel the humiliation burning through my skin, sending blush all the way to my ears.

"I told you to stay away from that woman," she says. Her entire body trembles as she walks around her desk, unlocking the topmost drawer. She lines a set of herbs to mirror mine, and my stomach twists as I realize what she's planning.

"How did you—Mama, I don't know what you think—"

"Do *not* insult me," she says. The words are a growl, a sob, a curse to the sky. "I've been worried for weeks, but after our last meeting, I *knew*. All it took was a simple detection spell, and I could see your fingers all over this office. Whatever this woman has told you, she is lying, Elliot. You were ready to burn our realm to the ground for her manufactured lies."

"Perhaps the urge to burn runs through my veins," I snap. "Perhaps I've learned from the best."

Mama doesn't respond. Her teeth are visibly clenched as she undoes one of the vials in her lineup.

"You can't take my memories, Mama," I say. "I'm not going to let you."

If Secora has taught me anything, it's that stealing memories is not simple. She only had mine because I opened to her, and that's the same reason Mama couldn't get mine from Secora. My mind may not be as powerful as Secora's, but I'll die before I lose that woman again.

"Foolish," is Mama's sharp reply. "A foolish child. Everything I've done was for you. A simple, pretty face and you've forgotten who you are."

Remembered, I want to correct. A complicated, vicious, beautiful face...and I've remembered exactly who I am. Who I'm not. Who I'm desperate to become.

"Mama," I repeat. Harder. "I'm not going to let you."

She doesn't respond now. She doesn't even look at me. She knows exactly what I'm capable of—exactly what happened to the last person who tried to take Secora from me. And still, her guard is down. She doesn't think I'll hurt her, and I hate that she's right.

Even when I wanted to save the vampires, I never wanted her to suffer. I was going to do everything in my power to keep her from harm, and I can't imagine inflicting pain on her now. Not Mama. The woman who knows my favorite meal and the surgeries I like best and the coworker I can't stand.

I keep my eyes on her, because though I know she won't physically hurt me, I can't trust her with my mind. I watch her every movement as she places the ingredients of a forgetting spell in a shallow bowl. Dismemrate, it's called. I've never taken it, but I've studied it. On a small scale, it can wipe a person's memory for the past few minutes or hours. With the quantities she's using, a child would likely forget his entire life.

I'd lose a year, if not more. I'd lose every second I've had with Secora since we were teenagers.

But like taking memories, Dismemrate only works on the willing. This alone won't make me forget, which means there's more to Mama's plan.

With my eyes still on Mama, I touch the glass vial in my pocket. When Secora gave it to me an hour ago, I'd been so confident I wouldn't need it. If it hadn't caused her to spiral, I would've insisted she keep it.

Now, I'm debating whether to use it.

Anything at all, Elliot.

She'd want me to signal, and that's exactly why I can't. There isn't a damn thing Mama can do to *me* that would break me, but there are plenty she could do to Secora.

"You're going to take this," Mama says. She takes a stone pestle and grinds the herbs against their bowl. "Or I'm going to track that vile woman down and kill her like I should have twelve years ago."

Red flares my vision, and magic pulses through me. My hands twitch with the sudden rush of power, and despite Mama's focus on her work, she tracks the movement. She glares at my hands, then at me, even as tears streak down her face.

"You will not touch her," I say. Magic pools in my hands, and I let the sensation build until I feel it everywhere.

Seconds.

That's all it takes, and I feel sixteen again. My body shakes exactly like it did in that augur house, facing down yet another person I thought I trusted. I hold too much power in my body, and I'm struggling to remember why I don't let it all out. Why I don't destroy this entire fucked up building, taking me and Mama with it.

"Did you know I loved her?" I ask. My voice barely sounds like mine. It is too venomous, too lethal to truly belong to me. "When you denied her and betrayed her and sentenced her to death...did you know I loved her?"

"You were sixteen!" Mama shrieks. Her hands fumble the pestle, and it clatters to the floor. She makes no move to grab it, instead leaning forward on her palms to glare at me. "You didn't know what love was! You were an impressionable child, and a Dark One saw your weakness and took advantage. She filled you with darkness until you could no longer feel the light. She convinced you to *kill* your best friend, Elliot! She is a *monster*, and I cannot let her win."

By the time she's finished speaking, Mama's chest is heaving and her hair has fallen loose around her face. She hardly looks like herself. She has come apart at the seams, and I'm forced to see her exactly as she is: a broken, angry woman, overtaken by hatred and fear.

Too many responses come to mind at once, and I'm temporarily stunned into silence. *I loved her and I love her still*, I could say. Or, *she has only ever given me light.* Or I could echo Margot and say, *Secora is many things, but she is no monster.*

Instead, I say the only thing that really matters:

"So, she wasn't lying." Because though I didn't need it, Mama has just confirmed every memory Secora showed me. I loved her. I killed Harrison. Mama helped me get away with it, and she betrayed Secora to do it.

"I love you, Mama," I say. I leave Secora's vial untouched in my pocket, then lay both palms toward Mama. "I know everything you did was because you love me. That doesn't make it okay, but I understand. So does Secora. If you truly want what's best for me, don't do this. Don't try to steal her from me again. Don't punish the vampires more than you already have. Come with me. I'll show you—"

Mama jerks back from the desk and bares her teeth at me. Despite the tears still drying on her face, something switches in her eyes. Gone is the desperate impulse of a mother, and here is the furious wrath of someone losing control.

"She's infiltrated your mind again," she hisses. "Made you confuse our enemies for innocents. You killed your best friend. Now, you advocate for the vampires. Your father's murderers!"

"Killing them won't bring him back!" I shove to my feet, leaving my hands on the desk. "Wiping my memories won't change the truth! I killed Harrison and I love Secora Reed. If you want me to forget her, you'll have to kill me. You'll have to—"

A violent eruption crashes against Mama's door. The wood splinters, and fractured pieces spray across the room. I stumble backward as a cloud of black dust and magic rips through the remaining parts of the door. I've barely righted myself before a final explosion takes the door off its hinges. It's no more than fallen against my chair than Secora is in the room, scrambling over the damaged wood.

"Secora—"

"You were supposed to signal," she says, glaring as she rights herself. Blood covers the left side of her tights, and through the ripped fabric, I can see the edges of a nasty cut.

"Fuck, get behind me," I growl, shoving her there before she has a chance to argue.

In the chaos of Secora's entrance, Mama fell to the ground, but she's already getting back to her feet. Her eyes widen as she catches a glimpse of Secora, and a hideous smile claims her mouth.

"I always hoped I'd get another chance," Mama says. Her arms lift, palms stretched for Secora.

"Don't, Mama!" I yell. "Don't make me choose!"

Because it won't be you, is the silent end to my sentence. Unspoken, and yet the room quiets as everyone hears it.

"Move, Elliot," Secora whispers. She's already shoving past, arms raised to take on the same woman who betrayed her too many times.

The next ten seconds are pure, unfiltered chaos. There's no time to process or plan, to pause or demand logic. I can only watch as Mama and Secora's magic collide.

Secora screams as she does unseen damage to Mama's mind. Mama's eyes roll back in her head, and yet somehow, she fights still. A flare of her palms, and she sends Secora back against the bookshelves in a violent thrust. I don't know how badly she's hurt. She might have hit her head, or Mama might have done far worse than just throw her.

I can't risk it either way.

Secora and I protect each other. We always have. We always will.

Mama lifts her hands again, ready to strike. She's so focused on Secora that she doesn't see me coming. She doesn't realize I've moved until my hand is clasped against her sternum, fingers clutching her shirt.

It is not a painful death. I do not rip her skin like I did to Harrison. I do not relish watching her suffer.

"I love you, Mama," I say. The words are barely audible through my choked sobs, but I swear, her eyes soften as I speak them. Her hands clasp my wrists. Perhaps in fear. Perhaps in resigned acceptance. "I'm sorry. I'm so sorry. I love you."

"Elliot—"

She doesn't get the chance to speak another word. I've held the blood from her heart for too long, and with eyes still wide,

Mama's body goes limp. She's lifeless in my arms, and I am struck with a hideous symphony of agony and relief.

I scream as her body hits the floor, collapsing to my own knees. I'm shaking, every piece of me whirling with violent disbelief. I just killed Mama, and I don't even have time to process it. I have to check on Secora. I have to get us out of here. I have to leave Mama behind.

31

WITH A RUSTED BLADE
CORA

When I wake up, I can't make sense of my surroundings. I'm in my bedroom at the manor, and much like the very first time, I have no idea how I got here—or *why*. I jolt upright, but my mind continues to lag. I have blurry memories of being in the Day Realm, of waiting for Elliot and Madam Lyrie. I remember he'd been late. I remember pacing the opposite side of the street, until finally, I'd walked through the council building's front doors. Then…

Nothing.

I touch my head. My entire skull is sore and a pulsing headache radiates all the way to my neck. By the thick bandage across my forehead, I must have an open wound.

I flip the blanket off my legs. I'm wearing a simple black frock, no tights. There are bruises on my thighs and another bandage on my calf. Whatever happened in that building, I likely didn't walk out of it.

"Well, I'll be damned."

My bedroom door swings open, crashing against one of the memory shelves. I startle, gripping my blanket as if it's a shield. Amelia leans against the door, surveying me with keen eyes. Her hair is twisted in a sloppy bun, and she's wearing casual attire. I can't remember the last time I saw her without a full face of makeup and a swanky outfit.

"You're in my quarters," I say stupidly. The wards should have made that impossible.

"Your lover let me in," she says. She taps the doorframe. "Wouldn't let me into your bedroom though. Apparently only *he* is worthy of touching you while you're unconscious."

He's alive.

Elliot is alive, and that makes everything else bearable. My aching body. Our failed mission. The likelihood the sun curse will get worse. If we have any chance of protecting the vampires, we'll need to act fast.

But first...

"Where is he?" I swing my legs off the side of the bed and stand, only to immediately lose my balance. With one hand to my temple, I use the other to keep myself upright.

"You've been out for five days," she says, ignoring my question. "Milas and Beatrice have a bet on whether you'll die."

"Milas is going to run out of weapons," I say. My vision spots, and I slouch back against the bed.

"Beatrice knows better than to bet against you," she says. Then, "You should lay back down. You're going to knock another hole in your head."

I grip the blanket again and close my eyes.

"Five days?"

"Five," she confirms.

I take a steady breath. The room is spinning, but I've already wasted too much time. If the council isn't already prepped for their ritual, they will be soon. I'm not going to fall asleep and risk losing another week.

"Where is Elliot, Amelia?" I ask. If he lowered the wards on my quarters, he must be in better shape than I am.

"He's having his first proper meal in days," she says. "He finally agreed—very reluctantly, might I add—to take a break. Of course you decide to wake up in the brief time he's gone. I imagine he'll be sour about that."

"Amelia—"

"Yeah, yeah. He's in the courtyard," she says. "I'll get him for you."

"I'm coming with you."

"Cora, I'm no healer, but your lover is. He insisted you rest—"

"I've slept for five days. I've rested plenty." I push back to my feet, taking slow, careful steps as I cross my bedroom. By the time I near Amelia, my head is fuzzy, but I'm confident I won't pass out. "Let me change, and we'll go."

I expect Amelia to fight me on it, but she only sighs, watching in amusement as I dig through my dresser. Above it, a collection of green and blue and orange memories flail in their jars, far fewer in number than they used to be.

My hands shake as I grab the first pair of leggings I find. I clumsily pull them into place and shove into a pair of black shoes. I'm too worried I'll fall if I try to tie the laces, so I leave them loose.

Once I'm out of the room, Amelia pats my shoulder. She doesn't hug me, like Grace would, and for that, I'm grateful. I've never enjoyed casual affection, and aside from Elliot, I prefer not to be touched. Amelia lets her hand fall, lips tilting.

"Glad you made it," she says.

"That bad?" I ask. I don't look at her as I head for the courtyard. I'm dizzy and slow, but Amelia doesn't complain. She keeps my pathetic pace and takes her time before responding.

"Worse," she says finally.

I nod. My throat suddenly feels tight, suffocated by too many unasked questions. I don't want to ask Amelia what happened—I want to hear it from Elliot. It's his mama at the center of this, and it's clear we never made it back to his home with her. They would've needed me to subdue her, and it's clear I didn't.

I slow as we near the final corridor. Through the floor-to-ceiling windows, I can see Elliot at the stone table. He's faced away, shoulders slumped and food untouched. His head hangs forward, clutched between his hands.

My heart seizes, misses a beat. Somehow, without knowing, I *know*. And the question I ask is far from the one I expected.

"Is she dead?"

Amelia stands at my side. She's taller than I am, but not by much. Even as I feel her staring at me, I don't take my eyes off Elliot.

"Yes."

I try to swallow, but that knot in my throat is squeezing tighter. It's hard to breathe, let alone speak. I force the words out. Before I see Elliot, I need to—I *have* to know.

"Was it me?"

Amelia's touch ghosts my shoulder.

"No," she says steadily. "It was him."

I close my eyes, squeezing so tight my head throbs. It's not that I wanted it to be me. I just really, *really* didn't want it to be him.

"He didn't say precisely what happened," she adds. "Only that he killed her. His friend cleaned up the mess. Made it look like a natural death. We'll see if the council believes it."

I assume she's talking about Henry. I have no idea how he'd make a murder look like a natural death, but I don't doubt he'd try.

"Is he okay?" I ask. It's an impulsive question, and I'm only asking because I already know the answer. Because I desperately want to be wrong. Before Amelia responds, I lift my hand, waving the question away. "Never mind. I'm...I'll go see him now."

"Do you want me to stay?"

I shake my head. My focus is still on Elliot, who has yet to realize we're watching him. He has the survival instincts of a child. If I didn't know otherwise, I'd never think him capable of murder.

My stomach twists, acutely aware that *I* am the common factor in both of Elliot's kills. He isn't a killer, but he does it anyway, to protect me. I may not have been the one to kill Madam Lyrie, but I have no doubt I was the cause.

Without looking at Amelia, I suck in a deep breath and enter the courtyard. I've made it halfway across the cobblestone before Elliot startles. He turns to look at me, his face quickly flashing through a series of emotions. Surprise. Worry. Annoyance. Back to worry.

"Secora," he says softly. He sweeps across the courtyard, and before I utter a word, he's pulled me into a gentle hug. Despite the wound on my head, I rest against his chest, breathing in his warm scent.

He's the first to pull away, and when I do the same, he's not looking at me. His eyes are scanning the windows behind me. Without looking, I know Amelia is gone.

"I insisted," I say before he can ask about it. "Amelia wanted me to rest, but I...I needed to see you."

"I would have come to you," he says. His attention is back on me now, his warm fingers brushing over my temples, down my neck. "You should be in bed."

"I don't remember what happened," I say. A sudden, unprecedented thought pierces through my mind. "Did you... did you take them?"

Elliot's lips twitch at this, turning into a gentle smile.

"No, I'm afraid I don't share your talents for that," he says.

His fingers return to my head, carefully checking the bandage. "You took quite the hit. What's the last you remember?"

"Going into the council building," I say. My hands tremble as I press them against his collar. He's wearing an unfamiliar black shirt with buttons. It's not his, I realize. It's one of the vampires, which means he didn't have time to pack a bag. He should have before we even left that morning.

"Ahh," he says. He crouches to inspect the bandage on my calf. "Well, you didn't miss much then. You broke down Mama's office door. Made quite the entrance."

I don't miss the way his voice cracks when speaking of Madam Lyrie. I need to ask what happened to her, but I don't. I *can't*. My throat is clogged with too much emotion. I may not remember what happened in the council building, but this is all starting to feel eerily familiar.

Me causing issues in Elliot's life.

Him killing someone to fix them.

"Elliot," I say. Nothing more comes, just his name, hanging in the cool winter air.

"She gave me no choice," he says. He tightens the bandage before looking up at me. The sun highlights every single color in his hazel eyes.

"I doubt that," I whisper. Now it's my voice cracking, but I can't help it. I keep talking anyway, fighting the sharp knot in my throat. "It was me, wasn't it? You killed her because of me."

"No," he says vehemently. "She tried to kill you, Secora. That was *her* choice. That is why I killed her."

Tears streak down my face, burning hot against the cold wind.

"Elliot—"

"She did not suffer," he interrupts. His voice is hoarse as he rises back to his feet, cupping my face between his large warm hands. "It was fast. Like a heart attack."

I swallow. My insides feel raw, as if they've been scraped with a rusted blade. I open my mouth to speak, but nothing comes. I only stare at Elliot, eyes burning and lips trembling.

"I had Henry clean it up," he adds. "Aside from some of the wreckage, it shouldn't have been difficult. I don't think it'll come back to me. If it does..."

I close my eyes. The simple movement makes my head spin, and I stumble over nothing. Elliot steadies me, bringing me closer.

"I love you, Secora," he whispers against my temple. I'm in his arms before I've fully realized what's happening. He cradles me to his chest and kisses the edge of my bandage. "I love you. Everything will be okay now."

"I'm sorry," I choke out. I'm still crying, and I'm not sure I'll ever be able to stop. "I'm so—"

"Shhh," he whispers. "I've made peace with it."

32

TWO MONTHS LATER
ELLIOT

"Fuck, you're pretty like this."

One of Secora's legs is over my shoulder and the other is bent at my side. She wasn't sure about the position, but she looks anything but uncertain now. Her eyes keep fluttering shut, and her mouth is tilted in a blissful, lazy smile. Every time I thrust into her, she moans and digs her fingers harder against my shoulders. She's close to drawing blood, and I fuck her harder, hoping she will.

When she rocks her hips to meet mine, I almost lose the last of my self-control. It's steadily disappeared since we woke up twenty minutes ago and her soft lips tickled my collarbone. I had grand plans to fuck her until her clan meeting, but now I'm clenching to keep from exploding inside her.

"One more, honey," I say. "Give me one more."

She lets out an incoherent string of curse words, her eyes closed and that smile still in place. She looks like an angel. A beautiful, deadly angel, so pure she's painful to look at. And yet, I'm desperate for those dark eyes to be on mine.

"Look at me, Secora," I say. My words are punctuated by the sharp slap of my hips against her thighs. When Secora does as

I've asked, when those pretty eyes meet mine, I brush my thumb against her clit, rubbing in tight circles. "Come for me."

"I can't," she whines, but she can. She's close. We've only been having sex for a couple months, but I already know her tells as well as my own. The way her hips lose rhythm the closer she gets. The way her breaths turn into louder and louder moans. The way her cunt tightens over my cock, taking me deeper with each stroke.

"One more," I say, and it sounds exactly as desperate as I feel. "You can do one more, can't you?"

When her eyes start to roll back, I capture her mouth with mine, kissing her until she's moaning too hard to kiss me back. Her entire body arches as she comes around my cock.

She hasn't finished coming down when my orgasm rips through me. I grunt against her neck, fucking her harder and harder, until I'm collapsed against her, my cum dripping down the inside of her thigh.

Once we're cleaned up and back in her bed, naked and sated, she sighs. "It's almost time."

I trail my palm over her curves, cupping between her legs. We cleaned up, and yet, she's already ready for me. Soft and wet and warm, beaconing me to thrust inside her and never leave.

"For me to fuck you again?" I ask, teasing.

"We can tell them whatever you want," she says, ignoring me. "And we don't have to promise any sort of timeline."

"I'm ready," I tell her. "We'll tell them today."

She kisses my bare shoulder, and I tug her closer. It really is almost time to go, but I allow myself another minute of bliss, pretending she and I are the only people who exist.

$\sim$

SEBASTIAN VULCE still does not like me. If killing his greatest enemy—my own mama—doesn't win his favor, I imagine nothing will. Even with Grace at his side, he sits rigid at the stone table, openly glaring at me. The others at the table no longer seem bothered. Amelia and Grace both greet me, and Beatrice pretends I don't exist, which seems to be the greatest compliment she can offer.

"Sorry, the trolley was late," Milas announces as he strides into the courtyard. There's a severed ear in his shirt pocket, and I can only hope it's the same one I've seen previously. For all I know, he gets a freshly severed body part every morning as part of some macabre routine.

My heart picks up as Milas takes his seat at the stone table. They're all here now. Beatrice sits opposite Grace and Sebastian, tapping her sharp nails against the table. She, more than any of the others, looks ravenous. Not for Milas's news, like I am. Like Secora is, and Sebastian too.

She's desperate for the update Secora and I will give. The one we've kept putting off due to failed experiments. Today, finally, will be different.

Across from Milas, Amelia slouches against the ivy-covered stone wall. She uses a knife to clean underneath her nails. She looks bored, resigned, as if this meeting were any other.

I stare at Milas as he settles into the spot beside Amelia. My pulse strums faster and faster, until I'm certain it will give out.

"Well?" I demand.

If no one else is going to ask, I will. I *have* to.

"The Gazette announced her official cause of death. Heart attack," he says.

He leans forward, propping onto his elbows. He's looking at me, rather than the others, and it makes my throat tight. I swallow roughly, determined not to cry for Mama. It feels wrong to mourn a death I caused, even if it wasn't a death I wanted.

With his eyes still on me, Milas continues. "My sources have heard nothing different. No mention of a killer or even a morning visitor. It seems your friend cleaned up well."

"He's talented with spells," I say. I'm not sure why. Perhaps to say something at all, to move this conversation from the topic of my mama and onto anything else.

"Yes, well, he's prevented a war," Milas says. He thumbs the ear in his pocket. "There are whispers of a new council leader, but nothing official. I imagine it will be another month before we hear."

"And Elliot?" Secora asks. Her voice is raspy, strained. When I look at her, she's absently touching the scar on her forehead, right above her left eyebrow. Mama had done far more than throw her that day in her office. She'd shattered her skull, and even with vampire blood and every healing spell I knew, I wasn't sure she'd wake up.

I never would have forgiven myself.

As if she can sense my wandering mind, Secora lowers her hand, placing it on my knee. She squeezes gently, offering me a timid smile.

"My sources all assume you're in mourning, but we'll need to be careful going forward," Milas says. "Once you're ready to return to the Day Realm, you'll need to be strategic. We don't want the council asking questions."

I don't look at Secora, but I feel her stiffen. It's been two months since Mama died, and still, we haven't discussed the logistics of our future. Her life is here. Mine was in the Day Realm. I lower my hand to my knee, until my fingers cover hers. She relaxes, but just barely.

"And what of the sunwalker spell?" Beatrice asks. Demands. Of all the vampires at this table, she unnerves me the most. Milas and Amelia are simple. They do their work and only speak when they have something to contribute.

Sebastian is as volatile as Beatrice, but at least I see where his heart lies. He wants to protect his people, and because Secora is in that group, I can't help but admire him for it.

Beatrice, on the other hand, is nothing but chaos. Greedy, power-hungry chaos.

She doesn't care that I killed my mother. Or that the witches are without leadership. Or that Secora nearly died.

She only cares about the sunwalker spells.

I glance at Secora to find her already staring at me. She doesn't say a word, but she doesn't have to. The encouraging look in her eyes is all I need. She could answer Beatrice as well as I can, but she wants *me* to contribute. To be part of her side of the world.

"We're ready to test," I say. I'm surprised how steady I sound, how effortless the words are. "Secora and I made a list of ingredients for Milas to collect. We'll bring Henry in to perform the ritual. If all goes to plan—which I think it will—the vampires will be free in a matter of weeks."

Beatrice doesn't reply, but her lips curl into a satisfied smile.

LATER THAT NIGHT, I lay in Secora's bed with her head on my chest. We spent hours after the clan meeting, watching the last of my and Secora's memories. We've been working through them for the past two months, and now that we're finally done, I feel an unexpected pang of sadness. There's nothing more to remember. My only comfort is knowing that now we'll be able to make endless *new* memories.

"Have you considered joining the council?" Secora asks.

My hand freezes halfway down her hair. She almost always wears it up during the day, but it's my favorite like this. Loose around her shoulders, tickling against my bare chest. After a long pause, I start playing with her hair again, letting the soft strands filter between my fingers.

"Not really."

"You'd be a great leader," she says. I turn toward her, grateful that we haven't turned out the lights. I can see every detail of her face, from the soft wrinkle between her brows to the light blush trailing her cheeks. She clears her throat, tipping her chin proudly. "The Day Realm would be honored to have you. You plan to return home anyway, don't you?"

I trace the soft curve of her lower lip, smiling when her cheeks darken in response. She's trying hard to hide her insecurity, and the fact she's uncertain at all is endearing.

"This is my home," I say, kissing her temple. "Right here. With you."

"I know, but..." she trails off, then continues in a torrent of words. "I don't want you to feel trapped here. I know you don't like the Night Realm. Even if you want to go, we could make it work. Don't feel like you have to—"

I flip us around, so that I'm floating above her. Her dark eyebrows rise in shock, that pretty blush still in place.

"You are my home, Secora," I say. "If you go, I'll go. If you stay, I'll stay. If you want to live in this wretched manor, then I'll live in this wretched manor too. I'll play nice with the bloodsuckers. Start a healing center in the Night Realm. Fuck you every night and every morning. And I will be the happiest man in the Echo."

Secora wraps her arms around my neck and closes her eyes. I can tell the moment she starts to cry, long before the tears actually fall down her face. I remain propped above her, letting her cry. I kiss each of the tears before they reach her chin, nuzzling into her neck once she's finally fallen quiet again.

"It sounds lovely," she says. "And I don't use that word lightly."

"No, I don't suppose you would," I say, chuckling against her collarbone.

"You're going to stay?" she whispers.

"Yeah," I say. I kiss the hollow of her throat, then kiss the softest part of shoulder. "I'm going to stay."

THE END.

ACKNOWLEDGMENTS

To my readers: Thank you for rejoining me in the Echo universe (or for trying it for the first time)! I fell in love with Cora's character while writing her in *This Violent Light*. Long before I finished the first draft of that book, I knew Cora would be getting her own story. She's the softest, prickliest character I've ever written, and Elliot quickly came to life as the perfect man for her. I hope you love them as much as I do!

To HJ Nelson: As always, thank you for being this book's midwife. Every time I felt stuck or tempted to give up, you were always there, demanding I see it through. You are the first person I call when I feel like I'm an utter failure, and you somehow always convince me to keep going. One day, we'll be laughing about this in our castle. For now, I'm so grateful we can laugh while wrangling our unruly kids.

To Katrina: I can't really thank you enough for all the ways you've made my life better. You've gone above and beyond the duties of a best friend, and I am forever grateful. Here's to many more years of author events, chaotic traveling, and you keeping track of all the things I forget.

To my parents and Jonni: Thank you for loving me and believing in me. It's been a bit of a rough year on the personal front, but you've made it possible to keep pursuing this dream of mine. Thank you endlessly.

To my ARC readers: Thank you for supporting this little indie author. I can't say it enough - you are the reason my books are finding their place in this world! Every time you share and recommend my book, you are helping my dreams come true. Thank you so much, and here's to many more ARC opportunities in the future!

To Brittany and Beau: Thank you for being my constant sounding board when I come up with ideas. Brittany, you are always down to plot crazy story ideas and you're one of the few people I trust with my early drafts. Beau, whenever I can't get a world to make sense, you're the one who helps me pull it together.

To Dyston: Thank you for your incredible character art and input on graphic design. You are beyond talented, and I can't wait to see your work for other authors (but you are required to prioritize mine, of course).

To Tiegan, Cooper, & Micah: Thank you for always supporting my books as they're released and helping me to spread the word. I love and appreciate you!

To Asterielly Designs: Thank you for the gorgeous book cover. You were wonderful to work with and made my fuzzy ideas shine. If any authors need a cover designer, be sure to check out her work here.

To Ink and Lore Maps: Thank you for the stunning map of the Echo. If any authors need a map made, I highly recommend her.

～

If you enjoyed *That Vast Hunger*, please take a moment to review this book on Amazon and/or Goodreads. It makes a huge impact for indie authors like me! If you want to stay up-to-date with my upcoming releases and bookish sneak peeks, join my newsletter! You can follow me on social media at @authorbreewilde.

ABOUT THE AUTHOR

Bree Wilde writes romance and romantasy books for adults. *That Vast Hunger* is her third novel. She lives in Washington with her daughter and spends most of her time reading, writing, and yapping about books.

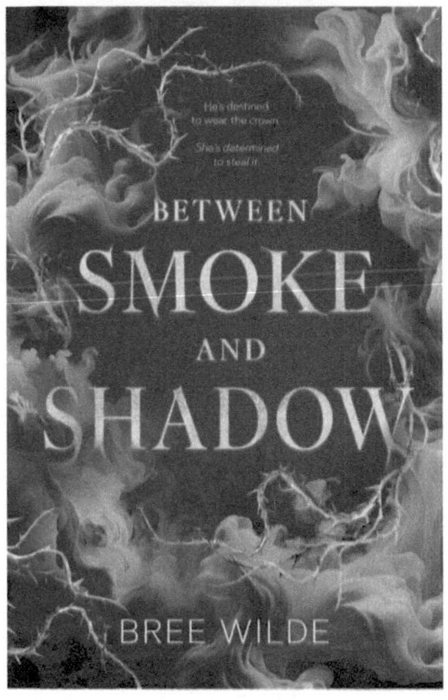

BETWEEN SMOKE AND SHADOW is an open-door romantasy with forbidden love, court intrigue, and a unique magic system. It is told in first person, alternating points of view. The perfect next read for fans of *A Court of Thorns and Roses* by Sarah J. Maas, *The Serpent and the Wings of Night* by Carissa Broadbent, and *The Ever King* by LJ Andrews. It is available to read in paperback, ebook, and through Kindle Unlimited.

THIS VIOLENT LIGHT is the first book in the Echo universe. It is an open-door romantasy with vampires, witches, and enemies-to-lovers romance. It is told in first person, alternating points of view. If you loved *The Vampire Diaries*, *The Serpent and the Wings of Night*, and *Bride*, you will love this book! It is available to read in paperback, ebook, and through Kindle Unlimited.